I0599721

# The Archivist's War

## History Is Written. Truth Is Erased.

By Vicky Wu

Fractured Ink Press

Copyright ©2024 by Vicky Wu

Published by Fractured Ink Press
All rights reserved.

This is a work of fiction. Names, characters, places, organizations, and events are either the product of the author's imagination or are used fictitiously. Any resemblance to actual persons, living or dead, or to actual events or locations is purely coincidental.

No part of this publication may be reproduced, stored in a retrieval system, or transmitted in any form or by any means, electronic or mechanical, including photocopying, recording, or otherwise, without prior written permission of the publisher, except for brief quotations used in reviews or other noncommercial uses permitted by copyright law.

ISBN: 979-8-9928978-2-1

For permissions, information about this book, or future publications, visit
https://TheArchivistsWar.com

Printed in the United States of America

**Fractured Ink**
PRESS

# PROLOGUE

## The Five Alignments

*Reality resists. But history is a patient liar.*

That phrase is often quoted in the Archives, though few recall where it originated. It is taught as reassurance, not warning.

The First Alignment was an accident. A single edit, an innocent correction in the margins of history. The world adapted instantly, as it always does. The lesson is simple: reality is resilient. Small errors can be fixed without consequence.

The loss of the scholar responsible is recorded as unfortunate, but necessary. Early history was unstable. Sacrifice, the texts remind us, is the price of progress.

The Second Alignment was a necessity. An empire erased, its people folded into myth. The Archives teach that certain knowledge, left unchecked, becomes dangerous. Erasure was not destruction, but mercy. A way to prevent endless war, endless contradiction. Knowledge unmade became knowledge controlled, and control became peace.

The Third Alignment was a war. Competing factions tore at the fabric of time, each claiming dominion over truth. Cities flickered. Histories overlapped. Reality itself became unreliable. The lesson is clear: when everyone writes history, no one can live in it. The war ended only when authority was centralized and truth was standardized.

The Fourth Alignment was a compromise. Laws were written—not to preserve every version of the past, but to regulate it. Dangerous texts were sealed away for the protection of the public. The Grand Archive was formalized. Oversight replaced chaos, and governance passed into steadier hands.

The Fifth Alignment brought stability. History no longer shifted violently; it is curated. Adjusted. Corrected when necessary. The public is taught that the past is secure, that the age of upheaval has ended. History, at last, was under control.

The Sixth Alignment is underway—and deteriorating.

## CHAPTER ONE

# The Impossible Document

*The street shouldn't have been empty.*

Nera turned the corner, her body angling for the familiar dodge around the apothecary's sidewalk display table. But her foot landed heavily on flat, empty stone. She stumbled, her internal memories slamming against a reality that refused to match it. Vertigo lurched in her gut.

The apothecary wasn't just empty—it was *missing*, like a thought wiped from memory before she could grasp it.

The smell of the bread baking in the little shop around the corner sparked the same hunger as it always did ... but she knew something was wrong.

Nera turned, eyes scanning the quiet alleyways. The world hummed, disturbingly mundane. A woman in a dark cloak walked past the intersection, carrying a bundle of herbs. A pair of young scholars in standard-issue grey cloaks lingered near the fountain at the Varethis square, their voices hushed as they traded notes. None of them reacted to the absence pressing at the edges of her mind.

Her ink-stained fingers twitched. She pressed her thumb against the shiny, puckered scar on her palm—a physical reminder that truth is flammable. She could still feel the phantom heat of the hearth where her mother had thrown her grandmother's journal. She had reached into the fire to save it, desperate to read the name of the father she never knew, but she had been too slow and the truth it contained had turned to ash in her hand.

This empty wall felt the same. Someone had burned the apothecary out of existence—but with ink.

When things felt unstable, Nera clung to physical sensations, something real. She knew better than to trust memory. The Archives taught that the Alignments spanned centuries because they were complete rebirths, history written from a blank page. Ancient drifts of time that no single human could perceive. But this didn't feel ancient. This felt raw. The absence she felt now wasn't a trick of her fallible mind; the physical world was real. The shop hadn't closed; the world had simply closed over it

She walked forward, the scent of crushed lavender still vivid in her mind, but the street ended in a blank façade of stone. Seamless. Untouched. As if the apothecary she visited yesterday had never existed at all. The cobblestones beneath her feet remained unchanged. There should have been a wooden sign hanging above the doorframe, a scent of crushed lavender and aged parchment, a kindly old man with ink on his hands who always slipped her an extra blank page of vellum.

But the space where his shop once stood was now a blank façade of stone. The buildings on either side looked identical to how they did before.

The hair on her arms stood up. Nera stopped mid-step, her vision swimming as the alleyway seemed to snag, the architecture bending momentarily like a reflection in a disturbed pond. Her dark eyes scanned over the scene, noting the details as fast as her mind could process them. A childhood spent memorizing delicate, fragile documents had honed her perception, but this was wrong. The street was empty in a way that unsettled her.

She fought back the urge to flee, to turn and run until the unnatural stillness of the street was far behind. But the memories of faces of those who trusted the Archive, who lived and died by its carefully crafted history, flashed through her mind, and she stood her ground.

She had always been this way—drawn to the missing, the misplaced, the rewritten, and early to notice what others would eventually forget. No one else noticed the missing shop because, for them now, *it was never there*. But she *remembered*. And that meant something was very, very wrong, and she was well aware of the risk she faced.

She stepped closer to where the shop should be, hesitant, as if the very act of acknowledging the erasure might unravel something deeper. A breeze carried the first hints of autumn past her, stirring up a couple of fallen leaves on the ground. At her feet, tucked in the narrow space where the stone met the street, she noticed a small scrap of parchment, so small that she could have easily missed it, fluttering against the ground, tucked between the cracks of a world that wants to forget.

She crouched, fingers hovering just above the brittle edge of paper. The ink was faded, nearly lost, but a few words remained intact.

*...Ink Holds Truth...*

A mantra among her Scribe peers, one that somehow felt heavier now. She paused briefly and wondered.

A tremor of movement down the street caught the corner of her eye.

She straightened, heart hammering. A tall, lean man in a dark black cloak with the hood covering his head, hiding most of his face, stared at her from the far end of the street. Unmoving. His gaze held her with unsettling familiarity—like a page from a book she once read but couldn't quite place. His head and face were covered in shadows where he almost blended into the darkness of the alleyway he had stepped out of. He tilted his head, just slightly, but didn't speak.

The world around them didn't pause, but the atmosphere thickened, the pressure dropping so suddenly her ears popped, as if the city itself was holding its breath. A faint, almost imperceptible drop in temperature prickled against her skin, raising the fine hairs on her arms like a raw charge. The market beyond the square hummed. The city lived. But for a single, stretched moment, it felt like reality was waiting to see what she would do next.

## Chapter Two

# Rewrite

Nera swallowed the unease creeping into her throat and forced her feet to move. She stepped toward the scrap of parchment, bending down to retrieve it with careful fingers. The brittle paper crackled at her touch, as if resisting being remembered. She turned it over and then scanned the faint, broken lines of ink.

More words, barely visible:

*"...If you remember, you are not alone."*

She hissed through her teeth. Not alone? *Someone else knows. Someone else remembers.*

Part of her wondered if it was a trap. She looked around briefly and tucked the scrap of parchment into the folds of her coat pocket, right next to the map she carried there, just as the mysterious man in the cloak moved slightly. A chill that had nothing to do with the air constricted around her chest as he took a slow, deliberate step towards her.

"You can still smell the lavender." Though his voice was barely above a whisper, it cut through the nearby noise of the market as if it was meant only for her, and carried a hint of familiarity. "That's the problem with erasing history, Scribe—the scent always lingers longer than the stone."

A flash of irritation cut through Nera's unease. *Archivist*, she corrected silently, the reflex instantaneous. She had earned her quill; she wasn't a student anymore.

But she didn't say it aloud. She didn't answer, instead forcing her breath to steady.

"Be careful, Scribe." There was a specific, deliberate cadence to his voice—a pause between words that felt startlingly familiar. Then, as quickly as he appeared, he turned and melted into the crowd of the bustling market in the street behind him.

Nera lingered for only a moment, her fingers moving around the fragile scrap of parchment hidden in her pocket. The market beyond continued, oblivious, voices rising in the usual chatter of haggling and gossip. But to her, the world had changed. *She had been seen.*

She forced her feet into motion, weaving through the press of bodies, heading toward the only place she could think of—the Grand Archive's lower chambers. If anyone had records of an erased shop or whispers of those who remember, it would be found there, with the stories of another place, one not bound by the Archive's rules. A place where the erased histories were kept, as truths waiting to be found.

* * *

The Grand Archive loomed over the outskirts of Varethis, a towering monolith of polished white stone that seemed to absorb the light instead of reflecting it. It stood as a testament to silent authority, its sheer size a physical manifestation of the institution's power to shape reality. Its halls were filled with scholars, Scribes in training and those who rewrote history with careful hands. But behind them, beyond the written records, there were others. The ones who made sure no traces of erased knowledge remained.

The corridors beneath the Archive twisted and turned, a labyrinth of cold, damp stone choked with dust motes that danced in the dim light. Her footsteps died instantly on the marble floor, swallowed by a silence so absolute it pressed inward. Few ventured down here without purpose, and even fewer were warmly welcomed.

Something moved in the periphery of her vision—a shadow that didn't just stretch, but detached itself from the wall. It looked ragged at the edges, like a sketch someone had stopped drawing halfway through. Nera whipped her head around, heart stuttering, but there was nothing but stone and silence. She rubbed her eyes, pressing until stars burst behind her lids. Just eye fatigue, she told herself. Too many hours staring at ink.

Nera walked faster, her footsteps a rhythmic echo in the oppressive silence, each one a deliberate affirmation of her resolve. A familiar wooden door came into view, slightly ajar, the dim glow of candlelight spilling from within.

Archive Master Soren Vale stood at his desk, framed by towers of fading scrolls and ink-laden pages—waiting, as if he had somehow expected her all along. He did not look up immediately, just dipped his quill into the ink and continued writing. The quill's shaft was black iron, its edges scorched as if fire had licked away its past—a relic of something rewritten, something erased. The dim candlelight cast shadows over the lines on his face, carving them deeper. His fingers, ink-stained like the pages around him, rested lightly on an open manuscript, but she knew better than to think he was at ease. Every movement was measured, every breath calculated.

When he finally lifted his gaze, dark eyes locking onto hers, there was no surprise—only quiet calculation. His voice reached her before she could form the words she wanted. His tone was quiet, steady—not a threat, but not entirely a welcome, either.

"You're late, Calloway."

Soren's voice was a low rumble, devoid of inflection, yet heavy with unspoken accusation. Nera met his gaze, feeling the missing apothecary pressing down on her. "Something's wrong, Soren. The world … it's changing."

At that, his tired eyes sharpened, weariness replaced by a flash of grim understanding. "Tell me everything."

Nera hesitated for just a moment, her mind racing to organize her thoughts. She placed the scrap of parchment on his desk, watching as Soren moved around and leaned in to examine it. The candlelight cast moving shadows across the ink-stained words.

"It was a shop, Soren," she said, forcing the words out evenly despite the unease curling in her gut. "An apothecary. I was there just yesterday. Today, it's gone. Not closed; erased, and no one else remembers it existed."

Soren lifted the scrap, his brow furrowing as he read the faint ink. She always believed he knew much more than he ever discussed and carefully kept it to himself. "And you found this there?"

Nera nodded. "Someone else remembers too. A man at the market. He knew what I saw, and he warned me."

Soren set the parchment down with more force than necessary. "You shouldn't remember. This is dangerous, Nera. You understand that, don't you?"

Nera felt a phantom heat throbbing against the scar on her palm. It always burned when she got too close to something the Archive wanted hidden—a physical warning that the truth was flammable.

"My mother said the same thing," she said, her voice dropping as she rubbed the shiny, puckered skin. "But ignorance didn't keep her safe, Soren," Nera whispered, looking at the scrap of parchment. "It just left her blind to threats. I need to know what this is."

The quiet hung heavy and unspoken. Soren finally looked up, searching her face as if weighing a decision he did not want to make.

"You won't let this go, will you?" he muttered, rubbing his temples.

"No."

A long pause. Then, with a reluctant sigh, he moved to one of the back shelves, pulling down a worn, leather-bound volume. He flipped through the pages, his movements careful but quick.

"If there are records of what was erased, they'll be here," he said quietly, placing the book in front of her. "But be warned—what's removed rarely stays buried without reason."

Nera pressed her palm against the rough cover, bracing herself. "Then it's time to dig."

Soren watched her a moment longer before nodding, his face a neutral mask. "Be careful, Nera. There are things in these records that were meant to stay lost."

She didn't answer, instead pulling the heavy volume closer and flipping through the brittle pages. The script was dense, written in precise strokes, but here and there were gaps, lines that faded into nothing, entire passages missing as if history itself had been censored.

Her heart hammered as she came across a half-erased entry. The ink was smudged, deliberately obscured, but a few words remained legible.

*...original Alignment... failure... memory instability...*

Her fingers gripped the book's edge. She looked up at Soren. "This—this is connected to the Alignments, isn't it?"

Soren's gaze darkened. He took the book and closed it with a deliberate thud.

"If that's true, Nera," he said, his voice dropping, "then we are treading on dangerous ground. Archivists don't admit mistakes. If something is being hidden, it was likely deliberate."

"But if I remember, and so do others —"

The candlelight flared violently. A sudden draft swept through the chamber, sending loose parchments skittering to the floor as Nera grabbed the scroll she had been reaching for.

She and Soren exchanged a glance.

"We aren't alone down here," he whispered.

Nera increased her grip on the scroll, her pulse quickening. The air felt charged, thick with something unseen but undeniably present. A soft rustling sound echoed from the far end of the corridor, just beyond the reach of the shimmering candlelight. Not the sound of parchment sliding across a desk, nor the scuttle of a rat—something heavier, more deliberate.

Soren's hand drifted toward the dagger hidden beneath his robes. "Stay close," he whispered.

Nera swallowed, nodding, and took a careful step forward. History loomed over her as a tangible force, her body flooding with adrenaline at the knowledge that whatever she was about to find could change everything. Another sound—a slow, measured footstep.

Suddenly, a woman's soft voice from the darkness cut through the silence: "You shouldn't have found that book, Scribe."

Nera moved her weight onto both feet, as though steadying herself before an impact, but she didn't back away. The voice was calm, deliberate—too steady for comfort. She couldn't see the speaker, only the vague outline of a figure lingering in the darkness beyond the candle's glow, somehow both there and not there at the same time.

Soren moved beside her, his stance subtly adjusting. He stared at the way her edges blurred against the dark, recognizing the impossible. "You were erased," he whispered, the realization striking him harder than fear. "Why are you still here?"

A slow step forward, just enough for the dimmed light to graze the edge of a brown cloak that almost seemed to not be there. The hem didn't fray; it dissolved. It looked ragged and grey at the edges, like a charcoal sketch someone had stopped drawing half-way through. " Someone who remembers," the stranger replied, her voice crackling slightly with a mix of age and wisdom. "Someone who has witnessed what happens to those who ask too many questions."

Nera exchanged a glance with Soren, her pulse drumming in her ears. "And what happens?" she asked quietly, forcing her voice to remain even.

The figure half chuckled, the sound low and knowing. "You already know. They disappear. And we are what's left." A gust of air swept through the archive, snuffing the candle in an instant. The chamber plunged into darkness.

Nera's breath caught as the air sat motionless, the stillness thick as the stone walls around them. She gripped the scroll tighter, as if it alone could anchor her to reality.

A whisper of movement brushed against her senses—a charge in the air, the sound of fabric gliding over stone. She could feel the presence still there, watching.

Soren's voice was steady, but low. "Get behind me."

Nera didn't answer, instead forcing her breathing to remain quiet, controlled. Her fingers searched blindly down to her calf until they found the small knife she kept hidden—a habit born from years of knowing that knowledge alone wasn't enough to keep anyone safe.

Then, another sound. This time, deliberate. A footstep, closer than before. "You don't belong here," the same soft voice whispered from the dark.

Nera straightened, refusing to let the fear curl around her throat. "Neither do you."

A pause, then the figure laughed—soft, but edged with something unreadable. "Perhaps not. But I am not the one now being hunted. Be careful, Scribe." And a whisper of her robes brushing past as she disappeared down the darker part of the hallway, melting into the dark.

Soren quickly lit a lamp on the desk, pushing aside some books and papers. He opened his mouth to speak when they heard a sharp, distant noise from the other direction; boots echoing against stone from the stairs to the upper levels near the entrance of the corridor. More than one set of footsteps.

Nera whipped her head towards the sound, but Soren didn't wait. "We need to move. Now."

Nera barely had time to react before Soren was pulling her back into his archive toward a narrow passage between the back shelves. The lamplight did little to pierce the shadows, and her heart pounded as they slipped through the dim corridor towards the rear exit. The sound of approaching boots echoed closer.

Just as they reached the exit, a deep voice cut through the darkness—calm, measured, and far too familiar.

"Aren't you supposed to be upstairs with the other first year Archivists, Calloway?"

Nera froze. She knew that voice. She would recognize it anywhere after hearing it daily for years during her schooling. Steady, unhurried, laced with quiet disdain—the kind that doesn't need to be loud to command attention. When she turned, she found High Archivist Master Belvar standing exactly as she expected him to: hands folded behind his back, his posture that of a man who never has to raise his voice to be obeyed. Considering he reported to none other than the Architect himself—Valen Kestor, the man who did not merely rule the kingdom but designed it—he felt that way for a reason.

Soren muttered a curse under his breath, pushing her forward. "Keep moving," he hissed.

But she couldn't, frozen in place with her pulse hammering.

"It was only a matter of time before your curiosity led you to something you shouldn't see," he continued, eyes darting toward the old ledger still clutched in Nera's hands. "Put the scroll down, and let's talk."

The corridor suddenly felt smaller, the walls closing in. She had seen Belvar angry over the years, cold and disappointed, but this was absolute. There was no frustration in his voice, only certainty.

Glancing just behind him, Nera saw additional men, clad in their standard solid black uniform with the single horizontal white stripe around their torso. She squared her shoulders. "If you wanted to just talk, you wouldn't have brought the Enforcers."

Belvar looked down at her, almost as if he pitied her. "You misunderstand, child. This is your one chance. Come to my office now and no harm will come to you."

Soren moved to stand between her and Belvar, his stance ready. "And if she refuses?"

Belvar regarded him coldly, unimpressed. "Then she will be corrected, as will you."

Nera didn't breathe. She stared at the single horizontal white stripe across the nearest Enforcer's chest. It was perfectly straight. The fabric was stiff. She memorized the weave of it, the way the torchlight didn't reflect off the matte black wool.

She didn't say a word; she didn't look at Belvar. She just gripped the scroll until her knuckles popped, turned, and ran.

## CHAPTER THREE

# The Chase

The moment her foot hit the stone floor, the corridor erupted into motion. Distant torches cast jagged shadows as she sprinted through the narrow passage, Soren close behind her. Footsteps thundered behind them—Belvar's Enforcers, closing in fast.

"Nera, right!" Soren barked.

She didn't hesitate. Veering sharply, she barreled through a side door, her shoulder slamming into it before it burst open. The scent of parchment and dust flooded her senses as she tumbled into another long chamber lined with towering shelves, dimly lit by lanterns hanging overhead.

Soren shoved the door shut behind them, sliding the latch into place. "That won't hold them for long."

Nera quickly scanned the room, heart pounding. "There—" she pointed toward an ancient metal grate in the floor hidden behind a row of shelves, barely large enough for them to squeeze through. A maintenance tunnel. Their only chance.

They dropped to their knees, wrenching the rusted grate free just as the voices peaked. Nera scrambled into the suffocating dark, Soren right behind her.

Above them, boots stomped onto the floorboards. "Find them," Belvar commanded, his voice vibrating through the stone ceiling.

Nera didn't stop to listen. She crawled until the stone scraped her raw, the tunnel finally widening into a crouch. A faint light glowed ahead—their only option.

She glanced back at Soren, who nodded once. No turning back now.

Pushing forward, the tunnel widened and grew tall enough for them to stand as she reached the opening and peered out. The tunnel emerged behind an old supply rack in a long-forgotten corner of the archives. The space was empty for now, but the voices behind sounded closer.

"We need to move—quickly," she whispered.

Soren didn't hesitate, slipping out first and scanning the room before motioning for her to follow. Nera stepped out, brushing dust from her hands, and took a breath—

A loud clatter echoed through the space as something toppled over. A crate, disturbed by their movement.

The voices from above halted. "Down!" someone shouted.

Nera didn't think. She ran out the far door of the room, Soren tight on her heels, and burst outside into an alley.

The alley was slick with recent rain and damp leaves and the uneven stones beneath her feet treacherously slick as she pushed forward.

"We need to split up if we want a chance of evading them," Soren said quietly between hard breaths. "I will try to draw them away since I won't be in as much trouble as you due to my position. We can meet back up later behind the old church at the edge of town. Be careful." Nera nodded and turned left, while Soren headed right.

The city was alive beyond the narrow alley passage despite dusk approaching—voices, movement, the faint glow of lanterns dancing against the towering buildings. If she could make it to the main streets, maybe she could disappear in the crowds.

Behind her, the shouts of Enforcers grew fainter, but she knew better than to slow down. The Archive's reach was long, and Belvar would not let her escape easily.

A turn ahead led her into the heart of Varethis, where clusters of late-night traders and weary travelers moved among stalls at the outskirts of the market in the town center. She weaved through them, quick but not running, keeping her head down and her breath controlled. Blending in was her best chance now.

Then, just as she dared to hope she'd lost them, she caught a glimpse of someone just beyond the edge of the crowd. A hooded figure, watching her. Waiting. She couldn't make out who it was from the angle or the distance, only that it wasn't the same man from outside the missing apothecary—yet they felt both familiar and unfamiliar all the same.

Hearing footsteps closing in behind her, she pivoted and sprinted, weaving through startled civilians in the narrow alleys.

She blindly ran into a stone pillar displaying a merchant's wares that suddenly toppled in her wake. Behind her, the Enforcers hesitated, distracted at the sound of falling rubble, giving her the precious seconds she needed.

Nera veered toward a side street, slipping between two stalls, her fingers brushing against the rough fabric of hanging tapestries along the way. If she could lose them in the maze of the market, she might have a chance to regroup, to think.

But the moment she emerged onto another street, she caught sight of the same shadowy figure a few buildings away, moving closer this time. Not a pursuer. *A tracker?* A warning flared in her mind. Whoever this was hunted with anticipation. It felt like they already knew her movements.

She quickly continued across the wide street and ducked into a narrow passage between two stone buildings, pressing herself into the shadows. Her breath was steady, controlled, but her heart pounded so loud she felt sure someone would hear.

A whisper cut through the night air, so low the voice couldn't be recognized. "You're running out of places to hide, Calloway."

Nera stilled, forcing herself not to react. She stepped deeper into the shadows, ready to bolt if necessary. "That depends on who's looking," she spat back as she continued moving.

The hooded figure continued closer and tilted their head, as if amused. "If I wanted to turn you in, I would have done it by now," they whispered.

That gave Nera pause. *Did she recognize this voice?* She studied the half-hidden figure in the dim light, searching for any hint of deception. Then, with an exasperated sigh, the figure pulled back her hood, showing a dark auburn haphazard braid that Nera would have recognized anywhere.

*Alis Tarren.*

"Took you long enough to get this far," Alis said slightly louder as she quickly moved closer, her usual smirk barely dimming by the tension in the air. "What, did you stop for a history lesson on the way?"

Relief warred with irritation. "You have a terrible sense of timing," Nera muttered, stepping closer.

Alis grinned, but there was tension behind her usual bravado. "And you have a talent for making a mess of things. A midnight meeting and a philosophical crisis, all before I've even had a drink? We need to move—now. You're not the only one being followed."

Nera snapped. "Shut up," she hissed, the words tearing out of her throat before she could stop them. "Just shut up and move."

Alis turned sharply, leading her away from her chasers, effortlessly keeping to the side streets and narrow alleys she had memorized where the Enforcers wouldn't follow easily. Once they were well out of immediate danger did she slow, scanning her surroundings before speaking. Nera followed, her mind racing. If Alis was here, that meant she had been keeping tabs on her—probably for longer than Nera would like.

They pressed forward in silence, Nera still shaken. Once she turned a corner and spotted a familiar figure leaning against a low wall behind an old empty church, she slumped against the cold brick, her lungs burning as the adrenaline finally crashed. Only then did Alis gesture for Nera to follow her toward the abandoned courtyard. A single lantern glowed under a tattered awning, where Soren stood waiting against the wall next to a gate.

His expression was tight as his gaze jumped between them. "Took you long enough."

"Oh, she's a joy to rescue," Alis deadpanned, crossing her arms. "Next time, maybe send an invitation before making half the city chase you."

Soren folded his arms. "We don't have time for bickering. If we're going to survive this, we need to move, now, together."

Nera took a calm breath, hoping to counter the adrenaline rushing through her body, nodding. "Where to?"

Soren gestured toward the gate to a narrow alleyway leading out of the courtyard. "There's an old friend with a safehouse nearby. Not Archive-controlled, not rebel-owned; neutral ground. We can regroup there."

Alis glanced over her shoulder, scanning the dimly lit streets. "Assuming we're not walking into another trap."

Soren shook his head, but didn't argue. "Then let's not waste any more time."

They wound through the city, keeping to the narrowest paths, avoiding open spaces. The tension was thick between them, but no one made a noise until they reached a weathered door tucked between two crumbling buildings. Nera realized she was not surprised that Soren would have a friend with a safehouse. Soren rapped a quick pattern against the wood, pausing just long enough before repeating it.

The door creaked open, revealing a dimly lit interior. An older man stepped back, dropping his arms to his sides. His gaze was sharp, but not unfriendly.

"You're late," he remarked.

Soren stepped inside, motioning for the others to follow. "We ran into complications."

The man's eyes flicked to Nera and Alis. "I assume this is her? The one causing all the noise in the Archive?"

Nera lifted her chin. "I prefer to think of it as asking the right questions."

The man chuckled, moving towards a fireplace on the opposite wall. "That remains to be seen. Come in. We need to get you safe."

The safehouse's quiet was a shroud, the twinkling lanterns casting nervous shadows along the cracked stone walls. Nera found her gaze drawn to the room's collection of old tomes; shelves lining all the walls which were cluttered with old books and loose parchment. Soren's usual calm was a brittle mask, stretched thin over barely contained irritation as he rested against the far wall, arms crossed. We don't have much time," he said, eyes moving between Nera and Alis. "Belvar won't let this slide. He'll be watching every move you make from now on."

Alis grabbed her braid and gave it an absent twirl. "And yet, here we are, risking our necks for the foolhardy pursuit of fake truth." She shot a glance at Nera.

Nera ignored the bite in Alis' words and let her gaze wander. Instead of answering, she drifted toward the shelves, her fingers gliding over the brittle spines. The shelves lining the walls weren't just clutter—they were filled with records. Old, forgotten, and likely forbidden.

One book caught her attention. It was somehow anomalous—leather-bound, its spine cracked from years of neglect. She pulled it free, dust billowing into the air.

"Nera," Soren warned.

She ignored him and flipped the book open, her pulse stuttering as her eyes skimmed the page. It was old and yellowed with time, the ink slightly faded but still legible. But something was wrong.

She faltered, the hesitation of missing words heavier than those spoken.

This treaty—the one outlining the foundation of her kingdom's rule—was altered. A revision was buried beneath the ink, its traces faint, barely visible unless you knew how to look.

Words had been corrupted, entire sections violently scratched out. Beneath a layer of newer ink, a faint, original script was visible. Nera squinted, reading the line aloud:

> *The Archivists were not invited by the Crown to preserve order; they were installed by the Council to bury the cost of the conquest.*

She pulled back, her breath hitching in her throat. The official history claimed the Transition was peaceful—a request from the people. This text didn't just contradict that; it called the foundation of their society a crime scene.

"What is it?" Alis asked.

"This is the Concord of Dominion," she whispered.

"Well," Alis said dismissively, "we've all seen that before. It's the Concord. We all memorized it ages ago ..."

"That's not what this says," Nera interrupted, her finger shaking as she pointed to the page.

Alis frowned, leaning in. "Then it's a forgery. A bad one. Everyone knows the Concord was a peace treaty, Nera. This says it was a surrender."

"But look at the ink, Alis," Nera argued, scratching at the page. "The official text isn't the base layer. It's sitting on top of the surrender. The peace treaty is the cover-up."

Soren stepped closer, his breath catching as his usually calm face drained of color while he studied the handwriting beneath the revision. "It's not a forgery," he whispered.

Alis caught the coin she had been flipping, her knuckles turning white as she trapped it against her palm. The smirk was gone. "I deal in contraband, Nera, not treason," she murmured, the usual sharpness in her voice dulled by a sudden, cold clarity. "If we walk out of here with that book, I don't get to go back to my life."

The words settled over them, heavy and suffocating. But before Nera could answer, their host moved abruptly near the window. He had barely spoken since they arrived, but now his fingers curled tight around the edge of the curtain as he peered into the darkened streets.

Soren caught the change in his stance immediately. "What is it?"

The man's mouth was a thin line. "Belvar's men," he whispered. "They're going door to door."

"Lights," Soren hissed.

The host pinched out the lantern flame instantly, plunging the room into darkness. "Don't move," he whispered.

In the sudden silence, the sound of the city filtered in. Nera heard the heavy crunch of boots on the gravel outside. Then, a violent crash from the house across the street—the sound of wood splintering, followed by a muffled shout. They weren't just searching; they were hunting. Nera stood frozen in the dark, the book pressed against her chest, listening as the boots left the neighbor's porch and crunched heavily toward their door.

Their host shook his head. "You need to go. Now." He gestured toward the back of the long, dark room. "There's an exit hidden behind the shelves—an old passageway, leads out the back. It'll put you into the lower districts if you move quickly enough."

Nera barely registered her feet moving, her hand contracting around the old treaty as if holding it alone could anchor her. The pages were solid, real—proof that not everything could be erased. But history had slipped through her fingers before. Soren was already motioning for her and Alis to follow, but her grip refused to loosen.

If she let go, would it vanish like all the rest of rewritten history?

The shelves near the far wall were wide, packed with aging records, but the old man was already pushing one aside to reveal a narrow stone archway leading into darkness.

"Go," the host urged, pushing them toward the shadow of the bookcase. "I'll stall as long as I can."

A heavy gauntlet pounded against the wood of the front door—once, twice. A quiet followed, more terrifying than the noise.

"Open by order of the Grand Archive," a voice commanded from outside.

Nera didn't wait for the host to answer. She shoved the heavy tome into her pocket, making the split-second choice to keep the evidence that could get them killed.

The wood around the lock shattered. The door burst open, and lantern light from the street flooded the room, illuminating the dust motes dancing in the air.

"Run!" Soren barked.

They started running down the dark stone passage which was crowded with even more shelves. *Hidden archives.* Nera moved fast yet couldn't help but be distracted by what appeared to be even older books and documents, wondering what histories they held.

Soren was right behind her with Alis, their footsteps shuffling against the stone floor. The dim light offered little guidance, but Nera kept moving, dodging between towering shelves stacked with forgotten ledgers and crumbling records. Their host told them there was an exit, but with adrenaline surging through her veins and Belvar's men closing in, rational thought blurred.

She looked up. The shelving units were old, made of thick wood yet rickety with age, stacked to the ceiling with scrolls and parchments long forgotten. An idea sparked ... risky, but better than a direct confrontation.

"Up," she whispered, gripping the nearest edge and beginning to climb.

Alis jumped up right behind her. Soren hesitated for only a second before following her lead. As they scrambled upward, their movement hidden in the shadows, the shouts grew closer. A moment after they scrambled out of view, figures spilled into the open space beneath them.

Nera held her breath. They were out of sight, but not for long.

Then, a single voice cut through the commotion.

"Keep them alive."

Nera held on to the dusty wooden shelf, her heart hammering against her ribs. Below, the Enforcers moved cautiously forward, their boots scuffing against the stone floor as they scanned the passage. They didn't know exactly where she, Alis and Soren were.

Soren carefully balanced his weight above her. He leaned in close, voice barely a whisper. "We can't stay up here forever."

She knew he was right. The Enforcers would figure it out soon enough. She scanned the towering shelves, noting the fragile joints, the brittle wood barely holding the weight of centuries-old books.

"We don't have to," she whispered back. "We just need a distraction."

She looked at the shelf. It was stacked with brittle scrolls—centuries of thought, perhaps the only copies in existence. *Do it*, she told herself.

She jammed her boot against the upright beam and shoved. The wood resisted, heavy and stubborn. Her foot slipped against the varnish, her knee banging painfully against the shelf. It wasn't moving. Panic flared—not just fear of capture, but fear of what she was trying to do. *I am an Archivist. I protect this. I don't destroy it.*

She gritted her teeth and threw her entire weight into a second, desperate kick.

The structure groaned, a sound like a snapping branch. The shelf tipped past the point of no return. In that split second of gravity taking over, Nera's stomach lurched. She instinctively reached out a hand as if to catch it, to save the falling scrolls, realizing too late that she couldn't undo gravity. And shouldn't.

The crash was deafening. It sounded less like wood breaking and more like bones snapping. The air instantly choked with dust and the violent, tearing sound of a thousand pages ripping at once. For a heartbeat she stood frozen, horrified by the dust, until Soren grabbed her arm.

"Go!" he hissed.

They leapt. Soren landed first, rolling to absorb the impact. Nera followed, barely keeping her balance as she felt Alis land next to her. They sprinted toward the farthest wall and promised exit. Behind them, shouts erupted as the Enforcers scrambled to dig themselves out from under a mound of books and regain their bearings.

A cold voice sliced through the chaos. "Stop them!" Belvar.

Nera hesitated. She knew what had to happen next.

"Go," she hissed under her breath.

Alis turned sharply. "What?"

"He wants me, not you," Nera said, already stepping away from them. "If you stay, you'll get caught too."

Soren looked concerned. "That's not an option."

"It is," she countered. "And you know it. You can still get out— both of you. Hurry."

Alis looked like she wanted to argue, but the sound of boots pounding toward them stole any chance for debate. Alis knew these streets and back alleys well, and trusted her chances there. Soren's expression flashed between frustration and understanding, but finally, he grabbed Alis by the wrist.

"We'll find you," he promised.

They ran.

Nera squared her shoulders, steeling herself as she turned back around and moved the direction they had come from.

Belvar was already waiting.

Nera paused and backed up slightly without thinking, her body pressing against the cold stone wall. The dim glow of a distant lantern cast jagged shadows across his face, his expression unwavering.

"You've always been clever," he said, stepping forward with measured ease. His gaze landed—just a moment—on the book he knew must be hidden in her pocket. A barely-there smirk tugged at the corner of his lips. He already knew. And he was letting her know that he knew. "But that can only take you so far."

Her mind raced, searching for options. There were none. She was trapped, and they both knew it.

Belvar gestured slightly, and two Enforcers stepped into view behind him, blocking any chance of escape. Their posture was relaxed, as if they already considered this finished.

Nera planted her feet, grounding herself as her fingers inched toward the small knife strapped to her calf. "If you're here to drag me back to the Grand Archive, you're wasting your time."

Belvar chuckled softly. "Drag you back? No, Calloway. I have already informed the Archivists to begin the rewrite of you. You were never here."

She swallowed against the knot lodging in her throat. "Then why are you still chasing me?"

Belvar sighed, a sharp, impatient sound, as if indulging a child's naive question. "Because, for now, you still exist. And that is the problem."

The Enforcers moved forward, reaching for her. Nera didn't think—she acted.

In a single fluid motion, she pivoted, letting the enforcer's reach miss by inches as she turned smoothly, her movement more instinct than thought. She redirected the force of the enforcer's grab, twisting his momentum against him, sending him stumbling into the far tunnel wall.

Nera turned and ran. She breathed in quiet, controlled bursts as she forced herself to move swiftly but silently. She didn't know these tunnels well, but she knew one thing—she couldn't afford to get trapped.

A turn ahead split into two paths; one leading upward reaching for shimmering lantern lights beyond, the other downward into deeper darkness. She hesitated for only a second before taking the lower route. They would expect her to go up, toward the surface and better light. But she needed to disappear.

The air grew colder, thick with dampness and the scent of old stone. Her fingers grazed the wall for balance as the floor sloped unevenly beneath her feet. Somewhere above, a muffled shout echoed, followed by the clang of steel against stone. She quickened her pace.

Then—a vibration of movement ahead.

Nera froze, her heartbeat hammering against her ribs. A shadow peeled away from the darkness, stepping into the dim light of a weak lantern. The mysterious man from earlier, his face partially obscured by his deep black hood, stood still as if he had been waiting for her.

His voice was smooth, unsettlingly calm. "You should not have come this way."

It was the same voice from the market. The same distinct pause. Yet she still couldn't place him. Nera stiffened, her fingers twitching toward the small knife she kept strapped to her calf. Almost without thinking, she pressed her free hand lightly against the rough stone wall beside her, grounding herself in the solid reality of it before forcing her focus back to the man in front of her. The figure didn't move, standing like a statue carved from shadow, but she could feel his gaze studying her.

"Who are you?" she demanded, keeping her voice low but firm.

The man tilted his head slightly as if considering whether to answer, the hood of his cloak casting shifting shadows across his face. "Someone who remembers things that should have been forgotten."

The tunnel's humid air seemed to drop ten degrees. The words rang with the same eerie weight as the parchment she had found.

"You know about the erasures," she pressed, adjusting her balance slightly, muscles tensed, prepared to spring into action. "You know what's being hidden."

A pause. Then, a slow nod. "Some. And so do you. That makes you dangerous."

The tunnels behind Nera were no longer silent—faint footsteps echoed from above, moving with purpose. The Enforcers were still searching. She didn't have time for games.

"Then tell me what I need to know," she said. "Before it's too late."

The man finally stepped closer, just enough for the dim light to reveal a glimpse of his features; a mouth set in a line of grim certainty. "You're looking for a book, Scribe. You should be looking for the ash."

Nera froze. "What?"

"The ink didn't dry on that history. They burned it. If you keep digging here, you won't find answers—you'll just fall into the same hole they threw the truth into."

Nera went still, straining to hear the footsteps from above, but she didn't let her expression betray the storm of thoughts racing through her mind. "Then where do I start?" she demanded, stepping forward. If she had already crossed a line, there was no use in holding back.

The man studied her for a beat. "You're asking the wrong question."

A flash of frustration flared in her eyes. "Then tell me the right one."

Another pause, then he looked slightly past her, toward the faint sound of approaching footsteps echoing from the tunnel. The Enforcers were still coming.

He turned his eyes back and stared into hers pointedly. "What does the Archive fear enough to erase?" he finally said.

They both turned slightly to the sound of footsteps getting closer. "Belvar's Enforcers check the upper outpost every hour on the hour. You have three minutes. I suggest you go left." Before she could respond, he vanished into the shadows, leaving her with only his words and the sound of approaching boots.

The Enforcers were too close. There was no time to hesitate. She pushed herself with one last touch against the stone and then bolted, plunging into the unknown.

The passage narrowed quickly, forcing her to twist and duck as the ceiling lowered. The air was damp, thick with the scent of ancient stone and something else—something stagnant and slightly oily. She didn't dare slow, not with the echo of footsteps reverberating behind her. They were relentless, closing in.

A faint light glimmered ahead. A way out? Or another dead end?

Nera pushed harder, her pulse hammering in her ears. The tunnel sloped downward, and she nearly lost her footing, catching herself just before slipping. As she rounded the final bend, her heart seized.

A wall. Solid stone, unyielding.

She skidded to a halt, fingers splaying against the surface. Panic lurched in her chest, but she forced it down. *Think. There must be another way.* Her hands searched frantically along the cracks while she sucked in air, fast and shallow, as if bracing for the inevitable.

A whisper of movement behind her.

"Nowhere left to go, Calloway."

*Belvar.*

Nera pressed her back against the solid stone, her fingers grazing the damp wall behind her. There was no clear escape, but she refused to show hesitation. She met Belvar's gaze, the dim torchlight reflecting off his cold, assessing eyes.

"You've run far enough," he said, taking a deliberate slow step forward. "Now is a good time to stop."

She scoffed. "You're assuming I ever planned on stopping."

Belvar tilted his head slightly, unimpressed. "I admire your tenacity. But the Archive does not admire disobedience among its Archivists, not even inexperienced ones."

She grasped the knife from her calf. She couldn't fight them all—Belvar wouldn't be here alone. And right on cue there was movement behind him, the subtle evidence of Enforcers just beyond the light. One moved in slightly to whisper into Belvar's ear. Belvar paused, an abrupt but slight change in his posture. He listened to the whispered message, his eyes narrowing in disbelief. "Are you certain?" he murmured to the enforcer. The man nodded once, a terrified expression on his face.

Belvar went unnaturally still, the veins in his neck straining against his high collar. The temperature in the tunnel seemed to drop as he stared at the Enforcer, his momentary silence heavier than any shout. "The Architect gave the order personally?" Belvar hissed, his voice dropping to a dangerous growl that made the enforcer flinch. "To let her walk?" so quiet that Nera barely heard.

"Explicitly, sir," the enforcer whispered, his eyes darting nervously to Nera. "He said ... he said the ink isn't dry on her yet."

Belvar went unnaturally pale. He knew what happened to drafts that Kestor hadn't finished writing. He slowly holstered his blade with mechanical precision. The authority he wore like armor hardened, revealing a man who understood that the Architect's design was more important than the kill.

Belvar turned back to Nera, but the cold indifference was gone, replaced by a sharp, dissecting scrutiny. He stepped closer, the torchlight casting deep shadows across his face as he searched hers. He looked at the set of her jaw, the defiant fire in her dark eyes.

A twitch of calculation passed through his eyes before he masked it.

"I always thought your defiance was a flaw in your training," he muttered, his voice low, almost to himself. "But I see now it is ... a permanent stain."

Nera frowned, gripping her knife tighter. "What?" Then she had a realization.

"You're wasting time," she said, schooling her voice into something controlled. "If you wanted me gone or dead, I wouldn't still be here breathing."

A flash of resigned indifference crossed Belvar's expression. "True. But you misunderstand your situation." He stepped closer, hands still clasped behind his back. "You are an error. The only question is how we correct it."

He was stalling. Which meant she still had a move left to play.

Belvar studied her, his face a mask of bored cruelty. Then, instead of giving the order to seize her, he clicked his tongue against his teeth, almost disappointed.

"You always were too stubborn for your own good, Calloway."

Nera kept her stance firm despite the pounding in her chest. She realized he was thinking, weighing something.

Finally, he tilted his head slightly, a shadow of amusement crossing his face. "Running was always pointless. You know that, don't you? You can't outrun the Archive. And you certainly can't outrun me."

Nera swallowed down the sharp retort pressing at the back of her throat. He wanted her to react, to lash out, to give him an excuse. Instead, she stayed silent.

"You're going back to the Archive," Belvar continued smoothly, as if it had never been a question. "But not as an Archivist."

Nera frowned, her grip on her knife loosening in confusion. "You're dismissing me?"

"I am reclassifying you." He took a half-step closer, his voice devoid of any anger, replaced by the chilling, detached curiosity of a scientist observing a stain on a slide "We do not immediately erase anomalies, Calloway. We study them. You are going back to your desk. You will sit among your peers. But do not mistake their silence for ignorance. You are no longer staff; you are on probation."

The air trapped in her lungs refused to exhale. It was a vivisection. The relief she should have felt was instantly strangled. This wasn't mercy … It was a stay of execution solely for the purpose of documentation.

"Your access is revoked," Belvar added, his eyes flat. "Your tenure is dissolved. You exist within those walls only because I am curious how long it will take for the rot in your memory to spread. Go back, Calloway. But know that the moment you stop being interesting, you stop existing."

Looking at the Enforcers blocking her exit, she realized she had no leverage. Out here, she was a target. Inside, she was a specimen to be watched. Her only play was to walk back into the trap and pray she could figure out how to dismantle it from the inside before they decided her usefulness had run out.

She didn't argue. Not now. The fight was far from over, but she knew she couldn't win it here.

Belvar motioned to his Enforcers, and they stepped back just enough to make it clear she wasn't being dragged back—she was being allowed to walk, but under his authority.

Nera said nothing. She turned back toward the Grand Archive. Belvar wasn't locking her up because he wanted to contain her. He was letting her back in because he wanted to see what she would do next.

## CHAPTER FOUR

# Reality Resists

Nera stepped towards the entrance to the Grand Archive. Varethis was the heart of the entire Archivist system. This was where the ink was mixed. This was where reality didn't just exist—it submitted.

Her heartbeat was steady but her mind raced. She had returned, just as Belvar wanted. But not as the same person who had left. She had unanswered questions that only the Archive could answer.

She reached inside her satchel, her fingers grazing the familiar shape of her quill. Raven-feathered, silver-tipped—a signature of her work. A personal artifact in a world that rewrote everything. Each Archivist selected their quill when they completed their Scribe attunement, and most went with a color scheme that aligned with their chosen profession within the Archive. As a Field Archivist, Nera had chosen black, reflective of all of its historical significance.

She turned sharply toward the narrow side corridor—the quiet shortcut used by Field Archivists to bypass the noise of the main atrium. Her hand reached for the familiar iron latch, but the metal held fast. Locked.

She tugged again, confusion flashing before memory caught up. *Your access is revoked.*

A heavy click echoed from the lock, but the door remained sealed. The mechanism recognized her ring, but it refused her entry. Belvar hadn't just demoted her; he was corralling her. He had sealed the shadows, forcing her into the open light of the main thoroughfare where there was nowhere to hide.

Nera straightened her coat, swallowed the lump of humiliation in her throat, and turned back toward the center of the room. If he wanted her on display, she wouldn't give him the satisfaction of looking afraid.

The echoes of her footsteps filled the marble corridor as she passed through the great hall. The usual hum of Archivists at work droned on, but there was an unease she now felt threading beneath it, something barely perceptible but impossible to ignore.

She knew why. *They were watching her.*

She could feel their eyes tracking her movements, whispers just at the edge of her hearing. Conversations would pause as she neared, only to resume once she had passed, quieter than before. It was subtle, but undeniable.

## Chapter Five

# The Safe House

The return journey was suffocatingly silent. Belvar finally stopped at the entrance, offering her a single, pointed warning before dismissing her. "You wanted knowledge, Calloway." His voice was smooth, almost amused, "Now you have it."

He stepped closer, lowering his voice just enough that only she could hear the warning. *"The Archive never forgets."*

Nera bit the inside of her lip and said nothing. She didn't know what he meant, but she intended to find out. For now, she had to act normal, whatever 'normal' meant when you were trapped inside the very institution rewriting history.

She made her way to her designated workstation, an unassuming desk tucked within the labyrinth of the records hall. A familiar stack of scrolls awaited her, the work of conservation and cataloging that had once been routine. But as she started to reach for the scroll she had already been working with, a shadow moved at the edge of her vision. A familiar figure approached, his steps brisk but measured.

She saw the tall form of Cyrus walking towards her. He moved with a disciplined stride—the gait of a man who regularly trained to counteract the damage of sitting at a desk for twelve hours a day. She noticed the red of his trim beard just beginning to show streaks of silver among the ruddy strands as he placed a bundle of scrolls on her desk with practiced ease. One of the Archive's most gifted codex analysts, he moved with the quiet confidence of someone who dealt in secrets.

"Decryption is complete," he said, his voice carrying smooth precision as he unconsciously pushed his glasses up. "The layers were intentionally buried but I extracted the primary text."

Nera glanced at him, arching an eyebrow. "Buried how?"

"Recursive cypher," Cyrus replied. He paused to wind the intricate timepiece strapped to his wrist, the sharp click-click-click of the gears cutting through the hush of the room.

Nera's gaze lingered on the movement. He was always fussing with it, a tic she had never understood.

Cyrus caught her stare. He didn't stop winding. "The Archive's clocks drift when history is edited. Gears ignore the narrative. A year can be rewritten; a machine cannot."

Finished with his adjustment, he pointed to a spot on the parchment with the royal blue feather of his quill, symbolic of those Archivists who chose the technical field of deciphering and encrypting. "The text was buried, not erased. That implies intent."

A quiet warning, though he didn't say it outright. Cyrus wasn't the type to speculate—his job was to extract information, not interpret its implications. But Nera had the distinct feeling that if he was bringing this to her personally, there was something he thought she needed to see.

She reached for the top scroll. The parchment was fragile but intact, the ink aged yet unyielding. "I'll take a look."

Cyrus gave a short nod, his blue eyes wide and unblinking behind his lenses, processing her reaction like she was data on a page. "Exercise caution, Calloway. Information is often encrypted because it is dangerous."

Then, just as quickly as he had arrived, he turned and strode back into the labyrinth of records, leaving Nera with more questions than answers.

She looked down again at the new scroll in her hand. A sharp throb spiked behind her eyes. For a heartbeat, the letters refused to sit still—the stroke of the "A" detached itself, floating like mercury on glass, before snapping back into the fiber of the parchment. Nera squeezed her eyes shut, fighting a sudden wave of motion sickness. It was like the history on the page had taken a breath.

Nera froze.

*A blink. A glitch.*

Looking again, the letters warped, reshaping themselves into something else before snapping back into place.

She held her breath as she stared, willing the words to stay in place. She had spent years memorizing documents, cataloging histories, training her eyes to see even the most imperceptible inconsistencies. Something was no longer holding inside the Archive. The air felt charged, thick with static.

She absently twisted the ring she always wore on her right hand as she realized she wasn't the only one who noticed. From the far end of the chamber, someone was watching her. A presence, familiar yet unsettling.

Nera inhaled sharply and looked up.

*Kieran Voss.*

Tall, lean, and coiled with a readiness that never fully faded, Kieran stood half-shrouded in the dim light. Something about him—his stillness, his patience—felt like an echo of something she should remember. His brown hair was slightly unkempt, and the faint scar along his jaw caught the light as he turned, the only sign he wasn't just another statue among the endless shelves.

His fingers ghosted over the hilt of a knife at his hip, not drawing it, not even adjusting it—just feeling its weight. A habit more than a precaution.

He waited at the edge of the chamber, his posture casual, almost indifferent, but his gaze sharp—too sharp. He was studying her, and Nera hated being studied.

She forced herself to hold his stare, unwilling to be the first to look away. It had been weeks since they had last spoken, since the last Archive project they had worked on together, and she wasn't sure if this was a coincidence or something else entirely.

Kieran took a slow step forward, now rolling the hilt of the small knife between his fingers with absent precision, a habit he only indulged when thinking deeply. But the way he looked at her—like he was waiting for something—made her skin prickle.

"You hesitated."

Nera frowned. "Excuse me?"

He motioned toward the scroll in her hands. "You hesitated before touching it. Why?"

The question unsettled her, because he had seen what no one else had. "I was ... distracted," she lied smoothly, intentionally adding a look that might make him think he was the distraction as a way to throw him off.

Kieran's expression didn't change, but something in his eyes darkened. He looked at the scroll in her hands, then back up to her eyes, his gaze lingering a second too long. He didn't say a word. He just stepped back, his eyes narrowing slightly, as if filing the moment away for later.

"You saw it, didn't you?"

He hesitated. Just long enough for Nera to catch it.

A chill crawled up Nera's spine. "Explain," she insisted quietly.

But Kieran only glanced past her, toward the hall where the other Archivists moved in their carefully rehearsed routines, oblivious to the fracture in their reality. "Not here," he said. "Meet me in the lower archives at midnight. Alone."

Then, softer, "I'll explain what I can."

Just as swiftly as he had appeared, he turned and disappeared through the bustle of Archivists and trainee Scribes who moved about the room.

Nera remained still, pulse thrumming in her ears. *Midnight. The lower archives. Alone.* It was a risk, but she knew she would go. She had to. She wanted the truth, and whatever Kieran knew, it was clear he wasn't willing to say it here, under the ever-watchful eyes of the Archive.

She forced herself back to her work, her fingers methodically unrolling the next scroll. But the words before her blurred, her thoughts lingering on the encounter. *Had anyone else noticed the momentary flicker?* She glanced around the chamber, scanning the faces of other Archivists. Luckily, none seemed to be paying her any more attention than usual.

Belvar wasn't present, but that meant nothing. His reach extended far beyond the halls he physically occupied. Even in his absence, his authority pressed against the Archive like a closing fist—unseen, but inescapable. She was certain there were eyes on her; there were always eyes on her now.

She forced herself through the motions of her work, keeping her head down and her expression neutral. The hours crawled by, each task feeling heavier than usual. Archivists moved around her in their quiet, methodical rhythms, but she was only half-aware of them. Her mind kept circling back to what she had seen.

When her shift ended, she had made her decision. Instead of heading straight for her quarters, she took a detour through one of the lesser-used corridors, where the walls held more secrets than most would ever notice. Once inside a seldom-used sitting room, she secured the door, reaching into the hollowed space behind a loose stone in the wall.

Her fingers brushed against the rough edges of the old, worn copy of the Concord of Dominion from Soren's safe house.

She had studied this treaty before—everyone had. It was one of the most well-documented texts in the Archive. But the version she held in her hands wasn't the same as the one everyone knew. This one had been altered, rewritten to bury something important.

She carefully opened the brittle pages, her eyes scanning the inked lines. She didn't know how much time she had before midnight, but waiting in silence wasn't an option. If the history she had been taught was indeed false, then she needed to understand why.

The hours dragged as she waited for nightfall. Each flutter of candlelight felt like a countdown, each quiet shuffle of paper like a warning. By the time she heard the last of her peers settle down in their quarters for the evening and the halls fall silent, her nerves were taut.

At the stroke of midnight, she moved.

Slipping through the dim corridors, she kept to the shadows, her steps measured and silent. The lower archives were rarely disturbed at this hour, their winding shelves a forgotten labyrinth of history. A perfect place for a conversation that wasn't meant to be overheard.

She reached the designated chamber, feeling the cold seeping through the stone as she entered. A single lantern glared at the far end, casting long, restless shadows around the corners of the room.

Kieran was already there, waiting in front of the fireplace, where a portrait of Valen Kestor was proudly displayed above the mantle.

He rested his lean frame against one of the heavy wooden tables, arms crossed, his sharp gaze moving over her as she entered. The lantern's dim glow cast shadows across his face, highlighting the familiar edge of wariness she had seen too many times before. He had always been like this—calculating, quiet, watching everything and revealing nothing unless he chose to.

"You came," he said, voice low but certain. "I wasn't sure you would."

Nera shrugged, forcing herself to remain casual despite the tension coiled in her limbs. "And miss the chance to be dragged into another one of your cryptic warnings? How could I resist?"

A twitch of something—amusement?—crossed his expression, but it vanished just as quickly. "This isn't a game, Nera."

She studied him for a beat longer. They had known each other for years, their paths occasionally crossing in the Archive long before she had ever suspected the depth of the history hidden within its walls. Once, she might have called him a friend. But things had changed, and now, every word they spoke carried weight.

"It never is with you," she muttered. "So tell me—what am I in danger of this time?"

Kieran straightened, pushing off the table, his posture changing into something more intentional. "You already know. You saw it today. The way the Archive is shifting. The way it's resisting."

She hesitated. "You think this round of rewrites are failing?"

He looked at the rows of silent books, genuine fear crossing his face. "I don't know what it is. I just know the ink moved, and that means something."

"But how?" she whispered. "All Archivists know that history is meant to be absolute. We were taught that once the Council decides, the world follows. There is no reason for reality to reject the ink while it's still wet."

The air grew thin, sucked dry by the unsaid, the scent of aged parchment mingling with the cold stone. She had spent years studying the past, learning how history had been shaped and reshaped by those in power, having trained under some of the best Master Archivists in the land, who were adept at carefully editing the past; but even she had never questioned whether the foundation of it all could unravel.

"And you?" she asked finally. "Where do you fit into this? You always seem to know more than you say. Why tell me?"

Kieran stepped closer, his voice barely above a whisper. "I don't have the answers, Nera," he admitted, his voice rough. He looked past her, at the rows of silent books. "I just know they're wrong. I look at the ink, and I know it's lying. And today, when I saw you hesitate with the scroll ... it was the first time I thought someone else saw it."

Nera's breath caught for half a second before she forced herself to mask it. She had spent years silently questioning the Archive's control over history, but she had never dared to ask if it had already rewritten *her own* memories.

The idea of it curled in her gut like a slow-burning flame. Nera swallowed. "You think it's happening to me too."

"I know it is." He searched her face. "You hesitated with that scroll because for a split second, the words weren't what you expected them to be. That's not normal, Nera. It felt like the ink wasn't holding."

Her fingers curled into a fist at her side. "If the Archive's power is weakening, then why does no one else see it? Why are we the only ones who remember?"

Kieran's gaze darkened. "Because the others never stood close enough to the truth to begin with."

The air was thick with everything unsaid. Nera felt his words settle over her like a cloak ... heavy, suffocating. If he was right, then she wasn't just uncovering lost history anymore. She was living inside of it, being pulled between versions of the past that should have never collided.

"And Belvar?" she asked finally. "What does he know?"

Kieran went rigid. "More than he's letting on. He's keeping you close for a reason, and it's not just to watch you. He needs you inside the Archive for some reason, Nera. I think he's afraid of what you might see."

His voice was steady, but there was something else. Something like hesitation.

A slow chill crept over her skin. She had spent so long digging for answers, only to now realize that she might already be a part of the story she was trying to uncover.

* * *

The following days passed in a haze of uncertainty. Nera carried Kieran's words, replaying their midnight conversation in her mind. *Could he be right? Were they on the verge of something crumbling?* The Archive was a place of order, of precision—rewrites were not meant to fail. And yet, she had seen it. She had felt it.

Every moment alone became a battle between reason and the gnawing compulsion to know the truth, and there was only one way to find out. Testing a rewrite herself was unthinkable, forbidden. Only Archivists of the highest level were permitted to alter history. Of course she was trained how, but it was something that she was still not officially allowed to do yet. Even if she could, even if she found a way, what if it went wrong? What if she unwittingly unraveled herself instead of the truth?

But that doubt was precisely why she had to do it. She couldn't trust anyone's records anymore. The only way to know was to try. To see if she had the ability to pull at the strings of history and glimpse what lay beneath the Archive's controlled façade.

And so, she carefully prepared. By the time she found herself sitting before the parchment, quill poised over the ink, the decision had been made. It had been made the moment Kieran looked at her with something close to recognition and said *You remember things you shouldn't.*

Nera sat in the dim glow of candlelight, her fingers tracing the faded ink of the document before her. This document was not of much consequence, just a copy of an order for supplies. The parchment felt both ancient and unsettlingly fresh, as if it had been rewritten more than once.

She hesitated. What if she did this and nothing happened? Worse—*what if something did?*

No. It was just a test—a routine which Archivists performed every day with nothing but ink and parchment. She could almost hear Soren's voice in her ear, sharp and warning during one of their lessons. *Do not reach for what you cannot hold.* He had always warned that the easier path was the trap—temporal edits were chaos waiting to happen. That's why Scribes were only allowed to test on simple basics with a teacher or mentor present, and the larger rewrites were reserved for only the most Master Archivists.

She paused, gathering her thoughts. A minor edit—just a test— nothing drastic. *Alignments build the house, but rewrites just patch the cracks*, Soren used to say. She dipped the nib of her quill into the ink and began. She settled her mind on the desired outcome and the extent of the small change she had planned, just 'patching a crack'. She wrote carefully, precisely, feeling the aching sensation in her hand and arm even though this was only a relatively small, contained physical rewrite, a simple change in quantity from an old, unimportant document.

The ink didn't just sit on the page; it pulsed, syncing with the thudding rhythm of her own heart. The muscles in her forearm seized, cramping as if she were lifting a stone slab rather than a feather. Heat flushed through her body like she had just sprinted a mile without taking a breath. She dropped the quill, her hand shaking so badly she couldn't unclench her fingers, gasping for air that felt too thin to fill her lungs. As the letters reshaped, the fibers of the parchment groaned, a microscopic screeching sound like tearing muscle. The world around the desk warped, the straight lines of the room bending toward the book momentarily as if the gravity of the rewrite was pulling the room into the dark.

This was unlike any feeling she had experienced as a Scribe. In the training halls, the Archive absorbed the recoil, making the alteration of history feel clinical—weightless.

But here, without the protocols to shield her, the shock went straight into her bone. She was touching the raw nerve of the world, and it burned. But trying was worth it.

She lifted the quill, admiring the line. It looked ... better. Cleaner. The chaotic, mismatched numbers were gone, replaced by a singular, orderly truth. A flush of relief washed over her. It was just a supply log, she reasoned. Just a small edit to test.

For a second, she didn't feel afraid. She felt *capable*.

Then, the room shifted. A subtle distortion rippled through the space, bending the edges of reality. Nera's vision blurred, her heartbeat thundering in her ears. Then, for a split second, she was gone. Not anywhere. Just a whisper.

A gasp dragged her back into existence. Her gasp. She groped the edge of the desk, her knuckles turning white, waiting for the room to stop spinning. Vertigo. It had to be vertigo. She smoothed the parchment to check the ink, but when her fingertips brushed the rough surface, she felt nothing. No texture. No friction; as if the skin of her fingers had gone blind. She pressed harder until the sensation returned—dull and distant, like shouting through water. Just numbness, she told herself. Just the cold.

She recalled vague tendrils of a memory of a stranger whispering, *Before the ink dried, there was another story,* desperately trying to grasp at the fringes of the memory before it dissipated into nothingness.

She stumbled back from the desk, breathing hard like she had run a race. The word *Benefactor* had flickered on the parchment, appearing, disappearing, reappearing.

She squeezed her eyes shut, but the letters burned behind her eyelids. When she opened them again, the ink was still wet.

Nera twisted the silver ring she wore on her right hand, a nervous tic, as realization dawned. There had always been vague stories during childhood, and a long history even before. Is it possible that the mysterious Benefactor was real—woven through the very fabric of recorded time? If so, had she just brushed against the thread that held it all together?

The implications of this near-erasure still clawed at her mind. If a mere stroke of ink could undo her, what would a more significant rewrite cause? She had been reckless, and now she knew: history did not like to be tampered with.

A knock at the door jolted her from her spiraling thoughts. She hesitated before slipping the edited parchment to the bottom of the stack on her desk and then crossing the room to open the door. Standing in the dimly lit hallway was a hooded figure in muted blue robes, their face partially concealed in shadow. The outline was just slightly wrong, as if the light couldn't quite agree where they ended. She could quickly tell this was someone she had never met before.

"You should not have done that," the frail man uttered, voice laced with something between caution and dismay. "You've been noticed."

Nera's pulse quickened. "By whom?"

The stranger stepped forward just enough for the candlelight to catch his features—etched with lines of forgotten time, eyes too knowing for a mere scholar. "By those who do not wish to be remembered."

The words made Nera freeze. If she had attracted the attention of the Unwritten, there was no undoing what she had set in motion.

## Chapter 6

# Seven Ledgers

The conversation still echoed in her mind long after the stranger had vanished.

She had tried to focus on her work, on the familiar scent of parchment and ink, on the way the Archive's halls stood unchanged—tall, orderly, unbreakable and unshaken. This was where she belonged. This was where she had always belonged.

*Then why did it feel hostile now?* Her steps slowed near a corridor she had walked a thousand times. She turned her head slightly, watching the space between the lanterns, the way the shadows should have moved but didn't.

*Had this hall always been this long?*

At her desk, a fresh stack of scrolls awaited her, bound in neat twine. She unraveled the first one, letting the familiar motion steady her hands. She fell into the numb, rhythmic comfort of the work.

*Ten crates of parchment.*

*Five barrels of ink.*

*Seven sacks of grain.*

Nera hesitated. Grain?

She frowned, scanning the order again. The ink refused to bond with the fiber, sitting atop the parchment like oil on water, the letters refusing to take a permanent shape. She blinked.

*Ten crates of parchment.*

*Five barrels of ink.*

*Seven—*

The word changed.

She carefully rubbed her thumb over the surface of the parchment. The ink held. Solid. Real. But she knew what she had seen.

Her heartbeat drummed in her ears as she forced herself to breathe.

She reached for her quill, dipping it into the inkpot beside her, looking at her hands until they stopped trembling before scribbling a note in the margins of the document. Just a mark. Just to see.

The moment the ink touched the parchment, it bled sideways, slipping across the fibers as if it had never settled into place. The letters unraveled, curling in on themselves before reforming.

*Seven ledgers.*

She recoiled, knocking over the inkpot. A dark pool spread across the fibers of the parchment. It should have smelled sharp— the metallic tang of iron gall. But for a long, terrifying moment, the air smelled like nothing. A vacuum. Nera blinked, and the scent returned, though it felt thinner than she remembered—flat, like a memory of a smell rather than the thing itself. She ignored it, wiping the mess with her sleeve. She stared at it, waiting, half-expecting the text to bleed again.

It refused. She slid the scroll to the bottom of her finished pile, but the ink beneath the stack was still trembling.

# CHAPTER 7:

# The Scholar's Rest

Later that week, Nera found herself seated at a familiar corner table in The Scholar's Rest, a modest tavern tucked into the outskirts of the Archive's district. It was her favorite spot in town because they allowed patrons to brew their own custom cup of tea by choosing from among the many options of tea leaves they carried.

The candlelight spilled over well-worn wooden beams, the scent of spiced wine, parchment, and steeping tea leaves filling the space. A musician in the corner played a mix of songs—scholar's hymns for the front tables, and traveler's ballads for the shadows—while patrons dropped coins in his cup with the quiet caution of people who knew even a tavern had ears.

Nera glanced around the entire room, taking in some familiar faces from the Archive. At a nearby table, Cyrus sat with his wife Sarina, her silken black hair tied up into a quick bun, their conversation quiet but animated as he gestured with one hand and then adjusted the timepiece on his wrist, checking the seconds as if timing the silence between whispers.

Across the room, Tavian, a self-taught historian and philosopher, sat with an aged tome balanced precariously on his knee. He looked young compared to the heavy philosophy he was reading—face smooth beneath a mop of dark curly hair. He was the kind of lean that came from forgetting meals in favor of reading chapters, yet his shoulders held the easy set of a man used to physical work, not just study. Tavian believed history was best understood by those who lived it rather than dictated from the top down. It made him an outsider among scholars, and a walking heresy to the Archive.

Across the table from her sat two of her childhood friends. Alis—her early school classmate and recent rescuer—smirked over her cup, her usual expression, especially after having played the role of knight in shining armor a few weeks ago.

Beside her, Cael Renwick, her closest friend growing up, reclined in his chair, his ever-watchful eyes scanning the room. One arm rested casually around the shoulders of his girlfriend, Livia, who slowly swirled her tea, seemingly disinterested yet listening to every word. She hummed along with the music in quiet amusement, the fingers of her free hand absently tracing circles against Cael's wrist.

It was a simple, absentminded gesture, but Nera caught the way Cael's hand closed around hers—just for a second, as if anchoring himself to something only he understood.

The clink of glass against wood announced Tyrek, the tavern's owner, before he even spoke. He slipped between the crowded tables with the tireless, fluid grace of a long-distance runner. He set down a fresh round of drinks, flashing a smile that felt warm and entirely disarming—the kind of genuine expression that made you forget he was charging you for the ale. "Alright, scholars, let's see who's drinking like an Archivist tonight. Veilshadow Ale, Ink-Stained Mead, and the sensible choice—Scholar's Blend Tea."

Cael gave a mock scowl. "We both know I'm taking the ale."

"Figures," Alis muttered. "Last time you drank that stuff, you started ranting about erased cities that never existed."

"They did exist," Cael shot back, grabbing his stein.

Tyrek chuckled. "That's what they all say. Veilshadow Ale has that effect—it lingers in the head like a half-remembered dream."

Nera sat silently in thought, picking up her own drink—tea, rich with spices that warmed the back of her throat. Scholar's Blend, meant for long nights hunched over detailed records.

"Smart choice," Tyrek noted. "You Archivists are the only ones who drink tea at a tavern," he said as he quickly handed Livia and Alis their drinks. "*To survival*, then." He raised his own mug slightly.

Alis tapped her cup to his, then looked at the others, her smirk widening. "To survival, and to history. May we always drink before we're erased." Cael noticeably rolled his eyes, but lifted his stein anyway.

Nera paused, tilting her cup slightly in return as she repeated an old scribe's phrase. "Ink holds truth."

A sharp clack nearby cut through the murmur. Tavian had set his mug down hard, refusing to lift it in toast.

"Ink doesn't hold truth. It only holds the memory of the hand that wrote it," he said, his voice flat enough to make Alis stop smiling. He pushed his cup away, the amber liquid sloshing over the rim, refusing the ritual entirely. "I don't toast to the cage."

Tyrek caught the words, and leaned toward Nera, unsmiling. "That's a damn fine toast," he murmured, his eyes darting to the door. "But keep it down. Two Enforcers were here an hour ago asking who rents this table. I told them ghosts don't pay rent."

Liaz, Tyrek's wife, stepped out from behind his shoulder, dropping a rag onto the table with a heavy, deliberate slap. She didn't look at Tyrek; she looked at the door.

"Maybe time to close the tab," she said, her voice like a gavel. Tyrek's charming smile vanished instantly. He knew better than to argue when Liaz sensed a predator.

At the next table, Cyrus froze. He looked down at the scroll he had been annotating all evening—a complex cipher he had spent weeks breaking. He glanced at the door, calculating the Enforcers' potential arrival time against the time it would take to hide the document. The math didn't work.

He didn't hesitate. With a pained grimace, he tore the scroll in half and dropped it into the center of the flame of the candle on his table.

"Cyrus," Sarina whispered, reaching for his hand. "I know you spent so many hours on that."

"Variable removed," he said quietly, watching his work turn to ash. He adjusted his glasses, his face blank, though his hand trembled slightly. "That could be dangerous. Now it is not."

"Right," Tyrek cleared his throat, still talking quietly. "Drink up then … maybe don't come back for a while. "Then he tipped his own glass to Nera's toast, voice louder, "Ink holds truth!"

Around the room, a few other scholars echoed it, their voices overlapping as their cups clinked together.

*"Ink holds truth!"*

It was an evening they had previously planned as a night to relax ahead of an upcoming group trip hosted by the Archives, the annual autumn Historical Review Tour to the town of Vornis, scheduled long before Nera's world had begun unraveling—a brief reprieve from the endless corridors of the Archive. Yet, even here, knowledge pressed against her chest.

Alis leaned forward, a grin playing at the corner of her lips as she slightly laughed from the tales from childhood they had been telling Livia. "Remember the restricted archives?" Alis said, nudging Cael. "Seven years old and you were already trying to reorganize the index while we were supposed to be stealing candy."

"I wasn't reorganizing," Cael corrected, swirling his drink. "I was fixing the catalog. And Nera was the one who got us caught because she stopped to read a warning label."

Livia, sipping her tea, raised an eyebrow. "I find it hard to believe Nera ever panicked over anything."

Alis smirked, tipping her cup toward Cael. "You've always been like that, though—never reckless enough to get caught, but never quite willing to let things go either."

One of the rebels at the next table—Jorin, a young, wiry man they barely knew but who was a regular at the tavern—overheard and chuckled as he refilled his drink. "That's the problem with you scholars. You lot always think there's a right answer." He grinned lazily, turning toward Cael. "So, tell me, Renwick—if you had to choose between the truth and love, which would you pick?"

Cael cleared his throat, embarrassed, quickly landing on Livia, the sound sharp in the sudden quiet, then turned his back on Jorin. "And then," Cael continued, grinning at Livia, "we got caught because Alis knocked over an entire shelf of scrolls. I've never seen Master Belvar so red in the face."

"We had to scrub floors for a month," Alis added, feigning a shudder. "Worth it, though. We got to hear Nera's mom lecture us about the sanctity of knowledge for hours."

Nera's smile faltered just slightly at the mention of her mother. Mirelle Calloway had always spoken of history in quiet, careful ways; never as something to be rewritten, only repaired. A skilled bookbinder, she had spent her life restoring what others had left to decay, a trade that paid their way yet also never let them dream too far.

Raising Nera alone, she had never spoken of the man who left them behind. Survival had been her priority, not questions. Nera always had the feeling this had less to do with what she might find, and more to do with who might find her. She remembered the way her mother used to check the locks on windows and doors twice every night; and as Nera grew older she realized something in her mother's mannerism said this was less about keeping out thieves and more about something else that she couldn't quite put her finger on, a topic that her mother would never speak of.

In childhood, Nera had resented her mother's silence, but as she grew older, frustration had grown into something more complicated. Had her mother chosen not to know, or had she simply known too much? And if she had still been alive, what would she think of who Nera had become?

Alis peered at her friend while rolling a coin between her fingers, then paused and suddenly tapped it on the table, breaking the silence. "You've been a ghost all week, Nera. Even worse than usual. You hiding something?"

Nera hesitated, glancing between her friends while nervously twisting the thin silver bands on her right hand, interlaced into one ring. Each was etched with tiny, forgotten symbols from an erased civilization; a relic that she had found among her mother's things once when she was young, and when she asked, her mother had snatched away and forbidden Nera from wearing it. "This is dangerous," she had said, "but it will be yours some day." Nera never saw the ring again until her mother died. She kept the ring and wore it as a quiet rebellion against those who sought to erase, a defiant reminder of what had been forgotten. Nera hesitated, glancing between her friends while absently twisting the silver bands.

Her friends lived outside the Field Archivists hierarchy. They weren't bound by the same rules. Speaking of the past so freely with them felt like standing on the edge of a blade.

"I saw something," she admitted quietly. "Something I shouldn't have."

Cael arched an eyebrow. "Then unsee it. We're here to drink, not commit treason."

Nera looked down, her thumb rubbing the scar on her palm. "I can't."

"Why?" Alis leaned in, her gaze dropping to Nera's hands. "You're shaking. You only shake when you've done something stupid." She grabbed Nera's wrist, exposing her ink-stained fingers. "You didn't just see something. You touched it."

Nera yanked her hand back. "I made a change," she whispered, the confession torn out of her. "I rewrote a record. It should have settled, but didn't."

"That's not possible," Alis snapped, her voice hard. "You aren't high enough in the hierarchy. You don't have the clearance to hold the pen alone, let alone change the ink."

"I know I don't!' Nera hissed. "That's why I'm terrified, Alis. Because it worked."

Alis whipped out her silver coin, twisting it between her fingers, as Cael looked down, suddenly vitally interested in his drink.

Livia tilted her head, setting her tea down with a soft clink and breaking the awkward silence that had settled over their small group. "I never really understood what it is you all do. I mean, I know the basics—Archivists maintain records, preserve history and all that—but it's not like I ever paid much attention to it in school."

The corner of Alis' mouth lifted in a half grin. "Cael and I started in Conservation. We were glorified dusters—keeping old paper from rotting. Boring, but safe. Unlike Cyrus over there," she pointed a thumb, "who breaks codes for a living. Or the ones in the basement who butcher history to fit the Council's narrative." She looked pointedly at Nera. "Nera is a Field Archivist. Her job is to find history ...not touch it."

Cael set his mug down hard. "Nera catalogs documents. That's it." He looked pointedly at Livia. "Boring, dusty work. Nothing to worry about."

"She deals with revisions," Alis corrected, ignoring Cael's warning glare. "She ensures history remains ... convenient."

Livia looked between them, sensing the sudden friction. "You're making it sound like a crime."

"It is a crime," Alis said, locking eyes with Cael. "Tell her, Cael. Tell her that the ink isn't drying."

"Alis, enough," Cael warned, his voice low.

"It should be set in stone by now," Alis pressed, leaning over the table. "But it's slush. It keeps trying to change back, and people like Nera are the ones holding the dam together."

Cael nodded, his expression dark. "That's where things get complicated. Some ruins and hidden histories refuse to disappear. Ghosts. And we don't talk about them."

Livia frowned, carefully hesitating. "That sounds … unsettling."

Nera absent-mindedly tapped her ring against her cup, a quiet *tink tink* breaking the tension. "They aren't ghosts," Nera argued, the need to be understood overriding her caution. "They are fragments, pieces of history that refused to be erased and still exist in some form. They're still here, Cael."

Livia frowned, pulling back slightly from Cael's suddenly increased grip on her hand. Cael released her instantly, but he didn't look at her. He glared at Nera. "The Archive doesn't want people questioning why the Alignment hasn't settled. Stop trying to solve a puzzle that's going to get us killed."

Alis jumped in. "The Archive controls which records survive. Sometimes, that means removing contradictions or making 'corrections' so history aligns the way they say it's supposed to. And sometimes, those corrections aren't as harmless as they seem. Which is part of the problem when you try to rewrite history."

Nera sighed. "That's why only high-ranking Archivists are supposed to make actual revisions. The risks are too great. One wrong adjustment, and entire events could unravel. I … " she hesitated even how to admit it, "I wasn't supposed to do what I did."

Livia glanced between them, eyes widening slightly. "But you did."

Nera nodded. "And now I'm left wondering what else has been changed—and who decides what version of history we're supposed to accept."

Cael leaned forward, studying her. "What exactly did you change?"

Nera hesitated. *The flickering ink. The wavering name Benefactor. The way conversations in the Archive had subtly shifted afterward.* She knew better than to say too much, but she also knew she couldn't keep it entirely to herself.

"Barely anything, but enough to know that history is resisting itself," she finally said. "And that we're not meant to remember what came before."

Her words silenced the table. Livia glanced toward Cael silently. Alis, usually quick with a quip, looked genuinely concerned.

"You need to be careful, Nera," Cael warned, his voice quieter now. "You're playing with something bigger than just records and ink."

She already knew that. But hearing it aloud made it feel even more real.

Nera drained the last of her tea, the dregs bitter against her tongue. She followed Cael and the others out, wrapping her coat tight, but the warmth of the tavern vanished the moment she hit the threshold. The heavy oak door swung shut behind her, cutting off the laughter, and she paused.

*The street shouldn't be this empty.*

A figure stood across the street beneath the shadow of an overhanging awning, half-hidden in the dim glow of the street lamps. His posture was unnervingly still, eyes locked onto her with a patience that made her heart hammer against her chest. Youthful strength radiated from him like it had every time she had seen him before, exactly like when she had found the scrap of parchment near the vanished apothecary.

Nera's breath hitched. This wasn't coincidence.

For a long time, neither moved. Then, just as the moment became unbearable, the stranger turned, continuing on his path, and melted into the darkness of an alleyway.

She knew, with absolute certainty, that this was no ordinary onlooker. He hadn't been watching her to see where she was going. He was watching to see if she was still real.

## CHAPTER EIGHT
# The Erased

Nera heard the tavern door open behind her and interior laughter spill out into the night; the voices of other patrons as they made their way into the evening.

She turned slightly to look at them, and when she pivoted back she noticed that the streets outside the tavern were now alive with the usual hum of evening conversation, warm lantern light spilling onto the cobbled paths. Merchants packed their stalls, the scent of spiced cider mixing with the sharp tang of parchment ink and the musk of old books. Scholars, traders, and rogue historians intermingled—some debating, some drinking, some selling half-truths in the form of rare texts.

This is what the street was supposed to look like when she had stepped outside the tavern doors. Normal.

"Nera...?" Kieran asked, in a tone that said he had already called her name at least once already.

Nera turned toward the voice, pulse quickening at the familiarity of it.

Kieran stood a few paces away, his gaze sweeping the street with a sentry's focus, the only evidence of any amount of concern. He was too still—watchful in a way that made the noise of the city seem dimmer, as if he were waiting to see whether she, too, would flicker and disappear. His coat hung just loose enough to suggest he could move at a moment's notice, and when Cael stepped closer, his own gaze hardening, Kieran barely spared him a glance. He wasn't concerned about Cael. He was watching Nera. Like he was waiting for her to catch up to something he had already done.

He hadn't been inside the tavern. He had been waiting for her.

"You're late," he joked, though there was no accusation in his tone—just observation.

"I wasn't aware we had plans," she shot back. She kept her voice even, but settled her stance ... rooted, prepared. If Kieran was waiting, she wanted to know why.

Kieran tilted his head slightly. "We never do. And yet, here we are."

Alis folded her arms, still wary. "And who exactly is this?"

Kieran ignored the question, his focus locked onto Nera. "You've felt it again, haven't you? The shifts?"

She hesitated.

But before she could answer, a strange stillness pressed at the edges of the street, sending a chill across her skin. Something felt ... *off*.

Her gaze drifted past Kieran and her attention fixed on an elderly man lingering just beyond the lantern glow. The light fractured around the old man; flickering, hesitant. As if reality itself wasn't sure he should be there.

He stood tall, yet his frame seemed stretched thin, weightless in a way that made him look like a half-remembered story. His white hair, tangled as if caught in a wind no one else could feel, framed a face that quivered between familiarity and absence. His gaze drifted past her—briefly unfocused—until it landed on Kieran. His whole body went rigid as if struck by a memory that shouldn't exist.

He was watching with a disoriented intensity, as if he had recognized Nera and was trying to place where from. His clothes were tattered; robes that might have once belonged to an Archivist but had long since been worn to obscurity. His gaze moved, unfocused, as if he were caught between two realities.

Nera took a step forward, her fingers automatically sliding into her pocket and tracing the uneven edges of the map tucked into her coat pocket. The parchment was the one truth she carried. Even when the world shifted, when streets she had walked yesterday vanished overnight, her map remained. And yet, something about this moment sent a prickling unease through her chest, as if even the paper itself could slip into revision.

Kieran noticed her demeanor and turned slightly, posture coiled, as if sensing something off.

The stranger across the street inhaled sharply. His fingers twitched.

"Your name ..." he muttered without coming closer, voice rasping as though he hadn't spoken in years. "I feel like I knew it, once." His voice trailed away quietly.

Nera froze.

"I'm sorry?" she managed.

The man blinked rapidly. "You shouldn't be here." His voice grew urgent, broken. "They will see you," he whispered, voice cracking. "The ones outside the pages. The ones who weren't meant to be."

Cael stepped in front of her, his stance solid, grounded. He wasn't entertained by riddles. He was looking for answers that made sense. "Drunken ramblings. Come on, Nera."

But the man's head snapped toward Kieran. His entire expression changed.

"You ..." his eyes widened with recognition before widening into a panic that had him stumbling backward. "You were supposed to—"

"Stop," Nera said. It came out sharper than she intended. A command.

Kieran turned to her, his silver eyes wide, waiting for her to ask the obvious question. *Supposed to be what?* He placed himself between Nera and the stranger, his hand resting casually on the hilt of his blade.

Nera didn't ask what he was supposed to be or do. She couldn't.

A cold, sick feeling uncoiled in her stomach—a terrifying suspicion that if she let the old man finish that sentence, the words would somehow attach to her, too. That looking too closely at Kieran was like looking into a mirror she had carefully covered up.

She stepped back, bumping into Cael. She grabbed his arm, her fingers digging into his sleeve, grounding herself in his solid, uncomplicated presence.

Nera's heart was hammering. "He's just drunk," she said, her voice high and brittle. She still refused to look at Kieran. "He doesn't know what he's saying. Cael, make him go."

The old man stopped, a violent tremor running through him like a man who had just stepped too close to a forgotten truth. His lips moved as if forming words that had been stripped from his mind before they could be spoken.

Then, as quickly as he had appeared, he stumbled away, his form flickering at the edges, as if he might dissolve into the space between seconds.

"Even I'm uncomfortable now," Alis muttered, fingers absently rolling a coin across her knuckles, a habit she fell into when weighing risk. Her gaze flicked toward the emptying street, already calculating the smartest exit route. "I don't know about you, but I prefer my nightmares to be things I can bargain with. Let's move before we start attracting the wrong kind of attention."

"You're right," said Cael. "We have to be ready for our trip tomorrow."

"We can't still be going," Livia whispered, looking at the empty spot where the man had vanished.

"We have to," Kieran said, his voice grim. "If we cancel now, after what happened to Nera, Belvar will know something is going on. We have to play the part."

\* \* \*

Vornis stood at the edge of old, fractured land, its architecture pristine but eerily untouched by time. To the Archivists, this was proof of their work's success. To Nera, it was a city that had been rewritten too many times and so thoroughly that it had forgotten itself, and the seams were starting to show. The air felt heavy, like pages stacked too tightly, and the foliage seemed delayed in time, moving seconds after the wind blew.

Alis was already scanning the crowd, not for history, but for threats ... or profit. Cael, however, had gone quiet. He gripped Livia's hand too tightly, grounding himself as if the world might slip away. And Kieran ... he didn't look at the city at all. While the others assessed the architecture, he was already mapping the exits.

"It feels ... delayed," Livia whispered. "Like the wind is blowing three seconds before or after the leaves move."

"It's a bad edit," Alis muttered. "Let's find the archives before the pavement decides to stop existing."

Nera pulled her map from her pocket, her fingers tracing over the gaps and inconsistencies as she walked, determining where she might be able to make updates thanks to this trip. There were missing places, names that had been scratched away by history itself. She had added to it for years, filling in details where she could, but it was always unfinished.

She had tried to focus on her tour friends, the other scholars and interested members of the general community who were participating, and on the carefully curated narratives of the past.

But from the moment she had felt the second shift, she knew she couldn't ignore it.

Vornis lay within reach of a glitch—a place where rewritten history frayed at the edges, where time itself hesitated. These locations were feared, avoided, or hidden, representing proof that history was not as stable as the Archivists claimed. This one, however, was tightly controlled by the Council of Revision. It's rare for anyone to visit, and only then as part of these periodic official tours.

Their tour started and the bigger group split into smaller clusters formed by people who knew each other, each going off in their own direction. Nera's group decided to explore the old archive building.

They found a man in the lower levels of the Vornis archive, where the air smelled of ozone and forgotten dust. He sat among stacks of yellowed books—an elderly man in robes that looked woven from smoke.

He wasn't completely solid.

The lantern light passed straight through his shoulder to hit the wall behind him. He flickered, his image tearing like wet paper before snapping back together.

"It's an echo," Cael whispered, stepping closer.

But then the figure looked up and his eyes were hollow, filled with a terrifying, impossible awareness.

"You returned?" the ghost whispered, his voice sounding like dry leaves scraping stone. "No ... the other one was taller. Older. He asked about the ink. He wanted to know why it didn't dry." The figure's form stuttered, his hands passing through the table as he tried to grasp it. "I told him what I told you. The ink bleeds because the wound is deep."

*Soren?* Nera wondered.

Livia took an uneasy step back, whispering to Cale. "Is he ... is he dead?"

The ghost ignored her, his gaze locking onto Nera. "You shouldn't be here. The ones outside the Archive … the ones that are not written … they will find you."

"The Unwritten?" Nera asked.

The figure recoiled, his form blurring violently. "No. Worse." His gaze darted toward Kieran. "You. You were supposed to be one who doesn't exist."

Kieran's hand drifted to his blade, though it would do no good here. "I'm standing right here."

"No," the ghost hissed, clutching a book that dissolved under his fingers. "I saw it, I wrote it. The ink was wet. You were gone."

"Who are you?" Alis demanded, her voice tight.

"I was called Edris Vayne," he whispered slowly, his hand drifting to stroke the spine of a ledger on the desk—a possessive, familiar gesture. "I kept these halls. I wrote the peace. Why is the ink still wet?"

Before they could ask more, the figure keened—a sound of static and wind—and dissolved into the air, leaving nothing but dust.

A coldness settled over Nera. Cael's voice held tension bleeding into frustration. "Enough of this. We're leaving."

## CHAPTER NINE

# The Glitch

That night, while they were all clustered in a side area next to the lobby of their hotel, Nera made her case to the group. The glitch location was just outside the city. They were here to study history—what better way to test the truth than to go where history refused to be rewritten?

There was some initial hesitation, but in the end, her friends all agreed, plus a few other participants from the tour. It was what they came for, after all. The trip was set. Cael, Livia, Alis, Kieran, and a handful of others would join. Some were skeptical, others curious. Some, like Nera, wanted answers.

\*\*\*

As they set out the next morning, she felt Edris' warning settle over her.

*One who shouldn't exist.*

The words wouldn't leave her. And by the time they stepped into the fractured, wavering reality of the glitch, she thought she might understand why.

As they crossed the threshold into the ruins, the air thickened, charged with an unnatural stillness. Stone pillars, half-formed and crumbling at the edges, stretched toward the sky, some shimmering in and out of solidity, unable to hold a single shape under the crushing pressure of two conflicting histories. Nera slowly slid her palm across the stone, part nervous habit, part to feel the history beneath her hand.

A gust of wind carried a whisper—too faint to discern, yet unmistakably human.

Then Nera's eyes landed on something.

A wall carved with the same intersecting curved lines she had seen before. Or maybe not seen … remembered? It sent a strange pulse through her. A memory she couldn't place, a life that wasn't hers, yet somehow had been. Her fingers instinctively brushed over the intertwined engraved rings on her right middle finger, though she didn't notice.

And then the *world tilted*.

Nera barely had time to react before the ground beneath her feet lurched sideways, sending loose stones tumbling into the shadows. A deep, resonant crack echoed through the ruins as the air seemed to warp, folding in on itself before snapping back into place. The others staggered, reaching for balance, each breath sharp with alarm.

Kieran caught Nera's wrist, grounding her just as the distortion rippled outward, dragging the remnants of the structure in and out of existence. The stone walls lost their solidity, turning into a geometric haze that refused to focus, phasing between masonry and empty air.

"What's happening?" Livia gasped, pressing a hand against the nearest column, which fluttered under her touch like a mirage. She quickly jerked her hand back, an uncontrollable reaction considering no one knew what might happen if her hand ended up inside one.

Alis stepped back, eyes darting to the symbols carved into the wall. "This place isn't just rewritten, it's breaking apart. The story is too heavy for the stone."

Nera looked down at her hand, tracing the matching symbol on her ring. A shadow fell over her.

She looked up to find Kieran standing too close. He wasn't looking at the wall. He was staring at her hand. His gaze was raw, stripped of its usual guard. He looked at the silver band like it was the only solid thing in a dissolving world. His hand twitched at his side, fingers curling as if fighting the urge to reach out and touch it—or her.

"Kieran?" she whispered.

He snapped his eyes to hers, the look of longing vanishing instantly behind a mask of iron.

"We need to leave. Now," Cael said, stepping toward her. He reached for her wrist—not to pull, but to ground her. His grip was solid, real. "We don't belong here."

But the ruins had other plans.

A shudder ran through the stone beneath them, followed by a low, guttural sound—not quite human, not really natural, not entirely mechanical. From the far end of the chamber, a shadow moved where no light should have allowed it to. It stretched unnaturally, sputtering along the uneven walls, its edges fraying like ink dissolving in water.

Someone, or maybe something, was watching them.

Kieran moved first, stepping in front of Nera, his hand gripping the hilt of his knife. "That's not a glitch."

The temperature dropped sharply. A whisper skated along the edge of the air, and for the first time since stepping into the ruins, Nera felt truly unwelcome.

A voice—disjointed, fractured, barely there. *"You should not be here."*

The flickering walls shuddered violently. The very fabric of the place groaned in protest. The markings on the stone—symbols she felt she should have recognized earlier but had not—began to glow, burning white-hot.

Then everything collapsed inward.

The air compressed, crushing the sound from Nera's ears. A violent pull yanked her forward, like a hook snagged behind her navel. The world liquefied. The stone beneath her feet melted into a roaring slurry of time and light, dragging her down into the friction between seconds

A fractured reality unfolded around her, layers of blurred images blinking in and out of focus. She saw pieces of a past that didn't belong to her memory: a city that no longer existed, and people whose names had been erased, a war that was unremembered, and fire on the horizon.

And in the center of it all, a figure standing at the threshold of an alternate history.

Nera turned, and for a second, time folded. She wasn't looking at Kieran standing beside her in the ruins. She was looking at Kieran from another place or time—his clothing foreign, his expression somehow softer yet filled with the same sharp determination. And then she saw herself—not as she was now, but as someone else entirely.

She turned to look at the present Kieran. Their eyes met. Recognition slammed into her like a force she couldn't explain. *We were here before.*

The thought was hers, and not hers. A glimpse of another life, another version of history that had been stripped away. She could feel it pressing on her chest, but when she tried to grasp it, it slid through her fingers like sand.

Kieran's face twisted, his eyes widening. He was staring at her—not the her standing here next to him in the ruins, but the her from the vision. He reached out, his hand cutting through the distortion.

He turned to look at her, but the second her gaze locked onto his, something in him shut down. His expression flattened, locking the memory away. Before either of them could speak—before they could question what this meant—the image collapsed around them.

Kieran's voice cut through the distortion, sharp and commanding. "Nera!" He grabbed her wrist. With a forceful pull, reality snapped back into place.

Next to them, Livia stumbled, clutching Cael's arm, her face pale. "The ground,'" she gasped, pressing a hand to her stomach. "It rolled like a wave. I thought the floor was gone."

Alis was rubbing her eyes and blinking rapidly against the dim light of the ruins. "Ground? It was a flash. Blinding. Like staring into the sun." She looked at Nera, squinting. "Did you trigger a flare?"

Cael shook his head, looking at the ceiling "It was pressure. The air dropped. My ears popped."

Nera looked at Kieran. He hadn't let go of her wrist. He wasn't looking at the ceiling or the floor. He was staring at her, his chest heaving, the memory of the fire and the war still burning in his eyes. But he didn't say a word.

Nera's fingers slid into her pocket and wrapped her hand around the map she carried. Something—or someone—had altered history, right before their eyes.

"We leave," Cael said, his voice shaking. "Move."

They didn't speak until they had returned to their lodgings. Nera reached for the door handle, but her hand passed through a pocket of cold air before finding the metal—a micro-glitch. A tremor in the history.

Alis saw it. She put her hand on her dagger. "We don't unpack," she said, her voice sharp. "We sleep in shifts. This isn't over just because we left the ruins. And we don't talk about it here, someone may be watching."

## CHAPTER TEN

# Unremarkable Things

The air over Varethis wasn't just thick with the heat of nature's last feeble attempt at summer. It carried a barometric crush that made ears pop and tempers fray. Near the fountain, a merchant shouted at a customer—not over a price, but over a coin that the customer insisted was gold and the merchant swore was copper. The argument escalated, hands flying, a crowd gathering to nod in shared, aggressive confusion. The city wasn't just holding its breath; it was choking.

The silence Nera had walked in for weeks was finally breaking. People had always whispered … quiet, fearful exchanges in alleyways or behind locked doors. But now, the confusion she had felt at the missing apothecary was spreading like a contagion. Whispers had become something sharper, more deliberate. Nera could hear it in the cadence of their words, the hesitation before naming places that no longer existed. The fragments of history, once wiped clean and forgotten, bled through the cracks—uneven, jagged, like ink resisting erasure.

It wasn't just memory fighting back; Nera could hear it in the arguments of merchants haggling with a desperation that went beyond business, in the way street performers changed their songs to reference old folktales that should have been long forgotten.

The names of lost places, erased people, rewritten rulers; they were bleeding back into speech, as if the past itself was fighting to be remembered.

Alis moved beside her, casually flipping a silver coin between her fingers. It looked like a mindless habit, but Nera knew that every flick of the coin was measured, every flick of her gaze cataloging movement, threat, escape routes; the honed instinct of someone who had lived too long on the edge of danger, on alert even though they were only casually shopping. Livia paused to walk to a stall selling beautiful tapestries. They passed stalls selling sculptures of Valen Kestor and one with life-like paintings of him as the Architect.

Cael's steps slowed behind them as they passed a jewelry stall nestled between a spice vendor and a mapmaker. Nera saw his gaze flick over the rows of silver and gold bands, their delicate etchings glinting under the lanterns.

The merchant—a young woman with silky jet-black hair and striking blue-grey eyes—stood beneath a sign that read Grimoire, a ring of keys hanging from her belt. She followed Cael's hesitation with a knowing look.

"For someone special?"

Cael didn't smile. He studied one ring longer than the others, his fingers hovering near the glass.

"For someone I need to keep," he said quietly.

A moment later, he dropped his hand back to his side and exhaled, a small, restrained smile tugging briefly at his mouth before it faded.

"Cael! Catch up!" Alis's voice cut through the din.

He blinked, stepped away from the stall, and fell back into pace, catching Livia's hand as he passed her and tugging her forward with a quick, playful pull.

As they passed a small book stall, the owner gave Alis a nod—so slight it could have meant nothing, except that Alis's fingers twitched in a barely perceptible response.

"They're talking," Alis muttered under her breath. She wasn't looking at the books. Her eyes were darting to the rooftops, to the shadows between stalls. Her hand drifted to her belt, tapping a rhythm against her daggers. "The guards are rotating too fast. Something's brewing."

Livia moved off to look at a display, oblivious. Alis instantly positioned herself between Livia and the open street. "Stay close," Alis snapped, her casual mask gone. "This isn't just a market today. It's a hunting ground."

Nera twisted the ring on her finger until the metal bit into her skin. That was what unnerved her. It wasn't only cautious speculation anymore. People were beginning to act on their uncertainty.

A bell tolled in the distance. Nera checked the sky; the light was failing faster than it should.

*  *  *

Livia's fingers trailed over the edges of a small leather-bound book, a shadow of momentary guilt fluttering across her face.

Cael watched her carefully, arms crossed. "You sure about this?" His voice was lighter than his gaze.

Livia smirked, slipping the book into her satchel. "What, you don't trust me to find something worthwhile for you in the Archives?"

He quietly laughed. "That's not what I meant."

She rolled her eyes, adjusting the strap over her shoulder. "I'll be quick. I just need to check something before the day is out."

Alis, watching the exchange with casual amusement, nudged Cael with her elbow. "Relax. She's not smuggling war plans, just indulging your bad habit of wanting books you're not supposed to have. You can come to the apothecary with us."

Livia shot Alis a grin. "Exactly. And besides, I like to create surprises."

Cael nodded slowly and almost said something to her, his mouth opening before he stopped himself. His jaw tightened. He frowned, but didn't try to stop her as she turned away, disappearing into the flowing crowd.

## CHAPTER ELEVEN

# The Apothecary

The shop was dimly lit, the glow of candles casting uneven shadows against the walls. The scent of dried lavender and burning resin mixed with the sharper tang of medicinal herbs, masking something more illicit—ink stains on the wooden counters, the ghostly remains of pages scrubbed clean.

Nera, Cael, and Alis moved through the narrow shop, passing shelves stacked with glass vials and crumbling scrolls. A few patrons loitered by the counters, speaking in low voices as the apothecary—a middle-aged woman with ink-streaked sleeves—measured out powders and tinctures with the precision of someone used to handling delicate compounds.

The younger woman at the front counter cleared her throat, silencing the conversation with a pointed glance. The patrons fell quiet, each retreating into their own business, but the tension lingered—thick, unspoken.

The door to the back room creaked open. The old owner sat at a heavy wooden table, rubbing a spot on the wood where a deep gouge should have been. "I dropped the pestle here twenty years ago," he murmured to himself, pressing his thumb against perfectly smooth, unblemished grain. "It made a crack shaped like a star.

Why is the wood new?" He blinked, looking up as they entered, the confusion not quite clearing from his eyes.

His gaze lifted as they entered, settling first on Nera, and then his fingers ghosted over the page, tracing a line that had long since vanished.

"Your name ... " he paused, voice scraping like ink on worn parchment. "I should remember, shouldn't I?"

Nera paused. "What do you remember?"

The man blinked slowly, as if pulling threads of thought from somewhere just beyond reach. "There was a girl ..." His brow furrowed. "But no, that city never existed."

Nera felt a shudder as if her own history was being edited.

Alis's posture locked, her fingers curling as if she could hold onto something slipping through her grasp.

Nera exchanged a glance with her, an unspoken question passing between them. Before either could press further, a sound from the street shattered the quiet—a surge of movement, hurried footsteps, voices raised in alarm.

Something was wrong. Cael moved instinctively. Livia was still out there.

The moment they stepped outside the apothecary, something felt altered.

The market that had been alive with its usual undercurrent of buzz and bargains had changed. The air had gone still. An unspoken urgency had taken hold, a transformation in the rhythm of the streets.

People were moving faster. Not quite running, not panicking. Not yet anyway. But their steps were clipped, their heads turning too often, their voices quick. And the streets were emptying, leaving an eerie feeling since usually these streets were crowded. The distant bells tolled again, their echoes pressing down on the streets like a warning that had yet to be spoken aloud.

Alis caught the movement first, her hazel eyes narrowing as she took in the flow of the crowd. "Something has happened," she stated absently.

Cael wasn't listening. His gaze was fixed beyond them, past the milling figures of merchants hurriedly closing stalls, past the cloaked figures ducking into alleyways to the Grand Archive.

Nera followed his line of sight. She could tell even from this distance that the Grand Archive's doors were still open, but something was off. The guards who always stood on opposite sides of the entry like unmoving statues were leaning in together to speak, their postures tense. There was a moment, a flash of movement, where one of them stood up and started to slowly pull the heavy doors inward; something which *never* occurred.

"Livia," Cael whispered, his voice barely audible. Then, louder, more urgent, "She's still inside."

Then suddenly he was moving, running as fast as he could.

"Cael, wait …" Nera called, but he wasn't listening.

Nera and Alis exchanged a brief look before chasing after him, their own unease mounting. Cael wove through the streets with a singular focus, shoving past bodies that blurred into meaningless shapes.

They pushed forward, faster, past a shopkeeper pulling down wooden shutters, past a man arguing with a guard about whether the entrance to the lower districts was still open.

The Grand Archive was ahead, atop a slight hill just over the bridge, pristine and silent against the growing unease of the city. The white stone reflected the fading sunlight in an unnatural glow, its towering doors slowly closing.

As they reached the steps on their side of the bridge, a gust of wind carried the scent of something sharp—burning parchment.

Alis cursed under her breath. "Whoa. That's—"

The scent was faint. Barely there. But it was real. Nera felt her pulse hammer in her ears.

"Go," she told Cael. "Now!"

He didn't hesitate and ran faster, crossing the bridge over the small river that separated the city center from the building, and sprinted through the slowly closing doors into the entry hall.

Cael heard fast steps running up behind him and turned quickly to see Alis and Nera panting heavily.

They moved fast, and it only took him a few moments to find her. Livia was exactly where he expected—tucked into a small, forgotten corner of the archives devoted to military drills, engrossed in her project, hunched over a desk in one of the lower halls, surrounded by volumes she hadn't yet finished copying. Her ink-stained fingers brushed over delicate parchment, her expression one of deep focus, as if she could will more time into existence.

She looked up at him when he entered, a small smile tugging at her lips.

"It's supposed to be a surprise!" she chirped. "You shouldn't be here."

Cael stepped closer, bracing his hands on the desk as his breath came uneven. His voice carried an edge he didn't bother to smooth away. "Neither should you."

Livia smiled softly, the kind of smile that meant she had expected this—him, his worry, his refusal to leave her behind.

She reached for a book beside her, one smaller than the others, its edges worn from too much handling. She pressed it into his hands.

"There's something I want you to see," she said. "But not yet."

His brow furrowed with concern. "Livia—" Then the alarms blared and they heard the big exterior doors of the Grand Archive finally slam shut.

A deafening clang echoed through the vast hallways as iron locks ground into place. The already dim candlelight danced as if the very air was evolving, the stillness ruptured by the sharp voices of Archivists further down the halls.

Then came the faint smell of smoke.

Thin wisps curled in far places almost out of reach, seeping through cracks like fingers searching for something to consume. The scent of burning parchment reached them.

Livia's head snapped up. Cael grabbed her hand.

"We have to go," he said, his voice tight with urgency.

For a split second, she hesitated, her eyes darting toward the shelves—the books.

Cael tightened his grip. "Livia."

That broke her free.

Together, they ran, Alis and Nera right behind them.

The corridors of the Grand Archive twisted into chaos. Scholars shouted, their voices tangled with the sharp commands of guards trying to impose order.

Cael pulled Livia through a side passage just as a section of the bookcases groaned, dust trickling from above.

Ahead, the main hall came into view—the towering shelves, the marble floors—now bathed in a faint, eerie orange glow. The fire hadn't reached this part of the Archive yet, but smoke was beginning to creep through the space.

Then, from the shadows near the entrance, a figure moved.

Kieran. He was already there.

His blade was drawn. His eyes were wide, his attention locked past Cael and Livia, landing squarely on Nera.

Whatever crossed his face when he saw her was brief and unguarded—and unmistakable.

She moved towards Kieran without thinking. Not a hesitation, not a question. Like something deeper had already decided for her. Just movement, instinctive and sure. Kieran had barely reached for her when she was already stepping forward, as if this was something they had both done a thousand times before.

It lasted less than a second. A shudder in the chaos. But as she reached Kieran's side, she caught Cael's gaze. For a fraction of a moment, his expression fractured; confusion warring with the panic, his eyes darting between them as if seeing something he didn't recognize.

"Move!" Kieran shouted. And then they ran for their lives.

## Chapter Twelve

# Ash and Aftermath

The flames began to move with a terrifying hunger, devouring shelves, curling parchment into blackened remnants of forgotten words. This was not just a fire. It was an execution. A final revision. A history rewritten in smoke and ash, sealed by the hands of those who refused to let the truth remain.

Already sections of the archives were being destroyed, far areas collapsing into wreckage as they ran down the corridor in the opposite direction.

The scent of burning ink filled the air, thick and suffocating. Smoke, curling around the ceiling of the thankfully ridiculously tall room, clawed at their throats as the Grand Archive—once a fortress of controlled knowledge—crumbled from within.

The heat became unbearable. Shadows danced wildly against the walls as the fire spread, licking at the towering shelves and curling up toward the domed ceiling. The crackling blaze was punctuated by the sharp snap of beams giving way.

"Are they destroying it themselves?" Kieran shouted over the chaos, his blade drawn, though it was useless against the inferno. "Is it that the Council would rather burn it than lose it? Or is it one of the rebel factions?"

"It's the Preservationists!" Cael shouted over the chaos, pointing toward a shadowed figure retreating through the smoke, clad in their signature dark lethal garb with faces obscured. "They must have found a way to breach the perimeter. They aren't trying to save the history here, Nera. They're scorching the earth so Kestor can't use it."

Nera held on to random salvaged pages she had managed to grab as she ran. Her hands were smudged with soot and ink, the words on the parchment half-melting under her touch. She coughed, her lungs burning, but she didn't stop.

A loud noise and a strangled cry cut through the destruction.

"Livia—!"

Nera's head snapped up. Cael shoved past the toppled shelves, his entire body coiled with panic.

Livia had been right there—right beside them. But now, suddenly, she wasn't.

It had only been seconds. Cael had been leading, running, his grip tight on her wrist as he pulled her toward the main corridor, eyes fixed on the exit. Livia had been a step behind him, clutching his arm, then she let go.

Cael stumbled forward, spinning around to grab her again, but she had stopped near a toppling shelf, her eyes drawn to a book with a violet cover.

"Livia, move!" Cael screamed, reaching back across the gap.

She looked up, terrifyingly calm, and reached for him. But the distance he had created by running ahead was just enough room for the ceiling to fail.

"LIVIA!" Cael yelled.

She paused.

Nera noticed it even through the haze. Livia froze, her eyes locking onto a specific spine bound in violet leather. Even through the smoke, Nera saw gold embossing: two twin, intertwined rings. The mark Cael had sketched into his journal a thousand times over the years. Livia wouldn't have known what the book was, but she knew Cael had spent years looking for that mark. She reached for it. And that was the moment that sealed her fate.

She stepped toward, her fingers barely brushing the spine of the old volume when another section of the ceiling groaned, threatening to collapse.

"LIVIA, RUN!"

Her head snapped up, realization dawning too late. She turned, started toward them—

The ceiling gave way.

A deafening crash shook the Archive as wooden beams and stone shattered into the floor between them, cutting her off completely. Flames surged in the sudden draft, devouring everything in their path.

Cael's entire body jerked forward with pure, unthinking desperation, responding before his mind could catch up. He wasn't just trying to reach her—he was trying to defy reality itself. Kieran grabbed him powerfully.

"LET ME GO!" Cael roared, struggling against Kieran's strong grip.

The flames began to roar higher, the air bending with the heat. Through the thickening smoke, Nera saw the last fleeting glimpse of Livia—her silhouette framed against the fire, turning to desperately try to find an escape.

Then they saw the roof above her collapse.

A sickening crack echoed through the hall as stone and timber crashed down, right where Livia had been standing and completely blocking her from Cael, the entire area immediately engulfed in tall flames.

The roar of the fire seemed to vanish, leaving only the sound of Cael's ragged breathing. A raw, wordless sound tore from his throat—a sound of absolute, shattering grief. He lunged forward again, but Kieran held fast, muscles straining as he wrestled him back.

"She's still in there!" Cael shouted, his voice breaking, his eyes fixed on a spot in the flames that no longer existed. "She's right there!"

Nera could see it in his face—the desperation, raw and uncontained. He fought against Kieran's grip like a drowning man, hands clawing at empty air as if he could pull Livia from the wreckage through sheer will alone.

Kieran didn't let go. His grip was iron, unyielding.

"She's gone," Kieran said, his voice harsh but steady. No comfort, no false hope. Just the truth, sadly laid bare.

"NO—! I can get to her—!"

"She's gone!" Kieran shouted, looking directly into Cael's eyes.

The words hit like a blow. Cael's frozen body sagged, his strength collapsing beneath the weight of it. He gasped, his breaths short, ragged; his hands shaking.

And then, suddenly, he went still.

The fire was spreading. The structure groaned above them. They only had seconds left if they didn't want the same fate.

It's like time froze. Kieran and Nera exchanged a brief look before Nera stepped forward. She gripped Cael's arm—not to restrain him but to simply anchor him, touch meant to remind him of the decades they had been close friends. Cael turned his head to look at her, but his expression was empty; Nera could tell that he barely registered her presence.

"We have to go," she said, her voice softer than Kieran's but just as firm. But as she pulled Cael's arm, a spike of quick anger flared in her chest. *Why did she stop? Why did she have to look?*

Livia had hesitated for a book. For a piece of history. For the very thing Nera had spent weeks insisting was the most important thing in the world.

Nera looked at Cael's shattered face and briefly resented him for it. She hated him for loving Livia so much that his grief felt like a personal accusation against her. If she hadn't pushed them, if she hadn't insisted that knowing the truth was worth danger, maybe Livia would be safe. She would be unknowing, but she would be alive.

She thought he wouldn't move as she tugged his arm. That he would stay there, that his grief would root him in place, that he would let himself burn along with her.

Then, slowly—barely—he shifted. Nera didn't let go. Neither did Kieran. Together, they pulled him away, with no moment to spare.

As they stumbled back toward the entrance hall, dodging falling beams and thick waves of smoke, a figure appeared above them—standing on the slowly collapsing upper level.

Master Belvar.

His robes were untouched by the ash, his face eerily calm despite the destruction all around him. He gazed down at them with the cold detachment of a surgeon cutting away rot.

"You think history belongs to you," he called over the roar of the fire. "But history is not a thing you hold, it is what we choose to leave behind." His eyes darkened with something resolute. "Memory is a weapon. We ensure it is wielded correctly."

Nera's body vibrated with fury. "Not anymore," she spat.

Belvar only smiled. Then the flames reached the supports, and the structure shuddered beneath them.

The main doors of the Grand Archive were just ahead, still sealed shut with smoke and falling debris turning the path into a gauntlet of fire and shadow. The heat had become unbearable, sweat and soot mixing on their skin. They were all covering their nose and mouth with their arm or shirt, bending down to escape the worst of the smoke as they pushed forward.

Cael was still in shock, moving on autopilot.

"Go, move!" Kieran ordered, pushing Nera forward as a massive wooden beam crashed down inches from them.

Just as they reached the final section of corridor, part of the ceiling collapsed, blocking the main doors in a wall of flame.

"This way—!" Alis's voice cut through the smoke. She was already ahead, motioning toward a smaller passage—a side entrance used for restricted visitors.

Nera didn't think; she just ran.

They barreled through the passage, small ashes of parchment floating through the air around them, weaving through the suffocating smoke, until—finally—a door loomed ahead.

Alis kicked it open. Cool air blasted them as they stumbled outside.

The city was chaos.

They kept moving while people were shouting, running, fleeing. Smoke curled into the sky in thick plumes behind them, the fire consuming the Grand Archive from within. Groups of brave men were sprinting towards the fire, towards the danger—the city's fire brigade with a mission to save what they could and rescue any Archivists still inside.

Nera and her group ran, and didn't pause until they had crossed the bridge, putting the river between them and the burning building.

Cael staggered forward, barely able to stand. He stopped, frozen, hands curled into his hair, his breath coming in broken gasps.

Nera pressed her palm over the intertwined rings on her finger, twisting them hard. The world around her felt distant, like she was watching through water—too slow, too quiet, too wrong. A heartbeat too late. As if something had morphed just out of reach, but she couldn't name what.

The pressure she felt in her chest spread to her throat. A swallow, tight and uneasy, as if she could choke down the truth.

"Nera?" Kieran's voice pulled her back from her silent musings.

She blinked. How long had she been standing there? The fire raged behind them, the heat licking at the night sky. Her fingers loosened from the rings, leaving red impressions on her skin.

"I'm fine," she lied.

Nera turned toward Cael, unsure of what to say. What could she say?

Cael was barely upright, brushing ash from his sleeve with methodical, jerky movements. He looked at the book in his hand—the one Livia had given him—and frowned, wiping a smudge of soot from the cover. "The binding is cracked," he said, his voice flat. "She hates when the binding cracks. I need to get some glue."

Nera felt her chest ache while witnessing the agony of her first and best friend.

Kieran stood beside Cael, silent. He didn't offer empty words. He didn't say *she wouldn't want this*. He didn't say *we had no choice*. He understood the words that wouldn't help. He just stood there.

And for the first time Nera had ever seen, Cael—who had always carried himself with sharp wit and quiet confidence—fell to his knees, unaware that he was still holding the book from Livia.

The fire roared behind them.

Livia was gone. Their history had just been rewritten in the worst and most permanent way possible.

Kieran's eyes glanced over the burning wreckage, sharp, searching. But when he spoke, it wasn't about the books. His voice was tight, controlled. A pause, too brief to catch, then softly, almost to himself, "Something else is gone."

Nera looked down at the fragments of salvaged texts in her hands. Ash smeared the ink. The edges were singed. She had saved some of the truth, although not much. She wanted to drop it in the mud. It felt heavy, useless, and cruel as if they had traded a living, breathing person for paper.

She felt like a thief who had stolen Cael's happiness to buy herself a mystery.

As they turned to disappear into the city, something flitted in the air. A piece of parchment floating, with a half-erased name shimmering on the scorched document.

Kieran paused, eyes flicking toward the building now falling into ruins. "Did you see that?" His tone was careful—too careful. Like he already knew the answer, but needed to hear her say it.

Nera had, yet was missing the mental and emotional ability to process what she had seen. Clutching the last pieces of history as she stared at her grieving friend sadly, she simply replied, "No."

\*\*\*

Nera hesitated to leave Cael, watching as he wandered aimlessly toward the center of the city. Everyone else had gone their separate ways, but something in Cael's posture—the way his shoulders slumped, the hollowness of his steps—kept her from turning away.

She followed at a distance, keeping to the shadows.

He stopped in front of the same jewelry stall, hands hanging empty at his sides. The market was mostly empty now, but the merchant hadn't packed up yet. Nera followed his line of sight to a small leather display. A ring.

She remembered him looking at it before. She remembered the secret smile he had tried to hide.

Cael stared at the stall silently, his body trembling with a silent, invisible weight. The merchant glanced up, ready to haggle, but something in Cael's expression made her stop. She said nothing as Cael reached out, his fingers brushing the ring before pulling his hand back.

He didn't speak. He just stood there, staring at a future that had burned down.

Nera turned away, her own chest aching. Some things were too difficult to witness. She headed slowly, absently, back towards the temporary quarters that had been provided by the city for all of the Archivists who had lost their lodging due to the fire.

\*\*\*

Kieran was gone for over an hour. When he returned to The Scholar's Rest, his boots were coated in a fine layer of dust. Not from the streets; from the fires.

He didn't offer an explanation and no one asked. He simply took his place at the edge of the hearth, the glow casting shadows against his face, and stared into the flames as if they held answers no one else could see.

## CHAPTER THIRTEEN
# Cael's Vigil

The map wasn't making sense.

Nera sat cross-legged near the dwindling fire in her room at The Bridle Inn, where she had ended up since Archivists were not allowed to return to any section of the archive complex until the living quarters were deemed safe. Luckily her mother had known the owners, a friendly elderly couple who were kind enough to save a room for Nera as soon as they heard about the devastation. Nera had the half-rolled map pulled out of her pocket and stretched across her lap, the worn edges curling at her fingertips. She had drawn these routes before, mapped the roads and landmarks a dozen times over. But tonight, the lines felt wrong.

She ran her fingers over the ink, retracing paths she knew should exist. The Archive. The Scholar's Rest. The burned remnants of history now turned to ash.

But then there were places she didn't remember marking. A crossroads she didn't recall sketching. A hollow space where a name had once been.

She frowned, angling the parchment toward the firelight, but the moment the glow touched the ink, it warped.

Not much. Barely a fraction of a second. But enough that she saw it. She pressed her hand flat against the map, grounding herself, but the sensation remained—a faint resistance beneath her palm, like the parchment was holding something back.

She folded the map carefully, deliberately. This was no time to question it; but she kept the parchment close as she lay down, staring at the night sky outside her window with her thoughts jumping from Livia to Cael, the fire, and lingering questions about everything going on.

She had spent her life trying to understand the shape of things, but tonight, the shape of the world no longer felt fixed, and she was even more focused on learning the truth.

## Chapter Fourteen

# A Kingdom That Shouldn't Exist

Nera spread the brittle, yellowed pages across the table. Another piece of the puzzle. Another attempt to hold together a truth that someone had tried to tear apart. The air held a sharp bite, a promise of winter not yet seen, but inside Theron's home, the heat was stifling.

It had been weeks since they'd arrived in the city, all finally settling in Theron's home as their safe house—a sprawling, timeworn structure nestled in the older quarter of the city, where the streets were tight, the houses were huge, and the walls whispered with history—not a comfort, but a low, unintelligible muttering that made Alis check the corners every time she entered a room. Nera ran her fingers along the uneven wood of the doorway, not to ground herself, but to make sure it was still solid. It hadn't changed. At least, she didn't think it had; yet some nights, she also wasn't sure.

She glanced at the floor where the doorframe cast its shadow. The angle was wrong. The light source was the fire to her left, but the shadow stretched forward, as if cast by a sun that wasn't there. She blinked, and the shadow snapped back to its proper alignment.

Theron's home was peaceful, but the air felt borrowed. He threw the door's deadbolt with a heavy thud, brushing dust from his coat. "I took the long route back with the supplies," he murmured to Kaelith, peeling off his gloves. "Had to skirt the Weaver's Arch."

Kaelith didn't look up from her book. "Is it active again?"

"It's skipping," Theron said grimly. "I saw a merchant cart go through the archway and come out three seconds too late. The locals are walking two streets over just to avoid looking at it."

"So it's getting worse," noted Kaelith.

Theron latched the heavy shutters, drowning out the rhythmic, mechanical crunch of Enforcer boots patrolling the street below, his shoulders relaxing as if the wood alone could keep the world out. But to Nera, the silence didn't feel like safety; it felt like breath held before a scream. It was too alive. It made the memory of the Archive's ash feel closer.

It was all wrong. The air should smell of dry paper and dust and the sharp, metallic tang of iron gall ink. For twenty years, that scent had been the only constant in her life. Now, when she closed her eyes, she didn't see the safety of Theron's walls; she saw the great dome of the main hall cracking, the white stone turning to black ash. The Grand Archive was a cage, yes, but it was *their* cage. It was where Cael had learned to laugh, where Kieran had learned to fight, where she had learned to read and write. It was gone. Burned off the face of the earth, and with it, the only version of themselves that made sense.

Theron himself was a man of contradictions, a young scholar with the sharp instincts of an athlete, his presence as solid as stone. He had once been a historian, before living with lost truths had turned him into something more. Now, his home had become more than just a sanctuary—it was a meeting ground, a crossroads for those who sought answers in the same shadows as Nera's group did and had become accidental rebels in the process.

The house reflected its owner: sturdy, deliberate, and filled with quiet knowledge. Shelves brimming with books, scrolls, and strange artifacts lined every wall, the scent of ink and old parchment thick in the air. As mandated by the Council of Revision, a painting of Valen Kestor rested above the mantle of the fireplace, a required presence in all households. His eyes were painted a cold, piercing dark—so dark they were almost black. Nera noticed that no one in the room ever looked at it directly. They moved around the hearth with their backs turned to the mantle, a collective, silent agreement to deny him the eye contact the portrait seemed to demand.

A shiver of repulsion went through Nera, not just hatred for a tyrant, but a deep, nauseating sense of familiarity. It wasn't his face—that was a mask of state propaganda. It was his hands. The artist had painted them gripping the quill with a specific, rigid tension in the knuckles.

Nera rubbed her own hand, feeling a phantom cramp in the exact same spot. Too much writing. She changed her grip on her mug, unsettled by how natural that tension looked.

Maps were tacked to surfaces, some so ancient their edges had curled with time, others freshly drawn with speculative theories scrawled in the margins. There were weapons, too—tucked between volumes or hanging within easy reach—because here, words and steel held equal weight.

It felt like a refuge, and yet, Nera had changed, like an innocence she had once possessed was forever gone, and always felt a prickle at the back of her neck, a quick blip of movement just beyond the candlelight—nothing she could ever place, but always there.

Theron's partner Kaelith had long, wavy red hair that cascaded like flames down her back. A scholar and a fighter, Kaelith balanced Theron's careful diplomacy with the fierceness the world had taught her. Nera had grown fond of her and her bubbly nature.

Alis, too, seemed changed since their arrival. Or maybe she had always been changing, and Nera was only now noticing how far apart they had begun to drift. The relationship between the two women remained strong, but subtle variations were beginning to appear.

Ever loyal and resourceful despite her disdain for history being edited, Alis helped her friends with the black market contacts, and through her, the fragmented histories of her own kingdom began to bleed through.

She was becoming quieter, more distant, absorbed in her own work. She had always slipped in and out of places unnoticed, her friends never asking about her questionable work on the black market. Now she was slipping away from Nera too—not in a way that felt accidental, but in a way that felt deliberate. Intentional. Like she was keeping secrets even from the people she trusted most.

There was a growing tension between them, one that Nera could feel but couldn't quite understand. Still, they worked together as well as they ever had—Alis's network of connections invaluable to their cause. But there were nights when Alis would leave the table early, disappearing into the wider city with a cryptic excuse. Nera never pressed, but it was clear that something was weighing on her friend.

Cael was seldom part of the group. He had been absorbed in his own grief that seemed to wrap around him like a fog. When he did appear, his presence felt thinner.

*** 

Nera found Cael by the window. The small, worn book Livia had given him lay open on a nearby table, pressed close to his hands. He wasn't reading. He held a quill, hovering over the margin of a page where Livia's handwriting—looping and delicate—abruptly stopped.

He reacted to the sound of Nera's approaching footsteps. He buttoned his coat with mechanical precision, his expression going carefully blank.

"She didn't read the text," Cael said, his voice stripped of its usual sharp wit. He looked down at the book. "She just recognized the symbol I was looking for. She folded the corner here—at the third stanza—to mark it for me."

He dipped the quill to the page, scratching a quick calculation into the margin. "She found the key, but I can't get the sequence to align, I'm missing a counter-sign."

He half-turned his head to the side while still looking at the book. "Liv, was there another symbol on the spine? Or …"

He stopped. The quill froze mid-stroke. The ink bled into the paper, a slow, dark stain spreading over the page.

Nera took a breath to speak, but Cael moved first. He carefully set the quill down on the table, aligning it perfectly parallel to the book's spine with steady, deliberate fingers. He snapped the book shut.

"Sloppy handwriting," he said, his voice bright and entirely empty. He turned to Nera, offering a sharp, brittle smile. "We should eat. I heard Tavian made bread that is almost edible today."

* * *

Nera could hear the size of the group that gathered in the study that evening before she even walked through the doorway. The space felt fuller than ever, the quiet hum of voices layering over one another, and she could feel the heat as she stepped over the threshold. The house was crowded.

Theron and Kaelith were deep in conversation with a handful of scholars, their discussion circling once again around the mysterious Benefactor—a name that refused to stay buried, no matter how many times history tried to erase it. Cyrus, his wife Sarina, and Tavian sat nearby, exchanging theories with Liaz and Tyrek, who had acquired yet another obscure text through his usual back channels.

Nera looked around the room, feeling as though she were separated from the others by a pane of glass, the knowledge she carried—and what had happened to her—keeping her isolated from the group.

A few others leaned in to listen, some faces familiar, others new—scholars, fighters, those who had begun drifting into their orbit, drawn by whispers of something bigger stirring beneath the surface. Nera spotted a weaver from the market, Tessa, and remembered her husband as one of the men who had bravely fought the fire at the Grand Archive.

Another newcomer—a tall young man with a mop of ginger hair—moved through the room with a tray of tea, entertaining adults and children alike with quiet jokes. He paused to chat with a brown-bearded builder and his tiny wife, a teacher Nera had met in the past, before stopping long enough to press a cup of chilled Scholar's Rest into Nera's hands. She nodded her thanks as he moved on, grateful for the cool drink in the stifling heat.

As the group kept growing Nera was having trouble keeping up with all the new names. More faces each time. Some familiar; some ... maybe not. She wasn't sure if it was just the streaming crowds or if she was forgetting people who shouldn't be forgotten. Who could tell any more?

She also noticed how the gatherings had grown to include whole families, evident in the children present this evening. Near the hearth, young Jaye sat upright with a book balanced carefully on his lap, his small fingers smoothing the page edges with careful reverence. At only ten, he was already in early training and had taken to these gatherings with the solemn air of a young Scribe, eager to absorb knowledge while still grappling with how to approach it. His gaze flicked toward Nera more than once, attentive and searching, before returning to the page.

A sharp laugh made Nera momentarily flinch, instinctively turning towards the louder noise. Across the room, six year old Clara twirled in a layered outfit, swaths of fabric draped over her small frame like an impromptu crown-and-cloak ensemble, declaring herself royalty of the old world. "I'm the queen!" she giggled, spinning until she was dizzy.

At her feet, Maria followed, determined to match every movement. Though only four, she had declared that she wasn't merely dressed like a princess—everyone was to address her as one. She made herself just as much a part of the group as anyone, enthusiastically offering 'help' even when none was needed. Earlier, she had climbed onto a stool to stir a pot in the kitchen, watched over closely by her mother who was teaching her how to cook. Her infectious laughter brought levity to otherwise serious meetings.

The youngest, Jhan, was just a baby—a sleeping bundle in the arms of Mave, the young woman Nera recognized from the jewelry stall in the market. She stood near the back of the room, happily watching over the children so their mothers could focus on other things.

Nera moved closer to greet the baby and was rewarded with the kind of wide, joyful smile only an infant could manage. Jhan's presence was quiet, but undeniable: a child born into a world still being rewritten, a future not yet decided.

While Nera enjoyed watching the children, and the sense of normalcy that their presence imparted, every time she looked at them she realized the cost of failure. Another timeline shift or an alignment correction and these children might never be born.

Cael had joined them that evening, to her surprise, but he sat quietly by the window, staring out at the dimming winter sky. He was there, but distant. His movements were slower than usual, his posture slack, as if effort itself had become negotiable.

Nera had seen this before—the way he held himself slightly apart, like someone bracing against an unseen current. At times his shoulders would tense, his jaw setting, and then ease again. In a room full of voices, his gaze would find hers and linger, not asking anything, not offering anything—just holding.

Once or twice, he looked as if he might speak. He never did.

The red-haired man passed by with a tray nearly empty, offering Cael a cup of the cold tea. Cael took it, cradling the cup in his hands without drinking, before turning back to the window.

By contrast, when Nera looked at Kieran, there was no stillness; only a sense of untamed motion. He paused mid-stride, his head snapping toward the window as if hearing a voice no one else did. His hand went to his chest, fingers curling into his shirt, eyes widening with a sudden, devastating familiarity—before glazing over, the memory dissolving into confusion.

She felt the strength of an unseen bond—an unspoken pull between them, shaped as much by what was missing as by what remained. He had been there when they first began uncovering fragments of a shared history, and the deeper they dug, the more entangled those fragments became. Even in silence, she felt his presence—not just beside her, but in the space between questions, in moments where understanding passed without words. It felt like knowing someone deeply and for a long time, despite how little of their shared past ... at least the past she remembered.

When she looked at Kieran, she saw the same questions reflected back at her, the same unspoken understanding that neither of them could turn away from this search—not now, not ever. But while her expression gave her away, his was always unreadable, sharp edges softened just enough to let her see past them. Just enough to remind her that he, too, was holding back.

\* \* \*

Alis stood by the door, watching Mave rock the sleeping baby. Her hand hovered over her dagger, not out of threat, but out of a nervous need to guard something fragile. She looked at the child, then at Nera, her expression hardening. She wasn't here for the books.

"Nera," Alis's voice broke her from her thoughts as she strode across the room. "I've found something." Out of the corner of her eye, Nera noticed how the interruption caused Kieran to involuntarily flinch and instinctively reach for his knife and his eyes darted towards the door.

Nera moved closer as Alis unfolded a crumpled parchment, the edges smudged with ink and dust. She spread it out on the table, revealing a map—one that was incomplete, yet unmistakably old.

"This," Alis said, tapping a section in the middle, "confirms my suspicion. This sector wasn't discovered; it was pasted in."

Before Nera could respond, Tyrek stepped over and cut in. "That's not all." He leaned back, a charming, dangerous grin playing on his lips. "I called in a favor from a supplier who usually runs wine, not treason."

Tyrek flipped a coin but didn't catch it. He let it hit the table. It didn't ring; it made a soft thump. "I had a payout from a smuggler yesterday turn to grey dust in my pocket," Tyrek muttered, staring at the coin. "Third time this month. We call it the Unwritten's Gold. That's bad business. You can't trade in a currency that either forgets its own value or dissolves."

He slid a worn book onto the table—carefully, like a high-stakes wager. "Royal treasury records. They list repairs to a fortress that doesn't exist. You can't spend gold on a ghost, Nera. Someone is collecting. It cost me a crate of vintage Veilshadow and a very uncomfortable conversation, but I figured the crown's dirty laundry was undervalued."

Liaz, standing silently near the door, spoke. "And three favors." Tyrek glanced at her. "Non-refundable," she added, her eyes locking onto him. "So make that book worth the expense."

"I returned from the northern outposts to verify the metrics," Cyrus said, winding the crown of his timepiece without looking up. "The locals report scorching. My analysis confirms the bedrock was deleted, not burned. The system attempted to remove the land mass but failed to draw the replacement terrain. It is not an error; it is full. You cannot write over the same spot a thousand times without tearing the parchment. The world has simply stopped taking the ink."

A hush settled over the room.

Theron, positioned between the group and the front door—habitually blocking the exit—adjusted his stance. He didn't look at the book; he looked at the map. "It's sloppy work," he said, stepping forward to point a calloused finger at it. "I've seen foundations that stop mid-brick."

In the corner, Cyrus closed his timepiece with a soft, final click. "The geometry is irrelevant. The data confirms it. Roads running straight into cliff faces. You can't cheat the weight, Nera. If you build a wall without a footing, it falls on you. This whole timeline is collapsing under its own ink."

Tyrek leaned forward, eyes gleaming. "Then we give it a shove? Let it fall?"

"No," Cyrus said. "We do not trigger a collapse until we can control the impact. We wait."

Kaelith folded her arms. "Then we stop pretending this is theoretical."

Nera's gaze flicked to Kieran. He hadn't spoken, but there was something in the way he held himself, as if he had already known what they would find, as if the words on the page were confirming something rather than revealing it.

It felt like they were moving closer. But closer to what?

A frustrated sigh left her lips, barely audible over the pounding in her ears, fingers tracing the edge of the map as she let knowledge of their discoveries settle. It was happening everywhere—the fractures, the missing pieces, the histories that had been erased and rewritten. Changes that should have already settled and revisions that should have already become permanent but had not. And for the first time, she felt it: this wasn't just history breaking. This was *her* history.

"Nera?"

The quiet voice startled her. She looked down to see Jaye standing at her elbow, his brow furrowed in a way that made him look far older than his years. He was clutching his school primer to his chest like a shield.

"What is it, Jaye?"

He hesitated, glancing over his shoulder at Theron and Kaelith, then held the book out to her. His finger pressed hard against a block of text near the bottom of the page.

"I'm confused," he admitted softly. "You and the others... you talk about the Benefactor like he was a person. Like a king who lost his throne."

Nera took the book, the leather cover warm from his hands. "Well, we believe maybe he was."

Jaye shook his head. "But my teacher says that's just a metaphor."

Nera frowned, her eyes scanning the text he had pointed to. The ink was sharp, the font precise—the hallmark of a recent press.

*...and from the chaos of the Void, Lord Kestor brought Order. He struck down the Formless One and paved the roads of the Kingdom over the wild madness that came before.*

A cold chill settled in Nera's stomach. They weren't trying to erase the Benefactor anymore. They were turning him into a monster.

"The Formless One?" Nera repeated, her voice tight. "We've never heard of that."

"She says that he represents the time before the ink dried," Jaye explained, his voice trembling. "That people who believe in him are just afraid of order." He looked up at her, his dark eyes wide. "If he stops writing ... do we just go blank? Like when you spill water on a page?"

"It's nothing to worry about, Jaye," Nera said, trying to offer the standard adult comfort. "It's just a way of teaching history to kids."

Jaye shook his head, rejecting the lie. He looked up at her, his dark eyes wide and terrifyingly lucid. "It's not a metaphor., right? If he stops writing, we don't just die. We stop being real."

Nera looked at the pristine pages. No burnt edges. No dangerous secrets. It was safe. But looking at the crisp, sanitized words, Nera finally understood the lie at the heart of the Archive. They claimed they erased the past to protect the future from chaos. But that wasn't it.

She traced the scar on her hand, remembering the smell of burning leather and the sight of her father's history curling into black flakes. If she didn't stop this, Jaye would never have to reach into the fire. He would never even know there was something worth burning for.

Nera closed the book, the snap of the cover sounding too loud in the room. "Yes, Jaye," she whispered, handing it back to him. "We remember it honestly. All of us."

She looked up, catching Cael's eye across the room. He saw the look on her face—the realization that the war wasn't just about the past. The Archive wasn't just rewriting history books; they were rewriting the children.

## CHAPTER FIFTEEN

# The Benefactor

Now, at last, they were beginning to understand—pulling the pieces together like a partially completed puzzle. The Benefactor had shaped the world in ways they still couldn't fully comprehend. But someone—something—had opposed him. The Tyrant.

Nera had always heard people like Belvar and the elders dismiss stories of the Tyrant as tools of control, warnings meant to frighten foolish scholars and restless children into obedience. No one could point to proof, not in any record that still remained intact. The same uncertainty surrounded the Benefactor. Mentions of either figure were rare in the archives, references fragmented and evasive, leaving scholars to argue whether they had ever been real at all—or whether they had been erased so completely that certainty itself no longer existed.

The gathering continued into the night, people coming and going, the room filled with hushed conversations and speculative theories as different groups reviewed the newly uncovered documents. But beneath it all ran an unsettling quiet, as if something were coiling rather than fading. The more they learned about the Benefactor, the more the shadow of the Tyrant took shape—not just in theory, but in fragments. His name surfaced in lost texts, in whispered stories, like someone waiting to be remembered.

Theron leaned toward Nera, his expression serious. "There's a rumor," he said quietly, "that the Tyrant has allies; those who want to see the kingdom return to its former glory—and they're actively supporting his work."

Nera's heart clenched. Having current allies would imply that the Tyrant still existed. If the Tyrant was still alive, and if he had supporters, they were not just hunting for answers. They were hunting for power.

The realization gripped her chest. They had stepped beyond discovery and were standing at the fault line of a battle that had never truly ended. "We aren't stepping onto a battlefield," Theron said, his voice dropping to a grim whisper as he looked at the children playing by the fire. "We're bringing the war right to our own doorstep."

## Chapter Sixteen
# The Shadow Histories

A sharp knock on the front door echoed through the study, cutting through the hum of conversation.

The room stilled immediately. Tyrek's hand drifted toward the dagger at his belt. Theron glanced at Kaelith, who had already moved into a position that put her between the door and the more vulnerable, youngest members of the group. Even Jaye, despite his young age, set his book aside with a wary glance at the adults around him.

Another knock. More deliberate yet less intimidating this time.

Nera stood, ignoring the way her pulse quickened. She felt like she had heard that knock before, the intent behind it. Had she? She wasn't sure.

When she opened the door, the dim candlelight from the study spilled over a familiar shape. She had seen his shadow before—at the edge of her flight from the Archive—speaking in cryptic phrases before vanishing into the night.

But this time, he didn't disappear.

This time, he had come to stay.

"I knew I'd find you here," the man said, his voice smooth but edged with something more—urgency, maybe even relief. "I came to talk to you."

The recognition hit Nera instantly. It was the same voice that had warned her at the missing apothecary. The same figure who had guided her in the tunnels. The mystery dissolved, leaving only a face she realized she should have known all along.

Without waiting for an invitation, he stepped inside, lowering the hood as he shrugged off his long jacket. The man beneath it was the tallest of them, though he didn't loom. He carried his height with a quiet, dense stillness. He was lean—muscle visible beneath his shirt, stripped of excess weight—and clean cut with his red curls tamed back to reveal features that were sharp yet softened by something familiar.

"Tobias." The name fell from Nera's lips before she fully processed it, as if she had known all along but never allowed herself to connect it. She still wasn't sure how she knew his name ... had he told her at some point in the past? It was hard to remember what was a real past and what was forgotten or rewritten.

He gave a half-crooked smile, then gestured behind him. "I'm not alone this time."

More figures stepped in behind him. Gaela, with thick black curls framing an infectious smile, scanned the room with open curiosity, her gaze bright with intelligence. She was followed by two others—travelers, fighters, their faces unreadable but alert.

Tobias turned to Nera, his expression sobering. "I have something for you," he said. "A text I've been holding onto for a long time, waiting for the right person to read it."

There was a note in his voice that sent a cold dread through Nera—not just about the history, but something personal. Like a thread of her past she hadn't realized was missing.

From beneath his coat, he pulled a thick, weathered tome, its binding reinforced with layers of stitched leather, its pages swollen from time and wear. The sigil on the front was barely visible, faded from years of handling, but Nera recognized the shape of it.

Intertwined curved lines. She looked at the ring on her finger and noticed the similarity.

She reached for the tome slowly.

"This isn't a history book, Nera," Tobias said, weighing the heavy volume in his hands before setting it down. "It's a weapon. I've held the line alone as long as I can; once you open this, there is no going back to the way things were."

Nera took it carefully and moved to a chair at the table and sat hunched over the tome, its thick pages spread open before her, the scent of aged parchment curling around her like smoke. She quickly became lost in learning its secrets. The longer she studied the book, the more the room thinned out—most of the group had gone quiet, drawn into their own conversations or slipping off into the night—but Kieran stayed, his presence a solid anchor near her side.

Tobias's gift was unlike anything she had seen. The book wasn't just old—it felt impossible, as if it had been stitched together from pieces of a world that shouldn't exist. Some of the ink had morphed, rearranging itself in patterns that made her stomach churn, and the dates ... The dates just didn't make sense.

She turned another page, her fingers running over the words, her mind grasping at the implications. The kingdom they lived in—the land she called home—wasn't real; at least not in the way history defined 'real'.

It had not risen through war and conquest, not been settled by early ancestors who carved out a civilization from the wilds, nothing like they had been taught from the earliest grades in school.

It had been written. *Created. By the quill.*

A passage leaped out at her, the ink sliding just enough to reveal itself, as though the book was waiting for her to understand:

> *In the year 3023, the boundaries of this land were sealed.*
> *It was made, not discovered. A kingdom formed from intent, from*

*will, from the remnants of something that came before. The past was stitched together. The people do not remember, because they were never meant to.*

She ran her finger under the date, her nail digging into the page. "3023? This is wrong." She looked up at Tobias, her voice sharp with the reflex of her training. "The ink implies age, but the voice seems new. You're showing me a forgery, Tobias. Like it was written today to justify a war yesterday."

She wanted it to be a lie. She needed it to be a lie. Because if it was true, she hadn't been just archiving history; she had been curating a fabrication.

"Keep reading," Tobias urged, his voice low.

"But this text ... it doesn't use the word unified. It says sealed." She looked up, the contradiction hitting her. "You don't seal a border you just discovered."

She looked back at the page, reading aloud, "It was made, not discovered. A kingdom formed from intent ..."

Kieran stared at the page, his voice low. "The history books say our ancestors conquered the wilds. They didn't."

Nera felt the floor seem to drop away. "They wrote over them."

Alis leaned against the doorframe, flipping her coin with a sharp clink. "Don't look so surprised. If you repeat a lie often enough, Nera, it doesn't only become the truth. It becomes the new law."

"We need to find—"

The book slammed shut. Kieran's hand was pressed flat against the cover, trapping the words inside. His breathing was jagged, loud in the sudden silence. He was staring at the leather binding as if it had burned him.

"Don't," he whispered, his voice rough with a fear she had never heard in him before. "If you read the rest, Nera, we don't get to pretend we're just archivists anymore. We become accomplices."

\*\*\*

After weeks, the walls of Theron's home had begun to feel too tight, the weight of recent revelations settling deep into her bones. Everyone was growing antsy as the weather edged toward winter, so the core group had gathered in the personal archive of another supporter.

Nera's fingers drummed absently against the table where she had spread out her notes—an old habit, an attempt to anchor herself to something tangible.

But even the solid wood felt temporary, like everything else she had believed in. She had always been interested in her country's rich history, which is part of why she wanted to become an archivist in the first place. Now to find out that the kingdom had been written into existence … not built, not forged, but written. And like ink on parchment, it could be smudged. Altered. Erased. It wasn't simply history that had been rewritten with every stroke of ink by an Archivist—it had become reality itself.

And now, it felt like they were running out of time to uncover the truth. Every day they spent feeling safe and normal was punctured by moments that pulled them from complacency—glimpses of families and children that reminded them what they were fighting for, and why.

A sharp knock echoed through the room, cutting through the hum of the small group of scholars and rebels who had lingered late into the night. The room stilled. Tobias and Theron exchanged a glance. Alis was already moving, drawing a blade from the folds of her coat. She never truly rested—always scanning, always listening, her fingers constantly brushing against the hilts of her daggers as if expecting trouble at any moment. Even now, she wasn't reacting to the knock—it was like her instincts had already expected it.

Another knock—harder and louder this time. The signal.

Theron jumped to his feet. "They found us."

The room snapped into motion. Tyrek was dousing the lamps, Cael swept the scattered documents into his satchel, and Alis muttered a curse under her breath as she reached for the nearest book, hesitating a fraction too long before shoving it under her arm.

Nera didn't move. She was still staring at the thick tome Tobias had given her—the truth about where they came from. Proof that the whole kingdom was built on a lie.

A firm grip closed around her wrist. Warm, steady, certain, like he had done this before. Kieran.

Cael walked up behind them, his voice was low, controlled. "Nera. Move." His posture was stiff, hands curled into fists at his sides—not in anger, but in the kind of restraint that made his presence heavier. He hadn't even glanced her way in days; but now, just for a second, he looked toward her—outwardly devoid of any emotion.

Nera was not quite steady, not quite broken as she forced herself to follow.

Alis threw open the door to the hidden passage behind a tapestry on one of the walls, revealing a descending stone corridor. It was old, damp, the scent of ink and earth so thick in the air that you could almost taste it.

Tobias motioned them forward. "You three go first," he said, nodding to Nera, Kieran, and Cael. "We'll cover the entrance."

Cael looked away, staring into the dark tunnel as if he could find a different path there. Since Livia's death, he had finally started to come around, but his usual sharp wit had dulled into something bitter and silent. Without a word he stepped past them, slipping into the shadows of the tunnel while the rest of the group quickly followed him down, underneath the safehouse, hearing the passage close behind them.

Footsteps thundered on the floor above.

A crash echoed upstairs. The air sharpened, reality bracing itself. They ran, dipping into the hidden entrance that would take them to the underground.

The tunnel was narrow, forcing them uncomfortably close. Cael hadn't spoken since they left Theron's home, his silence pressing against Nera's back like a wall he wasn't ready to cross. Nera reached out to steady herself against a wooden support beam. Her hand closed around empty air, missing the timber by a solid inch, even though her eyes told her she was dead on target. She stumbled, corrected her grip, and kept walking. When the path forked ahead, Kieran hesitated. Nera instinctively reached out, her fingers brushing his arm. "Left."

He quickly glanced at her—just a flash of a look, but in it, she saw an unspoken question. A test, a challenge, a choice. There was something in his eyes—recognition, maybe, or just quiet certainty. A conversation they weren't having out loud, but both understood. She nodded.

Cael clenched his jaw. "Just pick a path." His words were clipped, tight.

His gaze flicked between them, catching on the way Nera's hand hovered near Kieran's sleeve, the way they moved in sync even without speaking. Cael's shoulders stayed rigid, his arms crossed, fingers drumming a sharp, restless rhythm against his sleeve. He didn't step away. He didn't disengage. But there was a rawness to the way he held himself, like something stretched too thin and refusing to tear.

Nera tensed at the sharpness in his voice, but Kieran didn't rise to the bait. He simply moved.

The walls of the tunnel pressed in. Nera stumbled, a sudden wave of vertigo washing over her—not from the dark, but from the geometry of the passage. The distance between steps felt wrong, stretching and snapping back like a rubber band. The air tasted metallic, charged with the static of a history that hadn't quite settled.

A shelf lined the corridor ahead, its books snapping between versions of themselves—one moment an Archivist-approved text, the next, something far older, forbidden. In the flickering, for just a moment, a name appeared. A name that should not exist. Then it was gone just as quickly.

Nera reached out without thinking. Her fingers brushed the cover of one book, and for a split second, it wavered—then snapped back into place, rewritten.

Kieran caught her wrist. "Don't." There was something too quick in his voice, a reaction not just to her action, but to the consequences it seemed he already knew. His grip was firm, but not forceful. Calculated. He didn't pull her away—just held her there, waiting for her to decide whether to listen.

She pressed her lips together, swallowed, and nodded once. When she stepped away, he let go immediately. A choice given, not an order.

At the next bend, the passage widened into a hidden checkpoint within the Underground. Tobias and Theron caught up behind them, breathing hard. "We collapsed the entry arch. It bought us twenty minutes—thirty if they argue about digging," Tobias said. "Maybe enough time they won't find us at all. This is where we split. Nera, they're expecting us deeper inside. Kieran, Cael—you'll come with her."

Cael scoffed. "Since when do you give orders?" His fingers flexed, his stance shifting, the challenge undercut by how quickly he fell into place.

Alis, who had slipped in beside them with her daggers still drawn, tilted her head. "Since you're in no state to make your own," she smirked, before turning to continue with the other group.

Cael looked ready to snap back. But then—he said nothing. Just turned away.

Tobias set his lantern down with a heavy thud. "Master Belvar isn't done hunting you, Nera. He'll come for this place next."

Nera tightened her grip on the tome. "Then I'd better make sure this history survives."

Tobias nodded. "Go." And with that, they stepped forward into the rebellion's archive.

They meandered through the labyrinth of passages, their steps sure despite the repositioning corridors that made this place feel like it had been built from pieces of forgotten time. The scent of damp stone and ink mingled with something sharper—burned parchment perhaps, or something even older. The deeper they went, the more the walls seemed to press in, their surfaces lined with faded texts and fragmented records pinned haphazardly, as though someone had tried to rebuild history from scraps.

The underground was restless tonight. Nera could feel it in the way people moved, in the hushed voices vanishing just before she reached them. Like they knew she was coming. Like something else did, too. Like the air itself was adjusting, folding around old knowledge, like a whisper begging to be heard.

This wasn't the first time she had walked among rebels and outlaws; they had always been present in Varethis, but this was unfiltered. Here, she wasn't just a scholar visiting restricted collections under the watchful eye of the Archive. Here, she was an outsider.

The first underground chamber smelled of damp parchment and ink—but beneath that, something earthy. Ancient. As they made their way through this chamber, Nera felt confusion. She had expected books. Shelves stacked with stolen history, ink-smudged records crammed into every corner. And there were a handful here and there spread between a handful of rebels who occupied various spots in the room. But at the heart of the chamber, where lanterns burned low and voices dropped to whispers, stood a tree.

Cael stopped beside it, fingers hovering just above the markings. He didn't touch them.

"The Memory Tree," said the rebel tending its roots. She was young, maybe fifteen, dirt under her fingernails as she smoothed the soil. "It doesn't grow leaves. Doesn't even need light. But it remembers."

His gaze snagged on the bark. It was smooth, unnaturally pale, etched with curling lines that Nera realized weren't natural markings. They were names. Hundreds of names. Some bold and dark, others barely visible, fading as if time itself were trying to erase them.

"The ones the world forgot," the girl whispered, patting the soil.

Something cold slid through Nera's chest. She stepped closer.

Near the back of the chamber, a younger child hummed to himself, tracing patterns in the dust with his finger. His coloring and the careful way he moved made Nera suspect he was the girl's younger brother. The other rebels barely noticed him—or pretended not to.

Nera caught the tune first, light and uneven, like a lullaby sung by someone who only half-remembered the words.

> *"The ink was gold, the crown was red,*
>
> *The Tyrant wished his memories dead.*
>
> *One by one, the names were gone,*
>
> *'Til only hers was left alone.*
>
> *But ink is water, blood is stone,*
>
> *And he cannot hold the quill alone"*

The boy stopped, blinking up at her. Nera's throat went dry. "Where did you hear that?"

He shrugged, pushing himself to his feet. "It's just a rhyme. Everybody knows it."

But when Nera glanced at Cael and Kieran, their faces were unreadable. Not everybody knew it.

\* \* \*

They continued down the damp and poorly lit passages, dancing light creating shadows in the corners. They reached the main chamber, where a long wooden table was covered in layers of maps, half-assembled texts, and glass plates used for studying rewritten ink. Several figures were gathered around the table, deep in discussion, but two familiar faces turned as she entered.

Cyrus did not look up from the map. He tapped a specific coordinate on the parchment. "You're late."

Tavian merely crossed his arms. He had been standing still enough in the dim light that Nera hadn't realized he was there. He looked her over—not with annoyance, but with the exhausted recognition of a man watching a tragedy repeat itself.

"I assume the apocalypse followed you in? It usually does."

Nera realized she shouldn't be surprised that Cyrus and Tavian were part of the underground rebels, and she chose to ignore the edge in his tone. "It wasn't exactly optional."

Tavian adjusted the spectacles perched on his nose. "Catastrophe rarely is."

Cyrus leaned against the table, tapping his fingers idly against an open manuscript while Sarina sat nearby knitting by the candlelight. "The spies are whispering your name everywhere, Calloway. The danger surrounding you has compounded."

She froze as he said her name. Not Nera—*Calloway*. As if they were back in the Grand Archive, as if she was still one of them, as if that bridge had not been burned along with everything else.

"You have no idea," she muttered, but even as she said it, she wasn't sure that was true anymore.

Cyrus arched a brow. "Clarify."

Tobias entered and cut them both off before she could respond. "We don't have time for games. Belvar isn't knocking on doors any more; he's kicking them down. If you aren't packed, you're already caught."

"We've been preparing for Belvar since before you got yourself exiled," Tavian said flatly. "Your panic is noted. And unnecessary."

"No games," Tobias agreed, then tipped his head towards Nera. "But you need her to unlock this."

Tavian slammed his ledger shut. "We don't use people as keys, Tobias. That is the Archives' method, not ours. If we start treating her like a tool to unlock the timeline, we are no better than the people who broke it."

Nera didn't look away from Cyrus and Tavian, even as she felt the tension increase in the room. Some of the gathered scholars, rebels, and spies watched her with open skepticism. Sarina stared pointedly, wisdom evident in her dark eyes. Others looked with something closer to wariness.

Finally, Cyrus sighed. "We can table that discussion." He reached for a sheet of parchment, sliding it toward her. "The immediate priority is this data."

Nera stepped forward and took the page without thinking, her fingers brushing against the fragile edges. The ink was unstable, flickering ... rewriting itself even as she read it. At first, the words described a secondary treaty she had studied before, one she had memorized from her years in the Archive. But then—

The letters were reconfigured. The meaning changed. A name appeared where there hadn't been one before.

A shallow breath shuddered past her lips, uneven, uncertain. This wasn't just an edit. This was history trying to restore itself. Their home, their past—it had all been rewritten. And she was finally seeing the cracks.

She looked up, her heart pounding. "Where did you get this?"

Cyrus gave her a slow, knowing smile. "You are questioning the wrong variable."

Tavian's voice was quieter, heavy with exhaustion. "Catastrophes have a cadence, Nera. The rhythm is accelerating. The question is—why now?"

Nera shook her head. She didn't have an answer.

And then, after a heavy pause, from across the room someone spoke. "I know where Soren went."

The words shook her like ice water. She turned sharply, but the speaker—an older woman hunched over a pile of texts—didn't look up.

Nera's voice came out more unsteady than she liked. "What? Where?"

The woman hesitated, flipping a page between ink-stained fingers. "Depends. Are you looking for where he was, or where he's going?"

Nera stepped forward. "What does that mean?"

But the woman just shook her head. "If you're chasing ghosts, be careful." Her eyes flicked toward the moving text still clutched in Nera's hands. "Some of them remember being erased."

Nera stared at her, pulse hammering. Something about everything she had seen and heard made her realize that the rebels she had encountered over the years weren't just preserving history like she had believed; they were trying to bring back the original history.

* * *

The meeting chamber somehow always felt colder than the rest of the stronghold, despite also being brighter; the air swirling with dust and something else—something heavier, like a thousand forgotten stories pressing against the walls. The stone beneath Nera's boots was uneven, worn down by time and by those who had walked these halls before her, seeking answers in the fragments of history that refused to be erased.

Cael navigated the way, a lantern swinging in his grip, its dim light creating dancing shadows against the towering shelves that loomed over them. The room felt older from the others—not just hidden, but deliberately buried, as if the very foundation of the underground stronghold had been built to contain what lay within.

Two figures waited for them at the heart of the chamber.

The first was Gaela, Tobias' wife. She leaned against a desk, arms crossed, watching their approach with the quiet confidence of someone who already knew how this conversation was going to go.

"Was wondering when you'd finally bring her down here," Gaela said, flicking her gaze to Brieth next to her before settling on Nera. "We weren't sure if you would be coming as a guest or a liability."

Nera met her stare. "Still deciding?"

Gaela grinned. "Always."

Brieth, one of the most trusted scouts who also happened to be Jorin's girlfriend and ever the pragmatist, waved to the room around them. "You're here now. That's what matters. Tobias thought you needed to see something." She stepped past them, setting the lantern on a nearby table. The surface was covered in open scrolls, scraps of parchment, and what looked like the remains of a map half-burned at the edges. But at the center of it all was a single, leather-bound book.

Nera felt it immediately—the pull. The book's cover bore no title, but the leather was stitched with silver threads that shimmered in ways that defied the torchlight. It looked like a book that shouldn't exist.

Brieth tapped the cover of the book. "This may be what you've been looking for."

She stepped forward without thinking, but Gaela's voice stopped her. "Careful," she warned, her voice dropping the way a mother warns a child about a hot stove. "This book takes payment.

The last person who touched it didn't just lose their name on paper, they lost it in their own head. He stood there for five minutes yelling because he couldn't remember who he was. Don't touch it unless you're ready to pay."

Brieth winced. "They got it back. Eventually."

Kieran, standing just at Nera's side, frowned. "What kind of book does that?"

"The kind that remembers," Gaela murmured.

Nera didn't hesitate. She reached forward, her fingers grazing the worn leather. The moment she made contact, the text inside the tome began to change.

The ink rippled across the pages, twisting between languages, between forms, until finally, the text settled. Not in any script she had seen before—but one she understood all the same.

A sharp inhale cut through the silence before she could stop it, as if the air had turned to stone in her throat. This wasn't the first time she had read these words.

The moment the thought crossed her mind, the world around her fractured. A rush of air stole the breath from her lungs. The stone beneath her feet vanished as she heard a footstep behind her.

Kieran's voice cut through the charged air—sharp, instinctive. "Nera—!"

Then the world pulled them under.

## CHAPTER SEVENTEEN

# Search for Soren

The ruins stretched before them, not just rubble, not just the remnants of a forgotten city, but a battlefield filled with fire, smoke and violence. The sky churned slowly with unnatural colors, like an old parchment left too long in the sun with the edges curling inward. Buildings stood half-formed, some quickly switching between existence and erasure, others collapsing.

Nera stood in the center of it all, and she wasn't alone. Kieran was beside her, his stance tense, eyes darting across the devastation as if he knew this place. As if he had been here before. *Because they had.* The realization hit hard and fast. This wasn't just a vision. This was a *memory*.

She turned, searching the collapsing structures, the fire swallowing ink and stone alike. And then she saw them—the figures moving through the chaos, their voices carried by the wind.

Fighting. Arguing. Struggling to stop the rewrite. And in the center of it all, two familiar silhouettes. One was Kieran, slightly younger but unmistakably him. The other—

She went completely still. It was her. Someone else, yet also still her. She watched herself—a version of herself who had lived in a war that had never been; or had been erased.

The Kieran standing beside her in the fractured memory looked at her—at the real her.

The second their eyes met, recognition slammed into place.

He didn't look at her like a stranger. He looked at her like he had been waiting for her.

He reached out, his hand cutting through the smoke, but before she could take it, familiarity settled into her bones.

It was a war of preservation. She wanted to say something—anything—but the memory was already slipping, rewriting itself even as she watched. The past was being stolen again.

The version of Kieran in the memory turned, his gaze locking onto the present her, but before she could hear his voice—before she could reach him—

Everything collapsed.

*  *  *

The underground chamber snapped back into place. Nera staggered with a desperate gasp. Her fingers were still trembling against the cover of the book, but her mind was racing, spiraling, straining for something just out of reach.

She turned toward Kieran and found him already watching her. Not just watching—fixed, unblinking. His face was locked into careful neutrality, jaw clenched, chest rising and falling hard, as if he'd been dragged back into his body without warning.

Before she could speak, his hand caught her wrist. It wasn't calculated; it was instinct. His fingers closed tight, his breath ragged, eyes wide and unguarded as they searched her face. He opened his mouth, a word forming on his lips—then stopped.

She stared at him, stunned.

Kieran's grip faltered, his other hand flying to his temple as if struck. He squeezed his eyes shut, a violent tremor running through his arm that shook them both. He looked like a man trying to keep his footing on a floor that wasn't there. Then he gasped and snatched his hand away as if burned.

They turned and moved in unison.

The corridors twisted like veins through the hidden underground city, some sections flickering between eras, their stonework shifting as if the walls couldn't decide which version of themselves to settle on. The air still felt charged with whatever they had just glimpsed, even as the weight of the present pressed back in.

Kieran hadn't spoken since they left the meeting chamber. Nera knew better than to press him. Not yet.

He walked ahead of her, movements sharp and measured, his usual control strained at the edges. His posture stayed rigid, as though he were trying to outpace something neither of them had fully grasped.

Nera's mind still reeled from what she had seen. From what she had felt. That wasn't just a fracture. They had been there—together—moving in the same moment, the same struggle, bound by something deeper than history alone.

And whatever it was, Kieran had felt it before she did.

This wasn't the moment or the words she wanted—but it was what she had. "Kieran." He didn't stop. Her pulse ticked faster. "We need to talk about what just happened."

His steps faltered, but he didn't turn around. "No, we don't." The words were quiet, but they struck harder than they should have.

She moved closer. "Kieran—"

He turned sharply, his face blank, the shuttered look of a man who had learned to sleep in a trench, but his eyes—those silver-gray eyes—were anything but blank. For the first time since she had met him, she saw something raw in them. Something afraid. He stepped into her space, backing against the cold stone wall.

His hand rose, hovering inches from her face, trembling slightly For a heartbeat the air between them crackled with everything he wasn't saying. His lips parted, a name forming there.

"I can't," he choked out, the words ragged. If I say it … if I make it real … I lose you." He squeezed his eyes shut, dropping his hand. "We don't talk about things we can't change," he said, voice low but firm. "That's how we survive right now."

Nera stiffened. "So that's it? You just pretend none of it happened?"

He adjusted his balance as he firmly grasped both of his arms while staring deep into her eyes. "We don't even know what *it* was. Or if it was real."

A flash of irritation sparked in her. "Are you serious? We both saw it. We—"

"We don't know anything," he cut her off. "And until we do, we say nothing." The finality in his voice was a warning not to push.

She swallowed back the urge to argue, brushing his hands aside, trying to fight the stubborn streak she felt welling up inside like a barely controlled wave. He was shutting down, the way she sensed he always did when something shook him. But this time, it felt personal; he wasn't just guarding himself. He was guarding her.

And she wasn't sure what unsettled her more—that he thought she needed protecting, or that a part of her wasn't sure if he was wrong. Before she could push him further, a voice broke the tension.

"Well, this is new."

Nera turned. Cael.

He leaned against the wall just a few feet away, arms crossed, his presence both casual and completely deliberate. There was a sharpness in his eyes that wasn't quite directed at her, but at Kieran.

Kieran's thumb ghosted over the hilt of his blade, his fingers flexing once before he stepped back from Nera, turning to withdraw down the corridor without another word. A retreat.

Cael leaned against the wall and watched Kieran go, waiting until his footsteps faded. He didn't look at Nera at first.

When he finally did, something sharp had settled behind his eyes.

He moved toward her. "That's the first time I've ever seen him run from anything." His tone stayed casual, but his gaze didn't. It tracked the space Kieran had left behind, then returned to her.

Nera sighed, raking a hand over her face. "Not now."

Cael didn't move. He studied her too closely, then glanced back down the corridor. His jaw worked once before he shoved his hands into his pockets, shoulders tightening as if bracing himself.

He pushed off the wall and stepped closer. Smoothed his jacket. His expression settled into something polite and blank.

"He didn't leave because he was confused," Cael said quietly.

Nera stiffened. "Cael—"

"That wasn't panic." His golden-hazel eyes hardened. "He knew that place."

He took another step toward her. "He knew that place. Better than we did. If he remembers things that never happened, he's—"

"Stop," Nera snapped.

"He's a liability," Cael said anyway. "Or worse—"

"I said stop." She stepped past him, cutting the air with her hand, refusing to hear the rest of his comments. "We're moving."

She walked away before he could finish. Cael stood alone, the accusation hanging unresolved in the damp air.

## CHAPTER EIGHTEEN
# Third Seat

The underground never truly slept, but tonight, the endless energy felt different. Conversations were quieter, movements sharper, something unspoken pressing against the air like a storm about to break.

Nera felt it before she saw it. She had barely returned to the main chamber with Kieran and Cael when she noticed the change in the rebels' posture. The usual tension of secrecy had hardened into something sharper—anticipation, preparation. People stood in clusters, muttering in low voices, looking toward the central table where Tobias, Gaela, and a few others were gathered.

At the far end of the room, the elderly woman who had spoken to her about Soren stood alone, staring at the wall, lost in something only she could see.

Nera hesitated, her gaze flicking over the room again. Hadn't she just seen this? No, she had only just arrived. She was sure of that. And yet, for the briefest moment, the scene felt layered, like she was remembering something that had barely finished happening.

Tobias saw Nera first, waving her over. "You need to hear this."

She stepped closer, Kieran moving to her side, Cael lingering just behind. The parchment on the table was crumpled at the edges, as if someone had clenched it too tightly before deciding to let go.

Brieth stepped forward, her usual composure steady despite what she was about to share. She had always listened more than she spoke, but when she did offer information, it carried the sharp edge of someone who had survived in the margins and learned early that knowledge was survival—and guarded it carefully.

"One of our informants got this off an Archivist courier before it reached its intended recipient," she said, tapping a finger against the ink to draw attention to the key passage.

Nera read the first line and felt her stomach drop.

> *Calloway remains a threat. She is to be recovered, alive and unharmed, by force if necessary. By order of Valen Kestor.*

The second line was worse.

> *The underground faction is no longer beneath suspicion— it is confirmed. The network is to be dismantled. The orders are clear.*

Master Belvar knew what they were doing.

Nera's breath came slower, steadier than she expected, but inside, something cold twisted in her chest.

"So he's not just hunting me now," she realized. "He's hunting all of you."

Gaela's face was a fortress, but there was an edge to it, a barely concealed frustration. "You're not the first person Belvar has wanted gone. But you might be the first one he won't allow to disappear quietly for some reason."

Tavian frowned. "If history is any indication, he'll make an example of you since it seems he won't erase you."

Nera had already figured that out. It was what came next that sent unease curling through her.

Brieth spoke sharply. "There's something else." She hesitated, fingers pressing against the parchment before sliding it forward. "This isn't just about you. He mentioned something else in the orders. Something about … a seventh alignment."

The word sent a ripple through the group.

Cyrus stopped winding his timepiece. The sudden silence was louder than a shout. "If the foundation is fractured, the structure fails," Cyrus stated, his voice devoid of inflection. "Attempt an Alignment under these conditions, and history does not reset. It collapses."

"We don't know if they have the capability," Tobias said, assessing the threat level. "It's a theoretical option, not a tactical one."

Nera wasn't so sure. She took a step back, her gaze switching toward the old woman in the corner, the one who had not moved since she entered. Someone had told her this woman knew things—things that had survived past erasures, slipping through the cracks of rewritten time. Tonight, something was different.

Nera approached slowly. "You heard."

The elder didn't turn. Her outline wavered, edges thinning as if the candlelight couldn't quite decide where she ended.

"I remember," she said, her fingers twitching as though a quill still rested between them. A pause. A breath that seemed to stutter in the air. "He sat in the front row. Third seat."

Nera went still, anticipation tightening her chest. The elder's hand brushed the worn stone of the wall, her palm passing half through it before correcting, as if reaching for a classroom that no longer existed.

"He always pressed too hard on the parchment," she murmured, her voice thinning. "He wanted the ink to be permanent before he even understood the words. I failed him."

Her form flickered, momentarily transparent.

"Now…" Her gaze unfocused. "…I think he erased me for it."

Beside Nera, Kieran shifted. "Who?" he asked carefully. "Belvar?"

The elder blinked, confusion rippling across her face as parts of her faded in and out. Her mouth opened once more.

"Kestor," she whispered.

Tavian drew in a slow breath. "She's citing a biography that was never written," he murmured.

"I don't know what he was before," the elder said, her voice slipping, stuttering. "I only know what he becomes." She reached out, her hand passing cleanly through the stone table, as if neither of them were entirely real. "We cannot hold the quill, child. We cannot turn the page back. We can only whisper to the one who can."

Her pale eyes fixed on Nera's hands. "Write it true. Make history whole again."

Nera turned away, the warning settling heavily in her chest. Belvar was initiating a Seventh Alignment. They couldn't just survive this—they had to stop it. And there was only one person who had been tracking Belvar's history longer than she had.

She crossed the chamber to the strategy room. Tobias and Cyrus were already there, trading hushed words with Gaela and Brieth. The underground's intelligence network was a tangled web of informants, intercepted messages, and stolen scraps of knowledge that most people had already forgotten existed. If anyone knew where to find Soren, it was them.

"Soren?" Nera questions sharply, almost a demand.

Tobias ran a hand down his face. "Soren's alive. The network confirmed his pattern of movement."

Gaela crossed her arms. "No one's seen him directly, but word travels. He's leaving breadcrumbs. Coded messages. Just enough to prove he's alive, but not enough to compromise his location."

Brieth adjusted the strap of the bag across her chest, shaking her head. "It's deliberate. He's gone dark."

Nera took a step closer. "Then why leave anything at all?"

Cyrus didn't look up from the documents. "It is a data trail," he corrected. "Soren knows the Archive's ciphers. If he left traces, he calculated the probability that you would track him. He is not hiding; he is waiting."

The words sat uncomfortably in her chest.

Tobias gestured to the documents spread across the table. "Whatever he's doing, it's somehow connected to the Benefactor."

Nera stared at the pages. The ink had begun to fade in places, time eating away at words that once held weight. But one thing was clear from all the information they had gathered: Soren had never stopped searching for the truth. And now, it seems his search must have led him somewhere important.

Gaela tapped a finger against the map. "He left behind something you need. We don't know what it is. We don't even know where. But we know this: he wouldn't have risked leaving anything unless he believed it mattered."

Brieth nodded, her usual restlessness momentarily subdued. "And unless I'm wrong, he knew you'd be the one to find it."

Nera's gaze flicked back to the documents. Soren hadn't just left a map; he had left an invitation to help finish what he started.

A cold certainty settled in her chest, heavier than fear. If the timeline was truly broken, fixing it wouldn't be as simple as rewriting a line of text. It would require some type of anchor.

She looked at the empty space on the map where the answer should be. "He left a trail," Nera whispered, the realization tasting like ash. "And he knows I'm the only one crazy enough to follow it."

## CHAPTER NINETEEN
# Shelter in the Lie

The smell of warm bread and something spiced filled the air, curling into the corners of Theron's safehouse and breathing life into the morning. For all the uncertainty pressing in from every side, this moment felt normal—steady, almost untouched by the oppressive weight of history unraveling around them. The fire in the hearth crackled softly, and the long wooden table was scattered with parchment scraps, half-empty mugs, and the remnants of last night's conversations mingled with this morning's breakfast.

Gaela stood by the stove, flipping something in a pan with the ease of someone who knew exactly what they were doing. Cyrus sliced fresh fruit at the counter, his dry, ink-stained fingers wielding the knife with the same clinical precision he used to dissect codes. As the blade pressed into an apple, it bowed outward for a split second—curving like soft lead against the fruit's skin—before snapping back into a straight, rigid line. Cyrus didn't notice. He simply finished the slice.

Theron watched over a pot of thick porridge, his broad shoulders blocking half the firelight.

Maria stood beside Theron on a stool, stirring the pot with a careful rhythm that matched the nursery rhyme she hummed under her breath. She didn't look at the knife in his hand. She didn't notice the way the room had gone quiet. She just stirred, humming a tune about a sun that never set, while the adults exchanged looks that felt like things left unsaid.

Theron caught Maria watching him and pulled a ridiculous, cross-eyed face, flashing a crooked, rogue grin that softened the rugged line of his jaw. Maria giggled, and Theron winked at her, muttering about how some adults never stirred it the right way.

Clara hovered nearby, handing over ingredients whenever Maria asked, though she seemed far more interested in sneaking bits of fruit from Cyrus's pile when she thought he wasn't looking.

Jaye sat cross-legged on a chair at the table, already eating with some of the group, shoveling food into his mouth with the focus of someone who knew he needed to eat before anything else stole his attention. He pointed at a wedge of cheese on the table and shook his head. "I'm not eating that."

Cyrus didn't glance up from his cutting. He laughed, appreciating the momentary distraction. "Hunger is a variable you can control."

Jaye nodded, satisfied, and returned to his plate.

Tobias entered with fresh herbs from the garden for the kitchen; Tyrek, who had just arrived, trailed in his wake. "Three more arrests in the lower district this morning," Tyrek muttered, shaking the cold from his coat. "They aren't just taking people anymore; they're marking the doors with black ink. Belvar isn't investigating neighborhoods; he's *condemning* them."

He tossed Nera a small package. "One of my contacts who owed me a favor had this," he said. "Since you Archivists love your traditions, you might as well season breakfast with something from your peers."

Nera caught it, glancing at the label. The words were barely visible, etched into the smooth surface with careful precision. *Blackened Salt.* A delicacy.

She raised an eyebrow. "Where did you even get this?"

"Let's just say a supply clerk at the Academy over-leveraged himself. He couldn't pay in coin, so I liquidated his inventory." Tyrek said airily, biting into a slice of thick bread he grabbed from the table. "You lot supposedly use it for school initiation rituals, but it also makes damn good eggs."

Nera arched a brow but pinched a small amount between her fingers and sprinkled it over the food. The salt dissolved into the heat, leaving behind the faintest shimmer—like ink catching the light at just the right angle.

Liaz took the packet from Nera, sprinkling some over the pan with mechanical precision. "It also preserves meat," she told the room. "And we don't waste food. Eat."

Kieran leaned against the doorway, arms crossed. "Looks unnatural." He moved toward the table.

Nera reached for the tea canister, but Kieran was already there. Without looking at her, he slid the specific blend she needed—the calming hawthorn mix, not the stimulant she usually drank for work—into her hand. She took it, their fingers brushing naturally.

Cael watched the exchange, his mouth opening as if to offer her the coffee pot he was holding. He looked at the tea in her hand, then at the coffee in his. He closed his mouth and set the pot down.

She lifted the mug, watching the steam curl off the ceramic. It should have been scalding. But against her palm, she felt nothing. Panic spiked in her chest—a familiar, sickening drop. It was the same sensation from the Archive, when she had tried to rewrite the supply log and her skin had gone blind. The nerves weren't just numb; they were absent, severed by ink she had forced into the world.

She quickly shifted the mug to her left hand, and the heat bit instantly—reassuring and painful. She rubbed her right hand against her thigh, trying to wake nerves that had been edited into silence.

"Eat," Gaela ordered, flipping bread onto a plate with a thud. "Scholar's Bread is done. It's dense enough to sit in your stomach for three days. You can't rewrite the world if you pass out from hunger, and I'm not carrying any of you back if you drop."

She set the plate of bread on the table—a dense, hearty loaf with a crust darkened by the fire. Nera recognized it immediately. Simple, nourishing, and served regularly at midnight readings in the Grand Archive. It was a staple for those who spent too many hours buried in books.

Tobias picked up a piece and took a bite without comment. A moment later, he nodded approvingly. "Better than I remember."

"Everything tastes better when you're not sneaking it past curfew," Kaelith teased Theron, glancing at him with a knowing smile that carried echoes of their school days.

Across the room, Theron chimed in with a grin. "Funny. I always thought that was what made it better."

"Ignore him," Kaelith said, stabbing a piece of fruit with her knife. "Theron cooks like he fights—too much defensive maneuvering, not enough heat. He thinks if he stirs the porridge exactly forty times, the world won't end."

"Hey, I recall you burning the water last week, Kaelith," Theron quipped. "Pretty sure that puts me two points ahead on the 'keeping everyone alive through digestion' ledger. Unless you're counting the time you poisoned the guards, in which case, I suppose we're tied."

People moved around the room in slow, familiar motions, the morning routines of a house that had become a sanctuary. Others drifted in and out—some sitting, some leaning against the walls—their conversations easy despite the tension hanging beneath it all. Everyone gathered in loose clusters, the ginger-haired newcomer playing the jester and making the children giggle.

Nera had settled herself at the table, arms crossed as she watched the quiet rhythms of the morning unfold, and she let herself just breathe.

For an hour, maps were pushed aside, replacing talk of the Tyrant and the timeline with the smell of Gaela's bread and the sound of Maria laughing. Nera watched them, a lump forming in her throat. This was the "normal" the alignments were meant to protect—but it was fragile. If they failed, this laughter wouldn't just stop; it would never have happened.

Theron leaned back in his chair, stretching his arms with a satisfied groan. "The walls are solid. The fire is lit. Our bellies are full. And for now the roof holds."

Nera watched them, a lump forming in her throat. She wanted to believe him—that wood and stone could keep history out. She knew the normalcy wouldn't last and decided to enjoy it while she could.

Cael slid into the chair between her and Alis, setting a mug of tea in front of her—Scholar's Blend, just the way she liked it. He offered a small, tired smile, one that didn't quite reach his eyes but tried to bridge the distance that had opened between them. A plate of bread sat untouched in front of him; he kept breaking the crust into smaller and smaller pieces. But at least he was still here. At least he might eat.

"Just like the old days at the Scholar's Rest," he murmured, leaning in close enough that the world felt small again. Manageable. "Before the fires. Before the rewrites. We can get back to that, Nera. Once we fix this, we go back."

"You can't go back to a world that never existed, Cael," Alis said, not looking up from her plate. She tore a piece of bread with deliberate slowness.

"We were happy," Cael argued.

"We were blind," Alis corrected. "You're just missing a past that wasn't real. Don't let the lie comfort you."

He looked at Nera with certainty, offering her a future that looked exactly like the past she had lost. She wrapped her hands around the warm mug. She wanted to promise him he was right. She wanted to sink into the familiar comfort where the greatest danger was a lecture from Master Belvar.

Then her gaze lifted to the doorway.

Kieran leaned there, arms crossed, watching them. He didn't speak or step in. He simply stood, a silent, unyielding reminder of what they had seen in the dark—things that couldn't be unlearned. And in that moment, Nera understood there was no going back. The girl Cael wanted to save no longer existed.

Cyrus set down the fruit knife and wiped his hands on a cloth, his attention shifting to the room. Whatever ease the morning had offered, the work could not wait.

"We have a lead on Soren," he said, his voice cutting through the quiet. "Alis's contact sent word. The Nameless Market is moving. It'll be near the Sarith Hollow Outpost by midday. If we're going to intercept him, we move now."

\*\*\*

Nera sat at a long wooden table near the food stalls, her hand resting on the rough grain of the wood. The Sarith Hollow Outpost hummed with low voices, traders and rebels exchanging whispered reports of movement along the roads.

The heavy stone walls were lined with crates of salvaged documents, stacks of half-deciphered records, and the scent of wax-sealed scrolls that had never made it to the Grand Archive, or any archive. A heavy tapestry, faded with age, hung near the entrance, its threads depicting a history no one could fully remember. In the worn fabric, figures stood where none should; shadows in the weave, barely visible, their faces lost to time. Dozens of woven baskets overflowed with dried herbs carefully plucked from the local gardens, remnants of a harsh winter. This was contrasted by other containers filled with the first hardy shoots of Spring … a Spring which shouldn't be here yet.

The last few days had been a flood of information, pieces of lost history surfacing from the most unexpected places. Tobias and Theron had returned with an old ledger recovered from the outskirts of Varethis, one that contained more stories of an erased fortification near the Hollow Expanse. Cyrus and Tavian were preparing to investigate inconsistencies in border records from the eastern territories, places that had changed subtly over time, unnoticed by anyone except those who had lived there before the rewrites.

But the most pressing issue was Soren. Nera was certain he knew something about the past that mattered—things he may have always suspected but never proven. A woman from the outer trade routes, someone who had once worked in the Archive's lesser halls, claimed she had seen him passing through a town called Orswick.

It wasn't a place of any importance. But Nera remembered something—a long-ago conversation with Soren, when he had casually mentioned an old, forgotten library hidden in a town no one bothered to check.

"We split up," Kieran said. "Cyrus and Tavian verify the records you need in the east. Nera and I follow the trail to Orswick with a few others. The rest head toward the old waterways and the river towns—there are rumors of an old fortress near the Hollow Expanse. We check what needs checking, then regroup at the old Waystation. It's a good midpoint, and close to where the Nameless Market is often found."

His tone was level, practiced. When Nera glanced at him, he met her gaze, silver-grey eyes flicking over her expression before returning to the maps. Always assessing. Always prepared.

"Actually, forget Orswick," Alis said, checking her blade. "My contact sent word an hour ago. Soren didn't stay in the outer towns. He went straight to the source."

Nera turned. "The Nameless Market?"

"It's moving tonight," Alis said. "If we don't catch it today, we might lose the lead."

Cael tapped his quill against the table. The ivory shaft, the quill of a conservator, had a fine crack, not enough to break but enough to show wear—like a story half-forgotten. It was the one he had found in the ashes where Livia had stood—lying next to the charred remains of the violet book she had tried to save—when he had quietly returned to the ruins of the Grand Archive after it had burned.

He kept his eyes fixed on the map, refusing to meet anyone's gaze—especially hers.

"We divide our forces," he said, his voice clipped and overly formal. He drew a hard line across the Hollow Expanse, the nib of his quill tearing the paper. "I'll take the border towns. They're high-risk, low-visibility. If the Archive missed anything, it's there."

He began listing supplies they would need—rations for a month, three coils of climbing rope, redundant medical kits.

"Cael," Nera interrupted gently. "It's a two-day ride. We don't need rations for a siege."

He didn't stop. He didn't look up. "We take it all," he snapped, checking a clasp that was already secure. "We ran out of time last time. We aren't running out of anything ever again." He wasn't packing for a trip; he was fortifying himself against another loss.

Nera felt something niggling at her mind, an awareness of him in a way she hadn't before. He wasn't the same as he had been when they worked together in the Archive, or even when she had known him growing up. She could see it in the way his gaze lingered on the maps, the way his jaw stayed tight whenever certain names were spoken.

Nera set her palms against the table. "We leave within the hour."

The group split at the city gates. Cael took Brieth and a small contingent toward the border towns of the Hollow Expanse, searching for physical evidence of the failures, while Nera, Kieran, Alis, and Jorin turned toward the mountains where the Nameless Market was rumored to be hiding.

## CHAPTER TWENTY

# Cinders and Dust

The wind carried the scent of damp wood and rain-soaked earth, but beneath it lay something sharper—the metallic taste of ozone and static. It made Cael's teeth ache. The horses shied, tossing their heads and fighting the bit, their instincts screaming that the path ahead did not exist.

Cael forced his mount forward, his hand tightening on the reins. He didn't just need to see this; he needed to document it. He needed proof that couldn't be erased.

Brieth slowed her horse. "This isn't on any of the maps."

Cael exhaled. "That's the point."

They crested a small ridge, and below them stretched what remained of Fendrel's Hollow—a village that, according to every Archive record, had never existed. But it had. And it still did—but barely.

Half the buildings flickered, oscillating violently between solid stone and empty air. A cottage roof near the road didn't just collapse; it dissolved into grey mist before snapping back into existence a second later, perfectly whole. The sound was nauseating—a rhythmic thrum-snap, thrum-snap that vibrated in Cael's chest.

Cael pulled a charcoal stick and a blank parchment from his satchel. His hand shook, but he forced it steady, sketching the perimeter of the anomaly. He mapped the void where the well should be and noted the way the light bent around the watchtower, refracting like a prism through a cracked lens.

"It's not just a glitch," he muttered, scratching a jagged line across the paper. "It's a rejection. The land is trying to spit the revision out."

"It's like someone forgot to finish creating it," Brieth whispered.

"Or finish erasing it," Cael said. He turned his head to the right, the instinct automatic. "Liv, look at the archway, it's—"

The words died in the damp air. Beside him, there was only mist.

Cael's mouth clicked shut. He stared at the empty space for a fraction of a second, his hand twitching on the reins. Then, his jaw tightened, and he snapped his gaze forward, erasing the moment as if it hadn't happened.

A shift in the light caught his eye. Not a glitch this time—something solid. His jaw tightened. He pointed toward the far ridge. "Look."

A cloaked figure stood motionless on the horizon, silhouetted against the grey sky. They didn't carry a weapon, yet their presence felt heavier than a battalion. They weren't watching the road; they were watching the wound in the world, guarding it like a grave.

"The Hollow Watchers," Brieth muttered. "They believe this place is a scar that must not be reopened. They watch the glitch, not the world."

Cael looked at the figure on the horizon. It didn't move. It simply watched, waiting for the wound to open.

## CHAPTER TWENTY-ONE

# The Nameless Market

Miles away, on the road toward the mountain pass, the horizon felt heavy.

The entrance to the Nameless Market was never in the same place twice. This time, it lay tucked between sheer rock walls along the side of a lesser mountain range, just beyond the Southern Territories.

Nera followed Alis and Tyrek through a narrow cleft in the cliffs, their footsteps muffled by damp earth and the low hum of something not quite natural in the air. Those not entering with them remained behind, concealed in the surrounding terrain, watching for signs of trouble.

Tyrek led the way, moving with a loose-limbed rhythm that made no sound, his fingers idly tapping the hilt of a hidden blade. Alis walked just ahead of Nera, rolling her shoulders as if slipping into a familiar role, her usual smirk muted by focus.

The passage opened into a vast stone chamber—one that was clearly not part of any natural cave system. This place had been built. Or rewritten into existence. At the far end stood a set of massive wooden doors carved with shifting symbols. They never settled, the markings rearranging themselves like ink bleeding across parchment, forming new meanings as they moved.

Two figures stood beside the doors, cloaked in deep red, their faces hidden behind elaborate masks made of woven metal and glass. Alis approached without hesitation.

One of the masked figures tilted their head. "You bring guests."

"I bring business," Alis said flatly.

A pause. Then the second figure turned toward Nera, and something in the air shifted. It wasn't hostility. It wasn't even curiosity. It was recognition. Whatever they saw, it was meant for her.

Beside her, Kieran went still.

The first figure lifted a gloved hand and traced a small, deliberate symbol in the air between them. The carvings on the doors pulsed in response. Then, without another word, the doors swung open.

A rush of warm air hit them, carrying the scent of aged parchment, burning incense, and a faint, impossible drift of crushed lavender—the sharp, sweet smell of things that refused to stay lost. The lanterns overhead didn't cast light so much as bruise the darkness, emitting a low violet glow that made the shadows stretch toward her. It was too quiet for a crowd. Footsteps were muffled, leaving only the rustle of heavy fabric and the whisper of secrets being traded.

The Nameless Market had let them in.

Stepping inside was like stepping into somewhere that didn't entirely exist.

The Market wasn't a single place—it was a collection of spaces, pulled together from disparate times, conflicting rewrites, and forgotten histories.

High above, the ceiling stretched and arched in places that defied logic, giving it the feeling of an open-air market enclosed by stone walls. Stalls made of stone stood alongside structures of wood that looked too old for this world, while others were draped in ink-darkened cloth that shimmered between solid and unreal. It was unclear to Nera if the structures always remained the same or changed with each change in location.

People moved through the space in winding, intentional paths. No one meandered. No one wandered aimlessly. Everyone here knew why they had come and where they needed to be.

"Keep your voices down," Alis muttered, her gaze flicking across the crowd.

Kieran scoffed, but he lowered his tone. "You think someone's listening?"

Alis didn't look at him. "Someone is always listening." She nodded subtly toward the far side of the stalls—where a man who had been standing there moments ago was suddenly gone, his table empty, as if it had never existed at all.

Nera frowned. "Who was that?"

Alis gave a small shake of her head. "No one you'd get an answer from." She hesitated, then added, "But the Market doesn't run itself."

Tyrek crossed his arms, the leather of his coat creaking. "You mean the ghosts? The Unwritten?"

Nera turned toward him. "You've heard of them?"

Kieran's silver eyes tracked the flow of people through the stalls. "Everyone's heard of them. No one's ever met one."

Tyrek shrugged. "Because they don't exist."

"That's exactly what they want you to think," Alis said. "But we're looking for The Curator."

Nera let her gaze move across the merchants and traders. Some sold goods. Others sold knowledge.

A woman with an unreadable face sat behind a table stacked with ledgers and maps, each bound in unfamiliar coverings, their pages subtly shifting between versions of history.

Nearby, a man in dark robes held up a quill that he swore wrote on its own, bartering with a shadowed figure whose voice slid between dialects as they spoke. Some stalls held artifacts of rewritten worlds—weapons, trinkets, even clothing from places that had been erased. And woven between them, almost everywhere, were various tapestries.

Nera grounded herself by letting her fingers brush the edge of one as she passed. These weren't decorations. They were records.

Scenes played out in the threads—a battle that had never happened, a ruler whose name had been lost, a kingdom that had existed for only a moment before being rewritten. She pulled her hand back, the fabric almost too warm beneath her fingers, as if it remembered being something else.

She slowed at a stall where a vendor arranged rows of rusted iron keys, heavy and old. There were no locks in sight. Nera reached out, brushing the cold metal of one key etched with a crest she didn't recognize—a two-headed hawk.

"For the Gates of Orolis," the vendor murmured, not looking up.

Nera frowned. "There is no city named Orolis."

"Not anymore," the vendor said. "It was written out in the Third Alignment. The gates are gone. The walls are dust. But the keys ..." He looked up then, eyes milky and distant. "The keys refused to turn into nothing. They still try to open doors that aren't there."

Nera pulled her hand back as if burned. She was looking at the debris of a murdered reality.

Alis led them through the winding stalls with ease. This was her world. She nodded to some vendors and exchanged quick words with others. The people here knew her—trusted her, or at least respected her enough to acknowledge her presence.

Tyrek, by contrast, kept his head down. He'd dealt with some of these traders from a distance before, but this was the first time he'd walked among them.

Kieran remained silent, his gaze sharp, tracking everything. The Nameless Market wasn't a safe place, but it wasn't chaotic either. It had rules.

Alis glanced over her shoulder. "No stealing, no lying, no violence unless it's part of a deal. Break the first two, they kick you out."

Nera raised an eyebrow. "And the third?"

Alis's smirk returned. "Depends on who's watching."

Nera scanned the stalls, the sheer volume of merchants overwhelming. "So," she whispered, leaning closer to Alis, "What are we looking for?"

Alis's smirk vanished, replaced by a tight grimace. She kept her voice low, barely moving her lips. "Soren left us a note, Nera. Not much — just a fragment, passed through a courier before he vanished. It was supposed to give us a name."

She glanced toward the shifting stalls. "Without it, we're just tourists in a shark tank. If we ask the wrong person for the 'truth,' we end up dead before we ever find the Curator."

"So we're guessing?" Cael hissed.

"No," Alis said, adjusting her coat "We're gambling."

They passed another stall, this one lined with shimmering books, their pages swapping between blank and written, waiting for someone to choose a version of the story.

Alis stopped at a stall tucked behind a heavy velvet curtain, tapping a coin against the wood—two sharp clicks. A hand emerged, sliding a thin, leather-bound ledger across the counter.

"The invoices you asked for," the merchant rasped. "Records of the erased."

Alis opened it, her usual smirk vanishing. She traced a line at the bottom of the page. "This name ... this is the one from the Council records?"

"The ink didn't take," the merchant whispered. "That makes it expensive."

Alis slammed the book shut and shoved it deep into her coat, her face pale. "Whatever the price is, put it on my tab. We're leaving."

"Alis?" Nera asked, stepping closer. "What did you find?"

"Insurance," Alis said, her voice tight. She didn't look at Nera. "Let's find what we need and get the hell out of here."

Then, a voice from a nearby stall: "Didn't think I'd see you here again, Alis."

Nera turned toward the speaker. A man stood behind a table filled with fragmented records, loose parchment stacked in uneven piles.

Alis stopped, her expression clouding slightly—not quite pleased, not quite surprised.

"Enri."

The man—Enri—crossed his arms, smirking slightly. "Still chasing ghosts and selling forgeries?"

Alis arched a brow teasingly. "Still hoarding books you don't understand?"

Enri scowled, shuffling a stack of papers. "Better than the Archivist who came through three days ago. Didn't want books. Wanted maps of 'fracture points.' Paid in gold stamped with old runes." Enri shook his head. "He looked like he hadn't slept in a week. Kept muttering that he 'missed a pattern'."

"If he's a friend of yours," Enri muttered, "tell him the Market doesn't sell time travel."

Kieran leaned toward Nera. "Friend of hers? I think he's talking about Soren." he whispered. Nera kept her voice low, "Sounds like it."

Enri glanced toward Nera, then toward Kieran, his expression calculating. "And who are they?"

Alis didn't hesitate. "People with questions." Enri huffed a laugh. "A dangerous thing to have here."

Enri paused, his gaze on Nera's ink-stained hands. He reached under the counter. "He left this. Said if a young Archivist with ink-stained fingers came looking, I should give it to her. He called it 'a lesson for his student'."

He slid a small, sealed scroll across the wood. Nera opened it. It was a cipher key written in a hand she knew as well as her own.

*The ink does not dry where the wall is broken.*

Tyrek, moving beside them, spoke for the first time since they'd entered. "We need a name." Enri arched a brow. "Everyone does."

Tyrek leaned forward slightly. "We're looking for the one who runs things now." The smirk faded from Enri's face. "You shouldn't."

Alis's expression darkened. "I don't care."

Enri studied her, then rubbed the back of his neck. "You're going to owe me for this."

Alis tilted her head. "Already do."

Enri turned toward one of the larger stalls near the far end of the Market and pointed. "Start there."

Tyrek didn't look where Enri pointed. He stopped dead, his gaze locking onto a spice merchant three stalls down. The merchant was silently covering his wares, waving away a patron who was holding out a bag of gold.

Tyrek didn't speak. He simply slammed his shoulder into Nera, shoving her hard into the gap between two tents, placing his body between her and the open road. Kieran and Alis jumped. "He refused the gold," Tyrek hissed, his hand hovering over his blade. "Something is going on. Nobody here stops selling unless the currency just changed to blood."

Nera turned to look, but as she did, the hum of the market vanished. It didn't fade; it was cut. The vendor with the keys was gone. The woman with the ledgers had vanished. The crowd that had been pressing against them seconds ago had dissolved into the shadows, leaving the path entirely, terrifyingly empty.

"They're herding us," Kieran said. Before Nera could process movement, Kieran acted. He didn't ask, he didn't signal, simply stepped in front of her, placing his body between her and the shadows, his hand hovering over his blade. It was an unconscious movement, as if gravity pulled him into her orbit whenever danger appeared.

Figures emerged from the darkness—*Preservationists.* The leader stepped into the light; maskless, cold, and holding a curved blade.

"You can't run, Scribe," the leader said.

"We aren't looking for a fight," Kieran said, holding his stance.

"And we aren't here to fight," the leader replied. "We are here to collect." He looked past Kieran, locking eyes with Nera. "If you do not come with us, we will not chase you. We will simply go to the Old Quarter. To the house with the heavy oak door."

Nera's blood drained from her face.

"We know where they sleep, Nera," the assassin said softly. "The scholar. The redhead. The children—Clara, Maria, the others. Refuse, and we burn it down with them inside."

The threat hit her like a physical blow. The trap extended beyond the market; they were now holding her family hostage.

"There's no way out," Alis hissed, backing up until her shoulders hit the rough stone of the canyon wall.

Nera looked at the stone. It was solid. Real. But nature had failed them before.

*Reality resists*, she thought, reaching for her quill. Hopefully it still held some ink. *But ink persuades.*

Nera decided story was the only weapon left. She grabbed the map from her pocket and pressed the tip to the parchment and wrote, her hand trembling not from fear, but from the violation of what she was about to do.

*The wall in front of me does not exist.*

The quill dragged across the parchment. There were no Council dampeners here to filter the resistance; the ink didn't just fight the paper, it fought her. The tip dragged like she was carving into the stone wall itself. The ink burned, not against paper but against reality, using her arm as the conduit for the displacement.

Nera pressed the nib harder, and the stone wall twenty feet away screamed. Granite dissolved into two-dimensional static. The air tasted of copper and pulverized rock. On the parchment, the ink bubbled; on the wall, reality tore open revealing the raw, grey void of unwritten space. Nera tried to lift the quill from the page, but her arm didn't respond. The sensation from her elbow down was simply … gone. Not numb, but absent, as if the nerves had been severed from reality.

She used her left hand to pry the quill from her frozen right fingers. A tickle in her nostril drew her attention, and when she wiped it, her hand came away with a heavy smear of dark blood.

Kieran didn't hesitate. He grabbed Nera's arm and pulled her through the opening.

The others followed.

They tumbled down a steep incline of loose stone. When they hit the bottom, the Market was gone. The only sound left was their ragged breathing and the wind howling through empty ruins.

## CHAPTER TWENTY-TWO
# Illusion of Rest

Most of the group had returned to Theron's safehouse, while Tobias, Tavian, and a few others moved ahead through the underground tunnels. Nera paced near the low wooden table. The room was warm, the fire lit, and it felt like a home—but the feeling was a lie.

Theron checked the locks for the third time in an hour, stepping outside into the cold to watch the street. Tyrek and Liaz sat at a desk in the corner, quietly reconciling inventory ledgers. The room's silence masqueraded as peace, but beneath it lay the sense of everyone holding their breath.

Nera stopped when she saw Jaye building a careful tower of blocks near the hearth, baby Jhan close by. Clara and Maria slept curled beneath the table, worn down by a fear they were too young to name.

The assassin's voice echoed in her mind: *We know about the children. We know where they sleep.*

Behind her, a hushed conversation unfolded between Jorin Brieth and Alis.

"We can't risk it," Alis said, arms crossed, her ink-stained fingers tapping against her sleeve. "If the assassins remember how they tracked us here, they'll come back. And when they do, it won't be just us they find."

"Then we rig the entry hall," Jorin suggested, his voice cold. "We funnel them in, blow the main strut, and collapse the foyer on top of them. It's the only way to neutralize a squad that size."

"No," Theron said instantly, stepping back inside.

Cael frowned. "It's the best tactical choke point we have."

"I don't care if it's a perfect trap," Theron snapped, moving between Cael and the hearth, blocking the children from view. "The roof stays up. The people stay under it. Find another way."

Theron's gaze flicked to the corner where the children played, then to the table, then to the door. "I built this place to be a home," he said. "For warmth. For cooking. For sleeping." He turned to Nera, whatever illusion he'd been holding onto gone from his eyes. "You can't fight a war in a living room. We're sitting in a wooden box, waiting to be burned. The shelter is done."

The last time Nera had looked at the children, they'd been part of the background of the safehouse—a reminder of what they were protecting. Now, after the Market, after the rewrite, the room felt exposed.

They weren't just reminders anymore. They were the stakes—proof of exactly what everyone stood to lose if she didn't get this rewrite right.

She pressed her palms to the table.

Kieran, leaning against the far wall, finally broke his silence. "So what's your plan?" His eyes were sharp, unreadable. "Running isn't enough. You know that."

Nera knew he was right. Running only worked if the enemy had no trail to follow. In their haste to return to the safehouse after barely escaping the Nameless Market, they definitely had not been careful about hiding their trail. She had to erase that trail completely. Looking at the others and seeing nods from others in the group told her that they felt the same way.

"I'm going to remove the memory of how they followed us to the Market in the first place, so that they don't remember that encounter at all," she said, forcing the words out evenly.

Alis stiffened. "Absolutely not."

The firelight caught the warning in her gaze, but Nera shook her head. "If they can't retrace their steps, they can't find us again. It's the only way to keep the safehouse—and these people—hidden."

"You're spending capital you don't have, Nera," Alis snapped ... "You erase the path, you erase the footprints on it. You erase the footprints, you erase the feet. If you cut a bridge while people are standing on it, they don't just stop moving. They fall."

Kieran, unusually quiet, didn't object. He looked at Nera, then—slowly—he gave a single nod. Not approval. Not agreement. *Trust.*

"Fine." Alis threw up her hands in defeat as she stood to leave the room. "But don't act surprised if it goes wrong."

Nera watched her go, then looked back at the families huddled in the corner. Chaos. That's what this was. The truth was messy, dangerous, and uncontrolled.

A dark thought surfaced, unbidden. *Maybe the Council wasn't wrong. They curate history to prevent exactly this kind of fear.* But she hated them for it, and hated Belvar for calling her memory a weapon. But as she looked at the families, she realized truth was a luxury for the safe. For the vulnerable, reality was just a draft that needed to be tuned.

*It won't be a lie,* she told herself, the logic settling cold and smooth in her chest. It was a necessary cut to ensure survival. She felt a flutter of revulsion at how easily the Archivist logic fit her mind—efficient, detached. But she didn't push it away. She used it.

She inhaled sharply and pulled out her writing kit—ink, quill, parchment. Settling into the chair at the table, she pressed the tip of the quill to the page. Her hand trembled, just once. Trying to rewrite a sequence of events was like trying to pull a single thread from a tapestry without unraveling the whole image. She wasn't just changing a fact; she was severing an entire event.

The moment she started writing, the world contracted—like breath caught in the lungs of reality itself, waiting to see if she would go too far.

Everything else around her fell away like a blurred background as she focused, carefully shaping the rewrite: The assassins never went to the Market; they never found the right path to follow us neither to the Market nor here. They never knew we were even going to the Market.

The ink spread smoothly, each letter burning into existence. Then the upheaval came.

The air in the house bent—not physically, but in a way that made Nera's stomach lurch. Reality was groaning under a weight they weren't built to carry. The candlelight jumped violently. Somewhere in the distance, a child let out a soft, confused sound, as if sensing something unseen.

Nera grabbed the edge of the table and dug her fingernails into the wood until splinters bit back, anchoring herself as the room listed like a ship in a storm and a searing pain like a hot poker spread through her right hand.

A heartbeat passed. Then another. The world steadied.

It was done.

She paused, blinking as her vision refused to snap back immediately. Colors flattened to a washed-out grey. She looked down at the tool in her hand. A feather? No, a quill. Why was she holding it? The intent of the last ten seconds had vanished, wiped clean from her mind along with the assassins' path.

When she tried to speak, her tongue felt numb, thick in her mouth. She looked up at the others, struggling to place their names for a terrifying heartbeat before the memories flooded back, cold and disjointed.

Even through the blur, the moment Nera saw Kieran's expression, her stomach dropped. As her vision sharpened, she realized he wasn't looking at her at all—he was scanning the space around them. Searching.

"Where's Jorin?"

Cold spread through her as she froze.

Nera stood, her chair scraping loudly against the stone floor. "He went to the kitchen," she said, her voice tight. "He mentioned getting food."

Jaye rose from his spot near the hearth. "I remember... Jorin was in the kitchen earlier."

"Exactly," Nera said, moving toward the kitchen archway. "He's just—"

"Nera," Theron interrupted, brow furrowed. "Who is Jorin?"

The room went utterly still.

"He was here, wasn't he?" Cael said slowly, eyes narrowing. "He was at the Waystation. We traveled together on the way back."

Alis frowned. "You've forgotten," she said sharply. "He was here. He was outside the Market with you when the attack happened." Her gaze cut to Nera. "Did he come back with you?"

Nera looked at the table where she had thought Jorin had been sitting moments ago. His pack was gone. His weapons were gone. Only a single half-eaten crust of bread remained.

"He was with us," Nera said. "Everyone remembers him at the Waystation. Everyone remembers traveling with him. But after the Market ..."

Brieth picked up the bread, her hand shaking violently. She crushed it in her fist.

"He was just here," she said, her voice tipping toward panic. "The air is still warm where he was sitting, Nera. How do we explain this?"

Nera's throat constricted. Her rewrite had been precise, targeted solely at the assassins' memory. She had not unwritten Jorin. *She hadn't.* But reality wasn't a story to be edited—it was a tapestry. Had she pulled the thread too hard?

"I wrote that the assassins never found the path," she whispered, the horror of the logic settling in. "It seemed simple. A physical fix." She looked up at Cael, her face drained of color. "But Jorin was the one who found it." The silence in the room finished the sentence for her.

Alis sucked in a sharp breath, her fingers curling into fists. "I told you. I told you rewriting history is never clean—which is exactly why it should never be done."

"It worked," Nera said softly, her voice trembling but defiant. She gestured to the quiet room, to the children sleeping by the hearth. "The assassins aren't here. I calculated the risk, and I paid it." She rubbed at her throbbing hand as she spoke.

"You didn't pay it," Alis said, her voice dropping to something cold and precise. She pointed at Jorin's empty chair. "He did."

She crushed the coin in her hand until her knuckles went white. "That's the problem with the whole Archive. You think survival is just math." Her gaze cut back to Nera. "But you just traded a friend for a quiet night."

Alis stepped back, pointing at her as if Nera herself were the weapon. "I can dodge a blade. I can outrun a soldier. But I don't know if any of us can survive you."

Her voice cracked then, the cynicism breaking to reveal something raw beneath it. "This is why I never became an Archivist. No one should wield the power to decide who matters."

"Now Jorin's gone," she said, her voice sharp with accusation, "and we don't even know where—"

Before she could finish, a sickening hum tore through the room, vibrating straight through Nera's skull. The air pressure dropped so fast it felt like the space collapsed inward.

The stones behind Alis blurred into grey static, the wall stuttering out of existence before snapping back with a thunderous crack. Reality screamed as it tore.

For a terrifying second, Nera tasted the void—a flat, metallic static coating her tongue like ash. The silence that followed wasn't quiet; it was absolute, crushing. The shaking didn't just rattle her— it felt like it was trying to pull her apart, to loosen bone from body.

The vibration in the floor didn't stop. The soup in the pot on the hearth boiled over instantly, hissing as it hit the coals. The fire flared unnaturally green. Near the hearth, baby Jhan began to wail—a thin, terrified sound. Mave clutched him tighter, but the very stones of the fireplace were grinding together like teeth. The house wasn't sheltering them anymore; it was trying to shake them off.

Liaz didn't flinch as she stepped away from the desk. She placed a hand against the vibrating wall, felt the hum for a moment, then pulled back. "The beams are compromised," she said, her tone devoid of fear. She pointed toward the stacked supplies nearby. "The structure is failing. We load the carts. Now."

She and Tyrek moved immediately, efficiently lifting boxes of supplies and preparing to leave.

Theron looked toward the children, then to Kaelith. They both understood what needed to be done. The look that passed between them carried the possibility of a silent goodbye.

The air in the safehouse grew suddenly hot, tasting of brimstone and ash. The table Nera leaned on buzzed against her palms, vibrating as if it wanted to pull apart. The safehouse had become a wound in reality. Nera stepped back.

"I'm not sure this safehouse is safe any more," Theron said, his voice rough. "The foundation is liquid. We can't shelter people in a place that won't stand still. We need to evacuate the families." He turned to Tessa and Mave who were sitting with the kids in the corner. "Take the children. You all need to leave the city entirely."

"Where?" Tessa demanded, pulling Clara and Maria close. "The roads are constantly transforming. Nowhere feels safe."

Alis stepped forward, her expression grim. "The Nameless Market. It's near Varethis today, but it'll be near the Borderlands tonight. I have a contact—a caravan master who owes me a life. He'll take you. If you get into the Market just before it moves, you'll move with it. It's the fastest way to travel far. You'll be safer in the Borderlands."

Kaelith noticed Clara slowly stuffing her princess cape into a bag, crying. She crossed the room and knelt in front of her, voice low and sharp enough to cut through the tears. "Listen to me. Fear makes you slow, and panic makes you loud. You're allowed to be scared later. Right now, I need you to be boring. Be invisible. If you see something strange, you don't scream—you vanish. Do you understand?"

Jaye strode across the room with a confidence far beyond his years. "I should stay here to help."

Kieran, always a pragmatist, bent down slowly and spoke to Jaye gently. "We need you to go with the families," he said evenly. "We need someone who can help protect them—and look out for Clara, Maria, and Jhan."

Everyone could tell by Jaye's body language that he felt like he was being dismissed. Theron stepped forward, gripping Jaye's shoulders, his fingers pressing hard enough to be felt. He didn't smile. "I'm handing you the lead, Jaye. I can't be there," Theron said, his voice rough. "Don't let them wander off the map, and don't let them look at the sky if it starts glitching, ok? And Jaye?" He waited until the boy looked up, scared but listening.

"If the adults don't come back," Theron said quietly, "the mission doesn't end. It only changes. You keep moving until you find a safe zone that actually stays still."

Cyrus walked over and bent down. "Stick to the rules, Jaye. Watch the edges, and don't let instructions change without your permission. Order keeps everyone safe."

Jaye considered for a moment, then nodded and returned to the families to help.

Nera watched as the families quickly started gathering the things they most needed.

Gaela helped them pack up snacks and drinks for their quick travel in the kitchen. She stood up, her eyes dry but hard as flint. She looked pointedly at Nera. "We're packing them away like supplies so they survive your draft. I understand why. But if you get this wrong, they don't just lose a home. They lose the parents who sent them away. Maybe more. Make sure the ink holds."

Nera watched sadly, guiltily as Gaela closely hugged the children as they prepared to leave.

Tessa and Mave slowly moved through the room, hugging everyone in turn, while repeatedly swearing they'd keep the children safe. Jaye took Clara's hand and led her toward the back of the house, a newfound responsibility in his step. Mave followed with Maria, still clutching the worn cloth she had been using to help comfort baby Jhan, who now slept against Brieth's shoulder.

Brieth carefully transferred the sleeping infant into Tessa's arms, lingering long enough to brush a thumb over his cheek. "Get them to the border," she whispered, stepping back beside Cael and Nera.

Tessa nodded, pulled the blanket tighter, and followed the others into the dark.

There was not a dry eye in the room.

Jaye paused at the threshold, looking back at the glitching safehouse one last time. He adjusted his pack, the heavy weight of his school primer dragging at his shoulder. With a sudden, decisive movement, he stepped away from Clara and pulled the book out of his bag—the one with the crisp, lying pages about the Formless

One—and tossed it into the fire in the hearth. "Ink holds truth!" he exclaimed. He gritted his teeth, nodded at the adults, then turned and followed the others into the dark, leaving the lie behind.

Alis watched them go, her usual smirk gone. "If they make the Borderlands," she murmured sadly, "they might be the only ones who remember any of us if this goes wrong."

She and the others slowly moved back into the main room of the safehouse, which was noticeably quiet now, lacking the warmth and chatter that was usually present. The atmosphere had changed, a bit more charged and full of urgency than it had been before.

"Jorin must have been caught in the change," Kieran said quietly, dragging them back to the problem none of them wanted to name. "He should be here, but his history was revised. We need to figure out where he ended up."

Theron folded his arms, his voice lower than before. "You talk about this like you rewrote a simple sentence." He paused, looking at Nera. "You tried to bust through a wall, didn't you? That's a bold gamble, Nera—even for you. But you can't tear out a page without the whole story falling apart."

"That's exactly what happened," Alis snapped.

Nera slowly slid her palms down her face, grounding herself. She had to think. Rewrites didn't erase someone entirely unless you purposely erased then. She had altered the course of events leading up to the present. Jorin existed somewhere. She just didn't know where.

"We need to leave too," she said, forcing steadiness into her voice. Theron blinked, "What?"

"We can't stay here." Nera turned toward him. "The rewrite might have worked on the assassins, or might not, but we know reality has already updated. If Jorin is gone, other things have changed too. We don't know how far the effects will go. We must get underground before anything else unravels."

Alis shook her head vehemently. "*Now* you care about the consequences?"

Nera ignored her. She met Theron's gaze, steady and unyielding. "This safehouse is a home. If something went wrong, I won't risk it bleeding into this place. It needs to be protected."

Kieran leaned against the stone column, arms crossed. "The tunnels give us cover from soldiers. That much is true. But if the rot's already in the walls, then all we're doing is retreating into something that's already failing. I know how to fortify against people. I don't know how you fortify against a rewrite."

Nera met his gaze. "You think it's spreading?"

"I think we don't know enough to say otherwise," Kieran said. "And I don't like betting on unknowns."

Cael ran a hand through his hair and sighed. "Fine. Let's move." Nera pushed away from the table, still trying to recenter herself. The nausea of the rewrite still clung to her, but she forced it down. They had to move, and fast.

This was her doing. She hadn't just moved a chess piece; she had severed a lifeline. Staring at the shiny, puckered skin of her palm, she remembered being ten, burning her hand to save a history. Today, she burned a man to save a secret. For a lifetime, she believed the Archivists were monsters for editing reality to suit their narrative. But here she was, quill in hand, editing Jorin's life to suit hers. The line between protector and tyrant wasn't a wall; it was a choice, and she had just stepped over that invisible line.

Nera stared at the quill on the table. It didn't look like a tool anymore. It looked like a murder weapon. She reached for it to pack it away, but her hand recoiled, trembling violently. She couldn't touch it. If she touched it, she might erase someone else. Nera looked down at her hands. The ink stains on her fingers were gone. And she couldn't remember washing them.

A sick, cold realization settled in her gut. The horror wasn't that the magic had failed. The horror was that it had succeeded.

She had traded a piece of her friend for a safe and quiet night for everyone. And god help her, she was relieved.

## CHAPTER TWENTY-THREE

# What Changed

The underground tunnels weren't just a place to hide, not just another safehouse. There was an entire network of locations and places, making it the foundation of the resistance.

Old carvings still marked some of the corridors, remnants of a time before the Archive had rewritten the city's history.

Tobias was already waiting when they arrived, arms crossed, his usual air of controlled authority unwavering despite the tension in the chamber. He barely spared Nera a glance before speaking. "Tell me this rewrite of yours didn't just impact our entire safe zone." Nera stopped and stiffened. Tobias had never been one for subtlety.

The nausea still coated Nera's stomach, a sickening reminder of the friend she had just edited out of existence.

"It worked," she said evenly as she continued through the doorway. "The assassins can't find their way to Theron's safehouse."

Tobias pinched his lips into a thin line. "And what else did it break?"

Silent, Nera kept pace with the others as they moved deeper into the tunnels, her mind still tangled with the rewrite. She couldn't shake the hollow feeling in her chest.

Alis walked ahead, adjusting her pack, her footsteps sharp against the uneven floor. She had barely spoken since they left

Theron's safehouse, her anger simmering just beneath the surface. Kieran kept pace beside Nera, quiet as always, his gaze flicking to her now and then, as if waiting for her to admit she had made a mistake.

She wouldn't. Not yet. Not when they still didn't know the full cost of what had changed. The tunnel widened as they stepped into one of the larger gathering spaces. A few rebels were already there, speaking in hushed tones, their eyes wary as they took in the group's arrival.

Kieran was the last to enter, running a hand through his hair as he surveyed the room. "This'll do," he muttered. "It's safer than above. For now."

Cael glanced around before turning to Nera. "You need to rest." She only met his gaze, her silence an answer of its own.

"Whatever happened to Jorin," he pressed, his voice low enough that only she could hear, "we're not going to solve it in the next few minutes." Nera clenched her teeth, carrying words she wouldn't say, her eyes feeling tight with the stress of concern for their friend. He was right, but that didn't make it any easier to accept.

Kieran sat on an overturned crate, rolling his shoulders. "So," he said, his tone dangerously flat, "what's our next move?"

Nera hesitated. The confusion of the rewrite pressed against her like an invisible force. It wasn't just about the assassins anymore. The world had edited. Something had changed beyond what she had written, and she didn't know how far the ripples could spread.

"We wait," she said finally. "Until we know more, we wait."

Alis laughed bitterly. "For what? For more people to disappear?" Nera didn't answer. Because deep down, she feared Alis might be right.

***

The underground refuge had settled. Most of the group had dispersed—some finding places to rest, others speaking in low voices about what had happened. Stress still clung to Nera like damp air, making it hard to breathe.

She found herself sitting apart from everyone, near the edge of the chamber where the stone was cool against her back. The lantern light barely reached here, leaving shadows to stretch across the rough-hewn walls.

*Jorin should be here.*

She pressed her hands against her knees, trying to loosen the tightness in her chest. She had rewritten before, made small edits, carefully controlled changes under the tutelage of a Master Archivist—Soren and other teachers—as part of her training. This wasn't supposed to happen.

A quiet shuffle of boots on stone drew her attention.

Cael sank down beside her, stretching his legs out in front of him. He didn't say anything at first, just tipped his head back until it hit the stone wall. They sat like that, letting the quiet build between them.

"It's my fault," Nera grumbled finally.

Cael didn't look at her right away. "You did what you thought was necessary; what we all did." All the years they had spent as children growing up together let him understand that Nera needed calm and quiet in stressful moments like this.

"And now he's gone," she choked. She expected him to argue, to tell her she was wrong. Instead, he ran a hand through his dark hair, fingers lingering at the back of his neck. "Maybe. Maybe not."

She turned to face him, searching his expression, but he kept his gaze forward.

Cael pressed his body against the cold stone, like testing its weight. "Well. This is a disaster." His smirk twitched, just slightly, before settling back in place and then turning his head nonchalantly to look at the profile of her face. "Maybe you should try rewriting this conversation. See if it turns out better."

Nera shot him a glare, but he only half grinned, rubbing his jaw.

"Look. If you stop now—if you let this be the thing that makes you afraid to act—you'll never forgive yourself." The words slipped out quieter than he intended. "Trust me. I know."

Her voice scraped at the back of her throat. "You sound sure of that."

"Experience," Cael said, without humor. She turned her head slowly to face him.

"I waited," he said after a pause. "For too long. Thought I had time. Thought it was safer to hold back." His jaw tensed as he gazed deep into her eyes. "I was wrong."

For the first time since the rewrite, something shifted between them. Cael wasn't speaking like a strategist now, not weighing angles or planning three steps ahead. His voice was quieter. Stripped of polish.

Lamplight caught the gold in his hazel eyes. He didn't look guarded. He didn't look prepared. He just looked still.

"You're not alone in this, Nera." He moved closer, closing the space until his shoulder pressed against hers—a familiar, solid weight that pulled at memories of childhood days hidden among the stacks.

"It's always been us," he whispered, his voice rough. "Since we were kids. You and me. That hasn't changed."

He met her gaze, his eyes glassy, jaw tight. "But you need to know—I'm not staying because I think you're right."

He hesitated, then added, "I'm staying because if I leave... I don't know if I'd survive what you're becoming."

He held out his hand and waited.

She didn't.

She looked at his hand, then up at his eyes. She didn't see strength; she saw terror. And in that second, she realized he wasn't staying to help her finish the mission; he was staying to stop her from finishing it if the cost became too high.

A shadow shifted against the far wall. Cael froze and looked up.

Kieran was watching them. Not Nera—Cael. The usual edge of rivalry was gone from his expression. What remained was worse.

Cael noticed. He yanked his hand back as if burned, the closeness breaking instantly. Whatever softness had surfaced vanished behind a brittle mask. He turned away from Nera, jaw set, a vein standing out sharply at his collar.

Nera's attention flicked to Kieran, who had moved apart from the others. He rolled the hilt of his dagger absently between his fingers, gaze fixed on the shadows along the damp stone walls. He wasn't watching the room so much as listening to it—tracking something just beyond sight.

A warning prickled along Nera's skin.

*Something was wrong.*

Kieran's grip tightened on the dagger. Then he was moving, pacing a short line near the edge of the chamber, boots scraping softly against the stone. His movements were sharp, restless, as if the space itself refused to stay still around him.

He stopped abruptly and pressed the heels of his hands into his eyes, hard. When he lowered them, a muscle jumped in his neck, his pulse visible there—fast, uneven.

Then his head snapped up.

Kieran's gaze swept the room, searching, his mouth briefly opening as if a word had risen too close to the surface. His face hardened, his hands curling into fists.

"Damn it," he muttered.

"Nera," he said.

She pushed off the wall where she'd been sitting with Cael and crossed the chamber. The tension in her posture mirrored his the moment their eyes met.

"What is it?" she asked.

Kieran didn't answer right away. He just looked at her, something taut and unfinished in his expression—like he was braced against the edge of a thought that refused to form.

Nera felt it then. Not the word itself, but the space where it should have been.

The name from the parchment. Pulled from the fire. The one no one could place. She saw it in his eyes—the strain of reaching for something that kept slipping just beyond grasp.

They froze.

Neither of them said it.

Neither of them could.

## Chapter Twenty-Four

# What It Took

Three days passed in a suffocating blur. The group was still on edge, the consequences of the rewrite pressing down like a storm cloud that refused to break. Some of the rebels had begun questioning what had changed, their voices hushed in corners of the underground refuge. Nera had heard bits and pieces as she had moved around—mentions of forgotten roads at lunch, missing landmarks discussed by another group over dinner, places that didn't quite match their memories. She barely slept, the feeling of guilt keeping her mind running at night.

Every hour that passed confirmed their worst fear: the rewrite had removed Jorin. Some of the group had stopped looking at Nera entirely. The quiet in the underground wasn't peaceful; it was an accusation.

She wasn't sure how much of it was her fault.

The tension in the chamber thickened when hurried footsteps echoed from beyond the tunnel entrance. Someone was approaching, moving fast. Hands went to weapons. Alis tensed, reaching for the dagger at her belt. Kieran had already turned, ready for whatever came next.

Jorin stumbled into the light.

Nobody spoke. The world itself seemed to still. Then a sharp, collective exhale swept through the room.

Nera took an uncertain step towards him.

Jorin was breathing hard, his eyes wild with confusion. He looked like he had ridden through hell, and fast. His clothes were stained with mud and sweat, his face gaunt from days without proper food, and he could barely stand upright. His gaze swept over them, like he was searching for something—someone—to anchor him.

"What the hell happened?" he demanded, his voice rough from a long ride with too little to drink and too much road.

Cael took a low, disbelieving breath. "You're supposed to be here," he said.

Jorin's expression darkened. "I remember being here with all of you. I think. And then I wasn't." He ran a hand through his hair, fingers pressing against his temple like he was trying to force his own memories back into place. He looked down at his hands, trembling, then back at the tunnel entrance, as if expecting the path to follow him. "I stepped forward, but the floor was gone. I just fell." He winced, gripping his arm.

"Jorin?" Nera stepped closer, her eyes drawn to the way he was favoring his arm.

"I landed hard but it also felt like I was sort of being ripped in half," he gritted through his teeth. He slowly rolled up his sleeve and Nera gasped.

Instead of blood, a dark, jagged mark wrapped around his forearm—not a bruise, but a hole in the texture of the world. The ink didn't sit on the surface; it looked like a drop of corrosive oil eating through a canvas. If she looked too closely, she didn't even see skin—she saw a void beneath, twitching and fraying like a canvas stretched until it tore. The air around his arm felt freezing, a vacuum sucking heat out of the room.

"It doesn't always hurt but it's cold," Jorin whispered, refusing to look at it. "It feels like ... like part of me is missing. Like the magic didn't know how to put me back together perfectly. I was so confused that I didn't really notice it until I was halfway back here."

Nera stared at the mark, the realization hitting her with the full force of a physical blow. "Soren always said *physical changes resist because matter is stubborn*," she whispered, the memory of the quill snagging as she wrote rushing back to her. "*But memory yields because the mind is weak.*"

"I forced it," she said, the memory of the quill snagging rushing back to her. "The ink didn't want to go there. The path was gone, Jorin, but you were still on it."

She looked up at Kieran, face pale. "I tried to force the ink past the resistance. The timeline couldn't reconcile the path being gone while the person who found it remained."

Kieran stared at the mark. "It's not a wound," he murmured. "The truth is catching up. You erased the path, Nera. But he's still here." He looked up, his face grim. "The world doesn't know what to do with him. You wrote that he found nothing, so the ink is trying to make nothing."

"But why is he still here?" Cael asked, looking at the void eating Jorin's arm. "If the path he was standing on ceased to exist, he should have fallen into the gap."

"Because I knew the other roads," Jorin said, realizing it as he spoke. He rubbed his temple, the memory sharpening. "I landed on the Old Trade Road outside Orswick. I haven't used that route in three years, but I knew it well. I had it mapped in my head."

Nera let out a breath she didn't realize she had been holding. "You were your own anchor. Your maps and alternative routes."

"So I survived because I have a cluttered mind," Jorin muttered ironically, though his hand trembled.

Nera's stomach twisted.

"I tried to get my bearings, tried to find my place based on the bookkeeper's shop that I had been to many times. But the street didn't line up. The alleyway I always used, it's not just closed, Nera. It's structurally absent. The stone wall is seamless. Ancient. As if no alley had ever been cut there."

He looked up, his eyes wide with a specific kind of horror. "And the people ... I spoke to a merchant I've bought supplies from for years. She looked right through me. The rewrite didn't just move me; it erased the path I took to get there."

Jorin, and his new permanent ink on his forearm. It was proof that the shift had spread farther than any of them had anticipated.

Tobias crossed his arms, the movement pulling his sleeves tight against his biceps. "You're saying the street is gone? Completely? I can't secure a perimeter that doesn't exist, Jorin. If the street is gone, that route is burned."

Jorin nodded, his hands flicking in an unconscious gesture. "I make maps for a living, I know what Orswick looked like. The bookkeeper's shop should be at the edge of a side street—except now, that street never existed. The buildings that should have been there? Gone. The people I spoke to in the past, many times? Some of them don't remember me at all."

The chamber went still.

Alis crossed her arms. "What the hell does that mean?"

A wave of nausea rolled through Nera.

"I tried to follow the same path back," Jorin went on. "I swear, I took the same road we took to the Waystation. But parts of it didn't match up." His voice dropped slightly. "Some of the people I passed that I know didn't recognize me. And some of them ... they just weren't the same."

Kieran, still silent, stepped closer, eyes studying Jorin with something that looked almost like recognition. "You got caught in it?" he questioned.

Jorin narrowed his eyes. "Caught in what?"

Kieran didn't answer right away. His gaze flicked to Nera, heavy with a warning she couldn't decipher. "History doesn't just erase cleanly," he said finally.

"You got lucky," Alis snapped at Nera. "You deleted the path, so history threw him back to the start. What if it had decided the logical place for him was the bottom of a steep ravine?"

Jorin snorted. "Yeah? Well, tell whoever is in charge of the rewrites that they did a crap job putting me back where I was supposed to be."

Alis crossed her arms, still tense. "You're sure nothing else changed?"

Jorin hesitated. Then, slowly, he shook his head. "I don't know." There was a quiet gravity in his voice, something heavy and unspoken. "But I think we're going to find out; based on what I saw during my ride, I don't think it's done altering."

Nera swallowed hard. She knew he was right.

## CHAPTER TWENTY-FIVE
# Beneath the Ink

The underground chamber was stifling. Jorin's words hung heavy in the air, pressing against Nera's chest like an ink stain spreading across an untouched page.

Kieran drifted toward the narrow skylight cut into the stone ceiling, one hand resting near the hilt of his favorite blade, his fingers flipping the handle in a restless rhythm. Alis stood rigid with her arms crossed, the shivering light sharpening the tension in her expression. Cael's lips pressed into a thin line, his eyes tracking every movement in the room.

Something had changed. Not just Jorin. Not just the road in Orswick. Something deeper.

Nera's pulse hammered in her ears as unease slithered beneath her skin. She twisted the ring on her finger without realizing she was doing it.

Kieran stopped. His head snapped up toward the opening above them.

The others were still talking, but their voices faded into a dull blur. Whatever had caught his attention had narrowed his focus to a single point. His posture shifted—tight, alert, wrong.

Nera followed his gaze.

And then she saw the sky.

"What?" she breathed.

Beyond the chamber's arched ceiling, through openings carved into the ancient stone, a sliver of night sky was visible.

It took her a moment to see it.

The stars.

Or rather—the absence of them.

A hole in the heavens. A space where light should have been, where constellations should have stretched familiar paths across the dark. Instead, there was nothing. A dead zone.

The sky hadn't simply gone dark; it had been peeled away. A geometric patch of absolute nothingness hung overhead, too precise to be natural. It looked less like night and more like an ink spill on a painting—a flat, matte black void that swallowed the surrounding starlight.

Nera's stomach lurched. Looking at it made her dizzy, sick in a way that had nothing to do with fear and everything to do with error. This wasn't darkness. This was a place where the rules had stopped working.

Ice tightened in her gut.

Jorin's rewrite hadn't just affected him. And her own hadn't merely erased the assassins' path. This was larger. Broader. Something else was unraveling.

Cael stepped closer and looked up, then slowly shook his head—an answer without words. "That's not possible," he whispered, the sound too sharp in the stillness.

Alis muttered a curse under her breath.

Kieran didn't move. Didn't blink. He stood rigid, his gaze locked on the void, something like recognition flickering behind his eyes.

"I've seen this before," he murmured—more question than certainty.

Nera pressed her fingers into the scar in her palm. The room felt colder now, the air thinner, as if the sky above them was draining something vital away. She swallowed hard.

She had been so sure she could control the rewrites. That the consequences were hers alone to carry.

But is—

Kieran turned to her, the space between them heavy with unspoken understanding. "This isn't just you," he said quietly. "It's bigger than that."

And she knew he was right.

This wasn't hers.

It was something else.

And for the first time since she had begun altering history, Nera was truly afraid.

Kieran stood by the window, staring out at the empty street where the assassins should have been. It was quiet. Peaceful.

"They didn't come," he said softly.

Nera followed his gaze, then looked back across the chamber. At Jorin—shivering, glitched, clutching an arm that was slowly unmaking itself.

The room felt hollow without the families. Too quiet. Too still.

The children were safe. The threat had been diverted.

And yet something vast and wrong was tearing open the sky above them.

## CHAPTER TWENTY-SIX
# The First Archivist's Secret

The chamber felt smaller, the air pressed too close. No one spoke, but the silence was no longer just uncertainty—it was fear.

Nera's mind raced. She clasped her hands together to stop them from shaking.

Kieran was still staring at the missing constellations. His expression was tight, focused—recognition without language. He had felt it too. He knew something about this. But when Nera looked at him, he didn't speak.

Jorin jeered. "So... is this where we all start panicking?"

No one laughed.

Alis twisted her auburn braid, frustration pulling hard against the unease in her eyes. "We need to figure out what exactly changed. And more importantly—if it's still changing."

Tyrek, who had slipped into the room while everyone was watching the sky, let out a short, humorless laugh. "You don't have to look far. My people are already noticing it."

Nera turned to him. "Noticing what?"

"That things aren't where they used to be." Tyrek dropped into a nearby chair and leaned back, arms crossed. "The market is collapsing, Nera. My runners aren't just confused—they're losing ground.

A street disappears, a route folds in on itself, and everything built on it goes with it."

Nera exhaled a breath she hadn't realized she'd been holding. "We can't know what's changed unless we know what else has been rewritten." She looked at Jorin. "You're proof that things can vary without warning. If we don't figure out how far this has gone, we're working blind."

Cael frowned, rubbing the back of his neck. "Then we start looking. We compare what we remember with what's now."

Alis scoffed. "Great plan—except for the part where half the people in this room won't realize their memories are compromised."

Nera closed her eyes. Alis was right. This wasn't something they could see. It was something they had to recognize. And that was the hardest part.

Kieran's fingers slid over the hilt of his blade. Nera noticed he was suddenly on his feet, his attention pulled inward, his jaw set as if he were bracing against something slipping away. She could see it in his eyes—the strain of reaching for a memory that refused to hold.

"We need records," he said quietly. "Something old enough to remember when we can't."

The group turned to him. His voice was calm, but there was something tense beneath it, something certain.

"We need to find something written," he continued. "Something old enough that it couldn't have changed. If it has …" He hesitated for half a second. "Then we'll know how deep this goes."

There was a beat where Kieran froze. "The First Archivist."

Tavian, who had been sitting in the corner silently studying old ledgers, suddenly stilled. He looked up, his gaze sharp behind his spectacles.

Kieran shook his head, like a memory had surfaced too fast, too sharply. "The name—the one on the parchment outside the Grand Archive after the fire." His tone softened, but the steel beneath it remained, as if saying it aloud would make it slip further away. "It was the First Archivist's."

"That's not possible," Tavian said. "It's just a myth. There's no actual record of them."

Nera inhaled sharply, reaching for the missing details, but the name itself remained a blank space in her mind.

Cael narrowed his eyes. "You remember the name?"

Kieran's fingers twitched at his side. "No. That's the problem." He lifted his gaze to Nera. "I remember the title. I know the name was there. But I can't remember what it was."

Nera felt the absence like pressure behind her eyes. The First Archivist's name had been written on a scrap of parchment that burned in the Grand Archive fire. She knew it had existed. Now it sat just beyond reach, like a word on the tip of the tongue.

"Then we find it again," she said.

No one argued. The sky itself was changing. Whatever had begun was no longer contained.

\*\*\*

The chamber remained heavy with unspoken tension even though the decision had been made—find the First Archivist's records, track the missing name, understand what was happening before it spiraled beyond their reach.

But no one knew where to start.

Nera felt their stares, expectation tightening like a cold knot beneath her sternum. She had spent her life searching for truth— but this was no longer about history alone.

"We need a controlled archive," Cael said, breaking the silence. "Something untouched. If this rewrite is as big as it seems, most common records will have tipped with it. We need something preserved."

"Something the Archivists either wouldn't have either wanted to bother with or been able to alter," Alis added, rolling her shoulders as if shaking off the tension. "Which means we're looking for something older than the Archive itself."

Nera sighed, pressing her knuckles against her temple. "That narrows the options."

"Not really," Kieran muttered. His voice was soft, but edged with certainty. "There's only one place that fits."

Nera reached for the map on the table to clear space, but her fingers fumbled. She watched her right hand grasp the edge of the parchment, but she didn't feel the paper. There was no texture, no friction—just a visual confirmation that her hand was obeying a command her nerves had stopped reporting.

She quickly switched hands, rolling the map with her left, hoping Kieran hadn't noticed the lapse in motor control. She turned to him, waiting.

Kieran hesitated, jaw tightening. "I don't know the name. But I know the place."

Tavian went still. Then, quietly: "The Shattered Sanctum."

The words seemed to settle into the room like dust.

Nera frowned. "That's a myth."

Tavian shook his head once. "It's a fracture site. A pre-Alignment structure that never fully submitted. The records contradict each other because the building itself keeps changing its mind."

Cael's expression darkened. "That place doesn't even stay real."

Tobias spoke from the chamber's edge, cautious. "People disappear there. You can map it one day, and the next, the corridors rewrite themselves."

Alis scoffed. "Perfect."

Kieran finally met Nera's eyes. "If the First Archivist's name survived anywhere, it would be somewhere history failed to finish the job."

But Kieran didn't waver. He turned to Nera, eyes steady. "If we're going to find what's missing, we need to start where history has already fought back."

Nera had only heard of the Shattered Sanctum in fragmented whispers—an ancient ruin clinging to the cliffs near the Blackened Ink Sea, a place where history bled through rather than held shape. Stories said the walls still carried remnants of past versions of reality, inscriptions flittering between timelines like echoes refusing to fade.

A fractured place.

A dangerous place.

But if Kieran was right, it might be their only chance at finding something untouched.

Nera's pulse quickened, but she nodded. "Then that's where we go."

Theron, who had been standing quietly at the back of the room, finally spoke. "That's a risk," he said, voice even. "If you're right, and it still holds old records, what happens if they've been rewritten too?"

Nera hesitated. Kieran leaned back, hand brushing the hilt of his knife. "Then we'll know that nothing is safe."

A chill swept through the chamber. No one spoke. Nera inhaled slowly, forcing herself to steady.

Jorin had been rewritten. The stars had vanished. History itself was edited. And the only way to stop it was to go straight to the place where time had never held still.

She turned to the group. "We leave at first light."

No one argued. Because no one wanted to wait long enough to see what might disappear next.

\*\*\*

The path to the Shattered Sanctum archive was not marked on any map. No official records spoke of its existence, and even among those who whispered about the lost places of history, this one had become little more than a myth.

Yet somehow, mostly thanks to Tavian and Jorin working together, they had found their way and stood before it now.

They marveled at a structure of pale, timeworn stone, half-buried beneath creeping vines and the transforming landscape. The wind coming off the nearby sea tasted of salt and lightning, stinging Nera's eyes as it whipped through the crumbling archways. She pressed her palm against the entry pillar; the stone wasn't cold, but hummed with a faint, rhythmic vibration, like a heartbeat trapped in the rock. Unlike the grand, pristine halls of the modern Archivists, this place did not demand to be seen. It waited, hidden, only for those who knew how to look.

"This is it?" Cael asked, eyeing the overgrown ruins. His tone was unimpressed, but Nera noticed the way his gaze sharpened, cataloging angles, distances, people. He took in the ruins, then her—how her attention lingered on Kieran, how she waited for him without realizing she was doing it.

Cael said nothing. He didn't challenge it.

Tavian stepped forward, fingers skimming the worn stone of the entrance. "Not just any archive," he said. "This predates the Concord of Dominion—before Archivists became what they are now. Before rewriting history became doctrine."

Kieran paused at the threshold. His fingers hovered, then brushed the spiral carvings etched into the stone. He went still.

Nera watched his expression change—not recognition exactly, but something closer to restraint. His gaze flicked to the ring on her hand, his brow tightening for a fraction of a second before he pulled his hand back.

Then, before she could notice, before she could ask, he stepped back.

Tobias adjusted the satchel strap across his chest, watching the entrance with wariness. "You're sure the roof holds? I don't mind old places, Tavian, but I hate places that are held together by nothing but bad intentions."

"It won't collapse," Tavian said, fingers hovering over the stone. "But the *Mechanisms of the Old Gate* describe a cipher here that defies logic. The entry requires a specific tactile rhythm that—"

Kieran didn't wait. He stepped past Tavian, his hand moving without hesitation. He ignored the main glyph and pressed three hidden indentations in the stone—tap, tap, hold.

The mechanism responded immediately. Stone slid, locks disengaging with a low, grinding sigh.

Nera stared. He hadn't searched. He hadn't tested. He'd moved like someone who already knew where to place his hand—like he'd done it before and simply never remembered learning how.

With a low, grinding groan, the entrance split open.

Tavian stared at him, pale. "That cipher predates the Concord. How did you know the sequence?"

Kieran pulled his hand back as if the stone had bitten him, scrubbing his palm against his coat. "I didn't." He shrugged, staring at the dark opening. "My hands did."

A faint rush of air stirred the dust at their feet, and something—some presence, or perhaps only time itself—seemed to acknowledge their arrival.

Nera paused, deep in thought, then spoke slowly. "This place was never meant to be found by just anyone."

Tavian, sighed, still concerned but moving toward the entrance. "Well then let's hope we're the right ones."

Without another word, they stepped inside.

The air inside was thick with the scent of old parchment, dust, and something else—something that watched. The kind of stillness that came not from abandonment, but from conservation. This place had been left untouched, its records waiting ... like it was intentional.

Nera ran her fingers lightly over the walls as they moved deeper inside. The wide corridors were lined with shelves carved directly into the stone, filled with books and scrolls that looked far older than even the Grand Archive's oldest collection. Unlike modern archives, where history was carefully maintained and altered as needed, these records had been left alone.

"This isn't like any other archive I've seen," Tobias muttered, his voice low in the quiet. Filtered sunlight from high above, dissipating through some type of windows high enough above to not be easily seen, bathed everything in light bright enough to serve the purposes of any visiting scholars.

"Because it was never meant to be used the way modern ones are," Tavian said. He was already scanning the walls, his fingers twitching as if resisting the urge to touch everything at once. "They did not build this to rewrite the world. They built it to bear witness."

Kieran lingered near the entrance, his eyes darting around in the changing light. "Then why does it feel like something in here remembers us?"

Nera hesitated, feeling it too. The darkness of the corridor pressed close, heavy with stagnant air and dry rot. Not just history waiting, but a warning. A low vibration pulsed through the stone beneath her boots, a hum that made it feel less like a passage and more like the mouth of something that did not want to be disturbed.

She shook it off and moved toward the center of the chamber.

An old, intricately carved wooden pedestal stood there, untouched by time. A single book lay open atop it, the ink still sharp beneath a thin veil of dust, impossibly intact.

Nera reached out, her fingertips barely grazing the page when the air shifted. A faint charge crackled, like the breath held before a lightning strike. The ink wavered, its edges curling, then stilled again, as if deciding whether it would remain.

"This paper is pre-Alignment," Tavian whispered, reverence stripping his voice bare. "Look at the seal. It isn't the Council's." His breath caught. "It belongs to the First Archivist."

Kieran stepped closer, his hand hovering over the open page. His breath caught, sharp and sudden, as if something unseen had struck him.

"No," Kieran said, his voice rough. He pointed to a faded inscription at the top of the page. "The First Archivist wrote this, but he didn't write it for the Council. He wrote it for the Benefactor."

"This wasn't a record of control, Nera," he whispered. "It was a record of service."

Nera turned the pages carefully. Unlike official histories they had been trained to trust, this journal didn't attempt to shape facts into something palatable. It was raw, fragmented—filled with the thoughts of someone who had borne witness to history before it was altered.

She scanned the first few lines.

> *I was not meant to do this. But what other choice did we have?*

> *The war has taken everything. Cities burned, entire bloodlines erased. We were a nation of the dead before I made us a nation of something else.*

Kieran stepped closer, his eyes narrowed as he read over her shoulder. He didn't speak. He just stared at the ink as truth settled between them.

Nera turned another page, scanning quickly. Kieran, radiating tension beside her.

She caught the shudder of movement—his fingers grazing the edge before pulling away. He didn't turn the page. Didn't look closer.

She kept reading. The records grew more personal, detailing how the rewrite had worked, the resistance it met—how history itself had pushed back. How it had succeeded and resulting peace and prosperity.

But as she turned the page, she stopped. There, in the margins of the ancient text, was a note written in fresh, modern ink—a violation of every rule she had been taught. The handwriting was frantic, the ink barely dry.

*Edris didn't fail. He hesitated while rewriting.*

Nera traced the letters, her heart hammering. "Soren," she whispered. "This is his handwriting." She looked up at Kieran, the implication chilling her blood. "He doesn't think Edris died fighting the Tyrant, Kieran. He thinks Edris died trying to rewrite him."

She continued scanning the pages. The First Archivist had recorded his doubts, his guilt, his knowledge that what he had done would shape every generation to come. Yet it also detailed the successful completion of that First Alignment.

Then, toward the end of the entry, a passage that made her pause:

> *I fear that one day, someone will find this and try to undo it. And I fear who or what will try to stop them.*

Her fingers gripped the edges of the book. "Someone already wondered," she whispered.

Nera felt the stares of her friends like a physical force, unspoken questions settling like dust on the open pages. The First Archivist's words didn't just sit on the parchment; they seemed to suck the oxygen out of the air.

Kieran moved back from the pedestal. "So, the rewrite wasn't about peace?" Kieran muttered. "It was about making sure no one ever questioned who wrote history in the first place."

Tavian shook his head, a bitter smile touching his lips as he read the entry. "The *Codes of Erasure* calls it 'The Gentle Knife'," he murmured. "It started as mercy. But mercy doesn't keep you in power. Eventually, you stop erasing the pain and start erasing the people who are screaming."

Nera had already reached the same conclusion. It wasn't just about what had happened in the past—it was about what had happened since.

"The textbooks call the Second Alignment a 'sunrise'," Kieran muttered, looking at the chaotic scrawl on the page. "They taught us it was seamless. That the mountains moved without a sound. It was the Golden Age of Order—the beginning of a time that didn't need chains."

Tavian let out a breath that was half-sigh, half-scoff. He didn't look up from the text. "That is the nostalgia of the survivor, Kieran," Tavian said, his voice heavy with the fatigue of a man who has read too many tragedies. "We assume silence is peace, Kieran. Usually, it's just a hand over a mouth."

Tobias stepped closer to one of the stone shelves, pulling a book free and flipping through its pages. His expression darkened. "These rewrites didn't stop with the war. But this later one isn't just written; it's fortified. The words are guarded. Someone built a wall out of words here to make sure no one climbs over."

Nera joined him, slowly taking the offered tome. The ink here was sharper, the parchment newer—though 'new' was relative in a place like this. Still, compared to the First Archivist's journal, these were recent accounts, in steadily increasing numbers. And they were ... *wrong*.

"I wouldn't say it's locked," she mumbled, feeling a strange cold hum tingle lightly up her arm. She ran her thumb over a heavy downstroke. "Look at the ink. It didn't sink into the fiber; it pinned it down. The parchment is trying to reject the words, and the author forced them to stay." She looked up. "It's not strategy. It's panic."

Nera turned the page, her finger trailing down a column of redacted names—an entire village dissolved into static. And there, in the margin, the ink was still glossy. A note, written in a precise, cramped hand she had spent ten years memorizing on the chalkboard of in Belvar's classroom.

> *Narrative drift detected. The memory of the event has become more dangerous than the event itself. Correction is mercy.*

Nera recoiled, dropping the book as if it were hot iron. It wasn't just the cruelty that made her stomach turn; it was the familiarity. It was the same feedback Belvar used to write on her essays when she asked too many questions.

"These rewrites aren't corrections," she said, her voice tight. "They're cover-ups."

"It's … violent." She pointed to a jagged line of ink. "Look at the pattern. The First Alignment was woven into reality. But this? This is forced. The ink isn't sinking in anymore; it's sitting on top, crusting over. He wrote violently because the reality underneath has rejected the narrative. He's hammering it into submission to hide the seams. He'd rather break the world's foundation than let anyone see he didn't build it."

"It is exactly that corruption that has woken the fanatics," Tobias said grimly, looking at the door as if expecting an attack.

Nera looked up. "What fanatics?"

"The Preservationists," Tobias said. "They intercepted a supply wagon outside Varethis two days ago. They didn't steal the supplies, Nera. They burned the parchment and slit the throats of the Scribes."

Cael gasped. "They're killing Scribes now?"

"It's not about the paper,"Tobias corrected sharply. "They believe the Archive is a cancer. They see this—" he gestured to the violent structure on the page "—and they don't distinguish between the Tyrant and the Scribe. To them, anyone holding a quill to change history is a liar, and they have started executing to stop the ink."

Tavian paused thoughtfully, then moved to another section, pulling scrolls from the shelves. "The *Protocol of Unmaking* calls them 'drafting errors'," he said, his voice dripping with quiet disgust. "Whole cities have been purged as scraps. They didn't just write these people, Nera. They discarded them because they got in the way of the story."

Nera felt the blood drain from her face. This wasn't just about the past. The First Archivist's rewrite had been a singular event, done in the wake of a war to build a lasting peace, and from what they could decipher seemed completely stable. But what she was looking at now … this was something else. *This was ongoing.*

"The Tyrant," Cael asserted, his voice sharp with understanding. "He—or someone—is still rewriting history."

Kieran was already moving, pulling another text from the shelves. "Not just rewriting," he muttered. "Burying. Hiding."

"This isn't just history, Nera," Cael said, his voice cold and terrifyingly steady. "It's evidence."

He picked up a ledger, eyes scanning the defensive syntax. "The Tyrant didn't just rewrite the past; he left a paper trail of the murder. If we can prove the lineage—if we can prove the theft—we don't have to fight a war. We can walk into the Council and dismantle his reign with his own laws."

Tavian paused, his brow furrowed. "But it doesn't make sense."

Kieran looked up from the book he was holding. "What doesn't?"

"The *Laws of Succession* are absolute: men die." Tavian gestured to the records before them. "If this Tyrant is responsible for all of these … then this isn't a reign, Kieran. It's a stasis. He would have to have been in power for ..." he trailed off, pointing to the records as he did the math. "At least decades. Maybe centuries."

Tobias leaned back, casually. "You're saying the Tyrant isn't just a memory? He's active?"

Tavian shook his head. "No. I'm saying—if the rewrites are still happening, then either his successor has been continuing his work, or ... or it must be him."

Nera barely heard him. Her mind was racing. Everything they had uncovered, all the evidence of history being reshaped—none of it pointed to some distant past. It was ongoing. Growing.

"But that also makes sense. It wasn't just that the history has changed," Nera whispered, tracing the blurring ink. "It's the texture. Each rewrite wasn't a correction so much as a copy of a copy, and now the world has started to show degradation."

She turned sharply to look at Tavian. "But what if it *is* him?"

Kieran shook his head. "That's ridiculous. Check the dates. The First Alignment was centuries ago."

As he spoke, the ledger under Nera's hand shuddered. She looked down. Halfway down the open page, the ink boiled, turning to grey dust that blew off the page, leaving a smooth, blank line where a man had existed ten seconds ago.

"He's not just a contemporary," Nera whispered, staring at the fresh void. "He's working right now."

Everyone froze and silently stared at each other as those words took hold.

Nera gasped. "We've been looking at this all wrong. We keep thinking of the Tyrant as someone who lived far in the past. A figure from history. But what if we've been serving him this whole time?"

Tavian's fingers curled around the book he was holding. "That would mean—"

"That would mean the Benefactor wasn't just a myth," Kieran said slowly. "He must have held real power. Enough that someone needed him erased."

He hesitated. "And if that's true... then whoever replaced him made sure we'd never remember the transition."

Cael's expression hardened. He opened his mouth to speak, then closed it, looking at the records with a new, terrifying understanding. "He didn't rewrite history to save us from chaos," he whispered, his voice cold. "He did it to *hide his theft*."

They had spent their lives in a world that functioned, a world that had seemed—on the surface—peaceful, structured. Stable, until recently at least when the Sixth Alignment started to fail. The thought that their entire reality had been designed that way, that they had been made to forget an entirely different history ... it was too much.

Cael scoffed, shaking his head. "You're all jumping to conclusions. If it was him, don't you think there would be some record? Some sign of who he was before?"

Nera swallowed, staring at the countless rewritten accounts before them.

And maybe that was exactly why history had been made to forget it.

## CHAPTER TWENTY-SEVEN
# The Market Waits

They worked quickly, pulling texts from different sections of the archive, skimming, and cross-referencing. The deeper they looked, the more they found—entire uprisings that had vanished from the record, rebellions snuffed out not with force, but with ink.

And then, a single page that made a sense of panic seize Nera.

Tavian found it first, tucked between accounts of minor border disputes. The ink was darker, fresher, as if the words had only been laid down within the past few years. Unlike the others, this one wasn't a full rewrite—it was an *erasure*.

Nera scanned the passage.

*No record shall remain of the city once known as—*

The name was missing, blotted out, leaving only a ghost of ink where it had once been. Tavian turned the page, his fingers visibly shaking. Erased, but not gone.

"But Archivists are supposed to carefully edit," Kieran noted, "not erase. This wasn't a historical correction," he continued. "This was a purge."

Nera's throat went dry. The Tyrant, who they now believed to be Valen Kestor, wasn't just using the Archivists to maintain order. He was using them to remove anything that threatened his rule.

"This is what we need," Cael said, his voice measured but firm. "Proof."

Nera met his gaze, and for once, they were in full agreement. They had come looking for the past. Instead, they had found evidence of a hand still rewriting the present, and not for the reasons they were always told: good and for the benefit of the people.

The gravity of their findings pressed down on the group, but there was no time to unravel it all now. They moved quickly, pulling what they could, taking copies of the most damning documents. The room itself seemed to resist them, as if history did not want to be disturbed.

Kieran stood apart from the others, a book half-open in his hands. He wasn't reading. He traced a finger slowly along the inked lines, pausing, then going back as if something refused to settle.

He turned the page. His hand stilled.

A symbol was sketched in the margin—not the spiral they had seen before, but something else. An insignia. Nera watched his posture change, the tension pulling tight across his shoulders as he stared at it longer than necessary.

"Did you find something?" she asked.

He closed the book halfway, thumb pressing into the cover's lock. When he looked up at her, whatever he'd been about to say didn't make it out.

"Maybe, but I don't know why," he said quietly, "but I don't want to say it. Not yet."

Nera narrowed her eyes, but before she could press further, Cael spoke from across the room. "You're going to want to see this."

They moved toward him, gathering around as he laid a thin, brittle parchment on the table. Unlike others, this one had been rewritten but the original text still bled through in places, like a past refusing to be forgotten.

It wasn't a record of a ruler. It was a record of a betrayal.

Cael tapped a name near the bottom of the page. The ink had been nearly stripped away, but enough remained to see the outline of a name. Or rather, the absence of one.

"The one who tried," Cael said, his voice hollow. "And the fact that we don't know how—or why—tells you who won."

Nera leaned in, studying the passage.

*... Reality resists ...*

The records had been rewritten so many times that the truth was almost gone, but the intent remained. Someone had opposed the rise of the Tyrant and been erased for it.

Cael hesitated. "From what I can tell here ... the name isn't stable. It's been written and rewritten so many times it barely holds."

Kieran's expression twitched, but he said nothing.

They all stood there, staring at the fragmented piece of history, the pieces still coming together. None of them fully understood what it meant. Not yet. But whatever this was, it wasn't over.

A ripple passed through the archive, something subtle but undeniable. The air cooled with absence, as if the space had become less real.

Nera's fingers twitched as she looked up from the documents. The others felt it too. Even Tavian, who had been too engrossed in deciphering old passages, paused, his gaze flicking toward the shadows near the far wall.

Something moved.

Kieran reached for the dagger at his belt out of instinct, but the movement lacked hostility. It was observation—slow, nonthreatening, watching.

A figure stood there, partially in view, partially slipping between light and something else. Its shape morphed at the edges, as though caught between two versions of reality. Its eyes—if they were eyes at all—were fixed on them.

Then, it spoke. "Do you remember yet?"

The voice was soft but layered, as if spoken from a place just out of reach. A heavy weight settled in Nera's chest. It hadn't asked if she knew. It had asked if she *remembered*.

Kieran tensed beside her, and when she glanced at him, she saw it: a glimmer of recognition, buried beneath confusion.

Separating from the others, one of the drifting figures moved toward Kieran with a sudden, jerky intensity. It didn't glide; it stalked. The form narrowed its hollow eyes as it leaned in to study him.

"You ..." the voice rasped, layered with a sickening confusion. "You should be dead. The Tyrant does not leave loose ends."

Kieran's hand drifted to his blade, but he didn't draw it. "I'm still here."

The figure recoiled slightly, as if Kieran's very presence was painful to look at—too solid, too real for a place built on ghosts.

"No," the Unwritten hissed. "You do not belong with the erased. We are the ash, boy. You are the ember someone hid in the snow."

Kieran stiffened, stepping back as if physically struck. "Who?" But the figure had already lost interest, or perhaps it couldn't hold onto the thought. It drifted back, its gaze shifting to Nera.

Nera forced her voice steady. "Who are you?"

A pause. The figure moved, its outline changing. Then, another voice—distinct yet similar, another shape forming beside the first.

"We are not lost," the figure rasped, the sound grinding like stones in a riverbed. The air around the figure warped and thinned, sucking the heat from the room to fuel the projection. It was costing them something to be here—an immense, crushing effort to exist where they were not written.

Tavian inhaled sharply, stepping back. "*The Apocrypha* calls them 'The Breath Between Words'," he whispered. "Unwritten."

The Unwritten did not gather. They never had. Seeing more than one strain the same moment of existence made Nera's chest tighten.

"We are the ink that refused to dry. We remember the shape of the world before he broke it. We cannot fight him but we can show you where his hand shook. We have been here since the Second Alignment, watching him try to smooth the stone while we remember the truth."

The figure turned to Kieran, eyes narrowing. "You act surprised, boy. But you are the one who has forgotten. We are the scars. You are the open wound."

The Unwritten were notoriously rare and silent. They existed at the edges of history, remnants of revisions and erased names, but they were rarely coherent. And they almost never came this close. For the most part they were treated as old wive's tales.

Cael carefully stepped forward, his movements slow, calculating. "You know something about her, don't you?" He nodded toward Nera, but his gaze jumped toward Kieran too. "Or both of them."

The Unwritten closest to them tilted its head. The unfinished quality of its form was unsettling, a reminder of what happened to those lost between versions of history.

One of the figures, a woman, tilted her head, eyes narrowing as she looked at Nera. "I cataloged the errors," she whispered, her voice sounding like dry paper sliding together. "I know the shape of your face. You are not just a traveler here, Scribe. You are the weight dragging the story down."

Kieran took half a step back, placing himself between Nera and the spirit, his hand snapping to the hilt of his blade, but he didn't say anything.

Nera swallowed, her mind racing. She didn't look a t the woman or ask what she meant. She turned her back on the figure, eyes fixing on Cael and Alis. "We're done here," she said, her voice hard. "We came for a name, not a riddle. Let's go."

Then, the Unwritten simply said, "You will know. When you need to know." And with that, the figures faded, dissolving into history itself. A faint imprint lingered where they had stood—not footprints, not shadows, but something in between.

Cael ran his hand through his hair, gripping the back of his neck. "They're not just ghosts like we've always heard, are they?"

"No," Nera murmured, still watching the space they had left. "They remember the world the way it was."

Her own words unsettled her. Because for just a moment, she could feel something pulling at the edges of her memory. The only sound was the distant rustle of old pages turning in the still air.

"That ... was not normal," Tavian said in a tone that was too controlled, too careful.

Kieran turned away, rubbing his temple as if trying to press a thought back into place. "No. It wasn't."

"The *Book of Ghosts* describes a voice that is not a voice," Tavian said, his face pale. "We just spoke to a memory that has learned hate."

Nera just continued to stare at the space where the Unwritten had stood, the words still ringing in her mind.

*Do you remember yet?*

She didn't. But maybe, just maybe, she had started to.

Nera forced herself to move, grasping the pages they had gathered. They had come looking for the past, and instead, they had uncovered the present, evidence that history was still being rewritten—not to bring peace as originally intended, but to erase the truth.

What had just happened pressed on them, thick as the dust that lingered in the air. No one spoke at first, as if even the archive itself was waiting to see what they would do next.

She turned to Tavian, who was still watching the space where the Unwritten had vanished. "We need to make sure this information doesn't disappear."

He nodded sharply. "We'll split the copies, each of us taking one."

Kieran, still tense from whatever had unsettled him in that moment with the Unwritten, sneered, a quick, ugly twitch of his lip. "And then what? This is evidence, but it won't mean anything unless we know what to do with it."

Nera hated that he was right. The truth was only useful if they could wield it properly.

Tobias adjusted the strap of his satchel, already thinking ahead. "This isn't a text," Tobias said quietly. "It's an accusation. And if it surfaces in the wrong hands, we won't get a second rewrite."

"We take it to the Council of Revision," Cael said, his voice carrying a verdict. "Let them see what the Tyrant's been hiding. They're already questioning the changes—this evidence pushes them over the edge."

Nera looked at him. There was no hesitation in his eyes anymore. No grief. Only strategy.

"Then let's move," she said.

They finished their copies in silence, ensuring no trace of their visit remained. Nera didn't know if erasing their presence would be enough to stop the Tyrant from noticing, but she had no intention of leaving him an easy trail to follow.

As the others moved toward the exit, Nera caught Kieran's arm. He stopped, his muscles rigid beneath his coat. He hadn't spoken since the Unwritten appeared, and she saw the tension locking his jaw.

"They knew us," Nera whispered.

Kieran didn't look at her. He looked back into the dark of the archive, at the empty space where the ghosts had stood.

"Yeah," he said, his voice rough.

"And you felt it, didn't you? You knew this place."

He finally met her eyes. The silver-grey irises were wide, stripped of their usual guard. "I don't know how. But ... yeah."

Nera looked forward again, the weight of the book in her bag pressing against her side. "We're done looking for the past," she said. "Now we have to survive it."

She stepped out into the night. Behind them, with a sound like a tomb closing, the door to the Sanctum sealed shut.

## CHAPTER TWENTY-EIGHT

# The Council of Revision

The underground rebel safehouse was packed, the air musty with the scent of ink, wax, and dust from countless old books. Lanterns flared against damp stone walls, illuminating the makeshift workstations where maps, scrolls, and bound ledgers had been spread out in every available space. The room hummed with the quiet intensity of preparations, voices low but urgent as the rebels and scholars reviewed the culmination of their efforts—months of background research combined with the explosive new evidence secured from the Sanctum only recently.

The case they were about to present rested on a handful of questionable records—it was built on an exhaustive search through the remnants of a rewritten world. They had gone to the forgotten corners of history itself to uncover what the Council had long buried.

Theron stood at the head of one table, carefully unrolling a damaged scroll from the ruined archives of Vornis. "This is the original territorial record," he said, tracing a jagged line. "Gaela and I found regions that are literally bleeding into each other. It's like the Architect tried to force two puzzle pieces into the same slot and just hammered them until they stuck. The land isn't rejecting them; the foundation is breaking because there is too much ink in one place."

Gaela leaned forward, placing a hand flat on the map. "It's not just land. We found census records for towns that aren't there anymore. You're looking for glitches in the geography; we also found ghosts. Thousands of them."

"Proof is no longer required," Cyrus said, dropping a heavy, decrypted file onto the table. "These are internal Grand Archive reports I pulled from the deep vaults. They confirm the Council identified the failure years ago. They did not lose history; they encrypted it. These are not repair logs. They are sentencing frameworks."

Sarina, who had been scanning the documents beside him, reached over and flipped to another page, her sharp eyes darting over the text. "It wasn't a mistake. Look at the language here. It's panic. They drafted escape routes because they were terrified the narrative was about to eat them alive. They knew the history was sick, and they decided to bury the patient rather than cure the disease."

She shot Cyrus a knowing look. "Sound familiar?"

Cyrus shook his head emphatically. "It's the oldest trick in the book. Contain the failure rather than fix it."

Alis whistled softly. "So they all lied to their own people."

"Not all of them," Tobias said, shaking his head. "We've been tracking the money and the influence. The ones closest to Kestor are covering it up. The rest? They aren't blind, they're just comfortable. They won't ask questions as long as their share of history stays profitable."

Nera had been listening, but she wasn't just observing—she was calculating. Every map, every record laid before them had been pieced together under her direction. *This* was her fight.

It was all here. The contradictions, the half-erased names, the fluctuating borders, the unstable constellations. Proof that the

Sixth Alignment had not taken hold properly from the outset, that the Council had rewritten history not to stabilize reality but to maintain their own power.

"If this isn't enough for them to listen," she said, her voice steady, "then nothing will be." The others exchanged glances. No one wanted to be the one to say it, but the doubt was already in the air.

Cael leaned forward, lacing his fingers together. "We need to present this carefully. Make them think fixing this benefits them. If they feel threatened, they'll dig in their heels."

"Belvar is a rabid dog, but Kestor is a statesman," Cael reasoned, his voice gaining conviction. "He values structure above all else. If we can get past Belvar's blockade and get this proof into the official Council record, Kestor will have to act." Cael insisted, "He won't want his legacy to be diminished by incompetent underlings. We aren't just going there to complain; we're going there to appeal to the only man powerful enough to fix the machine."

"They should feel threatened," Kieran muttered. "This isn't about the Council or even Kestor. It's about reality itself unraveling. And they need to see it."

They had done everything they could to prepare. They had gathered more evidence than they ever thought possible. They had risked themselves for every scrap of information. Nera ran a hand through her hair, feeling the moment settle over her.

One by one, they began gathering up the documents, rolling the scrolls, folding the maps, tucking away the truth in whatever spaces it could fit.

Nera studied Cael. His voice was calm, his expression composed, but she knew him well enough to recognize when he was working an angle.

"The Council is still under the Tyrant's influence," she said. "They might bury this the moment we show it to them." Nera reached for the stack of ledgers, the ones containing names of the erased, the undeniable proof. Her hand hit the wood of the table. The ledgers were gone.

She looked up. Cael stood by his satchel, buckling the strap. He hadn't packed the ledgers. He had pushed them aside, planning to leave them in the safe house.

"Cael," Nera said, her voice tight. "Put them in the bag."

"No," Cael said. "Those ledgers are proof," Nera pressed, stepping forward. "People are missing. Not just places. Not just memories."

Cael finally looked up. His face was perfectly smooth, his eyes cold.

"Those ledgers are a death sentence," he said, his hand hovering over the heavy books before he deliberately pushed them aside. "If we walk in there accusing them of murder, we don't leave that room. We bring the maps. We offer them a way to save face, not a reason to execute us."

He shoved the celestial charts into the satchel—the safe, scientific proof. "We are going there to report a structural failure, Nera. We take the maps. We leave the bodies."

Nera reached for the ledgers anyway, her fingers brushing the spine. "I'm taking them, Cael. We owe it to the dead."

Cael moved faster than she expected. He grabbed her wrist—firmly. He pushed her hand back, hard enough to sting, and shoved the heavy books off the table. They hit the floor with a sound like breaking bones.

"You don't get to be a martyr today, Nera," he said, his voice shaking with a terrifying, cold fury. He kicked the ledgers under the table, into the shadows. "I am not watching you die for a stack of paper. We take the maps. We leave the bodies. And you're going to hate me for it, but you're going to be alive to do it."

Kieran scoffed. "You want to use history as a weapon, same as him."

Cael's eyes flicked to him, cold as glass. "I want us to win this," he said. "Does it matter how?"

Nera ran a hand down her face. "It matters to me."

Cael gave her a slow nod. "Exactly. Which is why we need to make sure they see the version of history that forces them to act."

Tobias leaned against the wall, crossing his arms. "He's right, Nera. If we lead with the ledgers, we lose the element of surprise. We show the maps to test their defenses. We hold the ledgers in reserve."

Tavian frowned, but even he couldn't argue the logic. They had the truth. But how they chose to use it would decide everything.

\* \* \*

The heavy doors of the Assembly Hall groaned open, revealing the crescent tribunal waiting in silence beneath a mural of the Architect.

Before them in the Council chambers sat ten Archivists, arranged in a crescent formation at the raised tribunal.

Nera's gaze swept the line of faces—impassive, distant, bureaucratic. Until she reached the center.

She froze. Beside her, Cael's breath hitched.

Seated in the highest chair, watching them with the bored indifference of a man observing an insect in a jar, was Master Belvar. The High Archivist.

And—unknown to the public—the presiding head of the Council.

He looked at them with disappointment rather than surprise, as if he had expected them to have the good sense to disappear. He didn't speak immediately. He simply let his gaze drift over them— lingering on Cael's defiance, Kieran's hand hovering near his blade, and finally settling on Nera.

He offered a thin, patronizing smile. "I see you haven't lost your talent for being exactly where you do not belong, Calloway."

Nera looked around at the rest of the members of the Council, hoping for a friendly expression. Some leaned forward, seeming interested. Others sat stiffly, wary. Nera noticed that next to Belvar, an older female looked up from the papers she had been writing on, and upon looking at her exchanged a quick glance with Belvar, unspoken questions. Each member was clad in deep grey robes, embroidered with gold or silver, their faces ranging from impassive to mildly disapproving. Some sat with their hands resting on the polished curve of the tribunal table, while others leaned back, observing with distant curiosity.

It was immediately clear that not all of them viewed this meeting the same way.

On the far left, a sharp-eyed woman studied them with quiet intensity, her fingers steepled in front of her. Two seats away, an older man already looked exasperated, as if they were nothing more than an inconvenience. Others simply watched, waiting to see how this would unfold.

Nera's gaze flicked back to the two at the center. Their expressions gave away nothing, but their presence alone made it clear that whatever happened here, the tyrant would know of it before the ink dried.

The assistant cleared her throat. "Presenting the petitioners—Nera Calloway, Cael Renwick, Kieran Voss, —"

She stopped, clearly reconsidered, then waved the remainder of the list away with a small, impatient flick of her fingers.

"—and their associates, representing the concerns of the Free Histories and the Conservation of Truth."

Tavian muttered, "I would have preferred 'Heretics.' It has more historical precedent."

Alis quietly laughed under her breath. "Could be worse."

The assistant stepped back, folding her hands again. "The Council recognizes your request to speak."

A pause.

Nera stepped forward, shoulders squared, fighting the urge to shrink back under Belvar's stare. "We've come to present critical evidence concerning the integrity of the Sixth Alignment. We have records that show—"

"Records you stole?" Belvar interrupted smoothly. His voice, though soft, silenced the room instantly.

He leaned back in his chair, steeping his fingers. "You stand there, covered in the dust of ruins you were forbidden to enter, holding documents you do not have the clearance to read, and expect us to listen to your theories on integrity?"

He looked at the other councilors, offering a small, dismissive shake of his head. "It is exactly as I reported. Former students unable to accept that their failure to understand history does not mean history is broken."

Nera stiffened.

Cael gave a practiced, polite smile. "We're not here to waste time, only to bring evidence we believe you will find important and impossible to ignore."

Another member of the Council, a younger woman with keen, hawk-like features, tilted her head slightly. "Then by all means," she said, her tone like a blade. "Let's hear this ... impossible evidence."

Nera glanced at her companions. Kieran's hand was hovering over a dagger that wasn't there; Cael was standing so still he looked like he'd stopped breathing. This was it. She reached into her satchel, pulled out the first set of documents, and set them on the council's table.

"Let's begin."

The parchment landed with a dull thud against the polished tribunal table, the thick sheaf of documents shifting slightly as the weight settled. It was a physical manifestation of weeks of effort, of sleepless nights, of stolen records and whispered secrets carried across the fractured remnants of history. The ink on some pages was still fresh, the scrawled notes in the margins a quiet testament to the frantic urgency of their work.

And yet, the faces staring down at it from the crescent tribunal barely changed.

A few of the members leaned forward, eyes attempting to scan the top sheets with mild curiosity, their gazes flicking over pages like they were humoring a child's drawings. Others, including Belvar and the woman seated next to him, did not so much as glance at the stack of evidence—Belvar's attention fixed instead on Nera, as if the papers themselves were beneath consideration.

Finally, an older council member to the right—deep-set eyes, narrow face, the air of someone who had long ago stopped listening to ideas that did not serve him—let out an audible sigh. He drummed his fingers against the desk, his patience already worn thin.

His voice cut in, dry and dismissive. "You bring us scattered documents and expect us to question the entire foundation of history?"

Nera kept her posture steady. "We bring you proof that the Sixth Alignment isn't holding. It's an active rupture. History isn't settling the way you believe it is—it's bleeding out."

The man barely concealed his distaste. "And where, exactly, did you gather this so-called proof?"

Cael smoothly stepped forward, his voice taking on that measured, persuasive quality he used when navigating dangerous discussions. "From across the remnants of written and unwritten history. From places that still bear the scars of failed realignments. From maps that contradict the very laws of revisions. From testimonies of people who should not exist and yet do. Every record we've gathered points to the same conclusion—the Sixth Alignment is fractured."

A woman seated to the left of the tribunal, her fingers steepled in front of her, arched a single brow. "And you expect us to take the word of students who are possible rebels and exiles over centuries of carefully maintained recordkeeping?"

Kieran finally spoke, his voice even but carrying an edge beneath it. "Then why is reality resisting?"

A ripple of discomfort passed through the chamber.

Alis, lounging against the side of the tribunal, took an exaggerated breath. "Let me guess. None of you have actually stepped outside of this chamber to check, have you?"

The sharp-eyed woman to Belvar's left tapped a single, perfectly manicured finger against the desk. "We do not act on every passing theory of instability. If we did, we would be entertaining unfounded speculation every day. Revisions take time to settle. If there are inconsistencies, they will smooth out. It is the work of the Archivists to make sure."

Nera slammed her hand onto the map. "But they're not smoothing out. They're widening." She pulled a second map from her satchel, rolling it open across the table. "This is a celestial chart from before the Sixth Alignment. And this—" she set another next to it, "—is one taken last month."

A few council members leaned forward, faces showing keen interest. The differences were stark, unmistakable. Stars that should have been fixed in the night sky had transformed. Constellations had reformed in ways that defied natural movement.

Tavian, who had remained silent up until now, stepped forward to add to the stack of star maps. "The stars don't care about our laws, Councilman," Tavian said. He gestured to the map, his expression hardening. "You can burn every book in this city, you can force every citizen to recite your version of the truth, but you can't rewrite the sky. These aren't errors to be corrected. They're stress fractures. History is collapsing under the weight of your ink."

The exasperated older man waved a dismissive hand. "Natural shifts. Miscalculations in the charts. This is hardly the first time—"

"There's more," Nera said. She reached into her satchel for the heavy ledgers—the undeniable proof of the erased lives.

Her fingers brushed against the rough canvas of the bag's bottom. Empty. She froze and remembered Cael pushing the ledgers aside. *We leave the bodies.*

She looked up, shooting a sharp glance at Cael. He met her gaze, his face perfectly smooth, unrepentant. He had forced her hand. She had to finish the accusation with empty hands.

"People," she said, her voice tight with frustration. "Places. Whole families who should not exist, but do. Or should exist, but do not."

The elder on the right frowned. "People being erased would amount to treason," he said sharply, flicking his hand at the empty table as if swatting away a fly. "And you bring us nothing but air."

His hand drifted toward the silver bell on the table—the one that summoned the guards.

He stopped.

Slowly, he drew his hand back and instead reached for one of the maps. His fingers trembled as he traced a coastline that should not have changed. The color drained from his face.

The arrogance in the room fractured. They were no longer looking at a theory. They were looking at their own extinction.

"This isn't instability," he whispered, the word failing him before he caught it with sudden, brittle anger. "This is a breach."

Kieran, for the first time since entering the chamber, let the faintest smirk touch his lips. "You don't have to believe it. You just have to explain it."

Nera pressed forward. "This is not just a minor inconsistency. This is a collapse waiting to happen. And the people outside this chamber—the ones living in the world you keep rewriting—are the ones suffering for it."

The sharp-eyed woman turned her gaze on Nera fully for the first time. She studied her, then glanced at the records again. Slowly, she exhaled. Then she spoke.

"I see no official record of a citizen named Nera Calloway."

The words were casual. But the moment they left her lips, something in the air changed.

She turned slightly, adjusting the parchment before her, tone deliberately neutral. "The records mention a request for discourse from a Calloway. But the first name listed here is not Nera."

She paused, scanning the page again.

"In fact, I do not see a Nera Calloway listed in any registry for that year," she said, her voice cooling. "The only Calloway listed is ..."

She paused.

Her fingers tightened on the parchment until the edge bent. The syllable escaped before her jaw locked.

"...Nerith."

The room stilled.

Belvar went rigid. His gaze snapped to the woman beside him, sharp and alarmed, before he masked it and looked forward again.

Nera didn't react. She didn't recognize the name. It meant nothing to her.

Beside her, Kieran inhaled sharply. The sound was involuntary. He stared at Nera, eyes widening—not in confusion, but in something closer to shock. As if a piece of a pattern had just snapped into place ahead of the rest.

The woman cleared her throat. She looked back down at the parchment, smoothing it flat.

"Strange," she said shortly. "A transcription error, most likely." She turned the page and continued.

Nera remained still, confused, waiting. She glanced at Kieran, but she could see that the walls slammed back down behind his eyes, the moment already locked away behind whatever blocks he had built in his mind.

"Tell me," the elder on the right mused. "If we were to consider your request, what exactly would you have us do?" His voice was too smooth, too patient.

Nera squared her shoulders. "Acknowledge what is happening. Act. Address the damage before it gets worse."

Another member, a stern-looking man with a heavy brow, sneered—a quick, ugly twitch of his lip. "Let's be honest with each other. We are not concerned with petty discrepancies in the memory of commoners. They adapt, as they always have. What we concern ourselves with is stability. Structure. The ability to maintain the world in the shape it was meant to hold."

Nera's patience was thinning rapidly. "Meant to hold, according to whom?"

"According to those with the wisdom to preserve order. That has always been the way of things." He turned to the scribe. "Strike their testimony from the record. We will move to a vote on their expulsion."

"There will be no vote," Belvar said. He didn't look at the older man; he didn't even raise his voice. He simply adjusted his cuff, the quiet movement silencing the entire room. The older councilor's mouth clicked shut, his face paling as he withdrew his hand from the gavel at his seat.

Kieran snorted. "You're not even pretending anymore, are you?"

The woman with sharp cheekbones sighed as if bored. "Why should we? Your argument is transparent. You came here to negotiate intervention. You assumed if you frightened us enough, we would rush to fix a problem for you. But you've miscalculated. The world has been rewritten countless times before this, and it will be rewritten again. That is power."

Nera could feel Cael's stare without even looking at him. He had been trying to sway them, but now, finally, he understood. They were never going to be swayed.

Cael stepped forward, his voice smooth. "We aren't asking for truth. We're offering stability. If you don't fix the timeline, you lose the kingdom. Help us patch the cracks, and you stay in power."

Rapping his gavel on the table in front of him, Belvar smiled, but there was no warmth. It was the smile of a man closing a trap.

"You make a compelling case for stability, Mr. Renwick," he said softly. "But you misunderstand the architecture. "We do not rebalance systems," he said. "We remove unstable pieces."

He slammed his hand onto the desk. "Initiate the protocol for the Seventh Alignment," Belvar said. "Burn it all down."

The command came too easily. He didn't consult the others or ask how far the damage had spread. It wasn't the reaction of a man facing an accident, but the terrifying reaction of a man recognizing a signal—like the instability wasn't a failure in the design, but a feature meant to be used.

The Scribe at the end of the table didn't flinch. He simply dipped his quill and logged the order, the scratch of the nib echoing like a final verdict.

Cael stared at the ink drying on the page, his face draining of color. He had come here thinking the law was a shield he could wield, a structure he could reason with. But as the Scribe sanded the page, sealing the destruction of the timeline as a bureaucratic necessity, the realization hit him. The law wasn't a defense. It was the weapon. And Kestor was the only hand holding it.

With that, the Council rose as one and filed out in silence.

The doors closed. The sound echoed too long.

A Seventh Alignment meant there would be no witnesses left to remember why they had fought at all.

"We didn't buy time," Kieran said quietly. "We started the clock."

Nera looked at Cael. He hadn't moved. His face had gone pale—not with fear, but with understanding. He had played their game, by their rules. And they had changed the rules mid-move.

"We have to go," Nera said.

"Now!"

## CHAPTER TWENTY-NINE

# Erased Allies

Theron's safehouse hummed with the low murmur of voices, the scratch of quills against parchment, and the occasional shuffle of chairs against stone. Stacks of stolen records and maps sprawled across makeshift tables, illuminated by dimmed oil lamps. The air smelled of ink, dust, and exhaustion which was causing tempers to rise.

Nera sat at the center of it all, fingers attempting to tap a sharp rhythm against the table.

But the sound was wrong. Tap … tap … tap. The noise hit the air a fraction of a second after her finger struck the wood. She stared at her hand, then lifted her index finger and brought it down again. She felt the impact, but the sound lagged, like a hammer striking in a canyon. A wave of nausea rolled through her gut. Her senses were drifting out of sync. She was becoming a bad translation of herself.

She clenched her hand into a fist, hiding the tremor, forcing her mind to race faster than she could process the words on the page in front of her. She stood up moving around restlessly, too distracted for her mind to rest.

Cael stood by the window, a stack of recovered papers in his hand, staring past the words. He was looking at the handwriting on a ledger—a delicate, looping script that looked painfully similar to the work Livia used to do late into the night. He traced the curve of an ink stroke; his expression fractured for a split second before the scowl locked back into place. The smell of the ink, the dust ... it all reminded him of her. And she wasn't here.

"We should be out there," Nera muttered, restless energy thrumming under her skin. "Finding the places where history is unraveling instead of—" she paused and waved a hand absently.

"You mean instead of sitting here going through books?" Cael drawled from where he leaned against a shelf, arms crossed. "Funny, I thought you were the one who worshiped the truth. You know, written records, history, the kind of thing we're trying to salvage."

Nera shot him a glare. "Go to hell, Cael."

"Already halfway there," he smirked. "But you first."

Her temper flared, sharp and blinding. "You think this is a joke?"

"I think you're unraveling faster than the history you're trying to fix."

His eyes flicked to the books piled around her, and the sneer fractured. He went rigid, his gaze locking onto her ink-stained fingers with a sudden, sick familiarity. The anger dissolved, replaced by a pale, wide-eyed fear. He took a sharp step back, breathing shallowly, looking at her not with judgment, but with the hollow stare of a man watching a tragedy he had already lived through once.

"Stop trying to be a martyr, Nera," Alis cut in from the kitchen, her voice bored but her eyes sharp as glass. "Martyrs are just corpses with better biographers. And frankly, I'm not in the mood to attend your funeral today. I have plans."

Kieran had been quiet until now, but at Cael's words, he finally moved. Slowly, deliberately, he set down the knife he had been idly rolling between his fingers, his gaze switching to Nera. "That's enough," he said. Something in his voice cut through her spiraling frustration like a blade.

He stepped into Nera's line of sight. "Look at your hands."

She blinked, startled. "What?"

"They're shaking," he said, his voice devoid of judgment, stating it like a tactical report. "You can't hold a quill like that. Sit down."

"We don't have time—"

"Sit down, Nera."

Kieran's face went blank, the way a soldier goes still when an order crosses a line he can't argue with. "You think throwing yourself at this wall will break it? You're not alone in this, Nera. You can stop acting like you have to carry it by yourself."

Something hot and unfamiliar curled in her chest—frustration, anger, something deeper that she didn't want to name. She looked away. "Then help me find the answer."

"We will," he said, softer now, placing a hand gently on each of her shoulders. "But not like this." He gave her shoulders a gentle squeeze. His words settled in her bones, a truth she didn't want to acknowledge.

Nera didn't move. Then, finally, she dropped back into her chair.

The tension in the room didn't ease immediately. Even Alis, usually quick to interject, remained still. Theron scratched something in the margin of a document, unbothered, while Gaela and Kaelith exchanged a glance.

No one laughed. Nera forced herself to refocus on the text in front of her, but Kieran's gaze lingered.

## Chapter Thirty

# Forged Records

The others had long since dispersed, but Nera remained behind, alone in the main room of the dimly lit safehouse.

She sat at the now-empty table, staring at an old map spread before her. The ink was smudged, the parchment curling at the edges, but none of it mattered. She wasn't seeing it—her mind was somewhere else, running in circles, chasing after answers that refused to be caught.

She caught her reflection in the darkened window pane. She turned her head back to the map, but for a single, terrifying heartbeat, her reflection stayed facing the window—watching her—before finally turning to follow.

A shadow moved at the edge of the lamplight—a hesitation in the air, as if the room itself was uncertain she was there. She didn't look up when Kieran stepped forward, but she felt his presence settle across the table from her. "He let us walk out of that chamber," Kieran said, his voice low, interrupting the silence.

Nera paused, her finger tracing the coastline on the map. "He was arrogant. He wanted us to run."

"No," Kieran said. She looked up to see him staring at the wall, his brow furrowed in deep calculation. "I watched his hands, Nera. He unconsciously reached for his blade, then stopped. He didn't spare you out of strategy." He looked at her, a sudden, sharp realization darkening his eyes. "It was constraint. I don't think he can erase you. Not the way he erases everyone else."

He paused briefly. "You've been quiet," he said, changing the subject before the terrifying implication could settle.

Nera huffed a quiet, humorless laugh. "That's a first, huh?"

Kieran didn't smile. He watched her, then pulled out the chair opposite her and sat down. The sound of wood scraping against stone was the only sound between them.

"You can't keep doing this," he said.

She knew what he meant, but she didn't acknowledge it. She traced the curve of the map's coastline with her fingertip. "Doing what?"

"Pushing until you break."

She froze.

"I know what it's like," Kieran said. "To keep moving so you don't have to stop."

Something shivered through her, a tension behind her ribs that she couldn't quite name. "You don't know anything about what's keeping me going," she said, voice quieter than before.

Kieran leaned forward, resting his forearms against the table. His gaze didn't waver. "I know more than you think."

"You don't," she snapped, the exhaustion fraying her temper. "You don't know what it's like to feel the ink moving under your skin. To feel like you're the only real thing in a room full of ... of ghosts."

Kieran's expression softened, the sharp edges of his vigilance finally dulling. "I don't know the ink like you do," he admitted quietly. "But I know the ghosts. I've been watching you look for a way out of this room, Nera. Not because you're busy. But because you're terrified that if you stop working, you'll feel like you're alone."

He reached across the table, his fingers brushing the edge of her map. He opened his mouth, the words hovering there—something soft, something dangerous.

*Crack.*

A log tipped in the hearth, the sound sharp as a breaking bone.

Kieran flinched, his hand snapping back from the map quickly. The openness vanished from his face, replaced instantly by the guarded mask of a solider listening for a threat. He scanned the room, then looked back at her, his eyes distant again.

Her body slumped slightly, overtaken by exhaustion, as she shook her head. "It's not about me."

"You keep telling yourself that," he said. "And I'll keep watching you prove yourself wrong." The words settled between them, heavier than they should have been.

Nera finally looked up, meeting his gaze. There was something calming in the way he watched her, something frustratingly patient.

She didn't know what she had expected—some kind of argument, some kind of fight—but this was worse, because Kieran wasn't pushing her away. He was staying, and that was something she wasn't sure how to deal with.

He watched her hand on the map, and for a split second, his expression fractured. The guarded soldier vanished, replaced by something devastatingly familiar. His gaze softened, unfocused, following the curve of her fingers as if he were seeing them somewhere else.

He reached across the table. Not for the map. For her. His hand hovered inches from hers, palm open, the offer instinctive, unguarded.

Nera didn't think. Her fingers uncurled, her palm turning upward to meet his. The movement was fast, fluid—too natural to be deliberate.

Her fingertips brushed his, angling toward his hand as if they already knew where to go.

Then the contact shocked her.

She froze, staring at her own hand as if it belonged to a stranger. The familiarity of his skin against hers wasn't just comforting; it was terrifying. It felt like coming home to a house she had never visited.

She yanked her hand back, covering the documents as if protecting them from a thief. "I don't need you to manage me, Kieran. I can finish this."

Kieran froze. His hand remained suspended between them for a beat too long—empty.

Whatever had crossed his face vanished instantly, his features hardening into something closed and unreadable. His gaze didn't return to the map she was holding. It lingered on the space where her hand had been.

Slowly, deliberately, he curled his fingers into a fist and drew his arm back to his side. "Right," he said, his voice devoid of the warmth from seconds ago. "Just the mission."

Nera opened her mouth to correct him, to say she hadn't meant it like that, but he had already stood up and turned his back, starting to walk away.

"You should get some rest," he said over his shoulder. "We need you sharp tomorrow so that you don't make mistakes."

"You should too," she countered. He lingered for a beat longer, as if deciding whether to say something else. In the end, he only nodded once before stepping through the doorway, disappearing back into the darkened halls of the safehouse.

Nera pressed her fingers to her temples. She hated that he was right. She hated that he had seen it before she had.

## CHAPTER THIRTY-ONE

# The Grand Archive

The next morning brought no relief, only a sharper, colder light. Cyrus sat at the head of the table, his maps already spread out over the remnants of a meal no one had the stomach to eat.

"We need to finalize today's plan," Cael said, his voice even, yet firm enough to cut through the conversations. People instinctively turned toward him, some still chewing their meal, others straightening in their seats.

Gaela cast a glance over her shoulder as she slid more food onto a plate. "Eat first, talk after," she said.

"I don't need to stop thinking just to chew," Cyrus replied, though he picked up a piece of bread and took a bite as if to appease her.

Sarina, seated beside him, set down a parchment she had been skimming. "We're at a standstill with what we have here. The next step is getting information from the outside."

Cyrus nodded. "The breakage follows a pattern. If the records and geography are cross-referenced against memory, the source isolates itself. Speed is essential," he said, tapping a coordinate on a map. "The Apothecary shop isn't just missing anymore. The void where it stood has expanded. It consumed the bakery next door this morning. The baker didn't disappear—he walked into his shop and fell through the floor of the world. We are running out of solid ground."

Nera forced herself to focus.

Cyrus turned to Theron and Kaelith. "You two are the variables I can't quantify but it seems like you are best at gathering stories. Take Gaela and Brieth with you. Stories are messy—too much babble, not enough truth—but they contain patterns the Archives usually ignores."

Theron gave an easy shrug, scraping his spoon against the bottom of the pot before gesturing with it like a weapon. "So we poke the locals until secrets fall out? We'll play the charming travelers, buy the drinks, and wait for someone to slip up. It's tedious work, shaking the tree just to see what kind of fruit drops, but I suppose it beats waiting around here."

Kaelith, standing beside him, flicked a glance toward Nera before turning back to Cyrus. "We'll get what we need."

Tobias stood still. His height and calm presence acted as a gravity well, pulling the restless energy of the room toward him until the group stopped moving to listen. "I can't secure a route that doesn't exist, Jorin. Map the voids. If a road is compromised, we mark it as lost and find a new line."

Jorin paused, rubbing his forehead, seeming overwhelmed. "It won't be perfect. Half of this information is being rewritten even as we track it."

"Do what you can," Tobias said. "Even unstable knowledge is still knowledge."

Jorin muttered something about how that wasn't how maps were supposed to work, but he didn't argue further. He reached to take the map, his arm jerking in a staccato rhythm like a puppet with a tangled string. The movement stuttered and blurred. As his left hand—the one wrapped in the pitch-black void—brushed the edge of the wooden table, the wood didn't just bump; it hissed. A notch of the edge vanished, eroding in seconds, crumbling into a fine, colorless powder that rained onto the floor.

"I didn't mean to," Jorin whispered, pulling his arm against his chest.

Brieth stared at him, eyes wide, fear evident in her tone. "You're accidentally erasing it just by standing there."

"It's still me," he whispered, hugging her lightly.

"Alis, Tobias, and Tyrek," Cyrus jumped in, shifting attention. "The black-market networks track instability for profit. They will have data we don't. Get access to the unlisted records and find the anomalies."

"The riots in the Lower District are escalating," Cyrus added, tapping a cluster of reports. "The Enforcers have stopped processing detainees. They are simply erasing anyone who disrupts the peace."

He looked up from the report, his expression not one of horror, but of cold calculation. To him, the brutality wasn't a tragedy; it was a variable to be leveraged.

"That desperation makes them reactive," Cyrus continued, his finger tracing the perimeter line. "They are terrified of the infection spreading. Use the confusion to mask your movements. If you incite further unrest near the perimeter, it will draw the Enforcers away from your target. It is the most efficient cover."

Tobias set his mug down—a heavy, final sound. "No. Once we weaponize the panic, we lose the city. I won't cross that line."

Cyrus didn't look up from his map. "It doubles our odds of getting inside. It's the most efficient cover."

"And it turns civilians into targets," Tobias countered, his voice leaving no room for argument. "If we provoke a riot, the Enforcers will fire into the crowd to reach us. We go in quiet—or we don't go at all. I won't turn the city into a meat shield."

"Why, Cyrus, it's almost like you think I have connections in places you disapprove of."

"I calculated for that," he said simply. "Your network is a necessary variable." Alis grinned but said nothing more.

Cyrus' gaze finally landed on Nera, Kieran, and Cael. "The three of you will track the fractures. There are places where the timeline isn't holding its shape. We need to find the stress points before the whole thing snaps."

Nera gave a short nod. She had expected that.

But before Cyrus could address the rest of the room, Jorin stepped forward. He was staring at the pile of dust on the floor where the table edge had been.

"I can't stay here," Jorin said, his voice tight. He gripped his unstable arm against his chest, the void ink pulsing beneath his sleeve. "Cyrus, you're talking about stabilizing the safehouse. Look at the floor. I'm not stabilizing anything. I'm erasing it."

The room went quiet. Brieth's eyes flicked from the floor to Jorin's arm, then to the map, before she moved to his side and nodded thoughtfully. She looked at Nera. "He's a liability in the city, but we can still help. We'll take the overland route to the Borderlands. We'll meet up with the families."

"If the roads are changing, you'll need a navigator," Jorin said. "Unstable terrain's sort of my specialty.: The corner of his mouth twitched, then stilled. "We"ll make sure Tessa, Mave and the children are safe on the other side."

Brieth shook her head once, more fond than amused, then turned to Nera. "We'll keep them safe, Nera. You just worry about fixing history."

"And we'll send word back as soon as we can connect with the families," Jorin promised. "It's safer for everyone this way." They moved through the room in quiet embraces and then with a final nod, slipped out the back toward the overland trails, leaving the silence of the room heavier than before.

For a few moments no one moved, processing the loss of another group of friends. "This doesn't change the plan," Cyrus said finally. "Those remaining will stabilize what they can. We reconvene in one week. If the environment degrades, you withdraw at once."

Cael let out a sharp, brittle laugh. "Reconvene where, Cyrus?" He pointed to the map, where the ink of the apothecary and bakery had already dissolved into a void. "If the streets shift while we're separated, we don't just lose contact. We lose the path back."

The room went silent. They all looked at the map—at the fragility of the rendezvous point.

"Then we don't look back," Nera said, her voice steady. "We finish it, or we don't come back at all."

His gaze hardened. "We do not spend lives to satisfy curiosity. Dead witnesses preserve nothing."

The Sixth Alignment had failed. They believed now that Edris Vayne had tried something—and that it hadn't worked. They didn't yet know why. But if they didn't find out soon, they would be doomed to repeat the same mistake.

A quiet understanding passed between them all. One by one, the groups began gathering what they needed. Maps were rolled, weapons checked, cloaks adjusted.

Nera pushed away from the table, her thoughts already turning ahead. She caught Kieran's gaze briefly as he moved past her. He didn't say anything, but something in his expression lingered longer than it should have. She slowly turned away.

There was no room for hesitation. They had work to do.

## Chapter Thirty-Two

# Preparation

The day passed in a blur of restless tension. By nightfall, the safe-house was stifling, the air heavy with questions no one could answer. Cael paced the floorboards until the rhythm became maddening, while Cyrus stared at his unmoving calculations as if willing the math to change. The shadows lengthened until they swallowed the room, leaving the group sitting in a gloom that felt less like evening and more like a cage.

The silence stretched thinner and thinner, pulling tight enough to snap.

The back door was thrown open, letting in a gust of cold wind. Alis stepped inside, slamming it shut with her hip. She looked exhausted, her coat stained with street mud, but her eyes were bright with a terrifying kind of triumph. She tossed a heavy, wax-sealed packet onto the table like it was a dead rat.

"I spent three favors and a pouch of gold I didn't have," Alis said, unwinding her scarf. "But I found out why the Sixth Alignment is rotting."

Cyrus looked up, adjusting his glasses. "Provenance?"

"Bought," Alis said, pouring herself a drink with a shaking hand. "From a fence in the low district. But he didn't set the price. The seller did."

She looked at Nera, her expression grim. "It was Soren. The fence said a man in a grey cloak dropped it off yesterday. He paid a premium to have it held for 'the girl with the ink stains'."

Alis tapped the document. "He didn't keep it because he couldn't." She glanced up at Nera. "The fence said Soren was looking for places where the Alignment didn't hold. Where the rewrite failed completely. He's gone to find Edris himself."

Cyrus frowned. "This isn't just a record."

"No," Alis said quietly. "It's a confession."

She exhaled and tapped the page again, slower this time. "We were taught Edris Vayne died fighting the Tyrant."

Her gaze hardened. "He didn't. He died trying to rewrite and *remove* him."

The room went still

"Edris tried to use the Alignment to erase Kestor entirely. To *unwrite* him. The ink rejected it. Kestor countered. And it took Edris with it."

Kieran's breath left him slowly. "That's why Vornis is broken."

He looked up, the realization settling. "Edris was its anchor. When the rewrite failed, the recoil didn't just hit him. It hit the city."

"I don't understand," Nera whispered, staring at the tremor in her hand. "Edris was a Master Archivist—he knew the system. So why did the ink kill him, yet I'm still here after what I did to Jorin?"

Tavian's jaw tightened. "Because Edris rewrote from inside the Archive."

He gestured around them, sharp and bitter. "The Archive dampens the recoil. It was built to absorb the shock. Here? The walls don't break. You do."

He met her eyes. "You're taking the full force of the shift straight into your body. Into your nerves. Into your blood."

His voice lowered. "You're not surviving because you're stronger. You're surviving because you're letting the ink burn through you instead of the system."

"And Edris?"

"He tried to unwrite the Architect," Tavian said grimly. "There is no shield for that."

"There's more," Alis added, her voice dropping. She slid a single, jagged page across the table. "Edris wasn't the only one marked for deletion. This is a salvage list—names that the Tyrant tried to erase, but couldn't."

Nera looked down. The list was short. And at the bottom, written in a hand that looked frantic:

*Nerith Calloway.*

"The Council didn't stutter yesterday, Nera," Alis said softly. "They weren't getting your name wrong. They were reading the only file they have left."

A sharp crash cut through the silence.

Kieran stumbled back against the hearth, his hand knocking a heavy iron poker to the floor. He wasn't looking at Alis. He was staring at Nera, his face drained of color, one hand pressed hard against his temple as if trying to hold his skull together.

"Nerith," he whispered.

It didn't sound like a question. It sounded like an exhale—a breath he had been holding for years.

## CHAPTER THIRTY-THREE

# The Forgery

The voices in the safehouse had quieted, reduced to ripples as people broke off into smaller discussions. Some were still processing what had just been revealed, others were already acting. Nera, however, felt caught between the two—neither fully present nor detached enough to escape it.

She needed air.

Slipping away from the table, she moved toward the back of the house, stepping through the narrow doorway that led into the small courtyard behind. The night air was cool against her skin, the sharp contrast grounding her more than she wanted to admit.

High above, a bank of clouds drifted across the moon. They didn't billow; they fractured. As they passed through a patch of sky near the horizon, the vapor folded into sharp, geometric angles—triangles of mist—before unraveling back into soft clouds on the other side.

She leaned against the low stone wall, breathing slowly. The name—which seemed to be her name, but also not—still echoed in her head.

*Nerith Calloway.*

It was hers, wasn't it? It had to be. But she didn't remember it. Didn't know why it would have been marked for erasure yet still be here. Didn't know why the council had called her by that name as if it were something unquestioned, something certain.

Footsteps behind her barely made a sound, but she wasn't surprised when Kieran appeared at her side. He didn't speak at first, just studied her with that quiet intensity he always carried, the one that made it impossible to ignore that he was paying attention.

"You don't know why it's on the list," he finally said. It wasn't a question.

Nera shook her head. "No."

Kieran looked toward the sky before settling back on her. "Do you believe it is your name?"

That was the problem, wasn't it? She didn't know.

Her fingers curled slightly against the rough stone beneath her hand. "I don't know what I believe. What I'm supposed to believe. Maybe."

Kieran looked at her thoughtfully, his gaze drifting from her eyes to the scar on her palm. His hand twitched, reaching out as if to cover it—a reflex, fast and unconscious—before he caught himself and pulled back.

"It doesn't change anything," he said, his voice dropping to a rough whisper. "I found you. The name doesn't matter."

Nera frowned. "Found me?"

Kieran froze. A flash of genuine confusion crossed his face, as if he hadn't realized he'd said it. "I meant ... in the ruins," he corrected quickly, turning away. "We should go back inside. It doesn't change anything."

Something about the certainty in his voice made her chest heave. She looked away, back toward the courtyard wall, forcing herself to relax. "We need to figure out what we're doing next."

Kieran nodded, as if acknowledging that the moment was over. "Cyrus will also want to understand everything first. But I think we both know where this is leading."

"The Nameless Market," Nera said.

"The market," he confirmed.

"We should go back inside," she said quietly. Kieran didn't move right away. But then, finally, he stepped back. "Alright."

They walked in together, reentering the safehouse just as the discussion at the main table was beginning to take shape. Cyrus had unrolled one of the newer maps over the table, while Tobias arranged the most important documents beside it. The others had gathered again, the earlier tension still present but sharpened now into something more focused.

"The Nameless Market is the logical next step to gather the type of information we need now," Cyrus said, confirming what most of them already knew. "We failed last time because we looked for the wrong thing. We didn't know the language for the question we were asking."

Tobias tapped a sheet of parchment, glancing at the others. "The Market trades in what the Archive discards. If Edris failed to erase the Tyrant, someone sold him the ink to do it. We go find the supplier."

Theron leaned back in his chair, arms crossed. "Is the Market is roaming again? Do we actually have a location, or are we just wandering the map hoping to stumble into the right box?"

"Last known location was three weeks ago, shifting east," Tyrek said, rubbing his jaw. "If it's holding the pattern, it won't be far from that."

"But we don't know for sure," Alis added. "Not until we start looking," Tyrek agreed.

Cyrus glanced across the table. "We divide the labor. One team targets the Market. The rest stay here to monitor the timeline for updates."

"I need to help Liaz gather information at the tavern," Tyrek mentioned, "so I'll stay here."

Nera was already stepping forward before anyone could finish deciding. "I'm going to the market."

No one argued, though she caught the way Cyrus studied her for a second longer than necessary.

Kieran, unsurprisingly, gave a short nod. "I'm going too."

Cael sighed. "Well, I hate being left out, so I suppose that makes three of us."

Sarina marked their names down, then looked to Alis. Alis smiled faintly. "Please ... as if I'm going to miss this."

Tavian leaned forward slightly, considering. "I'll stay and map changes here. Someone needs to document what's happening in real time."

Cyrus settled back slightly. "Then it's decided. Those of us staying will coordinate with the contacts we already have in place. The rest of you will head for the market at first light." The discussion lasted a little longer, but the course was set.

As the group dispersed, Nera felt the decision settle over her. The Nameless Market had always been dangerous, always been unpredictable.

Nera looked at the list—at the name Nerith at the bottom—and then at the map. She finally understood why Edris had failed. He had tried to make the world clean. He had tried to cut out the rot without damaging the host.

She looked up, her gaze hardening. "We aren't going there to investigate," Nera said, her voice steady. She looked at Cael, then Kieran. "We are going there to finish what Edris started."

"That risks a total collapse," Cyrus warned from the table, his fingers pausing over his calculations. "If you force a correction on a timeline this unstable, the architecture will not hold."

Nera picked up the quill, feeling the weight of it. "I know. But we can't fix this without breaking something."

## CHAPTER THIRTY-FOUR
# The Cost of Knowledge

They decided to leave the city under the cover of a pre-dawn grey, trading the uneasy quiet of the safehouse for the open exposure of the road Two days of hard riding had put miles between them and Varethis, but the distance hadn't lessened the tension of Nera's choice.

The road stretched ahead, winding toward the distant horizon, but something was wrong. The way it curved wasn't quite right—like a map being redrawn as they walked.

Nera shifted in her saddle, instinctively tightening her grip on the leather reins. Her left hand registered the bite of the strap, but her right felt nothing. The numbness was creeping past her wrist now, a cold, silent tide moving up her forearm. She wrapped the leather tighter around her glove, forcing the hold visually since she couldn't feel it, and kept her eyes forward.

They moved faster now, having covered most of the distance to where the market should be, pushing their pace to reach the coordinates Alis had purchased.

The group had left before first light, moving quickly along the lesser-used roads that wound toward the last known location of the Nameless Market. They had heard reports that Belvar and his

Enforcers were in the area, so they watched their surroundings carefully.

The journey had been tense but uneventful—until now. She realized they weren't alone.

Kieran was the first to notice. His shoulders tensed slightly, just enough to make it clear that something was wrong. Nera caught his movement from the corner of her eye. "What is it?"

Kieran only stared, his eyes giving away nothing. Then, in a voice just low enough for her to hear, he said, "We're being followed. And not by Belvar."

Alis, riding right behind them, smirked. "Took them long enough."

Nera's stomach dropped. The assassins. She hadn't seen them since the night they had first attacked, at the market where they were headed, yet the assassins had no way of remembering that if she had completed that rewrite correctly. Now, it seemed, they were back, although they had likely forgotten that encounter.

She slowed her horse slightly, shifting her weight, her hand resting near the dagger at her calf. The others followed suit, sensing the change. They passed a mile marker split clean down the middle, the wood scorched black not by fire, but by the same dissolving ink Nera had seen in the archive. Belvar had been here.

One moment, the road ahead was empty. The next, a figure stood in the center of the path, cloaked, masked, utterly motionless.

Kieran pulled his horse up, his hand hovering near his blade. "Don't move," he murmured.

Nera's gaze snapped to the treeline. Six more figures stood against the grey sky, having stepped into existence from the blind spots of her vision. Bows held low. Arrows nocked. Waiting.

Kieran's hand snapped to his hip. In the same breath, he spurred his horse sideways, forcing its bulk between Nera and the ridge.

Cael shouted, "What are you—"

*Twhip.*

The arrow struck dirt where Nera's horse had stood a second before. Kieran froze, blade raised toward the ridge, chest heaving. He hadn't seen the archer. Hadn't heard the bowstring. He had just moved.

"Three on the ridge," he said calmly, already tracking. He spoke to her like a combatant. "Ready?"

Nera tightened her grip on the reins and pulled free of Cael, her dagger sliding into her hand. Figures jumped from the treeline with the heavy, lethal grace of predators, sealing the path. Bows drawn. Blades ready.

They moved with certainty. They had been waiting.

The leader approached from the road, the same masked figure, his long curved blade still sheathed at his side.

"Stay your hand, Voss," he said, voice grinding. "We are not here to kill you unless you force us to."

Kieran didn't lower his weapon. He moved his horse between Nera and the ridge.

The assassin's gaze lingered on the scar along Kieran's jaw as he stepped closer. "Now we find out if you are useful."

Nera kept her hand near her dagger, heart hammering. "Useful how?"

His attention shifted to her, cold and transactional. "The Nameless Market has barred us, but it will welcome you."

"And if I refuse?" Nera asked, reins tight in her grip.

"We are not here to harm anyone, Scribe," the assassin said softly, sheathing his blade but not stepping back. "We are here to open a door. The Market has barred us, but it will welcome you. Enter the Market. Retrieve the record of the First Break."

"Understand our rule: we contain outcomes we don't understand. We do not know if you are the cure for history or just another poison. Prove your intent is to restore the truth, our interests align and we become allies. But until we know you serve history and not power, you are a risk we must manage."

"That still doesn't explain why we should help you," Nera insisted.

He leaned closer, his voice dropping to a lethal whisper. "Refuse, and we will ensure you never reach the entrance."

She looked left. Kieran was now boxed in by two archers, his knuckles white on his reins. She looked right. Cael was free and sat tall in his saddle, hand resting near his own dagger. He moved his eyes, measuring the distance to the assassins before looking up at Nera. She looked at him with a question in her eyes. *Do we fight?*

Cael's gaze flicked to hers. For a heartbeat, she expected him to draw, to bluff, to offer some clever deflection. Instead, he slowly moved his hand *away* from his weapon. He crossed his arms over his chest and settled back in his saddle. His face was perfectly smooth, perfectly cold. He sat idle, waiting for her to surrender.

Kieran's blade was half-drawn, his muscles coiled to strike. "I can take the leader," Kieran murmured to Nera. "On my signal."

"Stand down, Voss," Cael said loudly, his voice cutting through the tension. He looked directly at the Assassin leader. "We aren't fighting. My friend here is feeling protective, but he's not stupid. We'll do what you want."

Kieran whipped his head around, betrayal flashing in his eyes. "Cael, shut up."

"I'm negotiating," Cael said coldly, looking at Nera. "Because unlike him, I know you can't dodge an arrow at this range. Agree, Nera. Don't let Kieran get you killed for pride."

"Fine. Let's talk," Nera choked out, her gaze still on Cael. The assassin nodded once, as if unsurprised by the answer. This, whatever it was, had been inevitable. And they were running out of time to avoid it.

The group dismounted, stepping cautiously off the road and into the shade of the tree cover just beyond the path. The assassins had already moved ahead, choosing a clearing where the light barely filtered through the thick canopy above. It was quiet here, removed from the dust and openness of the road, an intentional choice.

Nera watched the leader carefully as he adjusted his stance—just far enough away to keep the advantage if this turned into a fight. It wouldn't. But the instinct was still there.

The masked assassin tilted their head slightly. "We aren't here to debate philosophy, Scribe. We are here for a trade."

Nera didn't flinch. "I didn't know you bartered."

"The Market hides the name of the one who broke history and you can access it for us," the leader said, stepping closer.

"And if we say no?" Cael asked. The leader raised his blade. There it was. No truce. No alliance. Just a reluctant acknowledgment that neither side could afford to be blind to what was happening.

He lowered the blade an inch, but his muscles remained coiled. "We do not tolerate those who twist history but you can get the name we need. Go in, and bring it to us. Otherwise we have no use for you."

Something in the way he said it made the hairs on the back of Nera's neck stand up. "And we correct the error of your existence right now."

"I wasn't aware I gave permission for an execution." The voice boomed through the clearing, smooth, cold, and terrifyingly familiar.

The Assassin leader whipped toward the road.

Master Belvar sat atop his horse at the crest of the road, blocking their retreat flanked by over a dozen Enforcers who had emerged silently from the trees. His face was a blank page, but his eyes were locked on the Preservationists.

"Belvar," the assassin spat. "Archive dog."

"Preservationist filth," Belvar replied calmly.

He looked down at the Preservationists with cold, imperious boredom. "You are trespassing on a revision in progress," Belvar said, his voice carrying effortlessly over the wind. He raised a hand, his Enforcers drawing their weapons in unison.

The Assassin leader looked from Belvar to Nera. "This isn't over." Then, they were gone, dissolving into the woods, retreating before the larger group of Enforcers could engage.

Nera gripped her reins, waiting for the order, the arrow, the charge. But Belvar raised a hand—palm out. "Hold!"

"You're letting them go?" one of the Enforcers muttered, confused.

Belvar's eyes locked onto Nera's. A faint, cruel smile touched his lips. "They are running to the Market," he said, loud enough for them to hear. "Let them run. They are only delivering themselves to the door I have already locked."

He pulled his horse around. "Come. We have prepared the stage; let the actors find their marks." The Enforcers turned and followed him, vanishing over the ridge.

Nera sat frozen, her heart pounding harder than if she had fought. "Why?" Cael whispered, the silence of the road suddenly deafening. "Why didn't they stop us?"

Kieran sheathed his blade, his face pale. "Because he thinks the Market will finish us for him."

Nera didn't respond. Her thoughts were still turning over what had just happened, what the assassin had asked. The one who stopped the rewrite. They had been looking for that answer, too.

"We should keep moving," Kieran said. Nera nodded, forcing herself to focus.

The Market was still ahead. Whatever waited there had already claimed its first bets.

## CHAPTER THIRTY-FIVE

# The Only Way Through

The road twisted before them, narrowing as the trees thickened. The last known location of the Nameless Market had been marked on an old, half-faded map, but they knew better than to rely solely on it. The market never stayed in one place long.

The first sign they were getting close was the stillness. The usual sounds of the forest had faded—no birds, no rustling leaves, just an unnatural stillness pressing against the air.

Alis adjusted the strap of her pack, casting a glance toward Nera. "Feels about right."

Kieran scanned the tree line with the blank focus of a soldier waiting for an order. "They don't want it to be found easily now."

"They never do," Alis stated.

"So, what now?" Cael asked. He turned his head to the right, a dry comment about the mud already on his lips. "You'd hate this part, Liv. It's all—"

He stopped. The empty space beside him screamed silently. His mouth snapped shut with an audible click, his eyes glazing over as the habit caught him mid-turn, reaching for someone who was no longer there. He shoved his hands deeper into his pockets, staring straight ahead, and didn't speak.

Without commenting on his slip, Alis led them slightly right. The path narrowed further, curving sharply before opening into a clearing that hadn't been there moments ago. Tucked between the trees, partially obscured by hanging cloth and lanterns that cast shifting shadows, was the entrance.

The smell of old paper and burning incense curled through the air, mixing with the faint metallic tang of ink, telling them they had reached their destination. The marketplace itself was barely visible beyond the entryway.

And at the entrance, arms crossed menacingly, were the two guards in their red uniforms. Their clothing blended into the deep reds and greys of the market's threshold. They stood at attention, eyes sharp and assessing—neither old nor young, neither hostile nor welcoming.

"You took your time," the guard on the left said, voice smooth, deliberate.

Nera met their gaze evenly. "Didn't know we had a schedule to keep."

The guard tilted his head slightly. "Everyone does. Whether they realize it or not."

Alis sighed. "Are you letting us in, or is this going to be another long conversation about the philosophy of time?"

The guard's lips twitched, but it wasn't quite a smile. "You assume you belong here."

"Does anyone?" Cael muttered.

The Gatekeeper ignored him, focusing on Nera. "The market chooses who enters."

Nera felt the statement settle over her. The people who ran it had always been careful about who they let through its doors. And they weren't about to make it easy.

The Gatekeeper blocked the way. "Your credit is thin, Alis. You have one marker left. You can use it to enter now, or you can save it for the exit when things go wrong. You cannot do both."

Alis hesitated, her hand hovering over her belt. She looked at Nera, then back at the Gatekeeper. "We enter now."

The Gatekeeper stepped aside. "You may enter. Then pray that you do not need to leave in a hurry."

Then, their gaze moved to Kieran. A pause. "You as well."

But when they reached Cael, they didn't speak. The quiet hung heavy between them. Cael raised an eyebrow. "What? Not charming enough for you?"

The Gatekeeper didn't respond immediately. Then, slowly, they said, "The market does not always welcome those who carry too many shadows."

Cael blinked. "That's incredibly ominous." The Gatekeeper remained silent.

Nera immediately stepped forward. "We came together. We're not leaving anyone behind."

The Gatekeeper's gaze flicked back to her, face devoid of all emotion. "Then be certain you can afford the cost."

Nera didn't waver. "We can."

The Gatekeeper studied her for another moment before finally stepping aside. "Then enter. But remember—once inside, you bargain with more than coin."

They moved back, allowing the group to pass.

As Nera stepped forward, the shadows of the Nameless Market swallowed her whole.

The moment they stepped through the threshold, the space around them warped with the fluidity of slipping into a story already halfway told. The paths were uneven, twisting in ways that made it impossible to get a sense of direction. Stalls leaned at odd angles, shelves stacked high with goods that defied logic—books bound in languages no one should remember, artifacts from places that never existed, trinkets that pulsed with something lost.

Soft lantern light cast shadows where there should have been none, and the crowd moved with quiet efficiency. There was no shouting, no haggling, none of the usual chaos of a trade hub. Deals were made in hushed voices, agreements sealed with nods or gestures, the exchange of goods quick and deliberate.

Kieran was already scanning the space, his movements careful, measured. He didn't like it here—not in the way of fear, but in the way of someone who had learned to survive in dangerous places instinctively recognized another one.

Alis, on the other hand, looked at home. She was breathing easy, her eyes flicking between the stalls, her fingers briefly skimming the edge of a wooden counter as she passed. She didn't pause long enough to seem interested in anything, but Nera knew. She was cataloging. Memorizing.

"Every time I come here, it feels changed," Kieran noted.

Nera glanced at him. "Because it is different."

He smirked. "Yeah. That's what worries me."

A figure moved past them, wrapped in deep grey, their face half-obscured by the jittering light. The market was full of people like that—traders, seekers, those who had long since stopped belonging anywhere else.

And then there were the ones who did belong.

Nera caught sight of a merchant whose face she recognized, though she had never spoken to them. Another who had given them information once, only to disappear for months after. The market was as much a place of secrets as it was of trade, and that was what made it dangerous.

She felt Kieran step slightly closer, not touching but near enough to be a presence at her side. "We need to find the leader," he said quietly.

Alis nodded. "And to do that, we need to start making the right people notice us."

The market chose who it let in. But it also chose who it answered to. And they were about to find out if it had anything to say. The trick to the Nameless Market wasn't just knowing where to look—it was knowing who and how to ask.

Walking slowly, Nera let the market move around her, resisting the urge to act like a seeker. If you entered the market looking too hard for something, you ended up leaving with nothing. Or worse, with a price you didn't realize you had agreed to pay.

Ahead, Alis brushed her fingers over the edge of a stall, stopping in front of a merchant she seemed to recognize, while Kieran and Cael flanked Nera without speaking, their presence solid yet unobtrusive.

The first merchant they approached was an older woman with ink-stained hands, her sleeves rolled to her elbows, the smell of parchment and pressed oil clinging to her. She barely glanced at them before turning a page of the book in front of her.

"You're not here for books," she said, voice quiet but knowing.

Nera didn't let the flash of surprise show. "No."

The woman nodded once, as if pleased with the answer. "Then what is it?"

"We're looking for someone," Kieran said.

She lifted a brow. "Everyone here is looking for someone."

Cael sighed, crossing his arms. "We need the leader of this place."

At that, the merchant finally looked up. She studied them one by one before closing the book in front of her with a slow, deliberate movement, recognition in her eyes. "And why would you need that?"

Alis stepped in before Nera could respond. "Because we have something worthy of their time."

The merchant's lips twitched, almost a smirk. "Do you?"

"Yes," Alis said easily. "But we don't waste information on middlemen."

The merchant hummed, leaning back slightly. "You assume I'm a middleman."

Alis tilted her head slightly, offering a sharp smile. "Everyone here is."

The woman slowly ran a finger along the book's worn spine. "There's a price for knowledge in this market."

"There always is," Alis said. The merchant looked at her with a mildly curious expression. Then, finally, she nodded.

"West end," she said. "Find the stall with the black lanterns. Knock twice, then once. If they want to speak to you, they will."

Nera nodded. "Thank you."

The woman smirked. "Don't thank me yet."

As they turned to leave, Cael muttered, "I hate this place."

Kieran adjusted the strap of his cloak, his gaze already moving toward the west end of the market. "Then let's not stay longer than we need to."

Nera considered what came next. They had the location. Nera had the uneasy sense that agreeing to speak was not the same thing as being allowed to leave.

## Chapter Thirty-Six

# The Curator

The west end of the market felt heavier.

The stalls were more spaced out, the people fewer, but the air was thicker with something unspoken. These weren't merchants selling to travelers or rebels looking for scraps of lost history. The ones who lingered here were those who dealt in knowledge the world wasn't supposed to remember.

The stall stood at the farthest edge, where the market met the heavy stone walls that seemed to form its ever-shifting boundary. Three black lanterns hung above the entrance, their glass panes dark, absorbing light instead of casting it.

Nera stopped just outside, resisting the urge to glance over her shoulder. She could still feel the market behind her, the silent watchers who had likely marked their movements the moment they stepped inside.

Alis was the first to move. She approached the wooden stall with the same easy confidence she carried everywhere, but there was a sharpness to the way her fingers traced the edge of the counter, as if testing for hidden traps.

She knocked on the countertop twice. Then once.

The moment stretched. Nera held her breath, waiting. Then, from behind the heavy cloth that covered the back of the stall, a voice.

"Who seeks the The Curator?" It wasn't an invitation; it was a test.

Alis glanced at Nera before answering. "Those who have something to trade."

The fabric parted just enough for a figure to emerge. The Curator defied expectation. No opulence, no disguise—just a dark tunic, clean hands, steady eyes. Their presence was quiet, but undeniable.

They studied the group before finally speaking. "You come looking for answers. But you are not the first."

A chill slid down her spine. Someone had been here before them.

The market's leader motioned to the small space behind the stall. "Come inside. Let us see if your trade is worth the price."

Nera stepped forward, knowing that whatever happened next, they had already stepped too deep to turn back.

The space inside the stall felt dense, the air pressing against their skin with the suffocating mass of hoarded secrets. It wasn't just the scent of aged parchment and oil-burning lamps—it was something heavier, something woven into the walls themselves. This was a place where knowledge didn't just live. It was kept. Guarded.

The Curator moved with quiet certainty, closing the curtain behind them before settling into a simple wooden chair.

Nera forced herself to meet their gaze evenly. "We need information."

The Curator folded their hands in their lap. "Everything here has a cost."

Alis leaned against the counter, her movements casual, but Nera could see the sharpness in her posture, the way she was already watching for the angles in this exchange. "We know that," she said. "And we're willing to pay it."

The Curator hummed slightly, tilting their head. "You assume the price is one you can afford."

Cael leaned back slightly, crossing his arms, body tense, whispering, "I hate how this place talks."

The Curator barely spared him a glance before returning their focus to Nera. "You seek something dangerous. Something that was meant to be forgotten."

"We're looking for the one who stopped the rewrite," Nera said.

The Curator did not react immediately. They didn't blink but something in the air changed, as if the walls themselves had inhaled.

Kieran, standing just behind Nera's shoulder, remained still, but she could feel the tension in him, his hand hovering near his blade.

Finally, The Curator spoke. "You are looking in the wrong place."

A twitch of frustration flicked across Nera's face. "What does that mean?"

The Keeper's gaze was steady. "You think the answer lies in a name. A single person. But rewrites do not fail because of one hand alone. There are always pieces left behind, traces of what was, lingering in the fabric of things."

Alis narrowed her eyes. "So you're saying no one stopped it?"

"I am saying," The Curator said slowly, "that it was not one. There were many. And it was not done with intention, but with something far worse."

"What was it done with?"

The Curator paused. "Desperation."

Goosebumps prickled across Nera's skin. *Desperation.* The word sat wrong, heavy, like something trying to find its place in her thoughts.

Kieran's voice was low, edged with something careful. "What do you know about the rewrite failing?"

The Curator regarded him before standing and moving to a shelf at the back of the stall, running their fingers along the spines of half-bound ledgers before pulling one free. When they returned, they put the book on the table in front of them.

It was old—older than most things Nera had ever seen. The pages were thick, yellowed with time, the ink faded but still legible.

The Curator opened to a marked section and turned the book toward them. Nera's breath caught in her throat. It was a fragment of something rewritten.

Kieran leaned in slightly, scanning the page. "This shouldn't exist."

"No, it should not," the Curator agreed.

Cael frowned, squinting at the faded script. "What does it say?"

Nera clenched her jaw, forcing herself to read it aloud.

> *It is done. The Tyrant is gone. The war is over. And history will never remember the names that undid him.*

Alis was the first to speak. "But he's still here." It was half question and half statement.

The Curator nodded once. "Yes. He is." Nera clenched her jaw. "Then why does this exist?"

Their expression was unreadable. "Because once, for the briefest moment, it was true." The words shook her.

Kieran straightened slightly, his voice steady but low. "The rewrite worked."

"For a time, yes."

Nera's pulse hammered. "Then why didn't it hold?"

The Curator closed the book slowly, resting a hand on its cover. "Because something pulled him back."

The room felt too small, the sentence pressing against the walls themselves. Alis raked a hand through her hair. "Undone," she whispered.

The Curator inclined their head slightly. "Something, or someone, resisted."

Nera stared at the closed book, her thoughts racing. If the rewrite had worked, even briefly. Something forced history to realign itself. Someone had reached into the fabric of time and ripped the Tyrant back into existence.

And they had no idea who had done it.

The Curator watched them carefully. "Now you understand why the market does not part with knowledge freely. Some truths are not meant to be found."

Their gaze dropped to Nera's hand—specifically, to the shiny, puckered scar on her palm. "And some truths leave a mark."

Nera instinctively curled her fingers, hiding the scar. "What do you want?"

"I have the record of the First Break," the Curator said, tapping the book between them. "But I also have the record you have been searching for since you were ten years old. The name your mother threw into the fire. The identity of your father."

The air left the room. Nera froze, her heart hammering a frantic rhythm against her ribs. She took a step forward, the mission momentarily forgotten. "You know who he is?"

"I know why he left, which is enough." The Curator leaned back, their expression unreadable. "The Market demands a balance, Nera Calloway. I can give you the history of the world. Or I can give you the history of your blood."

Cael stepped forward, his eyes wide. "Nera..."

The Curator's fingers stilled on the book. "This offer is not a door I leave unlocked. What you do not take now, you do not choose later."

She looked at the book—the key to stopping the Tyrant, to saving the timeline, to keeping Cael and Kieran safe. Then she looked at the Curator, her chest aching with the weight of the question she had carried her entire life.

She could finally know. She could finally understand why her father had left her behind. But if she took that answer, the Tyrant would win.

She closed her eyes, pausing, then exhaling a breath that shook her to her core. When she opened her eyes, they were hard. "I don't need to know who he was," she decided, the lie tasting like ash. "I need to know how to stop this."

She pushed her own desire aside, leaving her origin in the dark. "Keep his name. Give me the leverage we need." The Curator studied her, a flicker of something like pity—or perhaps respect—in their eyes. "A heavy price. But paid."

Nera forced herself to focus. "What do you want in exchange for the rest of the story?" her voice sounding steadier than she felt.

The Keeper looked at her, considering. "What makes you think I am willing to part with it?"

"Because if you weren't, you wouldn't have told us this much."

A memory of something—approval or amusement—crossed the Keeper's expression, but it was gone too fast to name. The Curator moved to the back of the stall again, pulling a smaller book from one of the shelves, this one wrapped in dark fabric. They ran a careful hand over the cover before setting it between them.

"I do not deal in coin," they said. "I deal in knowledge."

Kieran slowly moved to the side. "What kind of knowledge?"

The Curator looked at Nera. "Yours."

A sense of foreboding settled over Nera. Alis glanced at her before speaking. "That's a vague request. Try again."

The Curator didn't look away from Nera. "You seek answers about the past. I want something from the present."

Nera straightened. "What?"

"A name." The Keeper's voice was smooth, but there was something heavier behind it. "There is someone within the Archive who does not belong. Someone whose name should not exist in their records. I want the name of the person who forced me into exile. You will find them for me."

The words settled between them like a challenge.

Alis scoffed. "You're asking us to hunt down a ghost in the most protected structure in the known world."

The Keeper's lips twitched, just barely. "I am asking you to find a name."

"And if we do?" Nera asked.

The Curator tapped a hand against the closed book between them. "Then I will give you the rest of the story. The moment the rewrite failed. The names of those who were erased. And information that will help you understand how to revise it."

A sharp, quiet weight settled in Nera's chest. The name of the one who had undone the rewrite.

Kieran glanced at her, his mouth pressing into a thin, grim line, his posture screaming that he didn't like this. Neither did she. But they didn't have a choice.

Nera absently touched the pocket where she keeps her map. "We'll find the name."

The Curator nodded once, satisfied. "Then the market will be waiting."

The deal was sealed.

As they stepped back into the market's twisting paths, Nera felt the full implication of what had just happened. They had a new path forward. But it was going to lead them straight into the heart of the archives. And they weren't going to walk away unchanged.

They stepped away from the market stall, back into the maze of pathways, but the Curator's words followed them.

The task they had been given felt impossible. Find a name that shouldn't exist. A name hidden within the Grand Archive—a place that had burned to the ground.

Nera felt it like a stone in her chest. The Grand Archive had burned. She had been there. They had been there. Cael had lost Livia. She could still smell the smoke, feel the heat clawing at her skin, hear the collapse of the structure as fire consumed it.

But almost no one around them remembered the fire. The market continued as if nothing had changed, as if the world hadn't rewritten itself while they weren't looking.

Kieran's voice was low, steady, but there was something sharp beneath it. "This is wrong."

"You think?" Cael smirked. He gestured vaguely toward the rest of the market. "You know what's worse? No one's talking about it. No hushed rumors. No whispers about how the city lost its most powerful structure overnight. If the Grand Archive burned, people died, people should be trying to rebuild. They should be mourning."

Alis tilted her head slightly, her gaze thoughtful. "So it was rewritten. Then where is it?"

The question settled heavily between them.

Kieran shook his head. "If the Grand Archive still exists somewhere, we need to find out where. Fast."

"Assuming it still holds any of the prior records," Cael muttered. "For all we know, the rewrite wasn't just a location update. It could be entirely different now."

Nera pressed her lips together. The thought made her stomach turn. If the Grand Archive had been rewritten into something else, then the information inside could have been altered too. The truths they needed may no longer be the same.

Alis glanced toward the edge of the market, where the paths twisted out of sight. "We're not getting answers here. But I know someone who might know where to start looking."

Nera lifted a brow. "Someone we can trust?"

Alis smirked. "Of course not. But they like me better than most."

Cael sighed. "That's not reassuring."

Kieran was already adjusting the strap of his cloak. "Let's go."

Nera twisted the ring on her finger absently. The Grand Archive was gone, but it wasn't. And if they were going to walk into its shadow, they had to be ready for whatever was waiting on the other side.

The market stretched behind them, twisting into its ever-changing paths, but Alis led them away from the Curator's stall with the certainty of someone who knew exactly where she was going.

They moved quickly, slipping through narrow alleys and cutting through side streets until the hum of the market began to fade. The shadows deepened here, the lanterns fewer, the air thick with the scent of damp stone and something metallic beneath it.

Nera glanced at Kieran, but he said nothing, his attention fixed ahead. Cael was quieter than usual, his hands tucked into his coat, his sharp gaze flicking toward every movement around them.

Finally, Alis stopped outside a doorway that looked indistinguishable from the dozen they had passed before it. The wood was worn, the metal latch rusted, but the way she hesitated before knocking told Nera that whoever was inside wasn't just another merchant.

Alis knocked, paused, then a final, deliberate tap.

The door creaked open, revealing a dimly lit interior. A man stood inside, silhouette sharp against the lantern glow, features half-hidden beneath the hood of a faded cloak.

He didn't speak right away, just leaned against the doorway, arms crossed.

"I should have known you'd be back eventually," Enri said, their voice smooth, laced with something almost amused.

Alis smiled, tilting her head. "And yet you still opened the door."

He paused, then stepped aside. "Get in before I change my mind."

Nera hesitated for only a moment before following Alis inside. Kieran and Cael stepped in behind her, their movements careful, measured.

The door shut behind them with a quiet finality.

The space was small but cluttered, filled with shelves lined with old papers, ledgers, and objects Nera didn't immediately recognize. A desk sat near the back, covered in ink-stained parchment and stacks of unbound books. The air smelled of wax and aged parchment, with a faint hint of something burned lingering beneath it.

Alis leaned against one of the shelves, casual but not careless. "We need information."

Enri arched a brow. "Of course you do. And here I thought you just missed me."

Cael scoffed. "Yes, I'm sure we're all very sentimental. Where's the Grand Archive now?"

The humor in Enri's expression faded slightly. He moved to the desk, fingers trailing absently over the edge of an open book.

"It didn't burn," he said after a moment. "Not like you remember."

Nera felt the floor seem to tilt beneath her boots. "What does that mean?"

He looked up at her. "It means the Grand Archive still exists. But it's not where you left it."

"The fire was real," Enri continued, voice dropping low. "The smoke, the heat, the death—that happened. But the Council couldn't admit they lost their greatest fortress to the Preservationists. So, they didn't fix the building; they fixed the history. They rewrote the Archive to have always stood in the north, safe and untouched."

He leaned forward. "The world accepted the lie. It forgot the fire. But you... you were there. You carry the burns of a timeline that no longer officially exists. That is why your friend is gone, even if the records say she couldn't have died in a building that wasn't there."

Cael's jaw tightened, the logic grating against his grief. "But why move it?" he demanded, his voice sharp. "If they have the power to rewrite reality from scratch—to create books and halls out of nothingness—why bother relocating the whole structure to the north? Why not just rewrite the fire out of existence and leave the building where it was?"

Enri shook his head slowly. "Because you can write over a memory, but you can't write over a wound. The physical destruction in Varethis was too absolute. The scar on the land was too deep. To simply 'undo' the fire in the same spot would have required an amount of power that would destabilize the city entirely."

He gestured to the map. "It is cleaner to build a new lie in a pristine place, and fill it with a bunch of newly created 'records' than to bury the truth under a pile of fresh ash. They moved it because the ground here remembers the heat."

Kieran's posture tensed slightly. "Then where is it?"

A pause. Enri glanced toward one of the shelves before pulling out a folded map and spreading it over the desk, pressing down the edges with quick, precise movements.

"Here," he said, tapping a point on the map.

Nera stepped closer, scanning the marked location. It wasn't where the Grand Archive had once stood. This was further north, nestled deep within territory that had once been neutral.

Cael frowned. "That's impossible. There was never an Archive there."

Enri's lips twitched, but it wasn't quite a smile. "Wasn't there?"

Nera's pulse quickened. It wasn't just that the Archive had been relocated. History had been rewritten to place it somewhere new—somewhere no one would question its presence. Somewhere the world believed it had always been.

"How do we get in?" Kieran asked.

Enri met his gaze, then Nera's. "You don't," he said simply.

A lull settled over the room, heavy and sharp.

Alis sighed, rubbing a hand over her face. "Somehow I knew you were going to say that."

Enri shrugged. "Then you should know what I'm going to say next, too."

"What's the price?" Nera asked.

He leaned back slightly, gaze steady. "That depends. How badly do you want to walk into a place that shouldn't exist?"

The room felt smaller, the air thicker. They had found the Grand Archive. But now, they had to find a way in. And that was going to cost them more than just time.

Nera kept her eyes on the map, the mark that shouldn't have existed staring back at her. "If they were right—if the Grand Archive had been rewritten to exist somewhere it had never been—then they weren't just looking for a way inside." They were looking for a way into something that had never been lost. And that was more dangerous than anything.

Alis paused and fixed Enri with a sharp look. "You're not going to waste our time pretending you don't know how to get in, are you?"

He smirked, tapping a finger against the edge of the map. "I didn't say there wasn't a way in."

"Then say what you mean," Kieran said, voice quiet but firm.

The amusement in Enri's expression didn't fade, but it dimmed slightly. He rolled the map closed, tapping it against his palm before setting it aside. "There's only one way inside the Grand Archive now," he said simply. "And it's not just through the front door."

"Shocking," said Cael.

Enri ignored him. "The new location has evolved security. Fewer external defenses, but the ones they do have are ... absolute."

Nera squared her shoulders, bracing for the news. "Absolute how?"

The figure tilted their head slightly. "How do you feel about walking into a place that doesn't believe you exist?"

The words landed heavier than they should have.

Kieran's body tensed, a momentary thought flitting behind his eyes. "What does that mean?"

Enri reached for a small leather-bound book from the shelf beside him, flipping through its pages before settling on one and turning it toward them. The ink was smudged in places, but the meaning was clear. Identification records. A list of names. Except some of them were crossed out.

Nera scanned the page, her pulse hammering. "They're tracking who's been rewritten."

"Not just tracking," he said. "Filtering. "Only Archivists who belong to the newest version of history are allowed inside now."

Cael's shoulders stiffened, as if history itself had settled on him. "And let me guess—we don't."

Alis tilted her head slightly, studying the list with narrowed eyes. "That depends."

Enri arched a brow. "On?"

Alis flicked her gaze toward Nera. "If she's already on their list."

The air hitched in Nera's chest, a reflexive reaction she couldn't suppress. The room was too still.

"You think they already expect her?" Kieran asked.

Alis didn't look away. "I think they already believe they know who she is."

Enri watched the exchange with interest before closing the book. "Whether they do or not, you still need a way in."

"Then tell us how," Nera demanded. Enri smirked. "You need to be rewritten." The words hung in the air, heavy and suffocating.

"That's not an option," Kieran said. The figure shrugged. "Then neither is getting inside."

Alis tapped a finger against her arm, thoughtful. "It's not permanent, is it?" Enri studied her. "No. But it's dangerous."

Cael scoffed. "Oh, well, if that's the worst of it."

Enri ignored him. "The market has people who deal in forged histories. They can alter records, slip you into the Archive's wards just enough to make you belong—at least on paper."

Nera swallowed. "And what happens if they realize we don't?"

Enri smiled. "Then you disappear. Completely, this time." Everyone paused. Kieran was the first to speak. "This is a mistake."

Alis sighed. "Probably."

Cael shook his head. "Definitely."

## CHAPTER THIRTY-SEVEN

# The Unwritten

Nera had barely processed the plan after they left, before the first change in the air made her skin prickle.

It wasn't something visible, not exactly. Just a feeling, a weight pressing against the edges of the space, the way the market sometimes felt like it was folding in on itself.

To her left, a merchant reached for a shimmering, unstable lantern hanging from his stall. His fingers brushed the metal—and passed straight through. The lantern flickered violently, and the merchant screamed. Nera watched in horror as his hand didn't just phase; it unraveled, turning into grey dust up to the wrist before he yanked the stump back against his chest, collapsing in agony. The people around him didn't run; they just stared, terrified, as if wondering who was next.

Then she saw them. The first figure stepped from the edge of the stall-lined path, their movements too smooth, too careful. A second and third followed. More silhouettes hovered at the edges, watching, waiting.

Kieran noticed them the same moment she did. His fingers twitched at his side, instinctively ready for a fight that hadn't started yet.

Unwritten. And they had been expecting them.

The one closest to them—a woman that may have once had dark hair and sharp, assessing eyes—spoke first. The air around her smelled of dried flowers and old regret. "You shouldn't be here."

Alis, unbothered, smirked. "That's funny. We were just told we need to be here."

The woman ignored her, gaze fixed on Nera. "You are looking for something dangerous." The woman's form flickered, the edges of her silhouette tearing like wet paper in the wind. She shuddered, a sound like dry leaves scraping stone, as if the act of holding herself together in this reality was an agony she barely tolerated. "The other scholar was just here," the woman hissed, the effort thinning her voice to a static whine. "He did not listen either. He demanded to speak to the First Unwritten. He walked into the silence to find him... and he walks the path of the Tyrant's shadow now."

Nera squared her shoulders, exhaling doubt before it could take root. *Soren.* "We're looking for the truth."

"The truth doesn't want to be found," the woman stated directly. Cael shoved his hands deep into his pockets but stood silent. "Fantastic," said Alis. "We're talking in riddles now."

Kieran didn't take his eyes off them. "Why are you here?"

The woman studied him. "Because you are." That sent a chill down Nera's spine.

Kieran staggered, a guttural sound tearing from his throat. He doubled over, gripping his head as if the timeline was physically splitting his skull.

"Stop," he gasped, squeezing his eyes shut. But when he opened them, he wasn't looking at the Unwritten. He was looking at Nera.

For a terrifying heartbeat, his pupils blew wide, swallowing the iris. He reached for her—not for her arm, but for her face—his fingers trembling.

"You were gone," he whispered, the words slurring with the weight of a memory that didn't belong here. "Why are you here?"

"Kieran!" Nera shouted, grabbing his shoulders.

The contact snapped him back. The moment broke. He stepped in front of her, reducing the space between them to inches, his blade drawn. The hesitation was gone; he was guarding her now with a ferocity that hadn't been there ten seconds ago—the ferocity of a man who had already watched her die once.

The Unwritten had always appeared alone.

Once, she had seen that rule bend.

This was the first time it had completely broken.

One of them stepped forward, a man whose face wavered oddly in the lamplight. "Don't go back," he stammered, picking at his own sleeve. "The walls eat you. I only wanted to fix a date. Just one date. And it took my whole year."

"If we stay out here, we lose a lot more than a year," Nera said, her voice hard. "The timeline is collapsing. I'd rather face the walls inside than the void out here."

The first woman tilted her head slightly. She didn't look afraid, she looked hungry. "Let them go," she told the man, her voice sharp. "If they break the seal, maybe the rest of us can spill out. Break it. Shatter it. I want to be free again."

She looked carefully at Alis, as if considering. "You need to understand the price."

Alis rolled her eyes. "Yes, yes, everything here costs something. We get it."

The woman turned toward her now. "And do you know what happens when something is rewritten incorrectly?" For the first time, Alis hesitated.

The woman's gaze sharpened. "Tell me, forger, what happens when you stitch a lie into a wound that won't heal?"

Alis' posture remained steady, but Nera caught the tension in her eyes, the way she shifted her weight just slightly. It wasn't that she didn't have an answer. It was that she didn't like the answer she had.

The Unwritten woman's voice was quieter when she spoke again. "It doesn't collapse. It festers. A lie in a broken history is poison, Scribe. It eats the surrounding tissue until there is nothing left to save."

Alis went still, her coin stilled in her fingers. She glanced at the bag that held her forgery kit, then at Nera, the metaphor landing. She wasn't just risking a lie; she was risking contamination.

Kieran looked directly at the woman. "You're saying if we rewrite ourselves into the Grand Archive—"

"You won't just change yourself," the woman said. "You will infect everything else. The more lies you feed into a history that's already unstable, the more dangerous it becomes."

Alis finally spoke, but her voice was measured now, not dismissive. "So you're saying we need to do it carefully."

The woman pondered for a bit, then, finally, she nodded slowly.

Alis turned to Nera. "Then let me handle it."

Nera blinked. "What?"

Alis rolled her shoulders. "I don't trust some back-alley market Scribes to rewrite us correctly. You don't just forge names, you forge history. If we're doing this, we do it my way."

The woman's gaze sharpened. "You think you can wear the mask without it becoming your face? The Archive does not hold guests, Scribe. It holds prisoners. If you write yourself in, the ink will swallow you whole and keep you there."

Kieran looked directly at the woman. "We're getting in. Whether the ink likes it or not." The woman laughed—a dry, rustling sound like dead leaves. "Then prepare to be forgotten."

Kieran gave a quiet laugh of his own. "Maybe it wouldn't be the first time," he said under his breath.

Nera paused, thoughtfully, then gave a small nod. "Ok, let's do it."

The Unwritten lingered a moment longer, then, as quickly as they had appeared, they faded back into the slithering shadows of the market. But Nera could still feel them watching. Waiting.

And for the first time since they had set foot in the market, she wondered if this was the step they wouldn't be able to come back from.

## Chapter Thirty-Eight

# Too Far In

Alis didn't waste time.

She led them away from the Unwritten's lingering presence, deeper into a section of the market where the paths twisted into narrower corridors, lined with stalls that dealt in things most people pretended didn't exist.

Nera followed without hesitation, but the weight of what they were about to do settled heavier with every step.

They were going to rewrite themselves into a structure that shouldn't exist.

Alis stopped in front of a stall that looked unremarkable—no strange artifacts, no visible records. Just a simple wooden counter and a low-burning lantern that barely cast enough light to see.

The man behind the stall barely glanced up as they approached. He was older, his hands ink-stained, his posture relaxed in a way that suggested he had never once been afraid of the world finding him.

Alis didn't greet him. Didn't waste time with pleasantries.

"I need a quiet space," she said. "And supplies."

The man sighed, rubbing at the corner of one eye. "You always need something, don't you?"

Alis smiled. "That's why I'm still alive."

The man motioned toward a back room. "Go. But don't bring trouble with you."

Alis offered a razor-thin smile. "No promises."

Nera followed her inside, Kieran and Cael close behind. The room was small, filled with stacks of parchment and ledgers piled high, the scent of old ink thick in the air.

Alis put her pack on the table, rolling her shoulders before turning to face them. "This is going to be delicate. I'm forging documents that say we are allowed to enter for a special project and adding that one line to the archive. If I do this wrong, the Archive's wards will reject us before we even step inside."

Cael sat on the edge of the table, arms crossed. "And by 'reject,' you mean …?"

Alis tapped a finger against the wooden surface. "Best case, we get turned away at the door. Worst case, we get erased or flat out killed."

"Then don't do it wrong," Nera commanded.

Alis grinned. "That's the plan."

She slammed a heavy book onto the table, the sound echoing in the small room. "You heard what that ghost said. 'The ink swallows you whole.'"

"Not a ghost," Nera said absently.

She looked up, her eyes sharp. "She wasn't being poetic. The Archive doesn't build walls to keep people out, Nera; it opens a door and pulls you in. If I write these false identities, the ink will hunt for a place to settle. If it can't find the truth, it will make the lie fit."

Kieran leaned against the far wall, hand casually resting near his dagger. "So how do we stop that?"

"We don't stop it. We anchor it." Alis grabbed a fresh sheet of parchment. "We need a tether. A truth heavy enough to trick the door into thinking we're real, even while we lie to it."

She looked at Nera. "That means you."

Nera stiffened slightly. "Me?"

"You're already tangled in the Archive's records somehow. They think they know who you are. If I anchor us to you, the rewrite is less likely to fail."

"And if I become part of the lie?"

Alis hesitated for the first time, her hand hovering over her writing kit. She looked at Nera, the usual smirk completely gone. "If I write this, Nera, and the Archive recognizes the lie, it won't just erase the entry. It will hunt the hands that wrote it." She looked down at her hands, fear finally cracking her mask. "I'm not just forging a pass. I'm signing my own warrant."

She took a breath, sharp and jagged. "Fine," she whispered, opening the kit. "But don't make me regret it."

\* \* \*

Hours passed.

Alis worked in silence, her pen gliding across the parchment with practiced ease, while Kieran and Cael remained watchful, scanning the room. Nera sat at the edge of the table, watching as Alis rewrote them.

Not their lives, not their pasts—just enough of their existence to slip through the Archive's doors unnoticed.

It should have felt simple. Instead, it felt fatal. Something about the ink on the page felt too final, too much like something she wouldn't be able to take back.

Alis leaned back with a quiet sigh, stretching her hands. "It's done."

Cael raised an eyebrow. "Just like that?"

Alis rolled her shoulders. "If I did it right."

Kieran approached, scanning the newly forged records. "And if you didn't?"

Alis' eyes gleamed. "Then we'll find out when we get to the Grand Archive."

Nera reached for the first parchment, running her fingers along the edges. The ink was dry. Set. She had walked into the Nameless Market as herself. She was walking out as someone or something else, at least in the official record.

The lie was in place. Now they just had to hope the Archive didn't reject them as an error before they ever stepped inside.

## Chapter Thirty-Nine
# Rewritten

The new Grand Archive towered over them, its white stone walls smooth and unmarked, defying time itself. The entrance was quiet, the kind of quiet that wasn't natural, but controlled. Engraved in the stone over the entrance was a new addition; next to the insignia of the Archivists the words *The Archive Never Forgets* had been added. Inside, history was contained like a caged beast, dangerous but tamed by ink and silence.

Nera, Cael, Kieran and Alis stood in the student work area in the courtyard by the side entrance, where Alis crouched over one of the many small desks normally used by Scribes as part of their studying, illuminated only by the glow of a single oil lamp. She was working fast now, copying the seal directly from the stone above the main entrance. The Archivists hadn't published it. They hadn't recorded it. The only place the new seal existed was carved into the Archive itself. There had been no way to finish that in advance.

"You sure about this?" she muttered without looking up, her voice tight with concentration. "Because I am exactly one forged document away from never being able to show my face in this city again."

Nera looked away, thinking. "If we don't do this, no one will have a face left to show."

Alis huffed quietly. "Dramatic. But fine."

The quill moved across the parchment, but Alis frowned, her hand shaking. "Your record isn't fighting me," she murmured, watching the ink race ahead of her nib. "It's anticipating me. The ink is pooling into the shape of the letters before I even finish the stroke." She looked up at Nera, unsettled. "It's not resisting, Nera. It's like the Archive is holding the door open for you."

She paused, dipping the quill again, but this time her hand hesitated as she moved to the next name. She looked up at Kieran, her eyes narrowing in genuine confusion.

"And you? You're even weirder."

Kieran slowly scanned the dark street. "I'm not in the system. I've been told that many times. That's why we're doing this."

"No, you don't get it," Alis corrected, her voice dropping to an unsettled whisper. She dipped the quill again, pressing harder. The tip scratched the parchment, but the ink didn't take, it didn't smear, it didn't bead. It simply vanished, as if the paper refused to acknowledge the stroke.

"It won't hold you," she said, her voice tight. "I can force Nera's record because there's resistance and that's something I can fight. But you?" She looked up at him, and for the first time, she looked genuinely unnerved.

"There's no friction, Voss. It's like trying to carve a name into water." She tapped the quill against the page. "You're not just erased. Erasure leaves a rough spot. But this ... this is like someone scrubbed the parchment perfect."

Kieran stared at the blank page. His jaw tightened, the muscles in his neck standing out as if he were bracing against a blow he refused to name. "Just get us inside," he said.

Alis dipped her quill into the ink again, flicking her wrist in precise motions, her forgery so convincing it would fool an Archivist at first glance, maybe even second. The page was a direct order for high-level access to the restricted archives, sealed with a counterfeit emblem that even Nera couldn't tell apart from the real one.

Kieran, standing at her side, watched the empty street with his usual sharp-eyed wariness. His posture was loose, relaxed in a way that wasn't relaxed at all—coiled, predatory.

"This is taking too long," he muttered, redistributing his weight from one foot to the other.

Alis shot him a glare. "Forging is an art, Voss. If you want, I can just scribble some ink and we can see how fast we get erased."

"Just hurry up."

Cael paced restlessly near the entrance. "We shouldn't even need a forgery. If history worked the way it was supposed to, the doors would be open to the truth."

Alis touched the quill to the paper one last time. The ink bit down, sending a thin tendril of smoke curling up. Alis hissed, clutching her own wrist as if the quill were drawing from her veins instead of the well. The black liquid hissed and burrowed into the parchment like a parasite seeking a vein. Fibers turned grey and rotted around the letters, pulsing with a faint, sickly rhythm.

But it wasn't just the paper rotting. "Alis," Kieran warned, pointing.

Starting at her fingertips, the color was draining out of Alis' skin. A lifeless, flat grey spread up her knuckles, chasing the veins like frostbite. It looked like the pigmentation was being sucked down the quill and spat out onto the page.

"Don't look at it," Alis gritted out, her teeth clenched as the grey crept past her wrist. "It comes back. Usually."

"Is it safe?" Kieran asked, his eyes on the smoking ink.

Alis stared at the mark—a parasite made of ink—watching it pulse like a fresh bruise. If she told them the truth, they would stop. If they stopped, they lost.

'Yes," Alis lied, her voice flat. She rolled the parchment quickly, hiding the burn mark before Nera could see it. "It's safe. Just don't let go."

She started to hand the scroll to Nera, but when their fingers brushed, Alis flinched, jerking it back as if she had been stung.

Nera moved toward the entrance, where normally a guard stood at post, barely visible beneath dim light of the Archive's outer lanterns.

The post stood empty. In place of a sentry, a slightly shimmering barrier, barely visible to the naked eye. "Well, this is new," Cael said as they all paused.

"Do you see that? Or are my eyes playing tricks on me," Alis asked.

Nera slowly walked closer, extending one hand tentatively, feeling a tingling sensation and a light pull surrounded by a cool breeze. "Definitely something here, like some type of magic that I've only read about in some really old accounts. I don't feel anything unsafe but it's also a solid barrier," she said. "Hand me the parchment."

Alis stepped forward and placed the curled paper into Nera's outstretched hand. Nera moved forward slightly and turned back with a smile. "Yes, I can feel the barrier release, it seems your skills worked."

Kieran stepped forward and took Nera's hand. "I think we should all go together. We may all need the document in hand." Nera nodded. Kieran reached back for Alis, and Alis reached for Cael, linking them in a single line.

As Nera pushed the door open through the shimmer, a raw charge stripped the fine hairs from her arms—a high-pitched frequency vibrating in her teeth as she pressed through.

Behind her, the reaction was violent. Kieran stumbled, the air around him cracking like a whip as the barrier tried to reject his mass, a ragged grunt tearing from his throat as if he'd been punched in the chest. Alis doubled over, gasping as if the air had turned to solid glass in her lungs, her face draining of color; while Cael hissed in pain, raising his free hand to shield his eyes as if facing a blinding light.

"It felt like walking through fire," Cael gasped, straightening with effort.

Nera looked at her own hands. They weren't shaking. They were humming. The veins in her right wrist darkened, pulsing in perfect, synchronized rhythm with the thrum of the barrier. It felt more like a handshake than an attack. "It recognizes me," she whispered, the sensation far more terrifying than pain.

The doors to the Grand Archive whispered shut behind them, the sound final, swallowing the noise of the streets outside. Nera had walked the halls before, but never with this weight pressing against her ribs. The Archive was supposed to be a vault of knowledge, yet it now felt more like something else.

Alis shuddered with a full-body spasm like a wet dog shaking off rain, then rolled her neck with a wet *crack*, muttering, "Alright, we're in. Now what?"

"The name," Nera said. "We need to find it before anything changes again."

They moved quickly into the main corridor. The stillness was absolute; a suffocating vacuum. When Alis' boot scraped the floor, the sound didn't echo—it was severed the moment it was made. The architecture swallowed the noise instantly, as if the building itself was programmed to delete anything that wasn't already recorded.

Instead of old dust and decay, the air smelled of nothing—sterile, cold, and scentless as the rows of pristine white shelves that stretched endlessly into the dark, so perfectly aligned that looking at them made her dizzy, like staring into a mirror reflecting another mirror. They were organized with a precision that felt inhuman. There were no loose papers, no ink stains, no signs that hands had ever touched these volumes.

"It's too clean," Alis whispered, her voice sounding too loud in the stillness. "It looks like a graveyard."

Nera scanned the titles nearest to her. They were static, bold, and horrifyingly incorrect. *The Peaceful Annexation of Varnis. The Great Illumination. The Voluntary Abdication of the Northern Kings.*

Nera pulled the second one down. Her hands shook. The festival it described was a mask. The subject was the fire. The book described the burning of the Grand Archive not as a tragedy, but as a "sanctified renewal of resources." They had turned Livia's tomb into *remodeling project.*

"They didn't just rewrite it," Nera murmured, pulling another volume from the shelf. The leather felt cold, like dead skin that had never been alive. "They sanitized it. There's no blood in these books. No war. Just … order."

Cael stopped abruptly, his hand lowering over a ledger bound in blue velvet. He pulled it free, flipping it open to a random page. His face was drained of color.

"What is it?" Nera asked.

Cael traced a line of text, his finger trembling. "This is a registry of the Renwick line. It says my father died of a fever in the winter of the Fourth Alignment." He looked up, his eyes hard. "My father was executed by Belvar's men on the steps of the old academy. I watched it happen."

He slammed the book shut, but not before Nera saw the seal at the bottom of the page. "It wasn't a clerical error," Cael whispered, his voice trembling with a new, distinct kind of rage. "It's signed. Belvar authorized the change personally."

Kieran stared at the rows of books, his expression darkening. "It's a prison," he said softly. "They didn't just trap the history; they trapped the people inside it."

## Chapter Forty

# The Scrap

Cael walked beside Nera, his gaze sweeping the endless shelves. "And you're sure it's here?"

"It has to be. Somewhere."

The Curator had been clear—bring him the name, and he would give them truth. But standing here, watching it unravel, Nera couldn't shake the feeling that the name wasn't just lost. It had been taken.

Unless …

Nera felt like she was working on instinct more than any understanding of where information may be now. She turned to show Alis a volume on the Third Alignment, but the words died in her throat.

Alis was gone. So was Kieran.

There was no sound of a struggle, no crashing shelves. The corridor behind them had simply … ended. Where the path back had been a moment ago, a solid wall of books now stood, unbroken and seamless, as if it had been there for centuries.

"Kieran?" she called out.

"They're gone," Cael said, turning in a slow circle. He reached out to touch the new wall of books. It was solid. Real. "The room just sort of changed its mind about where we were standing."

The isolation settled over them, heavy and suffocating. They were alone in the belly of the beast.

They heard Kieran yell her name from what seemed far away.

Nera looked at Cael. He nodded once, stepping close to her, his hand hovering near her arm—protective, steady. "I've got her, Voss," Cael yelled out, hoping they could hear. "Just keep Alis alive."

Nera turned to the twisting path ahead. It was just her and Cael now. She moved forward and Cael followed, turning a corner sharply, leading them toward the older records—the ones from before the Third Revision, before history had been rewritten to serve Kestor's rule.

Nera moved deeper into the stacks, her mind racing. The Archive was perfect. Alphabetical, chronological, thematic perfection.

*That's the flaw*, she thought. Soren's first lesson echoed in her mind: *The Archive does not destroy; it displaces.* Look for the silence between the years. She ran her hands along the spines of the section labeled Pre-Alignment Chaos. The dates were sequential. 3020. 3021. 3022.

She stopped. Her fingers hovered over a gap between two volumes. It was barely visible, a shadow between 3023 and 3025. A space too small for a book, but large enough for a secret.

"Cael," she whispered. "Look at the numbering. They skipped a volume."

She reached behind the row of pristine volumes, her fingers brushing against something cold and rough hidden in the dark at the back of the shelf. She gripped it and pulled.

Dust billowed—the first dust they had seen in this place. In her hand was a thin, worn volume that looked like it had survived a fire.

The moment she opened the tome, the ink stirred. She opened it, flipping through brittle pages, past records of rewritten rulers and lost wars, until—

*A name.*

It flickered into view—unsteady, resisting. It knew it wasn't meant to be seen. The ink curled, dissolving before their eyes, the letters unraveling like whispered words lost to the wind.

Cael leaned over her shoulder. "Did you see that?"

She nodded. "It's here. We just need to—"

As her eyes traced the letters, a drop of black liquid hit the page.

Nera looked up. The ceiling wasn't leaking water, or even ink. It was bleeding *shadow*. Thick, coagulated strands of black dripped from the stone with a wet, sickening *slap* that echoed. The pristine white shelves around them began to darken and rot, the words on the spines dissolving into a sludge that poured onto the floor like an open vein. The air suddenly tasted of iron and stagnant water. The silence broke—not with a noise, but with a vibration that rattled Nera's teeth.

Cael cursed quietly, backing away. "It's bleeding."

*No!*, Nera thought. She wasn't just going to watch history disappear—not this time.

She reached into her pack, pulling out a thin sheet of conservation parchment—paper designed to hold unstable ink—the parchment of the very map that she always carried in her pocket. Pressing it against the fading name, she closed the book and held her breath. The air itself tensed, thick and heavy.

Nothing happened. Then, slowly, the ink bled onto the parchment, carving out the name before it could disappear forever.

"You got it?" Cael asked, sounding hopeful.

She lifted the sheet, watching the ink settle into place. The letters were warped, trembling, but they were there.

A name that shouldn't exist. A name that had once been erased from history. A name they didn't yet fully understand. But they didn't need to understand; all they had to do was bring it back to the Nameless Market.

Suddenly, a whisper — dry, rasping, amused in the same way it had been beneath the Archive in Varethis.

The old woman in the cloak. Unwritten.

"You shouldn't have found that," her voice echoed from everywhere and nowhere.

From the pooling ink on the floor, shapes began to rise. Faceless. Robed.

Nera froze. She recognized them now — the shadow in the lower chambers, the figure at the end of the aisle. They had been watching her the entire time.

The old woman's outline sharpened — not solid, but less unfinished than the others.

Nera felt it immediately. This one wasn't just Unwritten. She was closer to being remembered.

The Archive had woken up.

"You woke the ink, child. And the ink here is hungry. You need to leave, before it leaves the floor." A gust of air swept through the Archive. The ink started to twist up from the floor like rising shadows, forming tall, faceless figures draped in robes that absorbed the light.

*The Silent Keepers.*

"I suggest you leave," the old woman's voice crackled. The air shimmered. The solid wall of books ahead shimmered, momentarily overlaid by the ghostly image of an open archway—a memory of the Archive before the rewrite.

"Run through the memory!" she screamed. "I can hold it for you, but not for long because it will cost me."

Nera didn't need to hear more and was moving to the archway before the old woman had even stopped speaking, Cael close on her heels. One of the Keepers lunged, its touch sizzling against the stone floor where Nera had stood a second before.

"Don't let them touch you!" the Unwritten woman's voice yelled from the shadows, frantic now as Nera and Cael ran down the corridor that the archway had opened. "They don't just kill—they erase!" she yelled as she worked to distract the majority of them.

Running up to a spot where two halls met, Alis rounded the corner ahead of them and screamed, "Run!"

Kieran appeared right behind Alis and sprinted to Nera's side. They all ran at top speed through the stacks of books. The corridor twisted, shelves closing in like a throat tightening. A Silent Keeper materialized directly in front of Cael, its arm lashing out like a whip of black oil. Kieran slammed into Cael, knocking him out of the way just as the ink slashed through the air, carving a deep, smoking gouge into the solid wood of a shelf.

Nera slid under collapsing scrolls, barely avoiding a Keeper's dissolving touch. They scrambled and burst through the side exit, tumbling into the cool night air just as the barrier slammed shut behind them, sealing the howling darkness inside.

## CHAPTER FORTY-ONE

# Ink Holds Truth

The Nameless Market had moved again, and thankfully was very close to Varethis this time.

Tonight, it had settled behind a row of collapsed buildings, their skeletal remains framing the entrance like the broken ribs of a forgotten beast. The path ahead was lined with dancing lanterns, casting elongated shadows across the stone.

No one stopped them this time. The gatekeepers manning the entrance simply waved them in.

The figures at the edges of the market barely glanced their way, their expressions unreadable beneath the hoods and scarves that obscured their faces. They had been expected.

Nera kept the parchment with the name pressed between her fingers as they wound through the narrow pathways, past stalls selling books that shouldn't exist, maps of places erased from history, and trinkets inscribed with languages that no longer had speakers.

Finally, Alis stopped at the same doorway they had visited before. She rapped her knuckles twice against the door.

Then, the door creaked open just enough to reveal a sliver of the dimly lit interior. Without hesitation, Alis entered and the others followed.

The Curator behind the desk was exactly as they had left them. They did not stand as the group entered, nor did they offer any greeting, simply holding out a hand.

Nera stepped forward and placed the parchment in their waiting palm. The ink on the page flickered when touched, the letters blurring, resisting. At first, they only stared at it; then quietly spoke the name aloud.

The room shuddered. It was subtle, a ripple of something unseen, but Nera felt it in her bones.

The Curator folded the parchment and placed it inside the desk, then without a word reached beneath the table and produced a small, unassuming book.

Nera's breath caught as they placed it in her hands.

The reaction was instant. The ink didn't just sit on the parchment; it seized. The letters liquefied, shooting upward in sharp, jagged spikes that hardened into black glass before shattering back into dust. A high-pitched resonance—like a tuning fork struck against bone—vibrated through the small stall, rattling the jars on the shelves.

Kieran slammed his hand to his hilt. "What was that?"

Nera pulled her hand back, her fingertips burning. The book hadn't just rejected her; it had logged her. She could feel the connection still humming in the air—a thread pulling tight, leading straight back to the Archive.

"It's a beacon," Nera whispered, the blood draining from her face. "The text isn't just forbidden. It's bait."

She looked up at the Curator. "You knew."

The Curator didn't flinch. "I told you knowledge has a cost," they said calmly, closing the book. "You wanted to find the Tyrant's secrets. Now the Archive knows you are looking."

Nera realized the Archive had not just marked her. It had identified her as opposition.

"This is what you wanted," the Curator said. "The truth that was taken from everyone."

She ran her fingers over the cover, her heartbeat slow and deliberate. The book that would prove the Sixth Revision was a lie. The book that would undo everything Kestor had built.

"And something else I thought you might find useful," they hinted while handing over a bound volume, older than the Curator. Not in the usual Archivist style—this was personal, hand-bound, stitched with care.

Nera flipped it open. The ink inside was uneven, the lines slightly slanted—not an official transcript, but perhaps a copy of something even older. And then she found the passage.

> We believed we could control history. That we could prune it, shape it, erase the parts that no longer served.

> But we were wrong. Erasure is not silence. It is memory folded into the cracks of the world, waiting.

> They called them Glitches. Anomalies. Accidents. But they are neither.

> The first cracks were made by my own hand, the first fractures placed there by design. Because I knew—

> One day, they would see.

The room felt colder. Nera forced herself to breathe. The Glitches were not flaws in the Alignment. They were designed to exist. And if that was true—if someone had built them—then what else had they left behind?

For the first time, her hesitation wasn't about what to do next—but about whether they should have started at all.

## Chapter Forty-Two

# The Weight

They returned to the safe house in silence.

Nera gripped the small book tightly, pressing it against her ribs as if it might steady the storm building inside her. She barely registered the winding paths they had taken to avoid detection or the way Alis led with practiced ease, her pace quick but never rushed.

They reached the safe house without incident. Tobias was seated at the far table, deep in quiet conversation with Cyrus, their heads tilted toward each other as they conferred in low voices. Tavian was by the fireplace, book in hand, though his sharp gaze flicked up the second they entered. Tyrek stood near the door, chewing absentmindedly on a piece of dried fruit, his usual smirk absent for once.

Only six remained at the center table.

Nera set the book down carefully.

Alis collapsed into the nearest chair, stretching out her legs. "Alright," she muttered. "Let's see the damn thing."

Nera ran her fingers over the cover, feeling the rough, aged texture beneath her fingertips. Her pulse was steady. Deliberate.

She opened the book. The ink had faded in places, but the words remained. "Even erased from history, the truth had fought to survive."

She read a line aloud.

*The Benefactor did not fall. They were overthrown.*

A moment passed. Then another. Most of the group nodded slowly.

Cael sat down across from her, dragging his fingers through his hair, sharp eyes scanning the page with a growing frown. "That's it, then. That's the proof we needed."

Kieran had yet to sit. He stood behind Nera, his eyes fixed on the book, unmoving. "Proof isn't enough," he said, voice quiet but edged. "Even facts won't do when the world still believes the opposite."

Nera turned another page, pausing thoughtfully as she reached a passage written in unsteady, desperate handwriting.

> *There was an heir who should have taken over the kingdom.*
> *But they disappeared. No one knows what happened. Information*
> *disappeared. Did one exist, or not?*

Her blood ran cold. The room felt immutable now. She traced the words again, as if rereading them might summon more details, but the most important part was missing.

There was no name. Whoever had rewritten history hadn't just erased the heir's claim. They had burned them from the record entirely. A presence removed so thoroughly that not even this book—a relic untouched by the Sixth Alignment—could recover it.

Kieran finally moved. He pulled out a chair and sat, slow and careful. He leaned forward, elbows resting on his knees, his gaze dark with implication. "The Benefactor had a successor. A rightful heir that appears to have been killed or unwritten."

"Which means it must have been someone dangerous," Cael added, voice low.

Alis scoffed. "No kidding." She tilted her chair back, balancing on the rear legs. "Kestor?"

Nera swallowed, staring at the empty space on the page where a name should have been. Valen Kestor had rewritten after the

First Alignment for one purpose—to secure his rule. And he had erased the one person who had the right to take it from him.

Cael spoke directly. "So we do what we came to do. We will write it back."

Nera closed the book, her fingers still pressed against the cover. "Not just write," she said. "We make history remember."

Alis laughed softly, but there was no humor in it. "You think you can just undo centuries of revisions so easily? You really don't know when to stop, do you?"

"No," Nera admitted. "I don't."

No one argued. They all knew there was no turning back now.

## CHAPTER FORTY-THREE

# The Decision

The house remained quiet, the air waiting with the kind of silence that only came when something irreversible was about to happen.

Tyrek lingered near the doorway, his gaze flicking between the four of them and the book sitting on the table. He didn't say anything for a long time, just watching, weighing something in his mind. Finally, he shook his head.

"Well," he muttered, "good luck with whatever insanity you're about to pull."

Tobias gave a slight nod before following Tavian toward the back door. "The odds are bad, Nera. But they're the only odds we have. Don't miss."

Neither of them asked to stay. They understood that whatever happened next wasn't for them to write and they had other people they wanted close by if things went wrong. The door clicked shut behind them, leaving only the four of them inside.

Nera slid her fingers into her pocket, skimming them across her map before she looked up at Kieran and Cael.

"We do this now," she said. "Quickly."

Cael frowned. "Are you sure we shouldn't wait? Figure out the best way to—"

"There is no best way," she cut in. "If we wait, history has time to fight back. The longer this book exists without being rewritten out of the world, the more reality will resist it."

Kieran nodded thoughtfully. "She's right."

Alis, still balancing her chair on its back legs, sighed softly. "Then get it over with."

Nera looked down at her right hand. The hesitation was gone, replaced by a cold, quiet hum in her blood. She brushed her thumb over the intertwined silver bands, twisting them—once, sharp and rhythmic—as if unlocking a mechanism.

Nera reached into her bag and pulled out her quill; the one that had rewritten small fragments of history before. She dipped the nib into the ink. The black liquid clung to the quill unnaturally, pooling at the tip, eager to be used.

Her pulse steadied.

Then, slowly, deliberately, she pressed the quill to the page. The moment the ink touched the parchment, the room lurched.

It wasn't an earthquake, not even something physical, yet there was a deep, pulling sensation, as if the walls themselves were breathing. Wooden beams groaned while candle flames jumped— not from a breeze, but as if the light itself was uncertain of where it should be.

Alis swore quietly, lowering her chair back onto all four legs. "Yeah, that's not unsettling at all."

Nera ignored her, but she couldn't ignore the sensation clawing up her arm. As the ink sank into the fiber, she felt the familiar, sickening lurch of reality detaching; the same violent snap that had stolen Jorin away in the blink of an eye. The ripple surged outward, hungry and blind, reaching for the nearest threads to unravel. Through the haze, she saw Cael's silhouette flicker, his existence trembling at the edges, threatening to be rewritten along with the history of the kingdom.

*No.*

She pressed the tip harder, hand cramping as she seized the chaotic energy. She forced the ripple to bypass them, channeling the violence into her own bones. She would take the cost. They would keep memory.

The ink flowed faster than it should have, pooling in spots, sinking into the page as if it had been waiting to be restored. The words of the book morphed, not erasing, but settling, solidifying.

Reality didn't fight her. It rushed into the new groove like water finding the path of least resistance. It wasn't acceptance; it was relief from the strain. Like it understood that it was going back to the truth.

But across the table, Kieran lightly gasped. It wasn't a sound of shock, but of physical impact, as if the ink settling on the page had struck him directly in the chest. He grabbed the edge of the table, his knuckles turning white, his eyes wide and unfocused. For a heartbeat, the sharp, guarded soldier vanished, replaced by someone younger, someone vulnerable.

"Kieran?" Nera asked, her hand hovering over the page.

He blinked, eyes swimming with a sudden, terrifying clarity. "I felt..." He trailed off, pressing a hand to his heart, looking at the book with a mix of longing and fear. "It felt like someone just called my name. It's okay, keep going."

Cael dragged a hand through his hair, grabbing strands for just a second before dropping away. He glanced around the room, as if expecting the walls to do more than stand steady. "So what, that's it? We just write it back in, and history bends to our will?"

"No," Nera muttered. She finished the last word, lifted the quill, and the ink stopped moving. "It doesn't bend. It snaps back."

Kieran's gaze lingered on the book before he stood up and rested his hands on the edge of the table, staring at the ink that had now settled.

Something about him was drifting. He didn't look triumphant, or relieved, or even satisfied. He looked like someone who had just set something wild loose and knew there was no way to stop it. Because there wasn't.

The truth should now be back. *The Benefactor had not fallen; he had been erased. Kestor had never been a ruler, he was imprisoned as a thief.*

Nera swallowed, closing the book carefully. The edges of the cover still felt warm beneath her fingertips, as if the ink inside was still settling into its place in the world.

Alis rubbed her temples slowly. "Well. That's done."

Cael stood and ran a hand down his face, blowing out a hard breath. "Now we wait to see if the world survives it."

They didn't have to wait long, because the moment Nera set the quill down, a deep, silent ripple passed through the room. The ink in the book had settled, the words no longer bleeding across the page, no longer resisting. The truth had been written back into the world.

Then the flickers started.

Nera felt nothing at first. Just the solid weight of the book in her hands, the quiet hum of the safe house around them. Then Kieran stiffened beside her, his breath coming sharp and shallow. His fingers twitched at his sides, eyes unfocused, staring past her, past the book, past the room itself as he began restlessly pacing the room.

The air in the room grew thin.

Cael's breath hitched, a ragged sound like tearing paper. He gripped the edge of the table so hard his knuckles turned white, the wood groaning under the strain of his restraint.

Nera watched him, sensing the shift. He wasn't looking at her. He was staring at the quill she had set on the table—at the ink still pooled at the tip, waiting. To Nera, the black liquid seemed to pulse, alive and waiting. Like it was hungry for more words, indifferent to who held the pen.

But Nera realized Cael didn't react to the magic the way she did. His gaze didn't soften or drift; it sharpened. He stared at the page like a problem waiting to be solved. Every scholar knew the principles.

Her eyes followed his to the empty space on the parchment—where a name could fit. Where a name wanted to fit.

His breath hitched, ragged and uneven, and he reached suddenly for the quill. Nera saw his fingers twitch, hovering over the parchment. There was something in his eyes she had never seen before—a desperate, terrifying focus.

The tip grazed the page, leaving a single, jagged black mark.

"Cael, don't," Nera whispered.

"I can fix it," he snapped, his voice breaking as his eyes filled. "One line. I just need one line."

"You can't," Nera said, her voice shaking. "The ink can't find her where she is. If you try to write her back now, it won't be Livia. Do you want to love a forgery?"

Cael froze. The ink pooled at the tip of the quill, a dark drop trembling there, heavy and black. He looked at Nera, devastation warring with fury. She thought he might scream at her—or worse, ignore her.

A tear fell. It hit the floor, not the page.

Slowly, painfully, Cael pulled his hand back, his fingers curling into a fist against his chest as if crushing the hope before it could take root. The ink in the book stilled. The moment was gone.

Cael swallowed, his throat working around words that didn't seem to want to come out. Finally, he spoke, his voice quiet, almost disbelieving. "She's really gone."

He looked at Nera, panic suddenly flaring in his face alongside the grief. Livia was gone. He couldn't save her.

Cael's fingers curled into loose fists, but he didn't say anything else. He didn't need to.

Across from him, Kieran was staring into the distance, his breathing slow and controlled, but not steady. His voice was barely more than a whisper.

"Something's wrong."

The flicker lasted no more than a heartbeat before it vanished again, slipping between the cracks of rewritten time. But whatever it left behind didn't fade.

Nera watched them both, the way their expressions hardened, the way something unseen pressed at the edges of their focus. Whatever they were brushing up against, it hadn't fully surfaced yet.

She should have felt it too.

But there was nothing. No echo. No tug of a misplaced past. No sense of something trying to claw its way back into her mind.

Because *Nera* Calloway had never really existed in the timeline that had just been restored.

## Chapter Forty-Four

# History Unbound

The moment history settled, the world shuddered and exhaled.

Nera felt it first—not a sound, not a tremor, but something deeper, woven into the fabric of reality itself; so subtle that if she hadn't been the one holding the book, she might have thought it was nothing.

But it wasn't nothing.

She glanced up from the table, scanning the room. The wooden beams overhead, the glow of the lanterns, the dust floating in the still air—all of it looked the same. And yet, there was something just slightly off, something she couldn't place.

Then Kieran moved. Just a step. But the moment his foot touched the floor, he went rigid, his fingers twitching like something had just slipped through them.

Cael frowned, rubbing a hand over his face. "Okay, is it just me, or did—"

Before he could finish, the candle flames flared violently, guttering even though there was no breeze. The black ink convulsed, churning against the paper as if the words were fighting a current only they could feel.

The floor beneath them groaned as if the weight of the house itself had changed.

Alis muttered a curse and stood abruptly, her chair scraping against the floor. "I really hate when reality gets weird."

Nera flipped the book in her hands. The words had settled. She pushed back from the table and drew a steady breath. "It's loose."

Kieran's gaze lingered on the book, then flicked back to her. "How long before people notice?"

"They already are," Cael muttered. He gestured toward the window, where the dim glow of street lamps illuminated the stone alley beyond. Shadows moved, hesitant and uncertain, as if people were no longer sure where they were supposed to stand.

It was subtle now. It wouldn't stay that way.

"We need to go out there," Nera said.

Alis shot her a look. "Right. Because that always goes well."

"We need to know how much has changed. If the city is reacting, Kestor will too."

Kieran ran a hand through his hair, his fingers lingering at the back of his neck as if trying to shake something loose. He nodded once. "Then we don't wait."

Cael stood slowly. "Guess that means we're taking a walk."

Nera slid the small book into her pocket. Whatever fractures had begun, they were already moving outward now.

History had been altered. And the world was starting to remember something it didn't fully understand.

## CHAPTER FORTY-FIVE

# Reality Unravels

The streets weren't the same.

Nera had walked this path dozens of times, but now, every step felt uncertain. Not because anything had physically changed—the roads still stretched in familiar patterns, the buildings still loomed as they always had—but something beneath the surface was dissonant.

People moved cautiously, their steps hesitant, their gazes switching between buildings and streets as if waiting for something to vanish before their eyes. Conversations were hushed, the usual rhythm of the city faltering. There were no riots, no chaos, but the doubt was there. The kind that spread like ink through parchment, slowly seeping into everything.

As they crossed through a narrow side street, Kieran's voice was low. "They don't know what's wrong, but they can feel it."

Cael kept his hands in his pockets, scanning the alleys as they passed. "They will soon."

Nera grabbed the strap of her satchel. She had been expecting this—changes in history didn't go unnoticed—but she hadn't expected it to start showing this quickly. She stepped onto the bridge that spanned the river next to where the first Grand Archive had stood, but stopped halfway. The stones beneath her feet hummed with a sick, low vibration. Ahead, the road led to a gentle, grassy hill on the outskirts—empty and pristine. But the air tasted of old ash.

She gripped the stone railing, vertigo washing over her. The bridge felt like a hand reaching out to grasp something that had been severed. Across the water, the empty hill didn't look peaceful; it looked like a wound that had been scrubbed too clean.

"Don't look at it too long," Kieran warned, gripping her elbow to steer her back toward the city. "The ground over there is dead. They scrubbed the scorch marks, but the earth still knows the weight that used to be there."

A man stood at a street corner, flipping through an old book with shaking hands, his lips moving as he read. His expression twisted into something like confusion, then fear.

Further down, a merchant knocked over his own wares, his eyes fixed on a ledger that he had spread open in front of him. "That's not right," he muttered, half to himself, half to no one at all. "That's not—"

He closed the book too fast, shoving it under his arm as he hurried off.

Alis slipped a coin out of her pocket, twirling it between her knuckles as she watched similar moments unfold all around them. "Yeah. This is going to get worse."

Nera didn't respond, because she already knew she was right.

They stopped near an empty courtyard, just out of view of the main roads.

"What's the plan?" Cael asked, his tone sharp with a panic he refused to let surface. "Because right now, it looks like we're standing in the middle of a world unraveling with no real direction."

Alis stood defiantly. "Correction—we're standing in the middle of the world remembering."

"Which is just as dangerous," Kieran said. "Kestor is not going to let this happen without a fight."

Nera turned slightly, scanning the city, the people, the slow unraveling of a truth that had been buried for too long. "He might not have a choice."

No one spoke for a long moment. The city had always been controlled. Carefully shaped, every rewritten line upheld by belief. But belief was starting to crack. And soon, it would break.

## Chapter Forty-Six

# The Unmaking

The tension in the city was turning into something bigger.

Nera stood at the edge of the square, watching the panic ripple through the crowd. She felt strangely detached, her mind cataloging the chaos rather than feeling it. Nervously, almost as if she didn't realize she was doing it, her thumb brushed the rings on her right hand. She twisted them—once, sharp and rhythmic—before letting her hand drop to her side.

They had seen the first signs—the markers of misplaced memories, the books and ledgers that no longer lined up with what people believed to be true. But this was visceral. This was *panic*.

The group moved through the winding streets, keeping to the edges where the lanterns didn't quite reach. The markets were still open, but they were quieter than before, the usual loud bargaining replaced with uncertain whispers. A group of traders stood around an old woman who clutched a faded letter in her hands, her face pale and confused as she ran a finger over the ink.

"This was from my husband," she said, voice unsteady. "But he … he died before he could write this." The men around her exchanged wary glances. One of them mumbled something and left.

Further down, two merchants stood in front of their stalls, their voices rising. "You're lying," the first man snapped. "You've always owned this shop." The second man shook his head, his hands clenching at his sides. "No. I swear to you, yesterday I worked at the forge near the east gate. I've never been here before today."

More people were gathering. More whispers.

At an intersection, a scholar stood on the steps of a government hall, a book in his hands, his voice loud and shaking as he spoke to the small crowd before him.

"They changed it," he said, flipping through the pages with frantic hands. "The text, the history—we've been reading a lie." His voice cracked, breath coming faster. "This book wasn't written like this—I taught from it! I've memorized every line! But now ... it's different. I swear it wasn't like this before!"

Someone in the crowd shouted at him. "Then why does it match every other copy?"

"The words didn't change. We did." He clutched the book to his chest, his eyes wide and wet.

The gathering broke into heated arguments. People pointing to ledgers, buildings, each other. A woman was gripping the arm of a man beside her, voice frantic.

"You remember, don't you? Tell them you remember!" The man's face was pale, blank, his head shaking slowly as he took a step away from her.

Nera walked cautiously, keeping her steps even. Her shoulders squared as they wove deeper into the unease of the city.

"This is worse than I thought," Cael muttered beside her, keeping his voice low.

"It's not stopping," Kieran said knowingly. "It's spreading."

They turned another corner, and suddenly the street ahead was in chaos. A group of men stood in a loose circle, shouting, their voices cutting through the air. Two of them were shoving each other, their movements angry, edged with something sharper than just frustration.

"You're not from here!" one of them snapped, pointing an accusing finger at the other. "You're lying, I've never seen you before."

"You've known me for years!" the other man barked back. "I work two stalls from you, you're the one who's forgetting!"

A third man grabbed the first by the arm. "It's not him. It's the city."

The first man turned sharply, confusion flashing into something more dangerous. "What the hell are you talking about?" His voice rose, and others in the crowd echoed the question—too many, all at once.

"I don't know," the third man admitted, voice quieter now. "I don't know, but something's wrong. I can feel it."

One of the men swung. The punch landed hard, sending the other man stumbling back into a fruit cart. Someone else lunged, grabbing him by the collar. More people were moving now, stepping forward, caught between trying to break it up and being drawn into it themselves.

Cael watched the crowd carefully. "That's going to turn ugly fast."

"It's already ugly," Alis muttered.

Nera took a small step forward, but Kieran's hand caught her wrist. She turned to him, but he shook his head once.

"We can't stop this," he said.

She forced down the lump in her throat, refusing to let it show. He was right. This wasn't one fight. This wasn't one misunderstanding. The city was unraveling. People were starting to realize that they had been lied to for a long time, and they were not happy.

The crowd was still growing, drawn in by the shouting, the confusion, the growing desperation of people realizing their reality wasn't as solid as they had believed.

Nera could hear more voices now, arguments spilling out from other streets, merchants yelling at customers, people demanding explanations for memories that no longer fit.

She pulled her arm free from Kieran's grip, but she didn't move toward the noise. She didn't need to. She had seen enough. She wrapped her arms around herself, holding tight.

Cael moved beside her, watching her carefully. "What now?"

Nera didn't answer. She didn't know.

But she understood that not knowing didn't mean nothing was coming.

## CHAPTER FORTY-SEVEN
# The Quill

They didn't return to the safe house together. That wasn't the plan. The four of them had spent the last few hours moving through the city in separate directions, taking in what was happening. None of them could stop it, none of them could control it, but still, they had watched.

Kieran disappeared into the lower districts, listening to the kind of people who spoke in hushed tones and moved in shadows. Cael had wandered the main squares, ears open to the louder unrest—the arguments turning into shoving matches, the sharp crackle of voices demanding explanations for things that no longer made sense.

Tyrek said he had to go back to check on his tavern with Liaz. Alis had left with Tyrek, the pair slipping into the hidden corners of the market where whispers were currency.

Nera walked alone.

Wandering through a city that should have felt familiar but didn't, she watched the way people clutched books and documents, flipping through pages with shaking hands to find proof of what they thought they knew. She passed by a group of men standing in a circle, arguing about whether a shop had existed two days ago.

She had seen it in their faces. The same realization she had outside of the vanished apothecary. History was not just written down. It was something lived. And when it started to unravel, it wasn't just words on a page that lost their meaning. It was people.

When she stepped back through the door of the safe house, somehow she already knew what she would find.

Alis, bag packed, just as she was about to slip out the back door. She paused once she saw Nera.

"Look at them, Nera. We didn't fix it. We just broke it differently. I told you—I don't deal in lies, I deal in survival. And I can't survive watching you erase either yourself or the world."

"I have to finish it," Nera said after a short pause.

"I know," Alis said slowly, her voice sounding heartbroken and angry at the same time. "That's why I can't stay. Because I love you, but I can't watch you become ink. And I can't do this anymore, Nera. I've spent my life hating the Archive for playing god, and I'm too tired to keep pretending we aren't doing the exact same thing, even if it's for a good reason."

Silently, she approached Nera. For the first time, her hands were still. No coin rolling over her knuckles, no calculation of odds. She looked Nera in the eyes sadly before reaching into her bag and withdrawing a small item, placing it in Nera's hand before turning and walking away.

In a blink, Alis was gone.

Nera looked down at her hand, slowly opening her fingers. She stared silently at Alis' quill.

\*\*\*

The air inside was still, leaving Nera hollow with the loss of another friend. She stood in quiet reflection for several minutes, considering the toll that everything was taking on her, her friends, and everyone and everything she knew.

Kieran arrived next, moving slowly inside. Nera could tell he knew something had happened, even if he didn't yet know what. He settled near the far wall, his hands loose at his sides. Cael walked in behind him, rolling his shoulders as if trying to shake off something that wouldn't quite let go.

For a second, no one spoke. Then Tyrek's voice broke the silence.

"I was here when Alis got back. I saw her before she left." He stood near the back entrance where he'd just come in from the yard, his usual casual stance missing the easy arrogance it normally carried.

Nera turned toward him fully. "Did she say anything?"

Tyrek shook his head. "Didn't need to. Wasn't in a rush, but she wasn't stalling either." He hesitated for a fraction of a second, then added, "She knew you'd understand."

Cael dragged a hand through his hair. "Of course she didn't say anything."

Tyrek rubbed his thumb against the inside of his palm, like he was testing a phantom coin. "She saw me watching her leave. Didn't explain. Didn't ask me to stop her. She weighed the cost of staying and decided she couldn't afford it."

"And what did you say?" Kieran asked.

Tyrek shrugged. "I told her she was making the right decision."

That landed harder than it should have. Nera's chest tightened, and she wasn't sure why. She had always known Alis wasn't meant to stay. That she had fought for the truth, but never for the same reasons as the rest of them.

Tyrek reached into his pocket and tossed a small, wax-sealed strip of parchment onto the table. "She isn't the only one who made it out."

Nera picked it up. The seal was broken, the scrawl hasty but familiar.

"A courier came in from the ridge an hour ago," Tyrek said. "Jorin and Brieth. They're in the Borderlands. They crossed the perimeter with the families before the riots locked it down. Everyone is safe."

Nera let out a breath she hadn't realized she was holding, the knot in her chest loosening just a fraction. They had made it. Tessa, the children, Jorin, Brieth—they were all out of the line of fire.

"Good," Cael said, his voice rough. "At least we don't have to look over our shoulders for them."

Nera nodded, clutching the note.

One worry gone. A thousand more waiting.

## CHAPTER FORTY-EIGHT

# The Tether

The city was breaking.

It wasn't just unease anymore, and it wasn't just whispers or arguments on street corners. It was full-blown panic.

Nera could feel it in the air as they moved through the streets, something unraveling around them. The confusion had evolved. People were awakening.

A woman stood frozen outside a shop, her hands gripping the edges of a ledger so tightly her knuckles were white. She kept flipping back and forth between pages, her mouth slightly open.

"It changed," she whispered. "I wrote this. I know I did. I wrote this yesterday." A man beside her shook his head violently. "No, you didn't."

"I did," she insisted, her voice rising. "I signed this contract, and it wasn't like this. I remember."

"You're wrong." The argument wasn't loud, but it was visceral. The kind of tension that cracked something deep.

Further down the street, a group of people stood around a crumbling wall. It shouldn't be crumbling. The stone had always been smooth, polished. But now, cracks spiderwebbed through it, peeling away layers of rewritten history—revealing letters and carvings no one remembered placing there. Someone ran a hand over the rough edges, brushing dust away, revealing more beneath the layers of rewritten history.

This was the city remembering.

Kieran's pace slowed as his eyes flicked from one unraveling moment to the next. His jaw locked tight, the muscles in his neck straining against the collar of his coat. "This is happening too fast."

"We knew this would happen," Cael stated blandly.

"Not like this," Kieran said. His voice was low, steady, but there was something in his expression—the skin tightening around his eyes. "Not this fast. Not this violently. It's wrong."

The sky above them felt lower, the air too thick. Every movement and sound carried a new heaviness, like they were walking through something fraying at the edges.

Then a scream.

Nera turned sharply toward the noise, her heart hammering, her instincts locking onto the sound like a predator catching the scent of blood.

A man had collapsed onto his knees in the middle of the street, his hands clawing at his temples. People were gathering around him, stepping forward but not too close.

"I don't—I don't belong here," the man gasped. "I don't—I wasn't—" His breath came sharp and uneven, his body shaking. "This isn't where I am supposed to be."

Someone tried to help him, but he recoiled violently, scrambling away. "No, no, no, you don't understand—I was supposed to be gone."

The crowd around him was growing, voices rising in scattered confusion.

"I know you," a woman whispered, her face pale, hands clutching the fabric of her dress as if grounding herself. "But I—I thought you were erased."

"I was!" the man choked out, his head jerking up, eyes wild. "I was gone! I was nowhere, and now ... I'm back!"

A woman near the fountain wailed, a sound of absolute loss. She was clutching a small, hand-knitted blanket against her chest, her eyes wild as she looked at the empty space beside her.

"Where is he?" she shrieked at the man who had just reappeared. "Where is my son?"

The man next to her looked at her, his face pale and unrecognizable to her. "I don't know you," he whispered. "I've never had a son."

Nera froze. The realization hit her like a physical blow. By writing the "true" history back in, she had not just restored the past; she had overwritten the present. The child had existed in Kestor's lie.

She hadn't saved the city. She had just chosen which people deserved to exist. The world felt like it had stopped. Nera stared silently, the roar of the crowd fading into a dull, terrifying buzz in her ears. She took a step back, then another. Kieran and Cael were both watching the scene unfold, their postures tense, their focus sharp.

"This isn't going to stop," Cael muttered. "It's only going to get worse."

Nera felt something cold settle in her chest. She had thought this would be controlled, that unwriting the Sixth Alignment would simply restore the world to what it should have been.

It refused to settle. It was collapsing. This went beyond rewritten history breaking apart and it wasn't going to hold for much longer.

Suddenly, the words from the second book the Curator had given her finally made sense. Glitches were not flaws. They were *safeguards*, written to reject anyone but Kestor. The world was doing exactly what it had been designed to do. She could not fix a system like that. She could only remove its architect.

\*\*\*

The safehouse felt too small the moment they walked back inside.

Nera stood near the table, staring down at the book she had rewritten, her fingers pressing into the worn edges of the cover. The quiet in the room felt wrong, too deliberate, as if reality itself were holding its breath.

Cael paced near the doorway, his movements restless, unfocused. He ran a hand through his hair before slamming it against the doorframe. "We should be out there. We should be seeing what's happening. Listening. Talking."

Kieran sat near the far wall, his fingers tapping against his knee, slow and measured. "It's happening. We don't need to see it to know that."

Tyrek had stayed for a while after telling them about Alis, but he had left without a word, slipping out to watch over his business and family while everything going on was so questionable.

Nera turned as Theron stepped inside, his broad frame filling the doorway. He scanned the room, his sharp eyes moving over each of them before he shook his head.

"City's turning to hell out there. The streets are a powder keg," he muttered. "It's not just confusion; it's sloppy violence. I saw a mob tear down a stall just because the grain of the wood didn't align right for them. The perimeter is compromised. I can hold a door against one soldier, but I can't hold it against a city that's collectively lost its mind."

Theron paused, wiping grime from his jaw, his voice dropping. "But the mob isn't what worried me. I checked the horizon on my way in. The Watchers are here."

Cael straightened. "Moved?"

"They left the ridges," Theron said grimly. "They abandoned overwatch."

"Meaning?" Cael asked.

"Meaning they aren't positioned to strike," Theron said. "They're positioned to witness. They're kneeling. Facing Varethis."

Kaelith followed a few steps behind him, her movements more controlled, measured. She tugged off the scarf she had been using to obscure her face and pushed a few stray locks of red hair behind her ears. "They're having a collective breakdown. A terrified mind is violent because it needs to prove it's still real. If we go out there, they won't see neighbors; they'll just see targets."

Tavian, Cyrus and Sarina entered a moment later, speaking in low voices before falling silent when they saw Nera and the others standing there. Tavian gave her a knowing look, but he didn't ask what had happened.

"The house is officially full," he said, sliding the deadbolt with a finality that echoed. "That is every soul we can save tonight. Everyone is here or in the underground tunnels, and Tyrek and Liaz at the tavern. If anyone else knocks, they can stay outside and argue with the wind, because I'm not opening this latch for anything less than a battalion."

No one asked about Alis. No one needed to. She was gone, but they all believed she would be okay.

Tavian sat near the far wall, running a hand through his hair. "Is there any history left out there?" he asked quietly. "Or is it just noise now?"

Nera swallowed. "It's getting worse."

The house wasn't just full now. It was sealed. Everyone inside was safe—for the moment.

Then, a sound outside.

Not shouting. Not a fight. Something else.

Nera turned toward the window, breathing slow. There was movement in the street. Not a mob, not a riot—but people standing still. Watching.

Kieran's posture stiffened next to her as he followed her gaze. "Something's wrong."

Cael stepped forward, frowning. "More wrong than it already was?"

They didn't wait for an answer. Nera moved first, sliding the latch and slipping through the doorway and into the cool night air. Cael and Kieran followed, the door closing behind them with a dull thud.

It was only when she stepped fully onto the street that she saw what had drawn people out of their homes. A man stood in the middle of the road, hands gripping his head, his breath ragged. His clothes were plain, no different from anyone else's, but the way he held himself— like he had just been pulled from something unseen—and torn loose.

"I wasn't here," the man rasped. "I wasn't—"

People were stepping closer, hesitant, uncertain.

"I know you," a woman in the crowd gasped. She lunged, her hands gripping the front of his tunic.

The fabric didn't dissolve. Her fingers didn't pass through smoke; he was real. She yanked him forward, the sound of his boots scraping against the cobblestones loud and undeniable.

"You were gone," she screamed, shaking him, terrified by the warmth of his skin. "We buried an empty casket for you! How are you here?"

"I don't know!" the man choked out, grabbing her wrists with hands that were shaking but solid. He stared at his own grip, horrified by his own strength. "I was gone. I was nothing. And then … I just woke up standing here."

Nera watched the reunion, paralyzed. Beside her, Cael's face drained of color. "That's not supposed to be possible."

Kieran spoke slowly, his tone unreadable. "It's not stopping."

Nera turned her head slightly, scanning the street, the buildings, the growing crowd which was seeing things they shouldn't, remembering things they were previously supposed to have forgotten.

The crowd swelled, people yelling as tensions rose and agitation turned to action. Groups began chanting, their words obscured by the din, while others tossed merchant carts and threw rocks through store windows in a fit of terrified frustration.

Nera watched a stall collapse under the weight of a rioting crowd. This wasn't going to fix itself. She had expected fear, uncertainty, knowing they had set something in motion that couldn't be undone. She had expected the chaos in the streets, the unraveling of history, the broken memories. But she hadn't expected it at this level.

Something tensed inside her.

She didn't know what triggered it. A face in the crowd. A movement that didn't belong. A pressure behind her eyes, like a thought trying to surface without permission. But the certainty landed anyway.

She had seen this before. Not here. Not now. In the book from the Market.

Nera turned back inside without a word and sat at the table. She opened the small book again, but she wasn't reading.

The understanding didn't come as words. It came as intuition.

Edris had tried to erase the Tyrant outright. To tear him cleanly from the story. Something had stopped it. The world had snapped back, violent and exacting, shattering everything closest to the attempt.

She had done the opposite. She hadn't removed him. She had contained him. Wrapped him in law and process and permanence, believing that if she could hold him still long enough, the damage would stop.

Two different approaches. The same resistance.

The problem wasn't power. It wasn't precision. It wasn't even the ink.

The Archive wasn't a wall to break or a lock to force. It was a story refusing to move forward.

Both she and Edris had tried to solve that by stopping something—by cutting it out or sealing it in place—without understanding what was keeping it there in the first place.

You cannot erase a villain.

You cannot cage him either.

The story will push back until the obstruction is addressed.

And the truth settled, quiet and terrible. It wasn't that the Tyrant had survived the rewrite. It was that something else had.

Her breath caught—not in fear, but subconscious recognition. She didn't yet know what it was. Only that it wasn't the man himself.

Her fingers curled into her palms, nails pressing into skin as she forced herself to stay still.

No one realized the way the realization rooted itself deep, how something inside her shifted and locked into place.

They didn't know. And she wouldn't tell them, because now she was certain.

And certainty, she knew, was dangerous.

## CHAPTER FORTY-NINE

# The Anchor

The walls of the safehouse groaned, the mortar grinding as if the stones were trying to pull apart. The noise from the street wasn't just shouting anymore; it was a dissonance that made Nera's teeth ache—a cacophony of a thousand people remembering a thousand contradictory histories at once. It sounded like a choir screaming off-key. The air in the room tasted of copper and charged air—the friction of reality grinding against itself, charged with the mental dissonance static of a city tearing its own mind apart.

Nera sat at the table, her hands resting against the closed book. No one had spoken for a while. The others had spread out, keeping to themselves in the way people did when they weren't sure what to do next.

The fighters had instinctively taken the perimeter. Theron was standing at the stove but it was clear that his attention was elsewhere. He was stirring a pot of stew with mechanical, rhythmic precision, counting quietly to himself. "Thirty-eight Thirty-nine. Forty." He stopped, checked the spoon, then started again at one, while remaining ready to spring into action the second the door moved. Kaelith was nearby and watched out of a window, weapon ready. Kieran took up a post between the door and the table.

Closer to the hearth, the scholars waited. Sarina was distracting her mind with knitting while sitting next to Cyrus, who stared blindly out the window. Tavian couldn't sit still; he paced the length of the rug with restless, kinetic energy, his frame cutting back and forth like a pendulum while he waited for water to boil for tea, although it was clear no one was planning to drink.

He stopped abruptly near the hearth, pulling a crumpled document from his pocket—one Nera recognized from the Sanctum visit. He stared at it for a long moment, his thumb tracing a seal of authenticity. His hand was trembling, not with fear, but with the sheer weight of what he was holding.

"I spent twenty years digging for this," Tavian whispered, his voice cracking. "Names. Dates. Proof that they existed. Proof that they mattered."

He held the parchment over the flames. The heat curled the edges, threatening the ink.

"Tavian?" Nera asked, stepping forward, alarmed. "That is the pre-Alignment census. That is the proof we need to convict him."

"Convict him to who, Nera?" Tavian snapped, turning to her with eyes rimmed in red. "He owns the Council. The city is burning. There is no one."

He looked back at the document, reading a name only he could see. "If I walk out there and hand this to them—if I tell a mother that her son wasn't just lost, but erased by a man she can't touch—I am not giving her justice. I am handing her a ghost she can't bury."

"It's the truth," Nera said softly.

"Actually it's not a ghost; it's a stone," Tavian corrected. "And I am not going to hand a stone to a drowning man just because it has his name carved on it."

He opened his hand.

The census fluttered into the fire. It didn't burn instantly; it resisted, the heavy parchment curling slowly, the names glowing bright orange for a heartbeat before crumbling into ash. Tavian watched it go, his expression hollowed out, as if he were burning a piece of himself.

"The historian's first duty is to the truth," he murmured to the flames. "But his second is to the living. And right now, the living need to survive the night."

Nera knew they had moved past the hope of good news. There was no more news. They were waiting for certainty, but certainty had no place in a world that had stopped knowing itself.

They were waiting for someone to tell what needed to happen next.

* * *

Cael held them all in a stony stare from where he stood near the doorway. "This isn't going to hold."

No one asked him what he meant. They all knew.

Kaelith didn't look up from her weapon. Her voice was quiet, but firm. "We built shelter inside a lie," she said, her tone clinical. "You can't expect the walls to stand when the foundation doesn't remember what it's supposed to be holding up. Let it break. We fight better in the open anyway."

Nera looked down at her hands, fingers pressed lightly against the rough edges of the book. The truth was written back in. History had been restored. So why did it feel like it was falling apart worse than before?

She forced herself to speak. "If we wait too long, Kestor will make his move."

"The response has begun," Cyrus muttered from the window. All eyes turned toward him. He didn't turn back to face them. He just nodded toward the street. "I can see them."

He looked down at his wrist, his fingers going to the crown of his intricate timepiece—a habit he had performed a thousand times a day for twenty years. Click. Click. Click. He wound it, his eyes fixed on the gears visible through the glass face.

The second hand wasn't moving. It was vibrating, twitching back and forth between two seconds that refused to resolve.

"Even time is collapsing," Cyrus whispered.

"Cyrus?" Sarina asked gently.

He unclasped the watch. He held it up to the firelight, watching the brass gears grind against a time that was no longer truthful. "I thought if I could measure the collapse, I could predict it."

With a sudden, decisive motion, Cyrus hurled the timepiece into the stone hearth. It shattered against the back wall, gears scattering into the ash. "There are no rules now," he said.

Nera stood slowly. She felt the others moving with her, Kieran repositioning silently to her side, Cael following behind. They stopped at the window, peering through the glass.

At first, the street looked the same. Still cracked in places, still littered with people trying to make sense of their lives.

But then she saw. Figures moved at the edges—not part of the crowd, not searching, but tracking. Some of the Archivists seemed like they hunted.

Cael's voice was tight. "They're assessing the damage."

Kieran went unnaturally still. "They're looking for the source."

Nera closed her eyes briefly, then turned back to the room, to the people who were still inside, waiting. The safe house was holding. But the city wasn't. And soon, they wouldn't be able to stay in here any longer.

Nera let the thought settle long enough to feel the room shift with it.

Cyrus sat at the table, jaw tight, eyes fixed on his notes like numbers could bargain with panic. Sarina's hand rested on his forearm, steadying him in a way words couldn't. Tavian was still standing, book half-open, but he wasn't reading anymore. He was listening to the city through the walls, the way a scholar listens for the first crack in a dam.

Theron moved first. He crossed to the window, peered through the narrow gap in the curtain, then exhaled through his nose like he'd tasted smoke.

"They're not going to calm down," he said, quietly enough that it carried without becoming a speech. "Not tonight."

Kaelith was already at the cabinet, pulling out cloaks, wrapping cloth, anything that could obscure a face in bad light. Her movements were quick and practiced, not frantic. Like she'd done this before in a different kind of war.

"We move house," she said. "Now. Before the streets decide this house is the problem."

Tavian's throat bobbed. "Move house," he repeated, hollow. "Like it's a chess piece."

"It is," Kaelith said. She didn't look at him when she spoke. She was folding, stacking, counting. "And right now it's a piece the board is about to flip."

Nera pushed away from the table. The chair legs scraped against the floor, sharp in the tense quiet.

"Everyone hears it," she said. "So listen to me. This place has done what it can. But if we stay packed in here, we aren't a safehouse anymore. We're a target."

Cyrus finally looked up, his expression hard. "If we split, we lose control of the information."

"We already lost control," Nera said. She didn't raise her voice. She didn't need to. "The city is rewriting itself out there, and it doesn't care that we have maps and ledgers and proof of a different history. And Kestor will be angry."

Sarina's fingers tightened on Cyrus's arm, not a plea, more a warning not to argue the wrong point.

Theron turned from the window. "The underground routes are still clear," he said. "For now."

Kaelith nodded once, sharp. "We use them while we still can."

Tavian swallowed again, eyes flicking to the door as if he expected it to rattle. "Where do we even go?"

"We will go to my mom," Kaelith said. "Outside the city line. It's not fancy, but it's walls and it's quiet. And it's far enough that the crowd won't stumble into it by accident."

Theron's gaze cut to Nera. "We can get people out in small groups. Two or three at a time. No lanterns. No talking once we hit the first junction."

Cyrus stood abruptly, chair pushing back. "I'm not leaving you here."

Nera met his eyes and held them.

"You're not leaving me," she said. "You're leaving with Sarina. And you're taking Tavian."

Tavian blinked. "Me?"

"You know what the Council will do if they catch you," Nera said. "You don't posture. You argue. You correct people. You look like a problem even when you're being polite." Her mouth tightened. "Right now, that gets you killed."

Tavian's lips parted, ready to protest on principle, then he stopped. He pressed his fingers to the spine of his book.

"I should check on my mother," he said finally, the words rough. "If the city is cracking … she won't understand why."

Cyrus's jaw flexed once. "That works. Sarina and I can get him there."

"And then you keep moving," Nera said. "You don't come back here unless you're sure you weren't followed."

Theron was already moving toward the back of the house, toward the narrow door that led to the underground tunnels. Kaelith followed him, pulling a small bundle of supplies into her arms, then paused long enough to look back at the room. At the table. At the ash-smudged hearth. At the lives they'd tried to hold together inside these walls.

"This isn't abandonment," she said, as if she could read the guilt trying to rise in everyone's throats. "This is evacuation."

Sarina stepped closer to Nera, voice low. "Are you coming with us?"

Nera glanced toward Cael and Kieran.

Cael hadn't moved. His hands were flat on the table, braced like he was holding the room in place by force. Kieran stood a little apart from the rest, eyes unfocused, the way he got when something inside him was trying to remember the shape of a missing piece.

"Not yet," Nera said. "I want to gather some of these documents."

Sarina searched her face, then nodded once like she understood more than she wanted to.

Cyrus looked like he was about to argue again, then stopped himself. He stepped in close enough that only Nera could hear him.

"Don't be here when the street decides it hates this house," he said.

Nera's voice came out quieter than she intended. "I won't."

Cyrus didn't look convinced, but he backed off. He took Sarina's hand. Tavian gathered his book to his chest like armor.

Kaelith opened the back door and the cold night breathed into the room.

"Hoods up," she said. "Heads down. No names."

One by one, they moved, pulled into motion by necessity more than courage. Cloaks swallowed faces. Footsteps softened. The safehouse began to empty without ceremony, like a body exhaling.

Theron waited at the cellar door, counting them through with a grim patience. Kaelith was the last at the threshold. She paused there, hand on the frame, eyes flicking to Nera.

"Lock it behind us," she said. "When you're ready."

Then she was gone, and the door shut with a quiet final click that sounded like a decision.

The house didn't feel safer with fewer people in it.

It felt *sharper*.

And for the first time since Nera had walked into this fight, she felt the story narrow, not toward relief, but toward impact.

\* \* \*

The voices outside faded into the background, distant yet ever-present. Nera moved away from the window, letting the curtain drop back into place. They had seen enough.

She expected Cael to say something, to argue, to push forward with the same sharp-edged frustration he always carried. But he was quiet, his jaw tight, his expression blank.

Kieran hadn't moved from where he stood, staring at something unseen. Rigid and tense, his gaze remained unfocused, locked somewhere beyond the room and the safe house. Something was wrong. "Kieran?" Nera's voice was low, careful. Breaths coming slow and measured, he seemed to be struggling against something pressing into his mind.

Then, without warning, he took a sharp step back.

He pressed a hand against the edge of the table, fingers curling against the wood, his grip too tight. His other hand moved to his temple, rubbing slowly.

Cael straightened. "What is it?"

A muscle in Kieran's jaw twitched, but still, he said nothing. His eyes closed briefly, then opened again, and they weren't the same. For the first time, his expression wasn't guarded. It wasn't locked behind control or sharp-edged focus. It was shaken.

"I remember something," he said, voice quiet, but rough.

Cael frowned. "From the Alignments?"

Kieran inhaled sharply through his nose, shaking his head. "No. From before. From before I wasn't supposed to exist."

Nera's pulse slowed. His fingers twitched against the table before he let go, before he straightened. His expression wasn't unreadable anymore. The walls behind his eyes had come down, leaving him open, unguarded.

His voice, when he spoke again, was lower. Steadier. More certain. "I remember you," he whispered, voice raw—like the words had been waiting, buried, clawing their way back into existence.

No one moved. Nera was holding her breath.

Cael's voice edged with something close to disbelief. "Who?"

Kieran turned toward Nera fully now. His gaze dropped to her hand—to the silver bands twisted around her finger. The rings she had found in a lost archive. The rings he had given her in a life they weren't supposed to remember.

He looked up, locking onto her eyes with a weight she couldn't escape. The smell of smoke and singed air faded, replaced by the ghost of a scent she hadn't smelled since the empty street corner—lavender. "You," he said softly.

Nera's heart started racing. Not confusion. No hesitation. He remembered her. Not just here, not just now, not just in this broken, unraveling world. Before. Long before.

She didn't move, didn't step away, didn't break the locked moment between them.

His voice was softer now, but no less certain. "*Nerith.*" The name hung in the air between them, sharp as a blade and heavy as a grave marker.

No one moved. But the silence wasn't hesitation anymore; it was a countdown. Tavian was right—there was no one left to appeal to. Kestor owned the Council. The safehouse was failing. There was no shelter left, only the choice to stand. "We don't wait anymore," Nera whispered, the decision settling in her chest like iron. "We use what we know to this point, right or wrong, and we finish this tonight."

Cael sighed, barely audible, but it wasn't a sound of protest. It was the sound of a man accepting the fall.

Kieran had remembered something he was never supposed to. And now, none of them could ignore it.

The knock at the door was sharp, deliberate. Every head in the room swiveled. No one moved right away.

For a long, stretched moment, the only sound was their own breathing, the distant hum of a city fraying at its edges.

Then Kieran pushed off the table, his steps controlled as he moved toward the door. He hesitated only a second before unlocking it and pulling it open.

Soren stood on the other side. His coat was heavier than before, streaked with dust and road wear, his posture bent with exhaustion. He had been traveling hard and fast. His eyes, shadowed by sleepless weeks, swept the room once before settling on Nera.

"You rewrote it," he said, voice edged, sharp—not with accusation, but with something deeper. *Recognition.*

Nera met his gaze. "You already knew that."

A pause. Then Soren moved slowly, stepping inside.

"I spoke with Edris." He pulled the door shut behind him, locking it with a quiet click. "It took a while to find him, and then longer sifting through his fragmented memories. I rushed back here, and I tried to not draw attention but I worry I may have been followed."

"By Belvar?" asked Nera. Soren answered with a nod as Cael brang him a drink of water.

Soren raised his hand to wipe water drops from his chin. "I know why he failed to unwrite the Tyrant," he said.

Cael slipped a hand in his pocket. "So he finally decided to share?"

Soren ignored him. His focus stayed on Nera, his voice calm but carrying weight. "He couldn't control what he wrote. He thought he was fixing it, but history resists when it's pulled too many ways. And when it resists, it shatters."

No one spoke.

Soren's gaze didn't waver. "You did more than restore the past. It was unwriting the rewrite. Layers on layers." He pinched the bridge of his nose, squeezing his eyes shut. "And it's coming apart."

Nera's fingers curled against the back of a chair. She had known, somewhere deep inside, but hearing it out loud made it real.

Soren didn't sit. He crossed the room, grabbing Nera's shoulder—hard. There was no calm in him now. He looked like a man who had stared into the sun.

"Edris was arrogant," he said after a long pause. "He thought he could force history into shape. That if he wrote carefully enough, slowly enough, he could control the changes. That wasn't how it worked."

Nera swallowed. "What did he do wrong?"

"He didn't change; he cut," Soren said, his voice rough.

"And that's why he died," Cael snapped, stepping between them. "So why are we using his playbook?"

"We aren't!" Soren's voice rose, cracking his usual calm facade. He wasn't lecturing any more, he was pleading. "Edris treated the Tyrant like a disease to be purged. But you can't just cut out the skeleton and expect the meat to stand up! Edris tried to murder the past. Nera has to *heal* it."

She stared at the book, her fingers brushing its edges. "Then how am I supposed to keep that from happening?"

Soren nodded slowly and thoughtfully. "Edris believed, after considering where he went wrong, that there were ways. Smaller adjustments. Targeted corrections instead of full revisions. He thought if he could stabilize the rewritten points first—anchor them in something undeniable—he could stop the unraveling."

Cael scoffed. "Clearly the other way didn't work for him, why trust this?"

Soren shot him a sharp look but didn't take the bait. His focus stayed on Nera.

"He didn't have the same control you do," he said. "He was already a ghost when he picked up the quill; Kestor had already started to erase him," Soren said, looking at her with a mix of pity and awe. "History couldn't find him to pin the rewrite to. You can't anchor a ship with smoke."

Soren studied Nera's face, a flash of old grief softening his clinical gaze. "You asked why you can rewrite when others cannot," he whispered. "It isn't magic, Nera. The ink in your veins ... that belongs to him."

"He tried to write you out. But the ink wouldn't take. You are the residue of a reality he tried to murder. You are the one stain he can't remove."

Nera stared at him, a cold feeling spreading through her chest. Revulsion. It seemed she was nothing more than a glitch. Like every choice she thought she had made—every risk, every scar—was just a structural error in Kestor's architecture.

A sudden, violent urge to laugh bubbled up in her throat. She wanted to take the book and throw it into the fire. She wanted to walk out the door, grab Kieran, and disappear into some nameless town where history didn't matter. Let the world break. Let Kestor choke on his own ink. Why did she have to be the one to stitch it back together? She didn't want to be a variable. She wanted to be small. She wanted to simply be Nera, whose biggest worry was late fees and ink stains.

She didn't just want that; for a terrifying heartbeat, *she decided to do it.*

Her foot slid back, a physical retreat from the table. Far from noble or tragic, the thought was ugly. Let the sky rip open, she thought, a frantic, selfish heat flushing her skin. Let history dissolve. *I don't care.*

She looked at Kieran, standing there ready to die for a truth he barely remembered, and the urge to grab his hand and run was so violent it made her nauseous. She realized, with sickening clarity, that she would trade every stranger in Varethis—every innocent family, every rewritten life—just to keep waking up tomorrow morning. She would let the world rot if it meant she didn't have to be the one to bleed for it.

The Archive would settle under Kestor's hand into something that *almost* worked.

Cael would live. He would stand beside her in whatever shape the Archive allowed them to keep. But something in him would be thinned to make room for their survival. The sharpness would go first. Then the warmth. He would laugh when others laughed, but the sound would be wrong, like an echo arriving a beat late. He would survive her choice, and she would watch him pay for it every day.

Kieran would forget her more slowly. Not all at once—never cleanly. He would still know how to fight beside her. He would still turn when she spoke. But one day he would hesitate before saying her name. Another day, he would look at her like he was waiting for context that never came. She would stand in front of him, whole and breathing, and be a blank space his mind kept trying to step around.

The world would hold. Buildings would stand. Streets would remain. The Archive would settle into something that almost worked. But every correction would leave a residue. Every preserved lie would require another small theft—another name softened, another memory shaved thin—to keep her anchored in a timeline that did not want her.

It was a monstrous thought. It was small, and cruel, and human. And she hated herself for how easily it came to her. To choose Kieran's hand in hers over the integrity of time. But she knew the rot would follow them. A love built on a stolen timeline would always taste like ash.

Nera sat weighing it, turning it over in her mind, considering what was still left to salvage, when Soren finally leaned forward and studied the expression now on her face.

She shook her head. Edris had failed because he cut too deep. He had erased people, places, entire pieces of time, and the world had fought against it.

The Sixth Alignment was failing in the same way. Too much was being rewritten at once, or too many times, or both. A forced ending when maybe it needed redirection instead. Something different.

Nera looked down at her hands. They were stained with ink— not fresh spills, but the permanent, shadowed tint of a lifetime spent in the Archive. She reached for the quill, but stopped. Her fingers hovered over the shaft, trembling, before she slowly pulled her hand back. She didn't pick it up.

Instead, she pressed her palm flat against the open page of the ledger. The parchment didn't feel like dead paper anymore. It felt warm. It pulsed against her skin, a matching rhythm to the blood in her veins.

A thought landed.

*She would shift.*

She didn't react right away, didn't let the realization settle on her face. Instead, she looked at Soren, weighing his words, feeling her own decision forming around them.

"You already know how to stop it, don't you?" he whispered.

She nodded imperceptibly. But it wasn't the way he thought.

Nera stood, the book from the market still in front of her, fingers resting lightly on the cover. The book had felt heavy before, but now, it didn't. Now, it felt like it had already done what it was meant to do.

Kieran was watching her. He had been since they returned, since the moment they stepped back inside the safe house. She hadn't looked at him directly, hadn't let herself. Not yet.

Cael sat at the far end of the room, his posture tense. He had been pacing earlier, his frustration building the longer they had waited for something none of them wanted to say.

Soren was the only one who looked calm. He had seen this coming. Maybe he had always seen it coming.

"There's a way this doesn't shatter," she said quietly.

She slowly raised her gaze to Kieran. The pause stretched too long, heavy with everything he wasn't saying.

Suddenly, the noise outside grew. What had been a steady background of voices and movement burst into a cacophony of chaos; heavy footsteps running towards the safehouse door, the sudden clash of metal and steel ringing and voices yelling.

Nera jumped from where she was sitting at the table. Kieran quickly stepped over to the window, moving the curtain slightly to carefully peer out. "Belvar's Enforcers," he snapped as he reached for the knife on his belt. Cael quickly jumped up to look, then lightly put a hand on Kieran's shoulder. "Wait," he uttered.

Kieran paused, and noticed some of the people who they had assumed were Archivists moving around the outside of the crowd were actually assassins. "The Preservationists," he said. "But they aren't attacking us. They're stopping the Enforcers."

Suddenly, Kieran and Cael saw a tall figure break away from the skirmish and move quickly toward the safehouse, rapping twice on the door.

Cael stepped forward to crack it open as Kieran shifted instinctively between the doorway and Nera. She had jumped up, gripping the book from the table as if it might be taken from her.

"You found what we couldn't," the Preservationist leader said, breathless. "Now we need to make sure you survive long enough to use it. We'll hold them off."

Nera stepped forward, the question tearing out of her before she could stop it. "Why? You burn archives. You don't save them."

The leader paused, his hand tightening on the doorframe, blood already soaking his sleeve. His eyes never left the book in her hands.

"Because we spent years trying to erase the lie every way we could," he said quietly. "But erasure is just another kind of silence."

He met her gaze. "You can't kill a story with fire. You have to replace it."

He nodded toward the book. "You're the only one holding a pen. Don't let it dry." And with that he ran off to join the fray.

Cael pushed the door, slow and controlled, watching the street beyond as the sounds of clashing steel and shouted orders moved further away.

Then he stopped.

"Soren," he said quietly. "The street's clearing. This may be your only window. All of our friends already moved, and you should go while you can."

"I know," he said.

Nera stepped forward. "You don't have to—"

"I do," Soren cut in gently. He looked at her then, really looked. "If I stay, I become leverage. Or a liability. And I've already been both."

Kieran shifted, tense. "Where will you go?"

"Anywhere history hasn't caught up yet." A beat. "Someone has to stay mobile."

Cael nodded once. No argument. No sentiment. Soren looked at Nera, his expression hardening into something clinical—the look of an Archivist deciding which pages to burn. "Edris flinched at the end," he said, his voice slipping into the stern, expectant cadence of the teacher she had once revered. "He tried to save himself along with the history. That is why he failed." He leaned forward, his eyes locking onto hers with a terrifying expectation. "Don't make that mistake."

Nera felt the chill of his instruction settle in the room. He wasn't asking if she was ready. He was telling her not to stop.

There was no hesitation in her voice. "I won't."

Soren stepped out into the street.

"Lock it," he said. "And you shouldn't stay long either."

Nera opened her mouth, but Cael was already moving.

The door shut behind Soren with a solid, final weight.

The bar slid into place. Cael turned the lock just as the last echoes of fighting disappeared down the street.

\*\*\*

Sitting back down at the table, Nera looked slowly at each person in the room. "We don't have time to consider this more."

She thought of Edris. Of his failure. Of how he had tried to erase something, someone, completely, and history had refused to let go.

She thought of the Sixth Alignment, how it had rewritten too many times, how reality had resisted instead of accepting.

The rewrites tend to use anchors. But to fix the story, she didn't need to destroy the anchor. She just needed to *move* it. She pressed her hands against the table, fingers splaying out against the wood.

Cael's posture stiffened as he moved to the table. "You don't even know what a full rewrite will do."

If she fought the current, she would break the world just like Edris did. But if she let go ...

The thought wasn't elegant. It was terrifying. She didn't know if she would survive it. She didn't know if she would become something new or nothing at all.

But they wouldn't understand that. They couldn't. Not yet. So, she didn't say it.

Kieran's voice was quiet. "You're not just talking about another rewrite."

Cael pushed up from his chair, understanding beginning to show in his eyes, shaking his head, his hands resting against his hips as he took a sharp breath. "You don't know that this is the only way."

"I do."

Cael laughed bitterly. "That's it? You just know?" She met his gaze evenly, steady. "Yes."

Kieran still hadn't moved.

Cael turned, dragging a hand through his hair, muttering something before he looked back at her. "You always do this. You make the choice alone. You don't—" He stopped himself, his breath hissing through his teeth as he forced the words back down. His voice was low when he spoke again. "You won't even give us a chance to talk you out of it?"

She didn't look away. "Because you can't."

The room was too still. Kieran moved. His steps were slow, deliberate, closing the space between them, stopping just close enough that she could feel his presence. He searched her face like he was looking for something, but he already knew what he would find.

He appeared calm, but when he spoke, his voice wasn't careful anymore. It was solid. Grounding.

"I know," he said.

She looked up, startled by the lack of resistance. Fear was absent from his gaze, void of the desperate need to save her that radiated off Cael. He was looking at her with absolute, devastating clarity.

"You are the only one who can," he whispered, stepping close enough that she could feel the heat of him, an anchor in the storm she was about to unleash. "Do what you were made to do, Nerith."

Nera looked at him, and for a terrifying second, the mask slipped. Her lips parted. The confession was right there, burning on her tongue—*I remember you*. She wanted to tell him she remembered the war, the way he had looked for her in every lifetime, their love. She wanted to give him the truth he had been starving for.

She reached out, her fingers grazing the rough fabric of his sleeve. His breath hitched, his eyes widening with a sudden, desperate hope. He saw it. He saw her remembering.

But then she stopped. *If I say it, he won't let me go.*

The realization slammed into her. If she made it real, he wouldn't just stand there; he would burn the world down to keep her. She pulled her hand back, forcing the wall back up. She swallowed the memory, letting it die in her throat, and turned away. Not because she wanted to. Not because she was afraid. But because she needed to move before the world caught up to her.

The world wasn't rejecting her. It was *looking* for her. That was the problem. Kestor was looking for her. Always.

So she had to move quickly. The decision hardened in her bones, but she didn't let it show. She flexed her fingers at her sides once before she let go. Then she stepped forward. And the world blinked.

Cael made a choked sound, a word dying in his throat.

Nera inhaled slowly. Her fingers curled against the table's edge, just once, before she released it. She turned away. The decision centered her, coiled in her guts, but she didn't falter.

Still, she let herself look at them—just once, just long enough to memorize the moment before it was gone.

Kieran stood rigid, unmoving; his eyes locked onto her like he could will her into staying. But there was no anger there, no sharp edge to his expression. Just something quieter, something heavier, something close to recognition but laced with grief. He knew.

Cael was breathing hard, his body rigid, every muscle pulled tight as a bowstring. His eyes were bright, burning with something unspoken, something sharp and raw. He wasn't ready.

Nera spoke slowly, softly. "You'll both be fine."

Anger finally broke through his grief. "I let Livia go. I stood in the ashes and I let it be real. I accepted it because I thought ... I thought if I finally stopped fighting history, I wouldn't lose anyone else. I wouldn't lose you," Cael said, his voice shaking with a bitter, ugly hurt. "Livia died to get us that book. She died thinking it would save us somehow. You're making her death a waste."

He stepped closer, his eyes hard. "She didn't burn so you could become a martyr. She burned so you could live. And you're throwing it back in her face."

Nera looked at him. If she gave him even an inch, he would burn the world down to keep her in it. She couldn't let him.

Her expression hardened. She turned her back on him.

"Nera, look at me!" Cael shouted, his voice cracking.

Kieran finally moved. His control snapped. He crossed the distance in two strides, grabbing her shoulders tight. "Stop."

"Kieran—"

"Don't you dare," he hissed, his voice cracking, shaking her once. "I didn't wait this long just to watch you write yourself out of this timeline. You don't have to do this."

She smiled softly, but there was nothing amused about it. "Yes, I do."

He stared at her, chest heaving, searching for a lie in her eyes. He didn't find one. Slowly, his hands slid from her shoulders, defeated.

Kieran inhaled sharply, something wavering behind his eyes. He stepped closer, not to stop her but to memorize her, his voice lower than before. "*Nerith.*"

The name settled in the air between them, not a question, not a plea—just truth, pulling itself back into the world. She could feel it ... the name he had whispered in the dark when they were young, the name he had screamed when they were separated. It was the only thing that had ever been truly hers.

"No!" Cael lunged forward, the paralysis of a culmination of grief finally breaking into desperate action. He didn't care about the history or the world; he reached for Nera, his hand inches from her arm.

Kieran caught him. He slammed his arm across Cael's chest, holding him back with a force born of terrible, rigid acceptance.

"Let me go!" Cael called out, struggling against Kieran's grip, thrashing just as he had in the burning archive.

Then Cael's gaze flicked to his coat pocket. Nera saw the movement, saw the way his hand pressed there once as if the weight inside had suddenly turned heavier against his ribs mid-fight. The violet book. The one Livia had died for. The puzzle he had been circling for months.

The missing counter-sign.

His eyes snapped to Nera. To the ink staining her fingers. To the way the room seemed to bend around her presence, like reality was listening.

Something in his face changed. Not calm, not relief. A hard, sudden focus, like a mechanism catching a tooth.

The fight drained out of him so fast he actually stumbled back, his grip loosening.

He pulled the violet book from his coat with trembling hands and ran his thumb over the charred edge, right where the fire that killed Livia had touched it. He stared at that burn as if it were an accusation. Or proof. His jaw flexed once, tight enough that Nera felt the snap of restraint from across the space.

"I understand it now. This maddening script I could never translate," he murmured, the realization spilling out low and ragged. "Because it wasn't meant to be read. The symbols don't flow like a language, they interlock like rings. It's a lock, not a language." He looked up at Nera, his eyes burning with a sudden, terrible clarity. "Livia didn't die to uncover a secret. She died to secure a seal."

He had spent weeks grieving her choice. At the insanity of dying for a book. Nera had heard it in his voice every time the subject came too close, the way his words turned sharp like he could cut the grief into something manageable.

He stepped forward, and the grief in his chest didn't soften. It condensed. It hardened into something cold and usable.

He slammed the small book onto the table and flipped it open to the page he had been worrying like a wound for weeks. "She found the way to bind a story so it can't be rewritten," he said, voice rough but steady. "But she was missing the key."

He looked at Nera, and the look held too long to be accidental.

"If you erase yourself, the world collapses. Don't erase yourself. Seal it like it is now, at this point. Use the cipher she found."

Nera looked at the page Cael offered. It was a complex array of logic—a way to bind a rewrite so it couldn't be undone.

"You want me to trap us both," Nera realized.

Cael held the book out, his hands shaking. His thumb brushed the charred edge of the cover—-the exact spot where the fire that killed Livia had touched it. "Seal it. Lock him out. We can—" He stopped. He looked at her eyes—really looked at them—and saw the truth she had already accepted. There was no version of this where she stayed. If she sealed the timeline, she trapped them in the broken one forever.

His hand dropped. The offer died in his throat. He wasn't handing her a weapon; he was handing her a tomb. But he didn't pull back. With a shaking hand, he pushed the book across the table.

Kieran slowly, deliberately stepped back, creating the space for her to leave. His silver eyes were clear, devastatingly dry, steady on her face. He didn't reach for her again.

He let her go—and in that restraint, she understood what he valued enough not to bargain with.

Nera closed her eyes briefly, feeling the weight of Cael's offering. He had realized he may not be able to save her, but could ensure her sacrifice actually worked. She nodded at Kieran, then at Cael. "I will."

Then she sat, pulling Livia's book toward her, flipping to the final blank page. Her hands didn't shake. The ink was still wet in the well beside her. The quill was already waiting.

She picked it up—the quill Alis left behind, a tool of a forger used to save the truth. She dipped the tip, watching the black liquid gather, and moved it to the page.

## CHAPTER FIFTY

# The Forgotten Name

The front door exploded and turned to dust.

Master Belvar stepped through the smoke, his blade drawn, his face twisted in a snarl of realization. The composed Archivist had been replaced by a man cornered by the consequences of the master he chose.

"I told you to run," Belvar hissed, raising his weapon. "I have no desire to protect you any more."

Before Kieran could engage, the air rippled behind Belvar. A pressure dropped the room to its knees. Belvar froze. He looked up at Kestor—not with reverence, but with sudden, horrific clarity of a dog realizing its master had picked up a weapon. The High Archivist had vanished; he was just an empty, powerless shell.

Belvar turned his blade not on Nera, but on the figure behind him. He raised his weapon ....

Kestor didn't flinch, and didn't speak. He simply looked at Belvar, flicked his hand, and the space where the High Archivist stood collapsed. Belvar was smeared against the wall like wet ink thumbed across a page, sliding down in a heap of unwritten potential.

Kieran was the first line of defense, standing between Nera and the door with his blade raised. Kestor didn't even slow down.

He walked straight past Kieran as if he didn't even exist. He didn't strike Kieran; he simply ignored him, the air rippling with a pressure that forced Kieran's arm down against his will. Kieran was just a distraction from his goal.

Cael, standing by the table, lunged to intercept. Kestor didn't look at him; he simply flicked an ink-tipped finger, and Cael dropped to his knees.

Kestor stopped at the edge of the table, directly across from Nera, ignoring everything else. He had walked through her defenders like they were smoke. He regarded her for a silent beat, his expression unreadable. Absently, almost as if he didn't realize he was doing it, his thumb brushed the heavy signet ring on his right hand. He twisted it—once, sharp and rhythmic—before letting his hand drop to his side.

"Stop," Kestor commanded. The word hit with the force of a compulsion that should have frozen the blood in her veins. The air rippled with the force of it, causing Cael's head to hit the floor and was pinned by gravity.

But Nera didn't flinch. The command washed over her and vanished, absorbed into the ink, into her.

Kestor paused, his hand freezing in mid-air. For the first time, the absolute certainty in his eyes fractured. He looked at his own hand, then at her, his features flipping from command to a cold, dawning comprehension. His voice held no power here.

He lowered his hand, the expression in his eyes turning to something colder. He walked to the shattered doorway and gestured to the sound of riots bleeding through the walls.

"Listen to them," he said softly, changing tactics. "That is the sound of truth. Filthy, ungrateful noise. Do you hear them, Nerith? Those screams are an accusation, not a tribute."

He looked at her with genuine pity. "I gave them a lie that kept them warm. You want to give them a truth that freezes them to death. I held the chaos back. You just opened the door."

"You did not do that for any selfless reason," Nera spat.

He moved closer, over the dissolving floor as if it was beneath his notice. "Does the reason really matter if they're suffering now?"

He stepped back, searching her face to see if he had changed her mind.

"Do not mistake your survival for strength," Kestor sneered. "You think you are a warrior?" He stepped closer, his voice dropping. "You exist because I cannot cut you out. You are a clot in my veins."

He was not without weapons. He raised a hand, not toward Nera, but toward Cael.

"If you will not submit to the architect," Kestor said coldly, "then I will remove the characters who are no longer necessary."

A shadow detached itself from the folds of Kestor's robes. It hit the floor with a wet, heavy sound—thick, viscous ink pooling and rising in a familiar, terrifying shape. A faceless hood. Robes that absorbed the light.

*A Silent Keeper.*

"No!" Nera shouted.

The Silent Keeper flowed, poured past Kieran's blade—a splash of shadow ignoring the steel—and wrapped a hand of heavy, solidifying ink around Cael's throat.

Cael gasped, clawing at the black substance, but where the Silent Keeper touched him, reality simply stopped. Cael's skin began to ... *revert.* The complexity of flesh and blood simplified instantly into a flat, grey texture. He tried to grab the hand on his throat, but his fingers found no traction. He opened his mouth to scream, but the sound was erased before it left his lips. He was being edited out of existence, cell by agonizing cell.

"Give me the quill," Kestor demanded as he approached Nera.

The ring on her finger suddenly warmed as he moved closer, distracting her momentarily. Her inheritance. She looked up, their eyes locking.

Kestor paused. He didn't raise his voice; he didn't strike. He looked at her with a terrifying, familiar devastation.

"... Nerith...," he said quietly, the name like ash in his mouth; a bitter resignation of a narcissist forced to acknowledge his only failure.

The name hit her like a physical blow. It was the sound of the secret her mother had died keeping. Nera looked at the scar on her palm—the burn she got trying to save the journal that held her father's name. She looked at Kestor—the way he stood, the way he looked at her with expectation. Even the way he twisted his ring.

Unconsciously she lifted her hand to her chest, fingers fumbling numbly against the fabric, unable to find a rhythm. Her grandmother's journal hadn't been burned to protect a rebel, which is what Nera had always hoped or suspected. It had been burned to hide *him*.

"The name in the fire," she whispered to herself, her voice trembling as the horrifying truth locked into place. "The name I burned my hand to save ..." she looked up slowly at Kestor, speaking slightly louder, "it was you."

Valen Kestor. Her absent father. The world seemed to stop, the noise of the riots fading into a high-pitched ring.

"You tried to write me out," she realized, speaking louder now, angry, the truth hitting her. "But the ink wouldn't take because that would also erase you."

She felt a strange, cold peace settle over her.

"And my name is *Nera!*" The words filled the room.

She looked back at where her quill touched the book.

"Don't be foolish," he demanded. "There's nowhere to go."

"Then we go nowhere." Nera quickly looked at the book, and she wrote.

Focusing less on message than intent, she wrote the first word, and felt the memory of her mother's eyes dissolve into static. The hold on Cael loosened immediately, but she needed to write fast.

With the next word, she sacrificed the sound of Cael's laugh, and even worse lost the emotion that triggered it.

She could feel a paradox whirling around the room, looking for a place to snap. Another word and Nera could no longer remember the names of many of her friends.

"I deny this," Kestor commanded, his voice vibrating through the floorboards. "The story ends here!" The floor beneath Nera's knees dissolved into sand. The table under her hand turned to dust, collapsing into a pile of ash. Nera didn't look up. She slammed the book onto her own lap, driving the quill across the paper even faster as the roof above them tore open to a void of nothingness.

"The ink is dry," Kestor dictated. "The page refuses."

The ink on Nera's quill instantly turned to dust. She quickly dipped it into her inkwell again, pressing intentionally against the paper to force it to take the ink.

Kestor focused on the book itself. "That record does not exist." The book started to fade in Nera's hands. She continued writing, and the sensation in her fingertips vanished as they became transparent, devoured by the quill. It was a terrifying expansion. Her skin started to lose its weave, the fragile mortality of veins and pulse dissolving into the stark, black geometry of letters. It bypassed death; it was translation. Her heartbeat changed rhythm, syncing perfectly with the scratch of the nib against the page. She was no longer just flesh and blood; she was becoming ink and intent.

*I am his anchor and I write intent.*

She wrote faster, desperate to outpace Kestor's words. It wasn't like the wall at the Market; she wasn't trying to force the ink through resistance. She was letting the resistance flow through her. She accepted the erasure not as a penalty, but as the medium. The paradox wrapped around the room, snapping the stone prison before it could touch her skin.

"Do you really think you can unwrite me, Nerith? You are my blood! My ink does not work on you because you are my ink. Strike me down, and you shatter yourself!"

He meant it as a threat, but he didn't understand. He thought the blood was a shield that would stay her hand. But blood wasn't immunity; it was the tether. It was the only thing heavy enough to hold him. An anchor doesn't float—it drowns. And she was finally willing to go under.

The ink pulled itself into the paper, devoured by the page like a name swallowed. The final stroke. The last word. She stared up at Valen Kestor.

"You called me a mistake," Nera whispered, the quill digging into the page for the final stroke.

She looked up at him, her eyes hard and clear. "But ink holds truth." She dug the quill into the page for the final word.

There was a terrifying cold deep in her bones, as if she had poured her own marrow into the ink, the burn scar on her hand throbbing with new pain. The sensation in her right arm vanished entirely, the limb going dead and heavy at her side, a permanent price for the final stroke.

Kestor unraveled into grey static, a scream quickly silenced by the ink on the page.

Nera wrote the final period.

The quill slipped from her fingers.

It hit the floor with a hollow clatter; the only sound in a room that had suddenly lost its center.

The smooth shaft was still warm. The ink on the nib was still wet. But the person that had held it was simply ... gone.

Air rushed in to fill the vacuum where a woman had stood a second ago, swirling dust motes in a sudden, violent draft.

\*\*\*

Cael collapsed, coughing, his lungs gasping for air.

Kieran's knees hit the floor with a bone-jarring crack. He collapsed, his forehead pressing against the wood where Nera had stood, a ragged, airless sound tearing from his chest. He clawed at the spot, his fingers searching for a heat that was already gone.

He sat up and reached out, desperate to catch her, to hold her, to prove she had been there, memory quickly fading.

But his fingers closed on nothing but cold air and the scent of lavender.

# EPILOGUE

The world around her flickered.

Not violently. Not in a way that meant collapse. But in a way that meant it wasn't whole.

She took a step forward, her boots meeting something solid—until it wasn't. The ground beneath her dissolved. One moment, stone and sand pressed against her boots; the next, gravity vanished, leaving her stomach in her throat before slamming her back down onto the ground. The air pressure dropped, stealing the sound from the world, then surged with the humidity of a storm that wasn't there.

She reached for her pocket, an instinctive drift of fingers seeking the map she had carried for years. But her pocket was empty. There was no map here. There was only the territory, raw and unwritten, waiting for her to decide what was true.

She kept walking. The air hummed with tension. Waiting.

Where was she? She didn't know if this place was real. She wasn't sure who she was.

She turned slowly. There was no horizon, no sky—only warping fragments of structures, half-built, half-destroyed. A road that led nowhere. A city frozen mid-thought, waiting to be remembered. A temple with its doors sealed shut. A tower that had no entrance. A street sign written in a language she didn't recognize but somehow understood.

Inhaling slowly, she tried to remember—to pull something solid from the fog in her mind.

What was this place? What was she?

Nothing came.

When she turned again, she found a book sitting on a stone pedestal—except, no, it wasn't stone. The pedestal tilted beneath it, shimmering, the texture of it changing even as she looked at it. Wood, metal, sand, something else. But the book remained.

She hesitated. Then she reached out. Her fingers brushed the surface of the parchment, and the ink inside began to move. Words blurring, reforming, rewriting themselves. History was trying to decide what belonged here.

Then, for a breath, just one, a name surfaced—fragile, uncertain, like ink still deciding whether to dry.

She stared at it. It meant something. It felt like something she should know. She parted her lips, barely whispering, testing the shape of it.

But before the sound could leave her throat, the ink reconfigured again.

The name was gone.

The space around her remained quiet. Still unfinished. Still unwritten.

She closed her eyes. The feeling of something pressed against her—a name unsaid, a history unwritten. She couldn't name it. So she didn't.

In the distance, a sound echoed. Another person.

She took another step forward.

*\*\**

The world had settled.

The air was still. The strange hum that had filled the streets for days had faded, leaving behind a city that had stopped fighting against itself.

The safe house was quiet. Not empty, but quiet.

Theron sat near the hearth, methodically sharpening a blade. Tavian leaned against the far wall, his gaze distant. Cyrus had gone silent, staring at the maps laid out before him, though none of them needed them anymore. Tobias and Tyrek both brooded in the corner while Liaz and Gaela were in the kitchen. Sarina and Kaelith were quietly organizing a pile of things near the hearth.

Many of the other regulars sat around, none speaking, but the heaviness in the room said everything.

Cael sat across from Kieran at the table. He hadn't said much in hours. None of them had.

It was over. Balance was returning. That should have been enough, but the quiet wasn't peaceful. It was absence.

Cael sat stiffly, his fingers tapping against his knee. His face was blank, but his eyes weren't.

Kieran had spent enough time reading people to know when someone was feeling too much to let it show. He knew, because he felt it too. The world had moved on. But it felt like a piece was missing, yet something they couldn't identify.

Cael sighed, running a hand down his face before leaning forward, resting his forearms on the table. "We should sleep."

It wasn't a suggestion. Kieran's fingers slowly brushed the edge of the table—smooth, worn, familiar. But then, a roughness. His hand paused.

A mark. No, not a mark. A *symbol.*

He stilled.

A faint scratch. Two circles with curved lines, intersecting. It shouldn't exist. The scratch was shallow. Basically invisible unless you were looking for it.

It shouldn't exist.

His stomach tightened. He didn't know why, only that something had just slipped past him—something he had almost remembered.

He drew his hand back slowly.

Maybe forgetting didn't erase everything.

And maybe missing didn't mean gone.

# Sneak Peek
# of Book 2

By Vicky Wu

Fractured Ink Press

# The Benefactor's Return

*(Unknown Location | Outside of Time)*

The first thing she realized was that she was alone.

Peace eluded her. She remained fractured. She was not whole. She was a draft discarded in the dark, consciousness trapped in the friction between what was and what is.

As she turned to view her surroundings, the movement felt sluggish, as if the air itself were made of water.

She was unmade, like the world itself had forgotten she was supposed to exist. She existed, but she was also the cost. She reached out, and her mind sent the signal to move a hand that history no longer recognized. She was consciousness trapped in a white void, an inkblot trying to remember its shape before the page dried.

Time stretched, direction meaningless.

She knew she had been someone once, but the thought slipped through her mind like spilled ink. Then, a voice—distant, or perhaps entirely internal—cut through the fog.

*"Nerith, you're late."*

She moved, more in control of her body now. The dream was vague, details blurred, but the shape of someone stood in the fog—a figure half-familiar, half-lost, searching for something in her that wasn't there anymore.

Her pulse kicked up, an instinctive reaction to something she should know.

But when she tried to place the thought, she found only silence. Yet, for a heartbeat, she felt the phantom warmth of a hand grabbing her wrist—an anchor in the storm. The smell of rain and damp drifted through the nothingness. She didn't know his name, but her heart stuttered a rhythm it remembered: *Safe. Home.*

She blinked. The image disappeared into a whisper of fog.

And she was alone. But she felt a presence calling her from somewhere nearby and decided that somehow, some way, she would find it. She didn't even know if it was possible, but if there was a way, she was going to make it happen.

*** 

*(Veridion | Theron's Safe House | Three Months Later)*

Something was missing, although he saw evidence every day of a presence that once was, but was not entirely erased. Not an Unwritten. Something else.

Kieran felt it in the air, in the way maps wouldn't stay set, in the names that surfaced only to vanish again. Varethis was unstable while the false histories of each alignment slowly trying to unravel, and the rebels were closer than ever to understanding why.

He ran his fingers over a half-burned parchment, the ink bleeding at the edges. A word sat at the top, half-erased but not quite gone.

Not a myth or a name. A title.

*The Benefactor.*

The whispers were starting again—fragments in rewritten records, discrepancies in accounts that shouldn't exist. Whoever this person had been, their erasure hadn't held. Some memory of them still remained and were a growing presence every day.

"Kieran." Tavian dropped into the seat across from him, tossing a sealed missive onto the table. "New lead."

Kieran ran his thumb over the broken wax seal. They were catching up to the past, correcting history with every new piece of information they collected.

Kieran looked at the map. The city was stabilizing. The stars were right. He didn't know what had fixed the sky, but he knew a cost had been paid. He felt a phantom weight on his shoulder—a hand that wasn't there—and for the first time in months, he didn't feel afraid of the future.

They felt the identity of the Benefactor within reach. And this time, he wouldn't let it slip away.

\*\*\*

(*The Grand Archive* | *Varethis* | *Three Months Later*)

Cael traced his fingers over the spine of the book, its title changing beneath his touch.

The Archivists thought they had buried history so deeply that no one could find it. That rewriting a war meant no one would remember it had ever been fought. That erasing a name meant no one would ever speak it again.

They were wrong. And now the right people had taken over the Grand Archive and were carefully working to restore history.

He closed the book and turned to the others gathered around the table. Theron, Tobias, Cyrus, Tyrek and a half-dozen rebels who had seen too many battles that weren't supposed to exist.

"We found another inconsistency from the timeline continuing to settle," Tavian said, dropping a parchment onto the table. "Still small, but bigger than the rest."

Cael read the document.

A name flickered where it shouldn't be. A scar on the page.

*Nerith.*

Cael's jaw locked, a sharp, hot pain flooding his chest, an emotion he didn't understand. He traced the name, his finger trembling not with awe, but with anger.

\* \* \*

*(Veridion Borderlands | The Nameless Market | Three Months Later)*

Alis had left before the world forgot.

That's what she told herself, anyway. That she had left by choice, that it had nothing to do with the way history had started unraveling beneath her feet.

She didn't belong in a war about rewrites, nor did she care who was supposed to rule. Believing in what was real rather than rewriting, she had walked away.

She checked the horizon. She saw the families and children settled in the camp behind her, sleeping soundly in a world that no longer remembered the war they had fled. Jaye was teaching the younger ones to read, using every book she had smuggled out. Alis had moved the line of defense and gotten them out. She had done her job.

Now, all she had to do was figure out why she was the only one who remembered the name they had all forgotten.

Slowly she continued down the road to the local market. The rebels fought their battles in the city, while she fought hers in the black markets—among people who knew better than to trust written words.

"You're late," muttered her contact as she entered the alley.

"I was on time," she said, flipping a coin between her fingers. "You were just impatient."

The figure handed her a small, folded note. "This isn't one of your usual jobs."

She opened it, and her expression—which had disappeared these last few months—hardened.

A name that had been forgotten by everyone. Except her.

*Nerith Calloway.*

Alis folded the note, smiling slightly while staring at the horizon where the sky still looked a little too thin. The story was over, but the ink wasn't dry.

# About the Author

Vicky Wu writes speculative fiction exploring memory, power, and the instability of truth. Her work blends dark academia with dystopian fantasy, examining how institutions shape reality through control of history and knowledge.

She is also the author of the nonfiction bestseller Pivot to Success: Transforming Marketing Missteps to Milestones (2024). The Archivist's War is her debut novel.

She lives in Texas with her husband.

TheArchivistsWar.com

# ACKNOWLEDGMENTS

Every book begins as a thought, a whisper in the dark, and this one would never have found its voice without the people who stood beside me. It wa a labor of creativity that took me several years to complete.

To my family. To Tye, for your patience and steady encouragement, especially during the long stretches when I disappeared into my own Archive for hours and days at a time. To my children, their partners, and my grandchildren, who remain my constant inspiration and my why.

To my early readers and the Grimoire Gems book club. Your enthusiasm and thoughtful responses helped provide excitement that carried me through moments when finishing felt uncertain. To Shirley, for working with me through far more editing than I ever imagined this book would require.

And to the readers. Thank you for believing in stories that refuse to be forgotten. I hope you find something here that stays with you, long after the final page.

**Reality resists, yet together, we write our own stories.**

# OTHER WORKS BY VICKY WU

Nonfiction:

*Pivot to Success: Transforming Marketing Missteps into Milestones* (Unscrewed Publishing)